SLENDER WISH

KERRY CASEY

This is a work of fiction. In other words, I made it up and no one should get bent out of shape over content.

ISBN-13: 978-0-9769765-4-7

Library of Congress Catalog Number: 2016906968

Printed in the United States of America

First Printing: May 2016

20 19 18 17 16 5 4 3 2 1

Published by:
five friends books™

fivefriendsbooks.com

The best books come from friends. That's why Five Friends Books™ puts the destiny of a book in the hands of readers. Please pass along your bookmarks to five book-loving friends. How far this novel spreads depends on you. Find out more by visiting **fivefriendsbooks.com**.

five friends books™

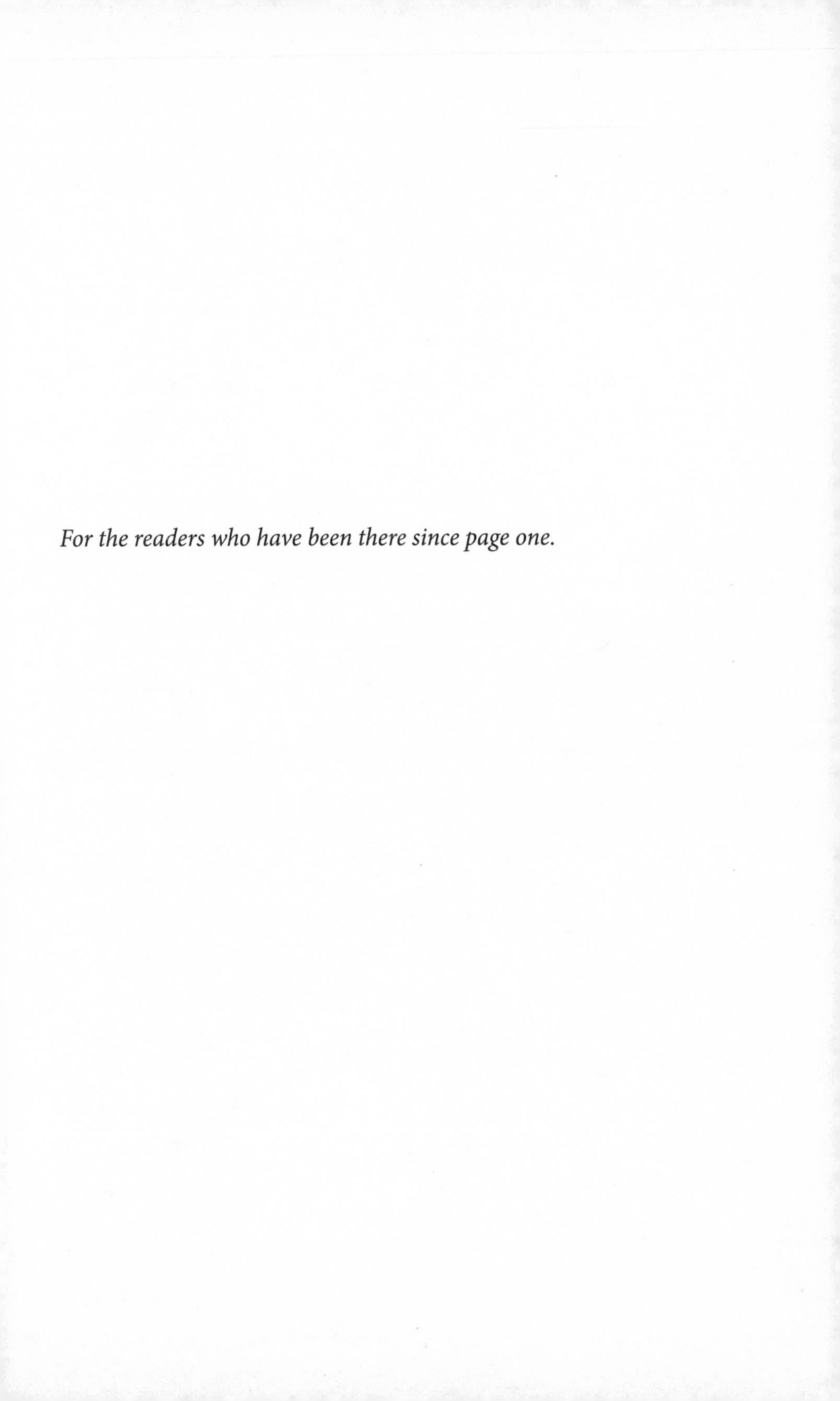

For the readers who have been there since page one.

In the time it takes
for a bird to turn its head
for a raindrop to break in your palm
for an eye to open
for a finger to sink a piano key
for a foot to slide out from under you
in that time
life as you know it
can topple off the head of a pin

BOOK One

DORMANT, WINTER 1986

There will always be innocent victims.

—Monsignor Kief

PART ONE

Baudette, Minnesota

VARKAS

The widow more sensed his presence than saw him.

Not that Varkas was an easy man to miss. His size was like an unpleasant odor. All heads pivoted. The hulking figure entered the funeral home, stomping snow from his work boots.

Despite the intense January cold, his only coat was a pressed navy sports jacket with an American flag lapel pin proudly affixed above the breast pocket. Those gathered in the funeral home's visitation area instinctively stepped aside.

With the room thus parted, a thin pathway of carpet now connected the widow and Varkas. Commencing, he had to stoop slightly under the painted plaster archway. She was standing near the room's farthermost wall, which was draped in mourning purple. Her small hand rested on the closed casket. She was surrounded by sprays of flowers and assorted photos of her smiling husband engaged in his life's many happy activities.

The wake's whispering voices hushed further. You could almost hear the individual carpet strands bend beneath Varkas's size 14 steel-toed boots. Then, a jolting scream left the widow's mouth.

"NOOUT!" The two words smashed out of her mouth as one. Her eyes wild, erratic—flashing white as her pupils tightened into focus. Her small fists rocketed into the air. "NOOUT!" she screamed again, throwing saliva as she shook her head in an attempt to physically negate his intrusion.

She was as much falling toward Varkas as running when the sight of the envelope in his hand yanked her to a stop. The Varkas envelope. Stark white. The widow's name boldly printed on the front. The red wax seal with a swooping capital *V* in cursive stamped on the back. Its insides were bulging with the over-burden of $100 bills.

The moment hung there, not unlike a tree will just before timber! is shouted. A fair enough metaphor, for her husband was a lumberman who had worked for Varkas. The job cost him his life. And now, on cue, here was Varkas, ready to square that cost with an envelope, as he had with others over the years. As had his father. As had his grandfather.

She came running at Varkas and were it not for the outstretched arms of her husband's coworkers she would have reached him with her tiny fists and kicking feet and bared teeth. She was carefully lifted off the floor and taken to the adjoining room where the wives of loggers attempted to console her. But what consolation was there, really, for the wife of a man so crushed by another's greed that he was laid in a closed casket?

Varkas turned the fat envelope over in his hands, reflecting. It was not the solemnity of the moment he measured, but the widow's behavior. *Is she worthy of my generosity?* Awkward silence descended upon the room.

He snapped the envelope with an oversized index finger like a judge striking a gavel. "You," his voice reverberated. He pointed a blunt index finger into the gathering. "I know you, don't I?"

The cluster of people leaned away from his aim. Varkas's finger sorted through them, until he found the man he was addressing. "You."

The man stepped forward. "We've met at your plant, yes."

"You're a shift manager," Varkas nodded.

"I am."

"Come. Take this," Varkas gestured with the envelope. "I trust you will see she gets it." Varkas hinted a smile. "Time has a way of making them reach." He nodded to the crowd. "Not sure about trusting any of the rest of you with this. Much money here."

The man stepped forward and accepted the thick envelope, glancing up at the towering Varkas.

"Didn't I hear you used to be a priest?" Varkas said.

"That's right."

"Your name?" Varkas's eyes narrowed as he searched his memory.

"Pat," the man said. "Pat O'Rourke."

"Good," Varkas said, satisfied with his decision. "Should be able to trust you. Even if you are an ex."

PAT

Dawn broke to an unforgiving blue sky.

Temperatures had not nudged above zero for the past ten days. Today was no different. Pat was angry, and that, too, had become a trend.

Tension wired through his jaw and neck and branched down his back. His typically open posture and wide shoulders were draw-strung. Certainly, Pat had kept diligent watch over his short temper throughout his adult life, with mixed success. But the concept of chronic anger was something he'd not known since childhood. Here it was back again.

The list of items responsible for his foul mood was not shortening. His truck didn't start. The farmhouse water heater was emitting strange dolphin-like pings and producing lukewarm output. And to top it off, he'd lost his left leather glove. Fine-grain cowhide. From a pair he'd been dutifully breaking in since two Christmases ago. He was just liking the fit.

He frowned and rubbed his face, there at the kitchen table. Pat stirred the remains of a spoonful of vanilla ice cream into his coffee. His running gear seemed to tighten around him, including long underwear beneath sweatpants with a well-worn Wisconsin Badger W imprinted on the leg. The Varkas envelope lay beside his mug.

Pat's anger reversed. Now he became angry with himself for letting such trivialities preoccupy him. What were dead truck batteries, unreliable water heaters and mislaid gloves compared to life's real losses? A wife of a lumberman now had to raise two in diapers without their father.

Truth be told, Pat was angry with God. He was angry to bear witness to the past seven weeks. Angry for so many losses that he and loved ones endured. Worry and sadness and confusion were mixed in. And guilt. Because his life—despite these tragedies—had turned for the better.

Pat didn't personally know the logger who died in the accident, nor was he familiar with his widow, but the three of them were indirectly brought together by Varkas. The logger had cut the Varkas forests. Pat managed a shift at the Varkas Forest Products plant—so, like many co-workers, he attended the wake. And the widow believed, as wives over the years in this richly forested area had always believed, that her young lumberman would outrun the felling of Varkas trees. She believed her man would evade the innate occupational peril. She believed *it* wouldn't happen to her family; *it* would take someone else's husband and she would be the one bringing dinner once a week to their grieving home.

Pat pushed away the Varkas envelope and returned to stirring his coffee. A melted dollop of vanilla ice cream both lowers the drinking temperature of a freshly poured cup and polishes off its bitter notes. More so, Pat thought, the act of swirling the black with the white encourages personal reflection. It reminded Pat that a good life—a real life—isn't all one thing or another.

The swirl of life takes you to the unforeseeable. You build relationships out of improbable dust and a home out of idealism that springs forth from a spit of ground. The question we eventually stare into is *How did I get here?* So diffuse is the answer, Pat could no more separate its layers than he could unswirl his coffee.

He didn't interrogate his fate. An ex-priest. A part-time counselor on the Rez. A manager at the Varkas plant. An alcoholic who hadn't had a drink in seven years, two months and three days. A man reunited with HomeSky, who was his life's love. A son of a deadbeat father. A surrogate dad to Meadow, and a stand-in grandpapa to her seven-week old treasure, Billy Little Tree.

How did I get here? was too big to handle right now. Pat needed a soupçon of progress. He needed to crawl out of an angry hole and fill it behind him, albeit slowly, with handfuls of ordinary moments.

He removed his weather-faded Red Sox cap and scratched his head. He drank his cup of coffee. He stretched in preparation for a seven-miler in the harsh cold of the second week of January. He tried to coax positive thoughts to his side.

Pat turned over the envelope and traced a fingertip across its red wax seal with its vaunted *V*, the same cursive letter found stamped onto the millions of board-feet of wood product trucked from the Varkas plant annually. Pat's thoughts zigzagged before locking on the one recurring truth that haunted him: *It easily could have been Cory lying in a casket.*

It has been seven weeks since Cory's fiancée, Hanna, was killed, a mistaken, violent death. There was hardly a person within 300 miles who hadn't in some way heard about Cory's truck chasing down the murderer's vehicle and their deadly collision on a remote highway. The media jackals scavenged off the story for weeks—which furthered Pat's anger.

He could only shake his head. *Where does all this come from? The persistent darkness?* Pat worked a dull ache out of his leg with a calf stretch. *How can Cory's brokenness be explained? I don't have a single answer? What did 15 years as a priest teach me!*

In two weeks, Cory would be coming to the farm to live. Since the crash, Pat's life was a blur. An unrelenting cycle of surgeries, recoveries and prayer—beginning with Cory on life support in a coma for four days at St. Luke's Hospital in Duluth and ending 230 miles south at the Mayo Clinic for traumatic brain injury care. Pat could drive to either hospital in his sleep, an idiom he came too close to accomplishing on the countless trips he'd taken.

The blur melded into a fog of waiting and watching and reacting as Cory's grievous injuries went from raw red to swollen purple to ugly brown to fading yellow. Incisions slowly scarred over.

There had been a mad rush to line up a compatible kidney donor—and the bizarre way Cory's mother responded to his need. It's for the best Cory knew none of this yet.

All of it was too much to untangle. Pat closed his eyes, leaning into the quiet of the farmhouse kitchen. HomeSky and Meadow and baby Billy Little Tree had gone to the newly built YMCA just outside town on the state highway. Tuesdays and Thursdays were lap days. Meadow swam while HomeSky waded in the shallows with the infant. That communal water did such good for them all.

Standing, Pat balanced on one leg and pulled his opposite foot up behind him, stretching his quad. He was bolstered by thoughts of his newly forming family. HomeSky, Meadow, Billy, and now, Cory. If there is such a thing as a provider gene, Pat's had been flipped on.

He had the last sip of coffee gone cold. Pat knew he must rid himself of worry that festered into frustration during the long hours of silence bedside with Cory. His frustration had cascaded into anger. Pat understood these emotions did him no good service. His temper had always been his Achilles heel. But he reminded himself that his Achilles heel fit comfortably into a size ten running shoe. Anger couldn't survive outdoors in the January elements of northern Minnesota. He'd run the outrage into the frozen ground.

Faith hadn't abandoned him. A small clue might be found in the wind-slapped cold. He wasn't asking for the answer—just a hint of what all this means for those who wake up every day to a harsh reminder of what they've lost.

HOMESKY

She smiled at the sound of her own humming.

The pool water lapped at her waist and HomeSky was reminded of how she once stood in a lake with her baby, Joseph, and taught him to float on his back just as she did now with Billy Little Tree. Swimming was a big part of her Ojibwe culture and allowing a baby to discover his instinctive buoyancy was an important tradition. More so, tradition is restorative. It can be a bridge over impossible tragedy, back to a place of optimism and hope and yes, humming. It's a long journey.

Billy's chubby legs frog kicked as he floated peacefully, his head cupped in HomeSky's outstretched palm. In a week, maybe two, he would backfloat without support—the start of building a spirit that would fly him far from the stifling borders of the Rez, she hoped.

HomeSky's quarter section of farmland sat north of the Rez. There, she and Pat and Meadow and Billy now made a home. It wasn't as simple as some whispered: that she took them in. They took each other in. They found much of what was missing in themselves in the others. Hopefully, when Cory joined them, he too would become more whole.

Her farmland was resting now, beneath the cold and ice and inches of dirty January snow. But come spring, there would be row after row of emergent green. Corn. Soybeans. Wheat. Field tied to field by a blue ribbon of winding creek and the dutiful pollination of bees and butterflies. On the south side of the farmhouse, an expanded ground space would be broken for a dedicated home vegetable garden.

Lately, Meadow had a sheet of paper in and out of her back pocket. Usually it carried the scribbles of a song but recently she was setting a grid for that family garden. She and Pat had big plans for the stretch of dirt, so HomeSky stood clear, only requesting that watermelon and beets be included on the seed list. Pat assured her with a wink that he would find a dry, weedy corner for her beets.

Meadow, breathing heavily, finished swimming her laps and dipped under the buoyed rope marking her lane. She drifted over to HomeSky and Billy.

"Hey there," Meadow quietly said. She blew air out her nose as her head surfaced, slicking her black hair back. "He's a little Olympian. Be doing the 200-meter backstroke in no time."

Meadow put her hand under HomeSky's as they exchanged responsibility for keeping Billy's head above the waterline. His precocious bloom of black hair spread out around his head. His dark eyes sparkled with joy as he calmly kicked and drifted in small circles around the pool's shallow end. They had the water to themselves.

"I don't want to get out," Meadow said. "Going outside freezes my hair. Reminds me of walking home after swimming in high school. That royally sucked." Meadow was working, slowly, on undoing 19 years of being surrounded by less-than-exemplary language.

"Do you miss high school?"

"Not a bit."

"Any part of it?"

Meadow shook her head.

"Nothing? Not even the simplicity of it?"

"Mine wasn't so simple." She looked at HomeSky. "Not to be a drama queen."

HomeSky smiled, looking down at Billy. "Not so simple now, either."

"Yeah," Meadow said. "This is a different kind of crazy. The worthwhile kind."

The two of them watched as Billy Little Tree's arms fanned out and splashed.

"I can't believe this life came out of me. I know it did—but it's still freaky."

"Not too long ago he was splashing around inside you,"

HomeSky said.

Meadow shook her head slowly as her hands squeegeed water from hair. "Pat says the miracle of birth is the most amazing thing other than the miracle of death. I'm not sure I'm buying that . . . the miracle of death thing."

HomeSky let her knees touch the pool bottom, bringing her head closer to Billy's. Water lapped at her collarbones. "I think he's right. But I can't say why, exactly. The miracle of birth is more apparent every day. Just look at this child. His development these past weeks. Every finger and toe and tiny nostril is a miracle, right before your eyes.

"But the possibility there's an equal miracle in death—one we can't grasp like we can this miraculous little hand—something that's a doorway to an afterworld or heaven, that is mind-boggling."

HomeSky paused. "For those of us left behind, death is devastating. Almost paralyzing." She looked at Meadow more intently. "For me, with RiverHeart and Joseph, only the passage of time allowed my eyes to open to the possibility that life and death aren't such far apart miracles.

"I came to understand the miracle of death as a doorway that survivors have to pass through, too. Things are not the same. They will never be the same. But once on the other side, we're able to find a greater appreciation. Especially in our relationships. Me and Pat. Me and you. Me and Billy Little Tree. Even my relationship with nature.

"From all my relationships, the loved ones I lost are still with me. The miracle of death, in my opinion, is something you can see only in the fullness of time. Tears fall away and you're able to stumble through that door."

Meadow's young face creased between her dark eyebrows.

HomeSky smiled. "Don't worry, beautiful daughter. Nineteen years is not enough time to know. My 45 are hardly enough."

"If the miracle of death somehow brought us together, then I know what you mean," Meadow said. "I believe in that."

"It didn't so much bring us together as it allowed this possibility."

Meadow looked away. "I used to curse my life. I cursed the Creator for it."

"Many do. Understandably so. We have no picture of the larger life in store. We're forgiven because we are whittled small and we can't see above the horror. Until we grow. Then we see in all directions. This new height is *bagosenim*. Hope."

"Like my Billy," Meadow said.

"So much so."

Meadow shuddered at a thought that rose goosebumps on her skin. "If I ever lost Billy, I'd lose my hope, right?"

"For a moment, yes."

"Then what?"

"Then you fight. To find your doorway. To find the death miracle that Pat speaks of."

"Is that what Cory will have to do?" Meadow asked.

HomeSky nodded. "He will very much need our help."

"Why can't he speak, HomeSky? Pat says he just sits in his wheelchair, staring at nothing."

"The doctors don't know, honey. They think it might be due to his brain trauma."

"When he went through the windshield?"

"Or when he struck the ground."

"Is it okay to talk about this?" Meadow's brow creased anew.

HomeSky had to again remind herself how young Meadow was, and that there was little in the way of emotional development in those years. "It's essential we talk about this. None of it does any good stuffed away."

"Do you really think we can help Cory?"

"I know we can."

"Maybe our little salmon can help, too." Meadow scooped her baby under his arms and lifted him above her head and looked into his eyes. Pool water ran off his little blue swim diaper. "We can help Cory, can't we?" she said in a singsong voice. "Can't we? Yes we can. Yes we can!" Billy writhed in the joyful pitch of his mother's voice.

Meadow took her child to her chest, feeling their skin touch. "His recovery won't be fast, will it?"

HomeSky stood. Her hair was long again, like before. She was strong, standing there, a few inches taller than Meadow.

"Not fast," HomeSky said. She softly put her arm around Meadow. "If you want to go fast, go alone. If you want to go far, go together."

SHERIFF

Rubbing his temples, he sat in his office chair.

The thumping pressure showed no mercy, setting up behind his eyeballs. Sheriff Harris blinked his computer screen into focus and grumbled. He was no fan of the newfangled contraption. But, in his opinion, the personal computer did offer one advantage over poking at typewriters. The computer made it much easier to correct his lousy spelling.

Paperwork, he thought. *Just thinking the word gives me a splitting headache.*

He tapped the right front pocket of his uniform shirt. A few years back, he would have found a pack of filterless Camels there. Instead, he found a pack of Big Red chewing gum. His taste buds were becoming fond of the sting of cinnamon. In his left shirt pocket he kept a pack of Trident sugarless wintergreen. He thought that tasted like chewing on swamp bark, and he told Kitty as much.

The Trident was her idea. She would tsk-tsk his bluster with a small kiss on the cheek before informing him zero calories were the ideal snack and zero sugar kept the dentist's drill at bay. It's almost as good as brushing your teeth between meals; she recited a huckster's adverting promise. He agreed to rotate in a piece between sticks of Big Red, but didn't promise. The Sheriff always kept his promises.

With the back of his oversized fingers, the Sheriff dusted his computer screen. He hoped by the end of the week he would complete his report on the Cory Bradford/Reg Cunningham case. He needed to be done with it. When he wasn't working on it—in the little time he set aside for sleep—he was dreaming about it.

He had teamed up on the case with a Duluth counterpart at the St. Louis County Sheriff's Office, the county where the deaths occurred.

After seven weeks of unrelenting police work, his report was nearly complete.

Reg Cunningham had booby-trapped Cory's cabin to have a gas leak. But because Cory's fiancée, Hanna, and her son, Singer, arrived at the cabin before Cory, she was killed in an explosion meant for him as she lit the space heater.

Singer was found an hour later on a nearby road, sleepwalking. Hanna had taken her napping boy from the car to the couch, and while she was preoccupied with unpacking, he walked out of the cabin before the explosion.

The Sheriff continued scrolling through the case details on his screen. Two sets of tire tracks in the snow left the scene. Vehicle One (Reg Cunningham) took the road north, winding around the field. Vehicle Two (Cory Bradford) crossed the road and drove through the adjacent field in pursuit. Vehicles collided one mile north of cabin. Speeds in excess of 80 MPH. One man dead (Reg Cunningham), one in critical condition (Cory Bradford).

The Sheriff's head fell into his hand, picturing the unspeakable violence of that day. In a bolt of anger, he smacked his desk with his fist, startling his seven-month-old pup from his half-nap. "Shitfire," he seethed.

Private stood and shook, his collar tag jangling. Tail tucked, he looked at the Sheriff.

"Ah, it ain't you, boy," the Sheriff said. "You're a good dog." Private let out a squeaky-old-door yawn before turning a tight circle and reclaiming his napping position. Then he had a better idea, lolling onto his back and presenting his pink belly.

"Oh, no," the Sheriff said. "Shame I woke ya, but I ain't taking the bait." He staunchly crossed his arms.

Private, with oversized paws thrust toward the ceiling, dogpaddled the air.

"I do not see you nor do I see your upturned belly." The Sheriff looked at the wall.

The standoff was scored to the quiet hum of his computer fan and the thin buzz of overhead fluorescent lights.

The Sheriff broke. He snuck a peek at Private, whose tail thumped the floor upon eye contact.

"Ah, the hell. You always get your way." The acquiescence in his voice put Private's tail into double time. Clearly, the dog had his master well-trained.

"Unconditional surrender." The Sheriff stood. "I can't accomplish anything with you giving me those eyes." In truth, he needed a break. A 15-minute walk around the block might be the best headache remedy.

The Sheriff couldn't escape the notion that he should have done more to stop Reg Cunningham. When a person goes back, gathers up all the pieces and begins to assemble the whole of it, suddenly there it is. Hindsight is its own kind of perverse hell.

"Shoulda seen it coming," he said to Private, scratching the dog's belly joylessly.

The Sheriff groaned, pulling on his rubber overshoes. He looped his arms through his coat and rolled up Private's leash and stuck it, along with a poop bag, in his pocket. "I'll take you off leash if you stay close. Got me?" The two of them locked eyes. "Are we clear?" Private cocked his head, non-committal. The Sheriff glanced out the window. The weather kept most people behind closed doors. "That cold out there will quickly have us standing an inch taller. Too many creature comforts dulls the edge."

The 1950 red-brick courthouse where the Sheriff kept office stood squat, framed by a stubborn gray sky. The building was designed as practically as the Baudette citizens it served. A simple, two-story rectangle, it had only as many doors and windows as called for by city code. There were no architectural refinements, embellishments or fandangles. No clock tower, no sweeping marble steps, no facade flourish.

As such, there was no visual irony in a square-shouldered, crew-cut-wearing, six-foot-five, 250-pound Sheriff making his way directly out of the courthouse's front door. An inch of light, wind-swirled snow was at his heel, along with Private. The dog stopped momentarily to stretch his length, rejoining his master on the muffled sidewalk.

The wind was untrained and nipped hard at the Sheriff's exposed skin. He wore no hat, no gloves, donning only the compulsory winter overcoat and overshoes. His red-brick philosophy—though some would call it redneck—was not backwoods, it was complementary. He belonged to this backdrop.

In Baudette, at 11 in the morning on an unseasonably cold Tuesday, there is little activity. The Sheriff's limp from a steel rod in his lower leg was becoming less pronounced with every step. Wounds heal, but a person never gets over being shot. He's jumpier. Less invincible.

The two of them walked their regular route: past the Dairy Queen, which was shuttered until the Friday of Memorial Day weekend. There was the Hardware Hank with its frosted display window serving as the only barrier between school children and the deluxe Lionel electric train set that climbed miniature snow-capped hilltops and chugged through idyllic verdant valleys. Farther along, at the street corner, the marquee of the Grand Theatre featured *Back to the Future* starring Michael J. Fox.

Smoke rose from the chimney of the post office. The Sheriff waited at the curb long enough to look both ways and quickly make the sign of the cross before stepping into the street.

Finally, they turned upwind, walking past the Mutineer's Jug. Private stopped to sniff the tavern's brick wall, on the alley side, which likely had been peed on by a dog of the two-legged variety the previous night.

This bar was a frequent watering hole for Reg, which made it one of the stops during the Sheriff's investigation weeks ago. He spoke with the bartender and a handful of regulars. A couple rounds of free drinks got them talking, revealing a disturbing story about Reg's youth that began to explain his violent, self-destructive behavior.

The Sheriff's thoughts drifted to the report on his computer screen. Reg had been found unresponsive in his overturned van. Cory was thrown through the windshield of his pickup truck. He was lying bloody and unconscious in the snow-covered field opposite the road.

After Reg's body was extricated from the vehicle, police bagged the evidence including a suicide note, a pistol with one bullet chambered and a camera. The developed film revealed pictures of Cory's cabin before and after the explosion. The suicide note said that the voice inside Reg's head would be silenced once and for all. But first, Cory must pay.

What a damn waste. The Sheriff gritted his teeth and looked through wind tears. Two blocks ahead, the animated neon coffee cup above Lu Ann's diner emptied and filled, complete with a swirl of rising steam. He shook his head at his failure. "I knew the guy was bad, but I didn't know he was bone-rotten." Private looked up at him. They began walking again.

As the murder investigation gained traction, everything came out. Three years prior, there had been a hellacious fight between Reg and Cory on the plant floor of the forest products company where the men were employed. Reg was left badly beaten with such long-term, debilitating leg and back pain, he thereafter walked with a cane in one hand and a bottle in the other. Every day, every step, was a stabbing reminder of what Cory did to him.

Immediately after the fight, Pat, who also worked at the plant, and the Sheriff created a cover-up saying that Reg's injuries were caused by a workplace accident: a fall from a high stack of pallets. That way the company's insurance would cover Reg's significant hospital bills and no charges would be pressed against Cory.

The Sheriff told investigators that Reg had invited the beating. For years, he had harassed, tricked and bullied a co-worker with Down syndrome. Cory finally snapped. Some kind of response was long overdue, the Sheriff argued. Cory went too far, yes, but Reg had it coming. So they covered it up. And it stayed covered until the Sheriff was obligated to uncover it to explain Reg's motive for booby trapping Cory's cabin to explode.

In the end, the Sheriff received a formal reprimand for his part in the workplace cover-up—something now on his permanent record—plus two weeks unpaid leave. As for Pat, he was knocked from first-shift supervisor to third, but that demotion lasted less than two weeks when plant production dipped by 10%.

This entire backstory to the murder was vomited out in the local and national news. Cameras and microphones were thrust in the Sheriff's and Pat's faces for weeks after the deaths. This had the Sheriff not only questioning his merit as a law officer, it had him driving home the long way and sneaking in his back door.

"Close ranks," the Sheriff commanded Private. He paused at Lu Ann's to exchange a word with a local coming out of the diner.

"Egg salad the special?" the Sheriff asked.

"Meatloaf," the farmer said, scratching his whiskers and looking at the threatening sky.

"Meatloaf is Thursdays."

The farmer worked a toothpick. "Always had been. But you know . . . with Lu Ann . . . how she is lately."

"A-yep." The Sheriff turned up his collar. "If you like wind, today's your day."

"It'll blow your mustache crooked."

The Sheriff joined the farmer in assessing the sky. "More snow comin'?"

"Bet your last nickel on it."

"Going to make for a long winter."

"Never known another kind."

"You could always move to California," the Sheriff said.

The farmer nearly swallowed his toothpick. "Yeah. And you could always become a ballerina."

LU ANN'S DINER

"Perhaps you need to get away."

Monsignor Kief said this with no small measure of forethought.

Lu Ann glanced at her watch. Two minutes to eleven. The brass bell above her diner's front door announced another early bird had lit in for lunch.

"What do you mean by *away*?" she said, her focus returning to their conversation.

"Away from work," the Monsignor clarified. "Away from Baudette."

She exhaled forcefully. Although her blind friend couldn't see it, the Monsignor correctly imagined the disconsolate look on Lu Ann's face. "I'm worn out by shame," she whispered. Dark circles had formed under her eyes. "Hanna. What a beautiful person. And Singer, without his mother." Her voice cracked. She squeezed her eyes shut.

The Monsignor slid his hands across the table until they bumped Lu Ann's. They sat in a quiet booth in back. He took her hands in his. "That was not your doing."

"Why would he . . .?" Lu Ann couldn't continue.

"Your father was deeply troubled."

She shook her head. "And I wouldn't even serve the bastard coffee."

"Lu Ann," the Monsignor said, "I never went out of my way to visit him, either. He was a member of my community. Perhaps none of us did enough." Monsignor Kief spoke with authority. "That said, the responsibility of his horrible act falls and rests with him. It is not a daughter's responsibility to direct her father's actions."

"Still, why?"

"That question, my dear, is ancient. Yet it gets asked anew every day. No one can say why. I don't believe your father intended to hurt Hanna. His anger was targeted at Cory, whom he blamed for his injures. But I believe his brokenness was actually sustained many, many years before their altercation. When your father was a boy."

Lu Ann spoke just above a whisper. "Do you believe the story?"

"If you're speaking of his abuse as a child, yes I do."

"Is that why he was the way he was?"

The Monsignor pondered. "The root cause of a thing is easily overlooked. So often, an extended time separates an act from its cause. Early experiences cast a lifelong shadow."

"I hate to think what that means for me."

"You, my dear child, are wonderful."

Lu Ann grew sarcastic. "Oh, absolutely. I can tell by the way conversations stop cold when I enter the room." She looked out the large front window at the sullen day. "I see what's going on. The whispering."

"That's among the things you need some time away from," the Monsignor said.

"Where? How long? How?"

The elderly priest's tone brightened. "I have been praying on those questions."

Lu Ann looked at the Monsignor. "By the look on your face," she said, "you've been praying and then some."

"Will you hear me out? Just ten minutes. I know you're distracted by lunch preparations, but I assure you, lunch can spare you a few minutes longer."

Lu Ann picked up her water glass. Her poached egg and toast were cold. "It's odd," she told the Monsignor. "I care about lunch prep, but I don't. That about sums me up."

"Ten minutes," the Monsignor gently repeated.

The Sheriff had returned to his office and dropped back into work. Private was asleep, tongue out, stretched on his back across the threshold. A small fox-shaped squeaky toy lay just out of his reach.

"Helluva guard dog," the Sheriff grumbled, fishing a stick of Trident wintergreen out of his left shirt pocket.

He turned away from the police report and thought about Kitty. Just last week, she became the subject of conversation while he and Pat played a few hands of cribbage at the diner. Pat had asked how the two of them were doing. Fine, the Sheriff had said, hoping a one-word response would douse Pat's smoldering curiosity. Just fine? Pat asked, undeterred . . . can you elaborate? I don't kiss and tell, the Sheriff announced, crisply shuffling the cards. Pat's eyes twinkled. Oh, so there *is* kissing? Cut the deck for cuss sake, were the only further words he pried out of the Sheriff for the next two hands.

Am I in a serious relationship? the Sheriff mused. His phone's speed dial buttons suggested he was. Written below one button: Kitty (H). Below the next: Kitty (W).

He pressed Kitty (W) and slid the receiver between his shoulder and ear.

"Shields Cards and Candles," Kitty chirped. "How may I help you?"

"Hello there." Pause. "It's me." Pause. "Thurgood." Phones and women flustered the Sheriff.

"Of course it's you, you silly goose. I'd know your voice in a windstorm."

"Oh. That's nice. Um. I was thinking about lunch?"

"A common thought this time of day."

"It's meatloaf at Lu Ann's."

"So is that an announcement or an invitation?" Kitty teased.

"An invitation. If you're free."

"What a perfect surprise! An unscheduled lunch date to warm a cold day."

"Well, yeah. You know."

"What time were you planning?"

The Sheriff's voice dropped into business octave. "It'd have to be sooner than later. I have a one o'clock call with the deputy district attorney and judge. We need to put the finishing touches on the case."

"Still going for self-defense?"

"All the way. No criminal charges pursued against Cory."

"I thought that wasn't an issue," Kitty said.

"It's not. Just protocol. In this day and age, you don't dot an i or cross a t, it comes back to bite you."

"You sound tired."

"Not really," the Sheriff sidestepped. He wasn't one to unload burdens, least of all on Kitty.

"How about I stop by in 15 and we'll walk up to Lu Ann's together?"

The Sheriff smoothed down his tie and wondered about the appearance of things.

"Let them stare," he said unwittingly.

"What's that?" Kitty said into the receiver.

"I'll be here," the Sheriff recovered.

Lu Ann capped the marker and inspected her small handwritten sign. A set of car keys had been found in her parking lot and she taped them to the cash register. She leaned the sign next to the keys. Normally she would have written something quippy like, *Car keys found. Next time leave your wallet—that I can use!* But her mischievous energy had gone flat. The sign read *Car keys found.*

As she rejoined the Monsignor at his table, Lu Ann slid a plated, warm caramel roll next to his coffee. He was so anxious to lay out his plan, he momentarily ignored what his nose correctly identified as hundreds of deliciously gooey calories.

He explained that he'd been talking to his friend Mick in the Twin Cities. The same Mick, he reminded her, who also owns a diner.

"I asked Mick how it was going down at his place. He said business was brisk. I said beyond business, though. Personally, how's it going? Like, do you ever feel burned out, doing the same thing day in and day out?"

Lu Ann watched the Monsignor closely for the answer to that question.

"Mick said it was never the same thing day in and day out. But he also said if you've ever burned toast beyond it really being edible, that's how he'd begun to feel." The Monsignor paused. "Guess what I told him?"

"You said something like you're sorry to hear it," Lu Ann said.

The Monsignor clapped his hands together in delight. "Quite the opposite! I said I was thrilled to hear it. You can imagine the awkwardness immediately ensuing."

"You mean like the one before us now?"

The Monsignor let the moment linger.

"He's right about that toast, by the way," Lu Ann commented.

The Monsignor snuck a small bite of his caramel roll. "Oh my. Oh my! Alert the Sheriff. This roll must be against the law."

"Thank you. But can we get back to the burnt toast?"

"Certainly, certainly. I asked him would he ever consider taking leave of his diner. For one month. Thirty days. To clear his head." The Monsignor took another sticky bite.

"And?"

"He apologized for being blunt and told me I didn't understand the restaurant business. He said 30 days is an eternity."

Lu Ann agreed.

"But . . ." the Monsignor's index finger shot up in the air, "when I continued to ask him why, that's when he started to really hear my question." A small memory smile came to the Monsignor's lips. "Don't you have very capable people working for you? Would business really dry up and vanish in 30 days? You can learn more in 30 different days than you'll ever learn in months of regular ones. Slowly," the Monsignor said, "Mick began to re-imagine the possibility."

"I could never do anything like that," Lu Ann said flatly.

The Monsignor wiped his mouth. "Lu Ann, I'm suggesting you do exactly that."

"You're serious?" Her abrupt tone lifted a few of the customers' eyes from their newspapers.

"Contrary to usual, I am. Here's my proposition. I think you should go to St. Paul and run Mick's place and he should come here and run yours. Leave your trusted lieutenants in place to keep the eggs crackin' and the coffee brewin'. Pick up the phone when you run into something you need help with. But that's it. Only communicate on an I-can't-figure-this-out basis. No checking in on daily or weekly rings. Urgent calls only. Get away from your typical day-to-day. Enjoy the energizing broadening that comes with a change of scenery. See what the good Lord opens your eyes to."

"Monsignor, I don't even know this man."

"You don't know the good Lord?" the Monsignor teased.

"You said you were serious."

"Agreed." The Monsignor waved a hand, banishing his silliness. "Lu Ann, I know the man and I trust the man. And guess what else?"

"I'm afraid to ask."

"He trusts you."

Lu Ann took a deep breath. "How? How can that be?"

The Monsignor smiled. "He's a good listener."

Lu Ann shook her head. "Come again?"

"I told him about you."

"About me?"

"I did. Upon listening he said any woman who at age 20 buys her own diner, raises two children on her own, puts them through college—while running that business—well that's someone he can trust in."

"Simple as that?"

"Is there really anything simple about that? About what you've accomplished?"

Lu Ann folded her hands as her thumbs tugged on her upper lip. "And he's . . . normal?"

"As normal as you and I."

Lu Ann exhaled. "I don't find that particularly comforting."

"Where are my two favorite men?" Kitty's voice bounded ahead of her as she came down the dim, fusty hallway of the county courthouse. Her nose reflexively crinkled, sensing omnipresent mold spores.

The Sheriff's office was the last one on the left. Kitty's cheerful voice rolled Private onto his feet, his tail whipping nearly fast enough to levitate his backside.

"Well hellooo Private." She offered her hand. "Do you smell Hansel and Gretel?" The spoken names of Kitty's Schnauzers, along with their aromas, got Private's entire back half writhing. "It's like being greeted by a brass band. Yes it is. Yes it is!" Her voice played with each word.

"His caboose is going to decouple," the Sheriff said, rising stiffly from his desk. He came over for a taut peck on the lips from Kitty.

Kitty settled into his bear-like hug. "It's cold as the dickens and you're a furnace."

"Built for winter, I guess. But if I don't get some meatloaf into me, that fire may go out."

"Well we can't have that. Has Private been out to do his business?"

"Check."

"Let's get him kenneled and get up there before they erase the special from the board." Kitty took a compact out of her purse. "This office could use a mirror." She quickly inspected her reflection. "Let's get him kenneled," she repeated, unsure of the hold up.

The Sheriff stood, looking down at Private. Private sat, looking up at the Sheriff. The pup sensed what was coming and was working the Sheriff with his best stuff: a sad-eyed droopy-ear combination.

"That dog is mind-controlling you," Kitty said.

"Kennel?" The Sheriff suggested.

Private seemed to shrink a bit.

The Sheriff swallowed. "What do you say? Kennel? Huh boy?"

Kitty snapped her compact closed in a clear opinion of the Sheriff's approach.

Now it was the Sheriff whose posture slumped. "Son of a biscuit. It kills me to stick him in jail."

"Jail? Nonsense," Kitty rebuked. "A crate-trained dog is a happy, bold, confident dog. Always has his own safe place."

She strode over, gathering the attention of both males in the room. "You don't ask. You instruct. Private, kennel." Her sharp, clear enunciation was followed by a hand gesture that cut the air like a sword. Private quickly ducked in the kennel's open door. "Atta boy! Good Private," she praised, before securing the latch.

"We'll see you soon, boy," the Sheriff said, trying to make the best of it. He went to the coat pole for his jacket.

Kitty straightened a few pens and paper clips on the Sheriff's desk. "Oh, I saw this in the paper, too." She put her fingertip on the front-page story from this week's *Baudette Region*, which was clipped out and pinned on the corkboard next to his desk. LOCAL LOGGER DIES IN ACCIDENT, the headline read. "I plan to stop by with a dinner. Poor woman."

One arm of the Sheriff's coat was bunched up, making a mess of getting it on. He joined Kitty deskside. "Twenty-seven years old is all. Two little ones at home." He shook his head. "Damn shame. Give me a hand with this coat here, can you?"

His request was music; Kitty lived to be helpful. "Why is that story pinned? I thought only open cases made the corkboard."

The Sheriff's arm wriggled through as Kitty made a few final adjustments. "Just between you, me and the coat pole, there's been too many 'accidents' on Varkas property lately. I'm going to have a look into it." He tapped the newsprint with his broad index finger. "Yessiree."

Kitty policed the collar of the coat, tending to a few flakes of dandruff. "Varkas isn't a man who likes people looking into stuff," she said, concerned.

"No matter to me." The Sheriff straightened. "I ain't *people*. I'm the law."

REAL AMERICAN

The morning's cold on the deck was forbidding. Varkas's hands were full. He made his way over to a corner post where he set his bowl of cornflakes using the same hand that held a quarter-pound of smoked venison sausage. His other hand gripped a rifle.

There had been multiple sightings of feral cats of late. In Varkas's experience, if you catch and bag a cat, drive it 15 miles up road and pitch it in the weeds, that low-back mess of fur will return to your ground the very next day. But if you substitute a bullet for the burlap bag, well then you have an altogether different outcome.

He sliced the sausage with a Buck knife pulled from a smooth leather sheath he had tanned, cut, stitched and stamped with his trademark cursive *V*. Cubes of meat rained down among the cornflakes, splashing drops of milk onto his boot tops. Cold left his breath visible, to be quickly ferried away.

The cornflakes and sausage were enthusiastically dispatched. Varkas frowned at the bowl's bottom, hungrier than if he had not eaten at all. The ephemeral light of daybreak left pink in the folds of clouds. Varkas blew into his huge hands, taking proud notice of calluses the size of bottle caps. He didn't submit to the luxury of placing his hands under his arms to warm them. *People are soft,* he thought. *Have the nerve of pastry dough. Hands to match.*

He faced the January morning wearing a flannel shirt, corduroy pants and a red, folded neckerchief in the fashion of John Wayne, whose surname Wayne Varkas was given at birth. Along with this name, Varkas inherited a misguided notion of what it meant to be a real American. Ever since his grandfather immigrated to America from the Czech lands—a skinny teenager in the early 1900s—with his lone suitcase, brush-cut hair, olive skin and few words of broken

English, the prospect of being a real American had been the family obsession.

Varkas stood monumental. As such, he was not altogether different than the old-growth forest he looked upon. People couldn't help but gawk at his stature—six foot ten inches tall, 300 pounds. Varkas wouldn't admit this to any person, but only two things frightened him: bats and church. Both were strictly avoided.

He was not an attractive man. Beneath his sloping, meaty forehead, the bridge of his thickset nose was deeply furrowed due to a permanent scowl. Sunk beneath black, wiry eyebrows were glowering eyes. Across his mouth were pressed thin, downturned, angry lips.

From his home's deck, Varkas scanned the land before him. There, under blue-crusted shadow, stood one acre of vast front lawn dormant below the snowpack. By creating this expansive clearing, Varkas made his statement. Wild forest, obey! You can be cut, cleared and leveled. And be sure, my chainsaws, harvesters and skidders will take more upon my whim.

Imagine Varkas's property like this: A long driveway angled in from the blacktopped highway. It was as if a storybook giant dragged a finger from the highway through the untrammeled emerald forest, clearing a path a full quarter mile in length. It was then as if that same giant sat down, crushing and leveling the forest beneath him. That was Varkas's clear-cut.

On this clear-cut, atop a small rise, stood Varkas's impressive two-story timber frame home. It was the product of his hands, his trees and his will. Out back, off the deck where Varkas had just finished breakfast, was his sprawling yard marked with the only two objects Varkas deemed worthy of such placement. First, marking the western corner, stood a 60-foot flagpole flying a ten-by-fifteen foot American flag. And in the eastern corner, set far enough into the clearing not to be windlocked by a curtain of 200-year-old red pines, a 1920 Baker Manufacturing steel windmill was positioned so the prevailing northwesterlies could find her galvanized blades in the summertime.

Here in a single sweep of the eye was the Varkas legacy. The rectangle of open ground taken from the forest. The proclamation of patriotism rippling on a flagpole. The steel windmill which, for Varkas, was emblematic of capitalism, driven by the free winds of an economic system that he came to love—and twist—for great personal gain.

Varkas's grandfather had been a windmill agent for the Baker Manufacturing Company, beginning in 1911. The young man gladly rode the rails north though drifts of snow, rivers of mud and clouds of biting flies to inhospitable northern Minnesota. Frankly, his territory was the one that no other salesman would touch with a skunk pole.

He sought out pockets of his fellow Czechs, as well as Poles, Bulgarians, Serbs, Hungarians, Ukrainians and Italians. These were men who were shortening their lives breaking the prairie, thumbing seed into the earth and kneeling on that very dirt to glorify or curse their God in response to the vagaries of weather.

With an ear for languages and a skin color that made his nationality difficult to place, Varkas's grandfather claimed to be a bit of everything. When a sales call took him to a Polish homesteading settlement, he was "at least a third Polish." When his prospects were Hungarian, he had a great grandmother who was from Hungary. In this new world, he was one of them. His words were trusted.

For a man a full head or more taller than the farmers he solicited, he had a knack for unknotting a man, for getting him to uncross his arms and page through a windmill catalog.

What a beguiling smile. What a firm grip and strong back. He had a patient way of finding opportunity under the smallest frozen rock. It took years and it took persistence but eventually the elder Varkas was selling Baker windmills across vast tracts of windswept northern Minnesota. As word of his success spread, he had to beat back other agents who lusted for the bounty this country unbuttoned around every bend.

Finally established, it was time to settle down and start a family, his legacy. He was quickly married and soon after he had a son at his side. Varkas's father only attended school through the seventh grade before exchanging his savings for a good pair of leather boots and taking up with his father, traveling the countryside, quietly accumulating experience. And wealth.

They soon came to discover that windmills were just the entrée into a larger conversation and a greater opportunity. Windmills got them invited to stomp about on land, but land was the treasure. Capitalism most favors the owner, not the salesman. So they set about owning land.

When the providence of weather flattened a farmer and money got so tight that a man was strangled by the very thing he'd toiled on, Varkas's grandfather would step in. He knew which men had large holdings and his proposition was consistent: let me lighten your load and take some of the less valuable timber stands in the wild backcountry. You keep your farm and fields and you're welcome to continue to take game from the forest. He'd tell them that sometimes you have to lose a limb to save a body. And so it was the Varkas family began to put large pieces of woodland together like an enormous jigsaw puzzle.

It was Varkas's father, though, who had the eureka moment. A few years of apprenticeship had made him savvy beyond his 16 birthdays. He came up with the destiny-altering idea.

The land surveyor. Quite often they crossed paths with these hardy men who not only set private and public property boundaries, but also classified land types and recorded ownership in government tract books. There were bargains to be struck, if you could find the right kind of surveyor and win his ear with a gift.

Whiskey. Prostitutes. Discounted windmills for close and distant relatives. These went a long way to win favor. Later, surveyors would demand a little off the top of each transaction, but at first, these partnerships were as wild and unorganized as the frontier itself. Deals were thrilling, cutthroat, lavish, reckless and sometimes violent. What a country! the Varkases proclaimed.

With friends in the U.S. General Land Office, the father-son team targeted swaths of timberland that could be misclassified as wetlands and bought cheap. Should any suspicion arise, they could attribute it to miscalculation, improperly filed survey plats, the inaccessibility of the land—not to mention the impossible hours and circumstances under which a surveyor was asked to work.

Another favorite ploy involved shaving off remote corners of traditional lands, ceded by the Ojibwe in deceptive treaties, and offering them for sale by public auction. Often, though, the only public to be notified about the auction was the newly created Varkas Lumber Company.

Like a giant sponge, the Varkas empire swelled. Timberland was amassed for pennies on the dollar, paid for with windmill sales.

"Trees grow slow," the elder Varkas counseled his clever son as they journeyed northern Minnesota's magnificent backcountry. "We have to be careful not to grow so much faster." They'd sit back-to-back having lunch in a sun-filled grassy draw, watching summer clouds spot the sky like puffs of Civil War cannon fire.

And so they went, off to the next homestead, walking into the rutted yard of a stranger's parcel of land. They'd step over a few chickens, the elder Varkas mussing the dirty hair of a curious child or two before greeting the owner coming out of a one-story clapboard. The sales pitch always began the same way. We just sold a windmill to such-and-such neighbor for a price almost too good to be true. And as the elder Varkas pitched, his son had his head on a swivel, looking at the woodland.

Back on the deck of his timber frame home, the wind gathered under a gaining sun and blew a chill through Varkas. Or was his shudder aroused by a thought? *The wind doesn't blow through the trees. It blows through my trees.*

He would spend the morning in his one-ton pickup burning diesel as he cruised between land holdings, updating meticulously notated index cards he kept stapled in his county atlas and plat book. He'd also check on harvesting crews, visit a few of his lumberyards and, as always, keep an eye out for potential land acquisitions. The Varkas empire was expansive, dotting across a vast wilderness from Baudette to International Falls in the north, and from Bemidji to Hibbing to the south. Nonetheless, Varkas was forever attentive for ways to add to his patchwork of timberland.

There was in fact one parcel that Varkas had been eyeing like a red-tailed hawk will a field mouse—a small quarter section that was most unimpressive at first glance. Just north of Baudette, the ground was fairly scrubby, rolling, with a few fields of underperforming cropland. To say the least, it didn't typify a Varkas acquisition. But back in the 40s his grandfather and father had circled this land in their atlas and inked a side notation: WATER!

Try as they did, neither his grandfather nor his father could interest the landowner in a windmill. The farmer, an Ojibwe who went about his work and said little, did once mention that water was the least of his problems on his land. The creek that cut through it was confirmation; even in drought years, water ran clear and high.

Land. Timber. Windmills. A hierarchy of beliefs had been ingrained into three generations of Varkas men. And at the top was the tenet that wealth can't grow without owning land.

Wayne Varkas did not challenge his forefathers' belief. He did, however, argue with its top position. Varkas had become certain that his grandfather had stumbled onto the ultimate source of power precisely from the beginning. It was always there, right under his boots.

Wealth can't grow without land, but land can't produce without water.

Suddenly, Varkas's eyes veered from the antique windmill to a feral cat slinking from the underbrush onto his clearcut. A slant of morning sunlight had thrust through the forest, laying down a warm rug of light on the snowpack. The cat took a moment there to attend to her cleaning.

She was promptly shot dead.

PART TWO

Middleton, Wisconsin

MB

Hell of a way to meet a guy, his clothes cut open, lying naked on the emergency room exam table.

Mary Beth Lancaster, known to all—even her mother—as MB, was working the night shift when a patient came in. It had been a slow night in the ER. Slow week, more precisely. But it was Friday. Anyone living within a siren's distance of a hospital knows when Friday night rolls around.

The 20-something male had been transported 25 miles to St. Mary's Hospital in downtown Madison, Wisconsin. He was quickly triaged and moved to surgery. Snowmobile accident. Excessive speed. Riding off-trail. Struck mailbox. Thrown into barbed-wire fence. Right leg badly lacerated. By the time the first responder arrived, he'd lost enough blood to be drifting in and out of consciousness. When lucid, he asked about the condition of his sled.

The on-call surgeon walked into OR2 and got started the same as always. "Good evening, ladies and germs. A guy walks into the ER . . ." He snapped the collar of his surgical glove for comedic effect.

"You mean good morning," MB said, checking the clock and making a chart notation. It was just past midnight.

The surgeon was undeterred. "Guy says, 'Hey doc, this apple juice tastes funny. However, I appreciate you warming it up.'"

MB groaned and finished for him. "Then the nurse interrupts, 'Anyone see my urine sample?'"

The surgeon's shoulders slumped. "So, I need some new material."

"Don't quit your night job," she told him.

He nodded, but quickly rallied, dropping his voice an octave. "May the forceps be with you." Then, turning his focus to the patient, "Okay. Let's see what we can do for this guy."

MB made a final check that the name on the chart matched the name on the patient's wristband. Mike Chevalier. That's as close as they came to an introduction. This time, that is.

Pretty much no one called Mike Chevalier anything but Chevy. It started when he was 11, playing a level up in PeeWee hockey. His coach pinned the nickname on him. It was an easy shortcut of the boy's last name, but there was more. The handle derived from the coach's almost religious belief that a Chevy was the most reliable brand of automobile to ever transport a human being. His dad was a Chevy man. His grandpop was a Chevy man. Chevys always started and they always ran. Likewise, he said, you could always count on Mike Chevalier to start the team's scoring and continue running up the score until the final horn. Chevy had the touch.

The second time MB and Chevy met was considerably less dramatic. And funny, actually. It was the summer following the snowmobile accident.

MB had just pulled a 24-hour shift in the ER, something the nurses call an "out and back." Three p.m. out to three a.m., and three a.m. back to three p.m. You end up where you started, just a day later. Occasionally, she did this for extra money, but this time she was filling in for her friend who was turning 29. MB told her that no one belongs in the ER on their birthday. Unless they were a patient, which was an all-too-frequent occurrence.

Behind the scenes, MB had arranged a surprise birthday party at the Lakeside, a bar-restaurant in Madison that had achieved landmark—if not deity—status. With its iconic, spiraling, two-level deck overlooking Lake Mendota, and the fact that it was walking distance from the hospital, the bar was very popular with her crowd. The Lakeside was usually loud and always friendly. Nurses and doctors often mixed with locals of all stripes. On this particular Saturday, the mix included thirsty softball players.

MB booked the party room from five till close. A smaller group of co-workers who got off at three agreed to meet early to be in on the surprise. The plan went like this: MB told her girlfriend she'd meet her for a quick birthday drink after her shift. I'll be coated in 24 hours of ER fuzz, MB told her friend, but I'm good for one. Maybe two. Then I'm going to bed, she had said.

The trap was set. MB wasn't easily excitable, but the adrenaline surge of an approaching surprise got her through her double shift. That, and a little something she got from her pal at the pharmacy.

That same Saturday, Chevy's softball team handily won their morning and noon tournament games. That was huge because it meant they didn't play again until Sunday at 11. Translation: plenty of time to wash down the dust and sleep it off. The team was pumped. They unbuttoned uniform shirts, swapped out baseball pants for shorts, cleats for flip-flops, and agreed to rally at their sponsor's bar. The Lakeside.

MB and her group were clustered at the comfortable, curved oak bar. The tavern was mid-afternoon quiet as they awaited the surprise guest of honor. The door opened and a softball team poured in, Chevy leading the pack. Through the raucous banter, Chevy emerged, hat backward, brandishing a weaponous white smile, heading for the bar. He had made the last error of the last game: E-6. That meant he was responsible for the first six pitchers of beer.

All of this makes a person wonder about life—about the fragile chain of happenstance that ushers in resounding consequence. Or at least, it had made MB ponder, in the years since that afternoon. What if a late-shift ambulance had made her miss the beginning of the party? What if Chevy's team lost a game? What if she didn't sit on the stool closest to the bowl of pretzels, the only snack food she had a weakness for? What if Chevy didn't double clutch and make a throwing error from shortstop on a ball he'd routinely handled all season long? What if his snowmobile hadn't clipped the mailbox? What if she hadn't been in the ER that night?

Who sets all this in motion?

"Six pitchers, Libby my darlin'." Chevy winked at the cute bartender. He edged into the bar close enough that MB could feel oven-like heat radiating off him. "Want to split 'em?" Chevy said to apparently no one. Then he looked at MB.

MB had secretly watched him approach the bar. She was pretty sure. She looked for a limp, but there wasn't much. His left knee was crusted over with infield gravel and dried blood, but when she closed her eyes and moved her hands to orientate her memory, she remembered it was the right leg she had triaged.

"Let's split 'em," Chevy repeated, this time with a smile that went beyond cute to someplace more addictive.

He's a pirate, MB thought to herself.

Chevy nudged the pretzel bowl toward her. "Two left. I'm willing to go halfsies."

"Big of you, seeing they're my pretzels," MB told him.

"Property of the establishment. Just like our team there." He gestured over to the boys. "We drink free. Can I get you something?"

"More pretzels, if you're intent on stealing my last couple."

"Stealing? A strong accusation." Chevy put his hand to his chest, purposely overdramatic. "I might feel some sort of heart attack coming on. Would you give me CPR?" Chevy had noticed MB's scrubs.

"It's a coin toss," MB said in her best bored voice.

Chevy took his time looking her over. "You work at the hospital. Isn't there an oath or something to aid the suffering?"

"Very observant."

"You're for sure too pretty to be a girl doctor."

The bartender, returning with the beer, overheard the comment and broke out laughing.

"Girl doctor?" MB shook her head. "Really? You do the male species proud."

Chevy grinned. "I mean female physician. Way too pretty."

More laughing from the bartender, who interrupted. "Chevy, you have no idea how right you are. She's way too pretty. And way not dedicated enough. At least that's what her mother repeatedly told her."

MB tightened as the bartender blew her bangs back. Chevy looked from one to the other. A protracted look at MB. Then the same for the bartender. "No way . . ." he said, smiling. "Really? Libby? This is your sister?" Chevy's tone switched from asking to telling. "This is your sister, the one you're always bragging on who works up at St. Mary's."

MB tried not to blush, which made matters worse.

Chevy took one of the two remaining pretzels from the bowl, broke off an upper ring, gently took MB's hand and slipped the ring on her finger. "Libby, I'm going to marry your sister. You are my witness."

"Get in line, sweetheart," Libby told him.

Chevy's fascination continued. "Just can't believe it." Chevy was talking more to himself now, looking at MB, memorizing her. "Sisters. It's a small world."

MB finally broke her silence. "You have no idea," she said to him, before she started laughing. It had been a long 24 hours helped by a couple amphetamines. She was a little loopy.

Chevy looked at Libby. His expression asked, *do you get what's so funny?*

Libby shrugged her shoulders as MB's laughter escalated.

"Sorry," MB said, gathering herself. She held out her hand and considered her pretzel ring before quickly chewing and swallowing it. *Look out,* she told herself.

Then her hand disappeared down below the bar where it nonchalantly came to rest on Chevy's knee. Chevy was more than a little startled, causing Libby to peek over the bar to see what was going on. MB's fingertip found the scar on the inside of Chevy's leg and slowly traced its course, up the thigh, stopping just short of the crotch. "Small world is right," MB said. Then she cocked her head. "In more ways than one, superstar."

CHEVY'S OFFICE

Pretty damn good. Chevy gave himself kudos as he hung the family photograph from Sears Portrait Studio on the wall of his new, small office. He'd been promoted and Boss Allen had made it clear: for a financial professional to be successful, his office must be properly dressed. In fact, that was rule number one on what he called TWL, The Winner's List. If you want to win in banking, his boss said, you start with family photographs in the office.

Puts people at ease, he told Chevy. We don't want clients who are edgy and tight. He'd say, do you know how an edgy, tight customer handles money? Then he'd clench his fists long and hard enough to get his point across, as well as leave deep fingernail furrows in his palms.

Chevy stood back and assessed the family portrait. *Little crooked.* A half-laugh escaped. *Ironic.* As he adjusted the picture, he was struck by the expressions captured on the different faces.

MB had a glued-on smile and her eyes couldn't have appeared more distant if she were looking away. Chevy was all-in, his head tilted slightly toward MB's, just touching, pronouncing their bond. And Singer, cuter than a four and a half year old had a right to be, stole the show, with his curls of blonde-brown hair catching some of the side lighting the photographer mentioned he was known for.

Together, they looked like the American Dream.

Chevy had been practicing in the mirror—which also hung on his office wall—how he'd answer the inevitable question from a client about the photograph. "How wonderful. Is that your family?"

"Thank you, yes. But, I must tell you, we are a work in progress."

"Oh?"

"Yes. My fiancée [lie: he was MB's live-in boyfriend] and my son are finally putting down roots here together after the court granted me custody of the boy." [Half-lie: as Singer's biological father, Chevy was granted temporary custody until the court decided the case.]

"That's so nice. What about the little boy's mother . . . if you don't mind?"

Chevy would pause here. "She died some time ago in an accident [half-lie: she died only seven weeks ago. Chevy wanted the appearance of a proper grieving period before finding a new life partner.] My son and I have been reunited and couldn't be happier, all things considered." [Lie: Chevy had serious doubts he wanted to be a dad and MB was trying her best not to let Singer penetrate her heart because she felt inadequate.]

Chevy sat down in one of the two chairs reserved for clients and scanned the office from their point of view. The walls facing this direction were dominated by framed wildlife prints. Deer, grouse, waterfowl, as well as the Wisconsin state fish: a leaping musky trying to shake a lure from its bear trap jaws.

Mandatory artwork, purchased from a stipend provided by Boss Allen, who couldn't have cared less that Chevy didn't own a fishing rod, know how to shoulder a gun or really care for outdoor pursuits. These were tools, Chevy was told. This is Wisconsin. The great Midwest. Outdoor prints make the client feel at home. If we were officed in New York, you'd have paintings on your walls so abstract it wouldn't matter if they hung upside down. But you're not in New York. These here, these are fire-starters. You know? They get a relationship going. And so it went with Boss Allen.

If queried about the outdoor prints, Chevy was instructed to reply he was a novice sportsman, before adding that they sure were blessed to live in God's playground. Then simply pause, he was told. The client will fill the vacuum. Get ready for story after mind-numbing story of massive swamp bucks and grouse shot over steady pointing dogs and trophy walleyes taken on slip bobbers.

Truth be told, his prized possession on the office walls was his framed 1981 Badger hockey team poster, the year the University of

Wisconsin won the NCAA championship. He and six other players had managed to put on fake buckteeth right before the shutter snapped.

Chevy looked at his teammates. There was Joseph, mugging the camera with those big plastic teeth. The practical joke was his doing. *I miss you, big man*, he thought. Chevy's gaze jumped to Cory, who had somehow agreed to go along with the prank despite being a stick-up-the-ass rules guy. He and Joseph were virtually inseparable; that must have been why he was in on it. *You were a player, kid. Now, it looks like you'll never skate again.*

Chevy's eyes left the team poster and came to rest on his recently earned loan officer certification. Framed, in a fancy script font, signed by the Secretary of State. He was moving up. It had been quite a trip.

Just over a year ago last fall, Chevy had joined Middleton Community Bank. It was after yet another winter of hockey with a semi-pro team out of Milwaukee followed by greenskeeping from April through October at the public golf course. Chevy loved the lifestyle, but his bank account was on fumes. And with the snowmobile accident the previous winter, his skating wasn't near what it once was.

To make extra cash back then, Chevy caddied on weekends. That's how he met Boss Allen, whom he then knew as Mr. Allen Sutton. Mr. Sutton: a lifelong resident of Middleton, which was a 15-minute drive to the public course in Madison. Mr. Sutton: a college hockey fanatic who could recite the score of each Badger game in the 1981 NCAA tournament when Chevy, the senior captain, led them to a national championship. Mr. Sutton: a man—socially and athletically awkward since childhood—who, star-struck, handed Chevy his business card along with a modest tip after a round of golf and said if he ever wanted a job in banking, he should look him up.

It was big-boy decision time. Chevy's life teetered. The golf course was closing for the season. He had met a very cool ER nurse. And his hockey coach wanted to know if his leg was 100 percent and would he be coming back for another season in Milwaukee. The beating you take in minor league hockey is not something you're supposed to think about, it's something you're supposed to do. Chevy thought about it. That's when he dug the wrinkled business card out of his golf bag and gave the banker a call. Then, for the first time in his life, he went shopping for neckties.

His promotion came just over a year later. Boss Allen called Chevy into his office to tell him he was no longer a bank teller. He was kicking him up to Small Business Banker. It would involve study and accreditation. Chevy assured him he was up for the challenge. Suddenly his career was on the rise. On top of that, he'd been seeing MB for over a year now, and had all but moved out of his apartment and into her house. A new life was starting to roll.

Then the phone call came. It was few days after Thanksgiving. Singer's mother had been killed. Cory was in a coma. Chevy was so stunned he didn't understand the upshot of what he was being told: his four-and-a-half year old son, who Chevy had only seen once as an infant, was in need of his birthparent.

Chevy adjusted the family portrait one final time before returning to his desk and looking at the appointments in his daily planner. Pretty standard. Two loan meetings—one scheduled for the morning, the other for the early afternoon. Lunch with Boss Allen. Not sure what he wanted to talk about but the tab would go on the company card and that was always a bonus.

Then at 4:00, Singer was in a music program at the Montessori school just ten blocks from the bank. That was one of the advantages of Middleton, its accessible coziness. MB was working the seven-to-seven shift but would try to get out of the ER early and be at the program, too.

Chevy also kept framed pictures of both MB and his mother on his desk—another Boss Allen mandate. When Boss Allen spoke of female clients he simply called them She. He told Chevy, when a couple comes in for a loan, the husband may think he's calling the shots, but more often than not, She is driving the bus.

She needs to trust you and this begins by seeing that your mother is important to you. Make sure Mom's photo is slightly angled out so clients can steal a peek.

Offering a discreet glance at a photo of your significant other is also critical, he was instructed. That way She knows you're in a committed relationship. Boss Allen would lower his chin—chins, actually—and whisper. Do you know what committed relationships are to our business? He held out his left arm and placed two fingers firmly on his wrist as if to take his pulse.

Chevy didn't need to be told to have a picture of MB close by. MB had him hogtied. For the first time in his life, Chevy didn't feel like he held the relationship controls. In no small part, this was due to the bizarre way they met. "She saw me naked first," Chevy would proudly tell his buddies. "The turnabout of the century."

What he didn't add was with his leg laid open to the femur, he had lost a life-threatening amount of blood and he was unconscious. How much more vulnerable could a guy get? She triaged him. She was with him through surgery. She helped him when he couldn't help himself. This was an altogether different foundation for a relationship than anything he'd ever encountered.

And though he could remember none of that, when they met for the second time, after his softball game at the bar, he had a sense of déjà vu. And this strange familiarity encouraged him to trust her. He was unusually open with her. His extremely human exposure to her had stripped away his artifice. "I have nothing to hide from your sister," Chevy said with a wink at the bartender that summer afternoon after the game. MB had replied in typical wry fashion. "Not to worry," she said. "Wasn't much to hide anyway."

Chevy chuckled, recalling the moment. He pulled MB's photo across his desk, closer to him. Her hair, near black, had a few well-placed highlights. Bangs high off her forehead, usually pulled into a ponytail, a habit from her athletic days in track. Because her bangs were pulled up, exposing her forehead, her eyebrows were showcased. Thin, dark and arched in such a way that one might think she was doubting or judging you.

At five feet ten, MB was not a small woman. This was a key criterion for Chevy. For him to be serious about a woman—to even consider her as a possible mate—that woman had to have size. If his children were going to be athletes, which he assumed they were, being bigger would be an advantage. Because MB was long, her face was long and thin. Her mouth was slightly downturned, giving her a hint of melancholy. It was part of her mystery. Attractive yet intimidating.

Chevy paused, thinking about her ears, which were a bit pointy and cool to the touch. He found them sexy. And her nose, which she didn't like ("it has a little bubble on the end") was, in his opinion, perfect. Thinking about her had him verging on an office erection. He considered paging her with the news: FLYING HALF-MAST, THINKING OF YOU but MB didn't like Chevy sending personal pages when she was on shift. Every time her pager buzzed, she told him, I get a little sick to my stomach. Someone's worst day is hauling ass toward me.

On the opposite corner of his desk stood a framed snapshot of Chevy with a strong arm around his mother. She was smiling a perfect mom smile with a roundish bob of perfect mom hair and a sparkle of perfect mom love in her eyes.

Chevy's mom was borderline saintly, rarely known to issue a complaint or a cutting word. Boundless love is what she had for her son. He grew up wanting for nothing. Mom was always there, utterly fulfilled in her role. A plated sandwich. An available Band-Aid. A Kleenex to mop his nose. Rides to the arena. Stacks of folded clothes. Endless inescapable hugs. He made a note in his planner: Call Mom.

In his desk drawer were his index cards used as crib notes. He pulled them out for a quick study. They contained bulleted talking points that Boss Allen told Chevy to weave into conversation when meeting with clients.

- Oil prices going down.
- Interest rates dropping.
- Commercial construction on the rise.
- Money is cheap.
- Capital investments are booming.

- Expand.
- Get yours before someone takes it.

Also drilled into Chevy's head during mentoring meetings was recognition of their true mistresses: fees and debt service. Oh, how Boss Allen got amorous around steady, small climbs in fees, rates and surcharges. "Paper cuts," he liked to call them. We just need a nickel here and a dime there, he told Chevy. They'll hardly feel our hand in their pockets. Especially as this economy revs up.

Soon, Boss Allen's eyes would widen inappropriately and a reflexive snort-laugh would come spitting into the room, which embarrassed him not in the least. No doubt, he told Chevy. 1986 was shaping up to be a banner year for banking!

And Chevy, sitting at his desk looking at his index cards, was determined to get his.

BOSS ALLEN

For every serious businessman officed within a 15-mile radius of the village of Maple Bluff, lunch at the country club was considered a badge of success. As the staff there was known to say, under their breath, many will come, but few are chosen.

Indeed, there was a lengthy waitlist to join the Maple Bluff Country Club, and advancement was slower than golfing behind senior citizens who had a better chance of turning 100 than breaking it. As a result, many applicants eventually dropped off the list rather than face the annual humiliation of completing yet another request-of-membership form.

But for six springs, Boss Allen had shown up on Application Day, the first Tuesday after Memorial Day, in his best golf apparel. His application was dutifully completed. The details provided were said to be held in the strictest confidence, including net worth, yearly income, workplace title, arrest record for the past ten years, as well as vehicle make, model and year. And, lastly, home address, which in Maple Bluff circles said as much about the applicant as could be found on any other line item. You are where you live, or so believed the admissions committee.

Each application required a $10 processing fee. False or misleading responses, the form stated in capitalized type, would result in automatic rejection. It was rumored that the nine-member admissions committee—responsible for the thumbs up or down of each applicant—included a prominent judge, a retired chief of police and the president of the Wisconsin banking commission. These men knew more about the applicants than their mothers did.

As one approached the maître d' stationed at the front of the dining room, if you were a member, you'd be greeted by name. If not, you'd be asked, spuriously, in a voice just loud enough to reach the dining room, if you were a member. This inquiry got noses lifted high, as the area's upper crust took a moment away from their shrimp cocktails to observe the latest interloper.

Taken on the whole, and rationally considering the expense, membership privileges here were not very impressive. You had access to an 18-hole golf course, pool, tennis and racquetball courts—venues that allowed non-members only as guests. Dinner reservations in the restaurant were for members only, as were private wine lockers that came with a name plaque and no corkage fee. Summer mooring privileges on the lake did cost extra.

Downstairs, the languishing exercise room was in need of new equipment. The steam room was fine, but overdue for new tile, and the teak benches had famously left slivers in some highfalutin rear ends.

The locker room was convenient but cramped and revealed more about your contemporaries than you wished to know. The complimentary drink at the bar after a round of golf or tennis match was a nice touch, and the valet would park and retrieve your vehicle at no cost. Yet make no mistake about it; members needed to be ready to write some hefty checks for annual dues.

But prestige refuses to be quibbled with and won't be squared on a ledger sheet. To be a member of the Maple Bluff Country Club, with its black, glossy ID card displaying two intersecting gold maple leaves, to have a polo shirt, tennis skirt or visor emblazoned with those same intersecting leaves, to have a MBCC window sticker for the back of your luxury vehicle was to quietly shout something of your rank in society.

Boss Allen lusted after such acknowledgment. He had ever since he biked across town in the dark of the morning as an 11 year old to deliver newspapers in the Maple Bluff neighborhood. It was a job he got because no resident child would stoop to such work—not to mention get out of his warm bed to haul heavy newspapers stuffed with coupons that his mother would never clip.

Like he was fond of saying, "Setting my sights on Maple Bluff is no bluff at all." Boss Allen would find his way into the respect and recognition of this village. He was sick and tired of arriving by the side door. He wanted to be greeted by his first name at the front.

"No. I'm not a member at this time," Boss Allen replied to the maître d'. "But I'm told I'm near the top of the list for new membership." His eyebrows lifted optimistically.

The maître d' smiled unconvincingly. "How many for lunch?"

"One more will be coming shortly."

Taking two menus under his arm, he instructed Boss Allen to please follow. Despite many open tables, he was led to a smallish one toward the rear of the dining room. At least it offered a view to the lake, Boss Allen cheered himself.

Were it summer, with Lake Mendota alive in sparkling waves and bobbing sailboats rather than flattened by a frozen slab of horizon, he wouldn't have been seated at this table. But that didn't occur to him. As the maître d' departed, he said he would watch for his lunch guest. Then his eyes seemed to briefly catch on the cut of Boss Allen's suit. Undoubtedly, the headwaiter concluded, his hands clasped behind his back, it came off the buy-one-get-one-free rack.

Allen Jerome Sutton was 44 years old. He saw his impending forty-fifth birthday as a "turning point." Those were his watchwords. Funny how he came by them. He was listening with one ear to a business radio program last week when the host mentioned something about a turning point. The words jumped out and bit him. They were no sooner broadcast than he felt directly spoken to.

He was a third-generation "President Sutton" at Middleton Community Bank. Dad had recently retired after 46 solid years on the job. Quite a career. Right out of high school, Allen's father had joined his father in the business. And thanks to diligent attendance in night school at the nearby University of Wisconsin, he slowly but surely gained the acumen and confidence to eventually take the baton from his dad.

Boss Allen's father was no boat rocker, and he told his family so.

I'm a boat captain, he explained. A captain never rocks the boat, he steers it safely to port—and then occasionally has a port. His father was fond of wordplay and would work on it daily at his desk during the many idle hours banking slathered on him. Wordplay is recess for the brain, so he said to his family.

Monday through Friday, he'd come home with a new one—or the start of one—to share over dinner. Boss Allen could picture his father. Always at the head of the table, in a laundered and pressed, white v-neck t-shirt, his office button-down and tie safely laid over a chairback in the TV room. He'd be working on his second of two Manhattans as he addressed the family. Okay, he'd start. What do you call an acorn you hold in your hand too long? His dad's eyes would scamper around the table. Clock is running, he'd tell them. Then he'd do a drum roll on the tabletop and say: a palm tree! Or: The bait store guarantees their minnows. If they die you get a re-bait.

And so it went, every night. A man content in his middle class, his wordplay and his blessings.

Upon retirement, Boss Allen's father couldn't entirely stay away from the bank. One morning a week he would put on a shirt and tie and come sit in the lobby and read the local paper while greeting familiar faces. He'd fill the tellers' candy dishes, be sure to brew fresh coffee, top off the water dish on the sidewalk for the dogs and then make his way past his old office—now Allen's—to a smaller one where he still kept a tidy desk.

He was left in charge of the bank's community participation, which meant keeping a calendar for the employees' mandatory ten hours of monthly volunteer work. Middleton Community Bank was proud of the "community" in its name. Since opening their doors, they demonstrated it by being good-neighbor people.

His father was also tasked with writing modest checks that the bank donated to the school, the chamber of commerce, the public library, the hospital, the scenic trail fund and the like. About one aspect of this, his father was clear: Allen was now the face of the bank. So Dad stood aside as his son stepped into the viewfinder during newspaper photo ops that captured checks exchanging hands between banker and good cause.

Allen had come to cringe when seeing those amateurish, run-and-gun pictures. For instance, a black-and-white shot in this week's edition was taken outside the warming house at the public ice skating rink, which his bank's contribution helped refurbish. There was Allen, freezing in his business suit, handing a check to a man in a snowmobile suit wearing a massive fur hat that looked like roadkill.

Ironically, the page opposite trumpeted a 4-color, full-page advertisement for First National Bank of Madison. Hell, they had national in their name and Boss Allen only had community in his. No wonder they were eating his lunch when it came to deposits, loans and mortgages. Not to mention prestige. Boss Allen knew full well he was ahead of the new president at First National on the country club waitlist—by two years—but the other banker leveraged his way to membership nonetheless.

No doubt, Boss Allen knew he was at a turning point. He was tired of being middle. He lived in Middleton. He was middle age. He was middle class. He was even born in June, the middle month of the year. Could life mock him any more than it already had?

No. He was going to do something with the life God gave him—other than watching his bank stunt in the shadow of larger competitors just six miles down the road. Other than returning to a home not three blocks away from where he grew up. Other than sitting at the head of a dinner table in a pressed, white v-neck t-shirt sputtering bad puns to his disinterested children. Other than being reminded regularly in the community page of the local paper that he was significantly overweight and his face had receded into a mass of fleshy chins.

Dammit all the way! He would extend his hand to this turning point, bow, escort it to the dance floor and spin it like there was no tomorrow.

Starting with a house in Maple Bluff.

Chevy, accompanied by the maître d', sat as quickly as he could without disturbing the water glasses.

"Sorry I'm late," he said, slightly short on breath. "These guys know how to live, huh?" Chevy's eyes sparkled like the French chandelier above them.

"Oh. Yeah. No problem."

"How you doing?" Chevy asked. Boss Allen had an odd twist in the corner of his mouth.

"Good. Yeah. Great. Glad you could make it." Boss Allen cleared his head, returning to the here and now. "How did your meeting go this morning?"

Chevy took a long swallow of water. "Excellent." He nodded enthusiastically, letting the gulp clear. "You know Polar Ice in town?"

"Sure. Penguins in bowties on the sides of their trucks."

"Yep. They want to add two ice lines by summer. One cubes. One blocks. Pretty standard cap investment loan. Could go two, maybe two-fifty."

Boss Allen whistled. "Not bad for a morning's work. How'd it come in?"

Chevy smiled wryly. "You know how I told you about my kid? About him singing at the Montessori school's holiday performance back before Christmas?"

Boss Allen did not remember. "Yeah," he said.

"Well this kid—my kid, I'm still not used to saying that—he sings like . . . I don't know, like a pro or something. He's up on stage for his part and goes off program and sings."

"What do you mean off program?"

"I mean he just gets the urge and starts singing Ave Maria. Including Latin parts. I have no idea. Must have been something his mom taught him. A regular little Pavarotti."

"Ave Maria?"

Chevy nodded. "Yeah. And it's not like they're a Catholic school. I wasn't sure what to expect afterwards, when everybody has cookies and juice. Thought the teachers might be mad about his improvising. Or parents upset 'cause my kid hogged the spotlight." Chevy looked at Boss Allen.

"So what happened?" he wanted to know.

Chevy smiled. "Unbelievable! Parents and grandparents were coming up to us left and right. The kid's a hit."

"Ah," Boss Allen said, nodding excessively. "That's how the business came in!"

"You got it. One couple turns out to be the owners of Polar Ice. We start talking about what we do, I say I'm in business banking, he talks about summers getting hotter and expanding operations and looking for capital. Next thing you know, we're sitting in my office discussing raising boys and variable interest rates."

Boss Allen had the proudest look on his face. "Did I not tell you this is how it works! Everyone needs a friend in banking—that's number five on The Winner's List."

"Yeah," Chevy said. "I never would of guessed. This kid shows up out of the blue and now doors are popping open."

"That kid's your golden goose."

Chevy hesitated. "What?"

"Activities, friends, parenthood—mark my words, they all lead to one thing. Business."

"I don't know if I'm ready for all that."

"That's why you have a girlfriend. She's a nurse, right? Best darn moms in the world, nurses."

"Slow down there a bit, Boss Allen."

His boss's face went lemony. "Why do you insist on calling me that?"

Chevy smiled, turning on the charisma. "It's just you. Boss Sutton sounds too formal and Allen sounds too informal."

"How about Mr. Sutton?"

"That sounds like I should be carrying your golf clubs. Boss Allen has the perfect ring."

"It's unprofessional."

"I'd say it's the opposite. It's like family. Like Uncle Bobby or Grandpa Bill. Isn't family and relationships on The Winner's List?"

Boss Allen made a face like he just missed a short putt. "I guess so."

After they'd finished lunch, Boss Allen again had an uncomfortable look on his face. This time he was calculating the tip. Not that the math was difficult; he was a numbers wiz. It's just that a 22 percent tip went against his nature, not to mention the lackluster manner in which their table was serviced. But Boss Allen had heard that the Club recorded the average tip of all non-members, and that was taken into account during membership review. Anything below 20 percent, it was rumored, was enough to sink your boat.

"Before we head back to the office," Boss Allen lowered his voice, "there's something I'd like to talk to you about."

Chevy heard the change in tone and answered by sitting forward.

"I'm just going to come right out with it." A sheen of perspiration rose on his ample forehead.

"Okay," Chevy said.

"How would you like to make 100K, tax free?" Boss Allen didn't blink.

Chevy did his best to remain casual. "I could get used to that idea."

"It's a one-time deal." Boss Allen's fleshy eyelids drooped. He looked a bit lizard-like.

"It sounds, I hate to say, like maybe it's illegal."

Boss Allen took a drink of water. "Chevy, the concept of illegal is more nuanced than one might think."

Chevy more expected Boss Allen to speak Russian than to utter those words. "How's that?"

"Getting here. You were late, yes?"

"Yeah. Sorry."

"Did you make a full stop at every intersection with a stop sign? Did you stay within the 25-mile-an-hour village speed limit?"

Chevy shook his head no.

"More nuanced," he repeated with a thin smile.

"Yeah. But it's hard to pocket 100K rolling though a stop sign at Sherman and Lakewood." Chevy opened his palms in a *just saying* gesture.

"Might be easier than you think, my good man." Boss Allen wiped his mouth with his napkin. "But we'll talk about it next week. Let the idea simmer."

Chevy was going to interrupt. He wanted more details. How can an idea simmer if all you have to work with is the idea's outcome?

Boss Allen folded his napkin and dropped it on the table. "Let's put this same lunch time down for next week. We can get more into it then, if you're interested. Meanwhile, I believe we both have appointments in less than 30 minutes."

Chevy checked his watch, surprised how the time had gone. And this latest proposition had his head swimming. He rose quickly from his chair.

"Oh, and Chevy . . ." Boss Allen said.

"Yeah."

"I suggest you make a quick detour to the men's room. The button on your left collar flap is undone. You'll want that corrected for your 1:30."

SINGER

Singer loved his Montessori school. More than twenty million ice cream cones. More than seven zillion dump trucks.

His classroom was just his size. Tables and chairs and couches and rugs and pillows all built for those who are low to the ground but aloft with imagination.

Large windows invited natural light to scatter freely about the room. Open spaces were decorated with gleeful voices, the hum of activity, teacher encouragement and respectful harmony. Walls were a keeping place for colorful student art.

Islands of flowing, open shelving were interspersed classroom-wide with stores of hands-on activities and mind-opening treasures. Squares of clay. Beads for counting. Cups of rice for measuring. Zippers for zipping and laces for tying and letters for learning. There were geography puzzles to conquer. Goldfish to feed. Plants to water. Singer's every sensory receptor was abuzz.

Singer's classmates spanned from three to five years old. It was an exciting day. The Music From Around the World program they'd been rehearsing for weeks was upon them. They lined up, quietly, in the hallway outside their classroom door, not an insignificant feat because they each held a musical instrument from a different culture in their hands.

A flute, drum, ukulele, spoons, finger marimba, bells, didgeridoo, harp, guitar, accordion, violin, maracas, harmonica, even a miniature bagpipe. They quietly watched their teacher who had her hand raised, the unspoken request for respect and order. Singer held no instrument in his hands.

The string of children made their way to the performance room. A small stage awaited with an old upright piano from which Ms. Anna, the music teacher, would lead the program. As she played, each of the 21 students would have their moment to step from the group to center stage to accompany her.

Folding chairs were set out in the small auditorium and filling fast with moms dabbed in a touch of makeup and grandparents in sweaters. Everyone craned to find their little musicians wrapped in colorful costumes on stage.

Chevy rolled up in front of the school but the better parking spots were long gone. He made his way to a side street and parked. Loosening his tie, thinking he'd stash it in the car, Chevy remembered he was still working. He used the rearview mirror to readjust his tie and give himself a wink.

The only two chairs Chevy could find together were near the back of the small auditorium. He put his overcoat across one and stood by the other as he continued to scan the room. Not many dads. The 4:00 weekday start time was not going to help Chevy with post-performance business small talk. *Where is MB?* he wondered.

Turns out, MB would not be making it. She did get home with time to spare. The hospital in Madison was only 15 minutes from her house. The performance wasn't until 4:00. She was scheduled to work seven a.m. to seven p.m.—double sevens, as they called it—but there were enough ER nurses to cover her early exit.

Home and showered by 3:30, she stood in front of her closet deciding what to wear. There, she felt it. It brushed against her ankle. She closed her eyes and tried not to think about it. But once the thought was acknowledged it would not be exiled.

Was she tired? She could take something for that. No, it was the idea of a crowd and the energy required to graciously meet strangers and Singer's beautiful face looking out in the audience for her. That was too much.

It took a fuller grip of both ankles now and held her feet fast to the floor. She wasn't going to the program, was she? She opened her eyes and looked into her reflection in the closet mirror. She was ashamed. She had let the idea in: *maybe I won't go.* A crack is all it took.

What's wrong with you? She challenged her reflection. But the idea of not going owned her now. *This is best for everyone. It's selfish for me to fall in love with Singer. It's not in his best interest. He belongs with the man who was more of a father to him than Chevy ever was.* She caved to the grip. *Neil Young and a joint.* She pulled on sweats and a sweatshirt. *Head for the ditch,* she thought.

Long before MB was an emergency room nurse or a joint-smoking Neil Young fan, she was Mary Beth Lancaster: a prodigy athlete and daughter of a 1956 American Olympic track and field silver medalist from Arlington Heights, Illinois.

MB's mother was an imposing six-foot-tall woman who competed in the 100-meter and the 4 x 100-meter relay. She and her team missed gold by 1.2 meters. This life-changing distance provided her with her first coaching point, which she relentlessly drilled into her developing daughter's head: 1.2 meters = 3 feet 11 and ¼ inches.

Her mother cut a hank of thin nylon rope to that length and it went with them everywhere they trained. When MB wasn't working to her mother's satisfaction, the small length of rope came uncoiling out of her pocket as she held it out from her body like a dead snake.

When a clock read 3:11, MB's mother would point it out. If they walked past a house with the address 311, they would acknowledge it. That number seemed to rise up from the surfaces of life and remind them both how close and how far they were from their best selves.

But 311 wasn't really a distance in MB's world. It was a reprimand and threat. Anything less than an A on a report card got a quiet, even response from her mother: "311." If MB was unfocused in training, or eating too much ice cream: "311." Her mother didn't raise her voice. She was proud of her disciplined German heritage.

Another favorite coaching point was that a team is only as successful as its weakest link. "Don't be that link," her mother said. MB never knew if her mom was the Olympic relay team's weak link, but it was unlikely. "Be the strong one."

MB, it turned out, was the strong one. Her younger sister by two years, Libby, was not so athletically gifted. She was shorter-legged and slower. "Be a go-getter, not a bed wetter," her mom would say after Libby lost yet another race. "Save those tears for the winner's podium." Libby tried and tried. She ran in the younger heats after watching her big sister win race after race. But MB had a born-in different gear. Before long, her younger sister was up in the stands with their dad, cheering.

MB had a scrapbook full of newspaper clippings. Her smiling freckled face, often standing next to her coach, her mother. They had a plan. They were going back to the Olympics. They were going to erase that 311 from the record book.

When MB was a high school sophomore she ran her way to a state championship. She easily won districts, sectionals, regionals and state at the end of the school year. That summer, in August, were nationals.

Nationals were the focus. The next milestone for MB. She didn't have a life, she had a calendar. She didn't have a mother, she had a coach.

But it was sophomore year. High school temptations danced before her eyes. Boys and girls started behaving very differently. Independence was raging to get out and it manifested itself in changing bodies and reckless thoughts. As much as MB tried to forestall or ignore this transformation, it was everywhere. Her focus slipped. There was a boy on the track team who was very cute.

Distractions or not, MB was too busy to be overly popular. She was not disliked, she was just, essentially, gone. Consumed by her sport. This placed her in a different category than other kids. When friends called and repeatedly got the same answer, "I have to train. Sorry." They eventually stopped calling. Soon, MB no longer occurred to them. She vanished.

That sophomore summer a lot of girls were at the pool and the beach hanging out and working on their tans. MB was indoors, resting. She would train in the morning when it was cool, and again in the evening, but when the blazing sun lorded over the day, MB was kept indoors. Her mother—her coach—made it clear that a beating sun devours energy. Read. Stretch. Nap. Nationals are coming. 311.

MB wanted to win nationals, but she wanted to get a tan, too. MB wanted to hang out at the pool and laugh at utterly stupid things. She wanted to be a teenager. And she wanted to catch that cute boy's eye.

So she did what she could. Like Rapunzel, imprisoned in her bedroom, she found a solution. Out her bedroom window she'd go with a bottle of Hawaiian Tropic, a beach towel and a folded piece of cardboard covered in aluminum foil. The roofline just below her window angled gently away and offered room enough for her towel. She'd lay back, hold the cardboard reflector open like a giant book under her chin and in 15 minutes get her tan. Everyone at school said a reflector, Hawaiian Tropic and fifteen minutes worked like magic. Her mom was busy downstairs. No one would be the wiser.

Until she fell off the roof.

The hot sun and grinding routine conspired. MB had nodded off. She was in the storm of a most vivid dream that had her sprinting, lunging for a finish line. Startled, she awoke to find herself sliding down the short roofline away from the curtains in her bedroom window.

Fingernails found no purchase as she clawed the hot asphalt shingles. Her sliding body gathered speed. The gutter was her only chance but her fingers grazed the lip as she went off the edge.

Her breath was bounced from her lungs as she landed on the porch roof below. Bones snapped. She rolled off that roof and dropped again, now headfirst toward the leafy ground shrubs. She remembered the earth coming toward her, slow and surreal, and spotting a red cardinal bursting from a nest in the foliage. There is a happy destruction in falling, she thought, before all went black.

Then she was awake in the ER. Had she dreamed of her mother's incessant yelling at her in the front yard, or did it really happen? Regardless, now everyone spoke to her in kind, soothing ER voices and gave her warm, fuzzy ER drugs and looked after her with bottomless ER attention. She was safe. No one could get her in the ER. The many hands that touched her wanted nothing but the best for her and had no other agenda above her health. This undisturbed peace she didn't want to leave.

A broken leg, three broken ribs and a chipped front tooth. Could have been much worse, the doctors said. Mom was silent. They would not be going to nationals.

Dad stayed positive, though. He always stayed positive. It was summer and she would be bedridden for a week and then housebound for many weeks longer. Dad went to the newsstand to get her magazines. Lo and behold, his favorite musician, Neil Young, was on the cover of the August edition of Rolling Stone. Neil Young hadn't done an interview in five years, which mattered not at all to MB. She thought his singing sounded like a cat whose tail was tangled in a house fan.

MB's dad brought home a stack of magazines and when he finished the Neil Young article, he flipped her the copy of Rolling Stone and said it was an amazing interview. When MB had exhausted all other content, she gave the interview a read.

She found a soul mate. What Neil Young felt was what she felt. What he said was what she wanted to say. He had grown tired of being the person other people wanted him to be. His manager. His wife—about to be ex-wife. Even his bandmates. He said you have to try new things to be alive. He said he had just experienced his greatest commercial success, but could care less about how other people defined achievement.

"*Heart of Gold* put me in the middle of the road," Young told the interviewer, referencing the biggest single he'd ever cut on the best-selling album he'd ever recorded. "Traveling there soon became a bore so I headed for the ditch."

MB started listening to her father's Neil Young albums. That summer, the needle on the record player gave out before her fascination did. And an affinity for the ditch came alive in her.

MB had burned a joint and was sitting at home on the couch with

Neil Young's *Live Rust* playing when it came to be Singer's turn to step forward and sing alongside Ms. Anna. All of the other children had played their instruments from around the world.

The piano returned to the melody and Singer's voice folded into a constellation of notes as he closed his eyes and saw Cory and his mother, shimmering, backlit in afternoon lake waves. In Singer's mind, Cory lifted him into his mother's arms where they splashed, laughing, and Cory splashed back. Then Cory went underwater. They looked for him. The sun shattered into a million pieces on the lake deck. *He will come. He will come. He will come,* Singer thought.

The boy continued to sing and Ms. Anna did her best to not join the others and fall mesmerized by the virtuosity of his voice. Her hands somehow kept playing while Singer's voice rose, higher and higher, richer and clearer. Each note, like Singer, was good all the way through.

Then there was only applause. The children had set their instruments at their feet and were clapping, too. Tears were falling from Ms. Anna's face. In all her years of music, she had never been in the presence of such a voice.

As the clapping subsided, heads and shoulders craned around—voices of the parents whispering—looking for the mother and father of the prodigy. Chevy sat momentarily at the center of attention. The chair to his right empty, save his overcoat. He'd been in this spot before, eyes and smiles directed his way. But it had been almost five years since he'd won the national hockey championship. Celebrity dissipates. It felt good to be part of this, even if he'd done nothing to earn it.

He looked at Singer. All he could think about was what Boss Allen had predicted. *Golden Goose.*

"Where's MB?" Singer asked as they drove home.

"Sorry, pal. She had to work."

Singer went back to his humming as the car pushed through the dirty snow.

MB's house was in the blue-collar section of Middleton in a neighborhood full of vehicles that didn't lack for rust. Thin, broken driveways narrowly separated close-set houses. Front porches drooped, gutters sagged, soffits yawned, all in need of a coat of paint.

When it snowed, like it had been doing since this miserable winter began in early December, kids might hitch a ride for a few blocks on your car's back bumper. After the holiday, Christmas trees were shoved out the front door, now half buried in snow. This was a neighborhood where people shoveled their own sidewalks and helped the elderly by clearing theirs. No one thought of wasting even one cent of beer money hiring out such tasks. This was family work.

After dinner, MB read Singer *The Cat in the Hat* and *A Very Hungry Caterpillar*, falling asleep four times along the way. Her house had three drafty bedrooms upstairs; one became Singer's, with MB's college futon mattress on the floor. Singer said it was a great way to sleep because it was like camping.

His mattress was tucked in a corner along with a floor lamp and the few possessions he brought with him, including his stuffed Magic Bear with an arrowhead tied around its neck. Before lights out, he prayed for his mother in heaven and Cory in the hospital. Then he told MB he wanted to write Cory a letter. He asked if she would help him.

"What would the letter be about?" MB asked as they lay next to each other on the mattress.

"I'd tell him about you and Chevy and my new school. And I'd tell him I should live with him and help him get better."

"Do you like it here?" MB asked.

"Uh-huh," Singer said, rolling onto his side and propping up his head on one arm. "This is my spare house. It's real fun."

"How do you know you should go live with Cory?"

"I just do."

"But remember, Cory is hurt, quite badly. Maybe he can't take care of you."

"Then I'll take care of him."

MB teased, "Are you old enough to do that? That's very brave."

"I can get lots and lots of help," Singer assured her, putting on a grown-up face. "From Pat and HomeSky and Meadow and Sheriff and Kitty." Singer thought some more. "And from Monsignor Kief and maybe Stu and Darlene!" Singer looked very confident. And why not, it occurred to MB. That was quite a list.

"Are all those your friends?"

"Yep. And Cory's."

"You're a lucky boy."

"Thank you," he said. "Can we write our letter?"

"How about tomorrow after school?"

"Do you work tomorrow?"

"Nope. Three days off now."

"Will you bring home more balloon gloves when you go?" MB had showed Singer how she could blow up a surgical glove, tie it off, and have a five-fingered balloon.

"I'll try to remember."

"My last one lost air."

"I'll get you more."

"I can't wait to show Cory how you do it."

"Time to brush teeth."

"I did before reading, remember?"

"Oh, yeah. Do you need to go to the bathroom?"

"Nope."

"Drink?"

"No thanks."

"All right then. I guess it's time for sleep." MB rose to her knees, ready to get off the mattress. "Goodnight then."

Singer tossed his little arms around her neck. "Goodnight." He squeezed tightly. "I love you. I'm not leaving because I don't."

"You are sweet. That's so nice to say."

"Cory just needs me more."

"Let's not talk about it anymore tonight, all right?" MB said.

"Okay." Singer slipped under his bed sheet and quilt. "Can I have

Magic Bear?"

"Will his necklace poke you?"

"It never has before."

"Okay. I'll tuck you both in tight," MB told him, doing so.

"Are you worried I'll walk in my sleep?"

MB stopped tucking the quilt under the mattress. "No, no. It's just cold out tonight."

"Not in here."

"Do you remember sleepwalking?"

"Nope," Singer said without hesitation. "I just remember people talking about it. Like that lady we saw with all the papers."

"Do you remember who that lady was?"

"Something like a special worker."

"Close," MB said. "A social worker."

"What's a social worker? She was funny."

"They help make sure kids like you end up living in the right house."

"What are kids like me?"

MB tried to put exhaustion aside. "Sorry, what?"

"You said she helps make sure kids like me get the right house to live in."

MB needed to choose her words more carefully. "I meant kids who have had something change in their lives and now they have to make changes, too."

"We should write her a letter."

"Let's start by thinking about writing Cory," MB said, forcing a smile, hoping to end the conversation.

"Don't worry," Singer said. There was a mysterious calm about him. "It's going to be okay." He settled his head into the pillow, gave Magic Bear a hug and began to hum a song that MB didn't recognize. She closed her heavy eyes to it and her breathing slowed.

"That's a pretty song, what is it?"

But Singer was already asleep.

In so many ways, MB was unprepared for all of this. She sat on the top step of the staircase. Behind her was a sleeping child. Below her, a boyfriend sat on her couch.

What the hell? In what felt like a minute ago, MB had a house to herself. She had a good job that she could bus to in the winter and bike to in the summer. There was a trusted, close-knit group of hospital friends who understood one another and the insanity of working around life and death. And she had her sister, Libby, tending bar ten minutes away. That was all she had needed. Well, not entirely true. She had her little magicians, which she kept hidden in a drawer.

When MB fell off the roof there was significant pain along with her healing. She was given Vicodin. She liked it. Quite a lot. She had become depressed, what with losing her shot at nationals, and the pills lifted her onto a warm, fuzzy conveyor belt and kept her moving through life. The pills ran out.

It was summer and all she could do was hobble around on crutches. With no training schedule to blindfold her, she saw she had nothing. No friends called. Nobody to hang with. Busy parents. A popular little sister. She had put all her eggs in one basket. And the basket just got flattened by a girl falling off a roof.

So she lied. She said there was still a lot of pain. The doctor prescribed something a bit stronger: fentanyl. That really swept the blues away. For a few more weeks. Until another prescription needed to be written and a new routine was there to catch and carry her. That summer, MB spent her days in the house with the three magicians: Vicodin, fentanyl and Neil Young.

MB sat at the top of the staircase and sensed a wave of depression gathering on the distant shore. She was all too familiar with her choices. She could ride atop the wave or get corkscrewed in its churn.

She tiptoed into her bedroom. In the back of her sock drawer was a prescription bottle of oxycodone. They were easy enough to get from the hospital if a person was careful. A few here, a few more there. Skim from the bottles that went home with patients. Misplace an occasional prescription. Tell your friend at the pharmacy your period is especially brutal this month.

There were a billion little lies and manipulations someone as smart as MB could pull off. As long as her usage was small and under control. Which it was. Or so she told herself.

She dry swallowed one 10mg tablet. That would have to be enough. She had to be lucid for the conversation that she and Chevy needed to have.

"He asleep?" Chevy asked from the couch, flipping through channels. "Nothing good on."

MB paused at the last step and listened. "I think so. Sure was a chatterbox." She sat down next to Chevy, but not too close.

Chevy scooted over and gave her a playful kiss. "You're doing great up there. How's it feel to be a mommy?"

MB tightened. "That's nothing to joke about."

"Who's joking? You're doing great."

"Chevy, no. I hardly have my shit together. I'm 28 and I feel like a 13-year-old babysitter."

"C'mon. You've got friends your age with two maybe three rugrats already."

"Yeah? Well, you have friends your age making two maybe three million dollars playing in the NHL already."

"Ouch." Chevy didn't see that shot coming.

"I know. Me too, ouch." MB frowned. "Let's stop talking about other people. Let's talk about us. And Singer."

"What's the big deal?" Chevy shrugged.

MB turned her palms up in disbelief. "Seriously?"

"I'm just saying, lotta people raise a kid."

"Shit, Chevy, we can't even get out of bed early enough on weekends to get to Clines before they stop serving breakfast. How are we going to raise a child?"

"Why do you not want this kid?" Chevy asked.

MB held up her hand. "Don't put this on me." She countered. "Can you tell me why you want him?"

"Just answer my question." Chevy remained calm.

"Let's start with I'm not ready and let's end with I'm not qualified."

"Qualified? Sweetie, what do you mean?"

MB looked away. "Capable. I'm not . . . the kid deserves more."

Chevy sat up from the couch pillows propped behind him. "Don't you want to have kids? Ever?" He asked in a quiet voice.

"Chevy, that's not the conversation we're having."

"Can't we take a side street?" He flashed a let's-loosen-things-up smile.

"No." MB said firmly. "We're talking about this. About Singer."

"I want to keep him."

MB was equally stunned and disturbed. "Keep him? God, Chevy. He's not a stray dog. This is a human being. It's a huge responsibility."

"Honey, I get that. But you need to be more laid-back about it. A lot of people who are bigger dipshits than us have kids."

"Laid-back. You want me to be laid-back?"

"Yeah," Chevy nodded, and casually reclined against the pillows. "Laid-back." He patted a pillow for her.

"Chevy," MB said, sitting erect, thinking about whether or not to say what she was about to say. "Do you know what another word is for laid-back?"

Chevy grimaced. "I think I'm about to find out."

"Clueless."

Chevy tipped his head back and closed his eyes. "That's pretty harsh, MB."

She continued. "When you're in a relationship, laid-back, taking things as they come, let's have another beer, let's see what happens, hey, I was just watching the hockey game on TV, I didn't notice the pile of laundry or the fact that we have no milk in the—oh, fuck it." MB threw up her hands. "Forget it."

"No, no." Chevy sat up straight and locked eyes with MB. "I'm listening. Do you think I'm too clueless to raise this kid?"

"That's not what I'm saying. I'm saying this is about me. Right now, I'm not ready. This is something I need to get my head wrapped around. Being a mom is a big deal and it's freaking me out. I don't want to screw up."

Chevy brought the conversation down an octave. "You mean like your mom screwed up."

"Yeah. I guess."

"You won't screw it up. You're good at everything."

"Chevy, we've lived together less than six months. We're not even sure if we're compatible as two, let alone three."

"MB," Chevy's voice dropped even lower, "I'm the father of that boy upstairs. The court has given me custody."

"Temporary custody."

"Yeah, whatever. I'm all he's got. He's got me and he's got you."

"I don't think that's true, Chevy. He's up there talking to me about names like Stu and Darlene and Sheriff and Kitty and Pat and HomeSky and Meadow and Monsignor Somebody—remember, the people the caseworker told us about. Singer told me tonight he wants to write a letter to Cory and tell him he wants to live with him."

Chevy got defensive. "Yeah? Well that's great. Cory might end up being a vegetable in a wheelchair for all we know. You're saying that's better for a young kid than living here with us?"

"I'm not saying that," MB said flatly. "I'm saying we should do what's best for Singer. And that might be back with the people he's known all his life."

"You know what?" Chevy stood from the couch. "What's best is for the court to decide." He shoved his hands in his pockets. "My life is a lot different now than four years ago, okay? I've got a good job. I'm moving up. I've met this amazing woman who I love, right? Have I told you I love you about a billion times every day since we first met and I proposed with that beautiful five-carat pretzel ring?"

"A billion and five," MB said.

"All I'm saying is think about it." Chevy sat back on the couch, closer, taking MB's hand. "Think about yourself as a good mom, because I have no doubt. Think about taking the next step with me." He rubbed her knee. "We don't have to decide tonight. Right?"

"I guess."

"We have a court date, April tenth—see, I'm not totally clueless. Let's just give this some time. We've got some time. Okay?"

MB shrugged her shoulders. Either the fight was beginning to leave her or the pill was beginning to affect her.

"Come here." Chevy wrapped her up in a tight hug. It felt good. Safe.

"I'll think about it," MB said, pulling back from the embrace.

"Awesome," Chevy said.

"On one condition."

"Okay . . .?"

"We help Singer write that letter to Cory. The two of them deserve that."

"What good does that do if the court decides in our favor?"

"It lets us know we did everything we could. If we are going to take this leap, we have to do it the right way."

Chevy could see there was no arguing. "Okay. We'll help him write the letter."

"Really?"

"Yep."

"Thank you," MB said, giving Chevy a strong hug. "Thank you."

The embrace lingered as Chevy's thoughts crystallized. *We'll write it. But I'll be dammed if it makes it to the mailbox.*

CHICKADEES

One week later, Chevy was back at the country club for a follow-up lunch. It was his turn to be early, or Boss Allen's to be late. The maître d' sat Chevy at the same table as last time. Considering all the open tables, it was a bit of a slight.

The expansive bay window offered Chevy a picturesque view of falling snow. Large and larger flakes parachuted down, occasionally disturbed by a breath of swirling wind, twisting them in opposite directions. The distant lake was obscured by a white veil, but closer to the window stood a line of deep-green, snow-topped dwarf spruce that offered a cozy atrium to busy chickadees.

The birds were having lunch, too. Flitting out to the pole-mounted feeder, politely taking one black-oil sunflower seed, and then disappearing back into the shelter of the downy boughs.

Chevy had always been a fan of snow. Snow meant hockey. Snow meant snowmobiling. Snow proved he wasn't too old to whip a donut in an icy parking lot. But this winter's snow had already lost its charm. Every day there was another three inches. Or five. Or last weekend, a foot. People were getting grumpy. It was only mid-January.

Chevy chose to make the best of it, as was his habit. Hell, he had on a decent suit and an expense-report lunch was in the offing. It was a nice step up being a player, seated among white tablecloths and walnut woodwork and business banter. Not long ago his view was quite different. He was sitting with a losing hockey team wearing stinky sweats at a crappy pizza joint with red and white plastic tablecloths in Moose Jaw, Saskatchewan, staring out a frosted window as the team bus idled in a dirty parking lot. Yep. Liked this view better. Mom and Dad would be proud.

Dad owned a dry cleaners. The bulk of his business was men's clothing—dress suits, shirts and coats and what you'd expect—but he expanded his services to include commercial work, like the upscale tablecloths and napkins now laid out before Chevy. The long draperies edging the dining room windows were like those that made it into his dad's book of business, too.

Dad didn't know how to say no to work. He took on anything and everything. Worked six days a week, sometimes seven if they were behind. Always smiling. Never complained. A born provider. He wanted Chevy and his two older brothers and their mother to be happy in their middle-class cocoon. He didn't want them worried about money.

Privately, his father worried plenty for them all. Especially during a lull. He hated a lull. He didn't trust a lull. The word looked like what it meant: lull.

During one particularly slow week, Chevy's dad had signs made for the store windows. Now taking wedding dresses! It required a lot of handwork, to protect the delicate fabrics and ornamentation from being steamrolled flat by the heavy machinery, but he did what he had to do.

During another slow stretch, Dad contracted—and paid cash—for a construction crew to knock a window through the front of his building and lay a blacktop driving lane that wound around the building from the parking lot. Suddenly, he was offering drive-thru and counter service.

And Mom, she just loved and spoiled her number three. She had all boys, and Chevy, her baby, stole her heart. She drove him all over kingdom come to practices and tournaments. Scrambled him a couple eggs before every game. Was always in the stands hollering out support for a sport she didn't very well understand—other than recognizing that her boy was always among the very best.

When she wasn't a hockey or baseball chauffeur, she was cleaning up behind Chevy, making sure his clothes were clean, folded and in the correct drawers, serving his favorite meals in front of the television, helping with homework and slipping him some walking-around cash when he and his buddies were heading out. All she ever asked for was a hug and a kiss in the morning and at the day's end. Her boys—especially her Chevy—were her purpose.

Chevy looked at his watch. It wasn't like Boss Allen to be late. Promptness was number three on The Winner's List. Nonetheless, it felt good to chill a minute. Having a kid was exhausting. Chevy rubbed his eyes until he saw dots behind them.

Singer was a cool little guy—Chevy said so, aloud, and meant it. Obviously, off the charts talent-wise when it came to music. Not to mention, the kid was a business magnet. Just this week, another parent from school had approached Chevy to compliment him on Singer. They got to talking and it turned out she was a music instructor who was thinking of opening a business space rather than teaching out of her home. He watched her drive away in a new Mercedes, which he thought odd for a music teacher, but maybe her husband was rolling in it. Chevy would find out more at school next week. Life was good.

Boss Allen was suddenly at the front of the dining room. The body language of the maître d' was aggrieved as Boss Allen whisked the snow from the shoulders and collar of his overcoat. After taking a step back, the headwaiter gestured to Boss Allen in the direction of the coat check.

"UN-believable," he said, finally situated at the table across from Chevy. Boss Allen drank a full glass of water before continuing. "Got in an accident. Totally my fault, though you didn't hear me say that."

"What happened?" Chevy asked.

"I was driving by a few houses for sale in the neighborhood and I'm looking over at this gorgeous Tuscan-Mediterranean when BAM! I hit a woman backing out of her driveway. She was still apologizing profusely when the police showed up, but just between you and me and the two-carat diamond earrings she was wearing, had I been looking where I was going I could have swerved or used the horn. I'll get a free paint job out of the deal, easy."

"Lucky you," Chevy said.

The waiter came over to refill Boss Allen's water glass.

"Excuse me," he said. "Can you bring four more water glasses?"

"You are thirsty," Chevy joked.

"Certainly," the waiter replied. "Are you gentlemen expecting other guests?"

"No. If you could you bring the glasses empty—and leave the water pitcher—it would be appreciated."

The waiter bowed slightly before leaving the table.

Boss Allen returned to their conversation. "Actually, we're here to talk about lucky you."

"By that I'm guessing you mean about what you brought up last week." Chevy's skin tingled. "About the 100K."

Boss Allen glanced right and left. The dining room was comfortably occupied: not too empty for one table to draw too much attention, not too crowded to promote eavesdropping. "Tax-free 100K," he specified.

"I'm all ears," Chevy said.

Once the waiter had returned with the glasses and left with their order, Boss Allen's voice dropped into a dull monotone, like he was explaining how to install siding on a garage.

"It goes like this. A fund manager I know slices five million dollars off his investment portfolio—which is peanuts compared to the whole elephant. He targets six very small startups to pump capital into. His business strategy, should anyone inquire, is if one of the little companies hits it big, the investment is well worth the risk."

Boss Allen reached across the table for an empty water glass. "The thing is, each of these six companies is a shell company."

"They're what?" Chevy asked.

Boss Allen peered through the glass at Chevy, tapping its side. "They're see-through. They don't exist. Except for a bank account, which we set up." Boss Allen arranged six water glasses on the table in a neat row.

"So our fund manager takes the five million he's shaved and parses it into modest investments, ones that won't pop any red flags—under a mil each—and loads them into the six fictional bank accounts."

Boss Allen picked up the pitcher of water and demonstrated this by filling each of the six glasses about three-quarters full.

"Follow?" he said to Chevy.

"Follow," Chevy said intently.

"Our job, after creating the fake accounts, is to help these companies," Boss Allen lightly tapped the rim of each glass, "move their money to an offshore account. One by one, they will transfer their balances," he emptied the water from the glasses back into the pitcher, "until, voila! We have the five million dollars back." He picked up the full pitcher. "Our investor has his original five million, but you know what?"

"What?"

"It's sparkling clean."

"Oh," Chevy said.

"With the clean five mil offshore, our investor is free to use this money however he pleases, AKA the stock market, which is currently on a rocket ride. Hell, last year, the Dow did 28%, and that's investing conservatively. Our guy is figuring 30-35% on his moves. That gets him, short side, 1.5 million annual return."

Chevy let out a low whistle.

"But, for the record," Boss Allen said, "the five million that he started with goes back into the six start-up shells. At the end of the year, his books show five million invested, five million returned, which is break-even, which is crap, so he pulls out of the little start-ups and the five million goes back to the fund, no harm no foul. We close out the accounts, and, like that, the companies vanish." Boss Allen snapped his fingers.

"But our guy's sitting pretty with an extra 1.5," Chevy said. "Not bad."

"Yep. The bank gets 500K for our trouble and he gets a clean million."

Chevy's brow furrowed. "But wait. If this investor is such a big shot, isn't that a lot of trouble for a million bucks?"

"A million dollars is a big bag of money."

"I guess." Chevy wasn't altogether convinced.

Boss Allen explained. "He told me it's because his wife wants to buy a place in Naples."

"Florida sounds pretty good about now." Chevy watched the snow falling outside the window.

"Naples, as in Italy. He says Italy is a total waste."

"What's the problem? Beautiful women, I hear."

"No golf courses. Says he doesn't want to spend a dime of his own money on it."

"What about the 500K that goes to the bank?" Chevy asked.

"It doesn't. It goes to us. Your cut is 100. Tax-free."

Chevy sat back and let it sink in. "I gotta say, I didn't think you had the onions for something like this."

"This is a one-time deal," Boss Allen said sharply, louder than he had liked. He looked off, deciding if he should say more. "I want to move to Maple Bluffs. I have my eye out for a house. This is my ticket to the neighborhood."

"That's cool. But why me?"

"Because you *do* have the onions to do it. And no one is watching you but me. If I were to do it, it would draw attention. Plus, you're a good kid trying to get a family started. Didn't you tell me your dad owned an auto body shop?"

"Dry cleaners."

"Oh, yeah. You know how many years your dad had to work to put away $100,000 for your family?"

Chevy looked out the bay window. He watched a chickadee go out against the wind, get his one seed from the feeder, and dutifully return to the shelter of under branches. "Probably 10 or 15 years."

Boss Allen nodded sympathetically. "Give my proposal a thought," he said. "We have a little time."

Chevy sat up straight, a spark in his eye. "You know what all my years of hockey taught me?"

Boss Allen said he didn't.

"One very valuable lesson: how to make a decision. That's hockey.

Decision-making. On a collapsed timetable. Most people, they hedge."

"So . . . what are you saying?" Boss Allen asked.

"I'm saying I'm in."

THE LETTER

Back at her house, MB was making brownies. In a contest between who liked them more—Singer or Chevy—it was a dead heat.

Every day for the past week, MB inched closer to the idea that maybe, just maybe, they could make a home and a fresh start with Singer. She was growing fond of the possibility of a new start because MB felt as though she had been running in place, or even backward, for years. A thought that wasn't without a stab of irony.

One of her mother's training secrets from her Olympic days was backward running. The Italian coach who helped her win the silver in Melbourne was a fanatic for it—how the foot lands with less impact, rolling toe to heel, strengthening different tendons and muscles, adding speed to legs that traditional running did not.

MB's mom would drive her to the high school track early—almost in secrecy so no other runner would be the wiser—and have MB run quarter-mile sprints backward. Eventually, she started challenging boys to a race. They could run forward while she ran backward. Soon, the boys got too smart to accept her challenge.

But then came the fall from the roof, a hastened recovery period, the lingering pain which evolved into a frustrating cycle of second- and third-place finishes, the deteriorating motivation and their endless arguments over training. After the last meet of MB's disappointing junior season, her mother said she was done as her coach.

Unbelievable, MB remembered thinking. I didn't even get to quit. She quit me.

There was a knock on the door.

"Open," MB shouted as her sister, Libby, zipped through the door, shutting the cold out behind her. She kicked snow from her shoes.

"I'm going to Mexico."

"One-way ticket?" MB asked.

"Don't tempt me." Libby grimaced. "I'm vulnerable. And hell, you pretty much mix a margarita in Mexico like you do in Madison. Only with more tequila in Mexico. And no long underwear."

MB wiped her hands on a dishtowel and came over to hug her sister. "Sorry I haven't been around lately. Busy busy. Jeez, you are cold."

"No duh. What are you making?"

MB picked up the pan and put it in the oven. "Brownies."

"What are they rated?" Libby asked.

"Huh?"

"PG or P-O-T?"

"Oh. Actually, G. As in Betty Crocker approved."

"Do you think Betty Crocker ever had sex?"

MB looked at her sister. "Is your brain frozen?"

"Seriously. I bet Betty could rock it." Libby picked up the brownie mix box and tapped the illustration of the prudish Betty Crocker on the side. "Rock IT!"

"Let me see." MB giggled, reaching for the box. She looked at Betty Crocker's white neck scarf, red sweater and shell of brunette hair.

"She's Bells of St. Peter rock it," MB said.

They burst out laughing.

"So, speaking of love lives, how's yours, little sister?"

"Don't go there. It'll put you to sleep. I mean that quite literally."

"Sorry. What's his name again?"

"Andrew. Don't get me started. Like I said, Mexico. Tequila. Skin."

"And maybe Javier?"

"Now you're talking," Libby said. "How's life here?"

"Getting good, actually."

"Look at you, Ms. Homemaker. Nice apron by the way."

"I don't know. I could get used to it. Maybe."

"Is that why you want me to take your pets away?"

"Uh-huh."

"Forever, or just for a while?"

MB shrugged. "We'll see."

"They in the basement?"

"Yep, we should get them out before Chevy gets home with Singer."

Libby frowned. "What's the story on that name, anyhow? Why Singer and not, like, Tommy?"

MB smiled. "You should hear him sing. If you don't believe in a higher power, one song might change your mind."

"Seriously? That good?"

"Otherworldly good."

"And Chevy is for sure the dad."

"Yep."

"We've never really talked about it. How'd it happen?"

"I think you know how it happens," MB said.

"I mean, was it a one-night thing or a serious thing?"

"He was in his senior season with the Badgers. Chevy says he was pretty wild back then, which is probably the understatement of a lifetime. His girlfriend, fairly serious I guess, tells him she's pregnant. He says she should consider an abortion. He's not ready to be a dad. She tells him to go to hell and breaks it off. He says okay if that's what you want. Chevy wins the national championship. He goes his own way, pursuing hockey, playing some minor league stuff that doesn't pan out. She has a baby."

MB stopped for a deep breath. "Four and a half years later he gets a call from a social worker saying his old girlfriend has been killed and he's the father listed on the birth certificate. Just like that. Whole new life."

"So she was a single mom? Didn't you say there was someone else in the picture?"

"Well, yes, eventually. A guy named Cory Bradford. He played on the Badgers with Chevy and was friends with this girl. They started hanging out after Chevy moved on. He helped with the baby. I guess, after a while, something clicked."

"It's all so sad for the little boy," Libby said. "Is he okay?"

MB shook her head, looking off. "Hard to know. He seems happy, normal. But it messes with my head." MB's voice tightened. "This is permanent. I have to do what's best for Singer. He's had enough uncertainty." MB was saying this to herself more than to her sister. "Chevy says Singer can have a great life here, with us. But Singer told me last week he wanted to write Cory a letter. Go back and live with him."

"How do you know what the right thing is?"

"The social workers weigh in, but ultimately the custody judge decides what's in the child's best interest. Our social worker said Singer is too young for the court to consider his opinion."

"What do you think?" Libby asked.

"I think this is a special kid. I think his opinion has to at least be made known. I got Chevy to agree and I helped Singer write his letter. I'm guessing it will eventually get in the case file for the judge to consider."

"What did it say?" Libby caught herself, "If you don't mind me asking."

MB thought for a moment. "It said I have a nice new house and go to a great school but I want to come live with you so you can be my dad like we said before Mom went to heaven."

"Oh, Christ," Libby whispered.

A tear rose in MB's eye that she blinked back. "Yeah," she said, shrugging. "Super confusing."

Libby pursed her lips. "Could be," she started slowly, "that here is a better place for Singer. Might be a fresh start here is what he needs."

MB nodded. "I was just thinking about fresh starts."

"Which brings us back to your pets in the basement. Shall we?"

"I guess so," MB said.

The pets, as MB called them, were named Terry and Jerry: two well-attended marijuana plants that she had been growing for years. In the summer, the plants were kept in her bedroom where she would, as MB liked to say, take them out for a walk. This meant carrying them, one by one, out of her bedroom window and onto the roof for some vitamin D. With Terry on one side, Jerry on the other, they would bask in 20 minutes of sunshine.

For MB, this was the equivalent of giving the middle finger to her fall from the roof in high school. Or maybe she was giving it to her mother.

Contrary to reason, her fall didn't obliterate all desire in MB to climb out onto a roof. There was a breathless moment of danger every time her foot went out the second-story window. To come down lightly on the unsteady granules of an asphalt shingle. To leave the indoor staleness for a kiss of fresh air. To taste the gradual slope toward possible flight. This, too, was a drug.

After she and Chevy had been on a few dates and he was beginning to accept the idea of MB being much more intriguing than any girl he'd known, Chevy drove to her place unannounced. It was a sunny afternoon filled with the songs of birds and the voices of running children.

As his car approached her house, he touched the brake at the sight of her on the roof, below an open bedroom window. Her shirtsleeves rolled up high. Her long, tan legs coming out of cut-off jeans. Her hair pulled back off her face with a yellow bandanna. Her aviator sunglasses. Her hands securing the plastic pots of two plants that appeared, from his vantage point, to be something other than common household varieties.

"She's six of the most interesting people I know," Chevy told a buddy. "I can't stop thinking about her." Cupid had released his arrow and Chevy was a goner.

"Which one is Terry and which is Jerry?" Libby asked.

"Terry is the taller one. T for tall, T for Terry."

"Shouldn't we take them out under a bed sheet or something?"

"Ah, give the neighbors a cheap thrill. You take Terry. I'll get Jerry and the grow light." MB picked up one plant and the fluorescent light and led the way. "You'll want to get them inside and under the light as quickly as possible. They're not winter-friendly."

"We'll get along great, then," Libby said.

With the passenger-side front seat pushed back as far as it would go, Terry and Jerry were arranged on the floor mat, ready to be relocated.

"Here," MB said, handing a note to Libby that read Taking Care Of Pets. Libby looked it over.

"One coffee cup of water every ten days. That's enough?"

"Yep. When they start to flower in spring, then you up it to a cup and a half."

"I'll have them that long?"

"Dunno. Probably. Have to see how this all turns out. But with Singer around, I pretty much don't smoke anymore. And Chevy never liked pot in the first place."

Libby looked closer at her sister. "What about the pills?" This was territory they usually steered clear of, but she loved her sister and she hated the pills.

MB matched Libby's eye contact. "Don't you worry, little sister."

Libby was hoping for more.

"Bye Terry. Bye Jerry," MB said. "Pop quiz, which one's Terry?"

Libby pointed to the tall one.

MB nodded approvingly. "Oh, and don't call them weed. They'll think you're disrespecting them."

Libby started the car.

"And they like Neil Young," MB said over the roar of the engine. "And David Bowie."

The sisters looked at each other. All the history between them had finally settled comfortably into a loving relationship.

"Thanks," MB said through the open car window.

"Love you," Libby said.

"Love you back," her big sister replied. She waved and quickly jogged through the dusty winter light toward her house, wondering if her brownies had burned.

Chevy had picked Singer up from school and they were making their way through the side streets of Middleton toward home. The roads were rutted and slippery with new snow. Singer was in the back seat in his booster, humming Christmas songs despite the weeks that had passed since the holiday.

Singer asked, "Did we get a letter back from Cory today?"

"I don't know, pal. I haven't been home yet. I've been slaving away at the salt mines."

"At what?" Singer said.

"At the bank."

"Oh, yeah." That triggered a thought. Singer hummed a bit more. "Do you know where snowmen keep their money?" he asked Chevy.

"C'mon, pal. You told me that one last week, remember? In snowbanks."

Singer laughed. "I like that one. I like where you work, too."

"You just like the candy dishes, am I right, big guy?" Chevy looked around to the back seat.

Singer was grinning. "I like the vault, too. Can we go in there again?"

"Sure we can."

"And the dog treats. Do dogs come in for treats in the winter?"

"Not as much, bud."

Singer was quiet for a moment. "Do you think we got a letter back?"

"We'll see when we get home. We'll check right away."

"I can't wait," Singer said, excited. "I want to tell Cory the snow-bank joke."

Chevy felt a twinge of guilt, but it quickly passed. Everything was going to be all right. He knew it. As long as Singer's letter went no further than the top drawer of his office desk, they'd be good.

The car turned onto their block, headlights sweeping across a dark yard. A rabbit was chased off the snow-drifted lawn by beams of light. It fled for cover.

PART THREE

Baudette, Minnesota

Cory

Hopes remained high that Cory would be able to speak again. He hadn't uttered a word since his swollen eyes opened from his coma. The bruising had faded, but much about his condition remained a mystery.

At the Mayo Clinic, some of the country's most respected neurologists and neurosurgeons examined Cory. And examined him again. And again. Despite the exhaustive battery of tests, no one could say conclusively why he was struck mute.

The focus of the doctors' concern was a large contusion over his left eyebrow. This was the impact point, the physicians believed, where Cory's head struck the windshield frame as he was ejected from his truck. The left side of the frontal lobe is where speech is formed as a person's thoughts are put into words and words are arranged in sequence to communicate.

The doctors' primary diagnosis was that Cory suffered a brain trauma causing akinetic mutism. Clinically speaking, however, akinetic mutism meant a loss of all voluntary movement as well as speech. But Cory had limited movement in his lower body upon coming out of his coma. Slowly, as healing progressed and brain swelling receded, all movement returned. Yet he remained mute. Right up to and including the moment he left the hospital.

There's a cruel joke in northern Minnesota: what do you call the end of January?

February.

And that's about where they were as Pat ignored his cold hands and pushed Cory's wheelchair up the ramp toward the porch of the farmhouse. Eight steps up the ramp, Pat realized the rise was too steep. His boots slipped backward and he nearly fell, if not for the wooden handrail.

"I should have tacked ribbing down," he said out loud, bending his knees and trying anew, moving slower up the snow-slicked grade. He'd have to dismantle the ramp and rebuild it. Under this realization, he grit a curse word between his teeth. But only momentarily. Until it dawned on him that to rebuild what was dismantled was the theme of his life. And, for that matter, Cory's too.

Pat chuckled. How could he be angry with false starts? He glanced skyward. Certainly, God was smiling with him. He was suddenly grateful for the lesson his miscalculation on the ramp provided.

Once the wheelchair reached the porch deck, Pat wheeled Cory around to face the quiescent fields. Sunlight banked off the endless frozen white, its squinting brilliance was almost bitter. But Pat's smile remained. Their eyes met and Pat could feel Cory asking him what in hell there was in that sweep of landscape to merit a grin.

"Just thinking to myself," Pat said. "I built the ramp wrong. Going to have to redo it. Go with two tiers, side by side, platform there in the middle, so it isn't so steep. Made me laugh. How many times I get things wrong the first time." He paused. The glare off the starched landscape was eye-watering. "Life, I guess."

Pat's smile endured. The wind scraped his face. He felt the sting of Cory's eyes still on him. Pat knew it was going to take time. Time, time, time. That was something Pat had in abundance.

The door swung open behind them. "What are you two doing out here?" HomeSky asked. "Come now, Pat! Before you both freeze. Please." It was not exactly the heartwarming welcome that HomeSky had rehearsed for Cory. And there had been rehearsing.

Neither HomeSky nor Cory was unfamiliar with loss. They both carried October 15, 1973 with them everywhere. HomeSky lost her husband that day. And by tragic coincidence, on that same day, 13-year-old Cory lost his father. What that day had stolen from them was what originally bound them together.

They both knew loss more recent, too. HomeSky, with the death of her son Joseph, Cory's best friend. And now Cory with the death of his fiancée, Hanna. What do two such people say to one another? Even if Cory could speak, HomeSky wasn't sure where she'd begin. But begin she did.

"I'm so grateful you're home." She leaned down to hug Cory.

He was cold and stiff and felt like the metal of his wheelchair. "Let's get you inside where it's warm."

Pat looked on. HomeSky nodded at him, acknowledged she was fine. It was fine.

"I'll get your crutches from the truck," Pat said, trying to sound upbeat.

HomeSky rolled Cory through the door.

Meadow planned to give them a moment alone downstairs. To reacquaint. She had met Cory briefly last summer. He, his fiancée and Singer came out to the farm for a visit. A sunny windless day filled with conversation and promise. That was when she was pregnant with Billy Little Tree.

Then, in an instant, smiles were wiped away.

Meadow finished nursing Billy and looked at her guitar. She put her son in his bassinet and the beginnings of a song came.

Take me to robin land
my robin land
brown and orange

orange and tan

let me free
let me soar
high above the ground

Take me to robin land
my robin land
green grass growing
all around

we'll sing from trees
we'll build our nests
high above the ground

Robin land
my robin land

robin land
my robin land

brown and orange
orange and tan

we're safe here
we're happy here
high above the ground

We're strong here
we're together here
high above the ground

we're singing here
we're resting here

high above the ground

Billy Little Tree watched his mother strumming her guitar and jotting lyrics in her blue notebook. Music had always been present for him as much as discord had always been present for her. From the womb, life is shaped. His eyes did not inherit what she had seen, and fled. His heart beat peacefully in ways impossible for her. Until now.

Meadow knocked twice on Cory's bedroom door. She paused before swinging it open. His wheelchair faced a window. Out beyond, snowbound fields sank into the horizon. He turned the wheelchair to face her and her swaddled son. There was no reaction. She stepped into the bedroom.

"I love that view. More in summertime than winter, though. Probably stating the obvious." Meadow felt herself pushing words at Cory. She paused for a breath. "I was on bed rest with this little buck for a couple months." She patted her son. "Spent a lot of time looking out that window. Talking to him."

As she came a few steps closer, Meadow saw Cory's wheelchair was equipped with a flip-up tray. A notepad had a pen on top, secured with a large rubber band. The word BEDROOM was written on the pad in neat handwriting. Meadow correctly surmised this to be Cory's response to Pat and HomeSky's question of what he would like to do next.

"I don't mean to interrupt," she said. "But I'd like you to meet someone." She took another step. "I'm Meadow, by the way. We met last summer." As soon as those words were out, she wanted them back. Would mentioning last summer dig up all he had lost? Cory was unreadable.

Meadow shifted Billy in her arms, taking one step closer. "He's an amazing guy. Can get noisy in the middle of the night. You might hear us up there. Walking and crying." Meadow looked up at the ceiling. "I'll be the one walking. Maybe a little crying." Her half-smile garnered no response.

She lowered her son toward Cory. "This is Billy Little Tree—"

Cory winced.

"I'm sorry. Are you in pain?" She pulled Billy back to her chest.

The sight of the tiny boy jolted memories. A beautiful face emerging from tight swaddling. Eyes happy, alert. Perfect nose. Rounded lips, like he might be attempting to whistle. It yanked Cory back to Singer. Those early days. The hours he walked with that boy. Spelling his exhausted mother. Trying to remedy the unremitting colic.

Cory shook his head no, he wasn't in pain. But Meadow could see it, like he was bloodied. She stood uncomfortably, out of ideas.

Cory picked up the pen from the tray. He gripped it more like a knife, but in the same neat penmanship wrote: TIRED.

"Sure, sure," Meadow said backing up. "Big day. Big transition." But each little step she took away from Cory told her with increasing volume that she was moving the wrong direction. Cory was making her escape easy.

She stopped, as Cory was turning his wheelchair toward the window.

"Cory," she said.

He paused, looked at her.

"Billy and I are happy you've come. This is an amazing place. There is magic here. I'll leave you now, but I want you to know, we aren't going anywhere. We'll be stubborn, Billy and I. We are going to keep coming back and talking to you. Hopefully, not bothering you too much. But stubborn."

Cory's hands remained on the wheels of his chair, which sat in profile to her. The radius in his left arm had been severely fractured. Because it wasn't healing properly, three weeks after it was set, Cory was taken into surgery. The bone was rebroken, stabilized with a metal plate and kept in traction with a gruesome-looking external fixation rod whose pins penetrated the skin into the bone on either side of the fracture. Using his opposite hand, he completed the turn in his wheelchair, leaving her his back.

"We'll go now," she said, leaving Cory at the window. "Glad

you're here."

Pat and HomeSky were talking at the kitchen table when Meadow and Billy joined them. Their moods immediately brightened. Pat's arms shot out, as did HomeSky's.

"Dibs," Pat blurted. "Mine were out first." He waggled his fingers toward Billy.

Meadow shrugged sympathetically to HomeSky and put Billy in Pat's arms.

"There's my sack of beans," Pat said, cooing. "Who's your favorite? Am I not your favorite? There's my boy."

Meadow sighed, sitting down. "He wrote a note. Said he's tired. Could be, but I don't really believe it."

HomeSky understood her frustration. "He's mourning, Meadow. On levels very hard to comprehend. We need to give him time and room."

Pat agreed. "For sure. But—"

"No," HomeSky interrupted uncharacteristically. She held up a hand as if to stop him. "I saw you left crutches in his room. It's too early for that."

"I was thinking—for motivation. But I know. I hear you. I just don't want to leave him so much time and room that he . . . disappears into it." Pat looked at HomeSky. *Now* she understood. Pat was afraid Cory might grieve as destructively as she did.

Reaching across the kitchen table, HomeSky laid her hand on Pat's. "We all cope in our separate ways."

Pat nodded, knowing what she said was true, but was not comforted. Billy started to squirm so Pat put him to his shoulder. "Got a gas bubble?" he asked. Meadow put a spit-up towel on Pat's shoulder.

"What do the doctors say we should do? Or expect," Meadow asked.

Pat was rub-patting Billy's back, intoxicated by the baby's smell and touch. "His surgeons have pretty much turned him over to his physical therapist now. I've sat down with his therapist a few times. He says maybe two more weeks till the wrist is ready for crutches, and then start easy, but get him going. The hip is doing just okay. Dislocations can be slow. The MRI or the X-ray—I forget which—shows the hip capsule is torn but the tendons and ligaments only got hyperextended, not detached. The wheelchair lets everything settle back and heal, keeps the joint in place, but it's the scar tissue we have to watch out for. It can build up and permanently rob mobility."

"Right or left hip?" HomeSky asked.

"Left," Pat said. "They think the leg caught on the steering wheel as he was ejected."

HomeSky and Meadow shook their heads.

Pat continued. "So, a schedule of getting him upright out of the chair, every three hours or so during the day is what's best. He has a few simple exercises right now. But all this has to be supervised. And we know how much Cory is going to love supervision. But movement gets healthy blood flowing, breaks down scar tissue, speeds healing, begins to redevelop muscle—all the important stuff. We can't let him just sit there."

HomeSky's tea was long cold, but she finished it. "Overall, what's the recovery look like? Months? A year? Longer?"

"Literally baby steps. They want him on crutches or better yet back on his feet in a month. That means end of February. But he's behind. He's 'unengaged'—that was the word his physical therapist used. It could be brain trauma, could be depression, maybe both. It was the PT folks who suggested I put the crutches in his bedroom. Start to set an expectation."

"I'm sorry about jumping on you about that," HomeSky said.

Pat shook his head. "No. A day or so won't hurt. This is physical and psychological and it's all very individualized. There isn't a manual we can pull out."

"What can I do?" Meadow asked. "How can I help?"

"What do you see? You're closer to Cory's age than we are."

Meadow paused in thought. "What you said about Cory, not letting him check out and just sit there, I get that. I've unplugged. It's destructive. Maybe I could talk to him about the Rez, and how my situation changed. He knows about my old man, right?"

Pat nodded.

Meadow spoke softly. "I didn't used to think there was anything to live for, really. That's scary now—how right you can be in your head even when you're totally wrong." Meadow looked up from her thoughts into the brightness of the room and her eyes settled on Billy Little Tree. "Cory doesn't trust anything."

HomeSky agreed. "You're right. I've been there. It's overwhelming to think about all that darkness, even for me today. Some of it, Cory must walk through alone. But he has to know others have walked there, and come through."

Meadow was looking out the windows over the sink at the early dark of January. "He can't be told. He needs enough room for the words to find him."

"Say more about that," Pat said to Meadow.

"He's lost. We need to keep talking to give him orientation but he can't be told everything is going to be okay. Because it's not."

Now it was Pat who spoke with conviction. "Everything's going to be different."

HomeSky nodded. "Meanwhile, we need to be loving friends."

"Onishiwabe," Meadow said. "Family."

Pat nodded.

Just then, the bubble that had been irritating Billy was set loose. There's something about an unbridled baby burp that can undo just about any tension in a room.

"Well lookie here! The Midas touch." Pat kept patting Billy's back. "My boy, anything you need, I'm your man."

He handed Billy to Meadow. She raised him up, bringing his diaper to her nose. "Whoa!" she said, recoiling. "Tell your man what you need is a change." She handed Billy back.

"Oh," Pat said flatly. "Well then, let's get you cleaned up."

HomeSky spoke, but in fits and starts. "Pat. I think we should talk to Meadow. You know? About the situation. With Cory's mother. At the hospital. Do you agree?"

Pat rubbed his face. "I do," he said yawning. "Excuse me. Long day." He looked at HomeSky. "Do you mind telling her while I change Billy?" He gave Meadow a little smile, trying to remove the worry crease from her forehead.

"Sure," HomeSky said.

In the end-of-day light, she saw a slackness in Pat's face, and deeper rings under his eyes. All the trips back and forth to hospitals and the rehabilitation center and the physical therapy facility, the continuous cycle of breakthroughs and setbacks, the conversations with medical professionals—the strain wore on him. She hardly dared ask. "When will you tell Cory?"

"Not today. Maybe tomorrow. Soon."

SHERIFF & KITTY

"Pot pie," the Sheriff said aloud in the foyer, his nostrils sweeping the air. He stomped the snow off his boots and left them in the rubber boot tray Kitty had purchased for days just like today. Squalls of snow had blown in and out of Baudette, each leaving just enough accumulation to create a mess.

At the sound of his master's voice, Private came tearing around the corner of the dining room, his nails finding ample purchase in the loop pile carpet. Ears pinned back, the pup accelerated as though sent from a slingshot toward the front entryway where the joy of his life stood.

"Private!" The Sheriff bellowed.

An excited whimper leaked from the blur.

The Sheriff patted his chest and said, "Hup!" The eight-month-old Lab leaped from a distance of 15 feet and sailed through the air to be caught by the mighty outstretched arms of the Sheriff. "Hey you little butter stick," he said. "Hey you basket of muffins!" Whines and licks commenced.

"Well if that isn't a welcome home," Kitty said, coming out of the warm kitchen with an apron tied at her waist. "Should I leave you two alone?"

"Ah, hell," the Sheriff said. "Been a long week. Nice to be appreciated."

"Speaking of which," Kitty hinted.

The Sheriff let the lean pup pour out of his arms onto the floor.

"I do look forward to Fridays and having you here when I arrive home." He gave her a kiss and a hug. "Sure as sugar."

Private circled around them and let out a high bark. The Sheriff backed him off with a glare.

"No need to be jealous," Kitty said in a happy voice. "There's enough huggin' here to go around." Private's tail came unhooked. She bent to the pup. "Attaboy, " she said, fingers scratching his side and under his chin. Private fell to the floor like he was tranquilized, rolling onto his back, begging for more.

The Sheriff had pretty much the same response when a steaming wedge of pot pie was set down on the dinner table before him. Chicken. Beans. Carrots. Corn niblets. And a flaky crust as golden as the Holy Grail. *But what bite to have first? A taste of crust? A hunk of dark meat? No, the—*

"Thurgood!" Kitty said to him for the third time.

"Huh?" the Sheriff said.

"Bless your heart for the admiration of my cooking but would you please first bless this meal?"

"Are there pearl onions?" was all he could say.

"You mean in this world? Or something more specific?"

The Sheriff gestured to his pot pie.

"You goof. Yes I made it with pearl onions."

"If this town harbors a luckier man, I certainly have not met him." The Sheriff sucked an imaginary string of chicken meat from his back teeth. Then reality stormed into the conversation. "Wait," the Sheriff straightened. "Isn't this over our calorie count?"

Not the most expected question out of this man. The Sheriff had never been small. Not a small baby. Not a small boy. Not a small man. But he was 250 pounds small, down from his high of 300. Quite an accomplishment, though the impetus of this weight loss left much to be desired.

He had been shot last summer. The Sheriff came out of surgery and an extended hospital stay 37 pounds lighter, with a renewed appreciation for life. Since then, Kitty's routine of regular walking and mindful calorie counting—not to mention the fact that a snack now equaled a stick of Big Red from his right front pocket or a piece of Trident Wintergreen from his left—the Sheriff was as light as he'd been in boot camp before shipping out for Korea.

Kitty put her napkin on her lap. "Granted. We are a bit over our count. But we are celebrating."

The Sheriff was well-trained. "How much over?"

"Don't be silly. I said we're celebrating. Did you hear me? Thurgood, I swear you have potatoes growing in your ears."

"Would that also go against my calorie count?"

"If you would please just say the blessing I'll be happy to fill you in on our reason for celebration," Kitty said with a pinch of superiority.

The Sheriff held out his hand for her to take. "Dear Lord, I am thankful. Not always the most vocal in that respect, but for this food and health you've blessed us with, we say thank you. And for this companionship, I am moved to say one last thing . . . so I might prove . . . I'm not the forgetful oaf . . . I may sometimes seem . . ."

The windup in the Sheriff's voice left the next sentence teetering. Kitty's eyes widened. Private sat up. "Kitty," he said, "happy one-half year anniversary of our first date."

Kitty's hand trembled in his as she beamed. The Sheriff leaned in and gave her a kiss. "Surprise," he said, physically acting out the word. Then he handed her a card in a lovely red envelope.

"You dickens! How did you know?"

"A law enforcement professional never gives up his sources." Very pleased with himself, he placed his napkin on his lap with a flourish.

"Should I open it now?" Kitty asked, knowing dinner was cooling.

The Sheriff smiled. "I should say so."

"Such a beautiful envelope—hate to tear it—I'll use my butter knife." She carefully removed the card. Two colorful birds sat on a branch under the words Happy Anniversary written in the leaves. On the inside flap, a handwritten note:

Dearest Kitty,

Six months ago we had our first date.
If you'll remember, we took your dogs for a walk up to the high school.

Then you served lemonade in the back yard.
My glass has been half-full ever since.

With deepest affection,
Thurgood

Kitty's eyes filled. "I'll treasure this. You are a good, good man." She kissed him softly. "Let me put this somewhere safe. You get started now before the food goes cold." Her voice broke, which put a lump in the Sheriff's throat almost large enough to restrict any intake of pot pie. Almost.

As they were drying and putting away dinner dishes, Kitty looked at the Sheriff. "You're suddenly quiet. Is it work?"

"I guess," he said. "Couple things rattling around inside my head. I am relieved to have Cory's case put to bed. I expected there'd be no charges filed, we all did, but with this new judge in Duluth, well, she's a she. I didn't know how she'd rule 'cause a woman behind the bench is something I've not dealt with. Turns out she cut through it like new scissors. She agreed with our plea of self-defense and since there was no one prosecuting, it ended there and then. Now Cory can get on with healing."

"Yes, thank the good Lord. How is he?"

The Sheriff shook his head. "The boy can't speak a word. His limbs all function, but Pat tells me Cory's only going through the motions on his physical therapy. Now that they got him home to the farm, Pat's hoping things will get settled and turned around."

"Time heals all wounds," Kitty said confidently.

"I shoulda done more," the Sheriff said, unconsciously tapping the countertop. "Shoulda seen something. All this going on under my nose."

"Honey, we've talked about this. That man, he stalked Cory. In Duluth. At his cabin. That's nowhere near your jurisdiction."

Sheriff heard none of it. "Those two go way back," he said. "They had a big fight over at the plant and it left Reg in a pretty bad way."

"What was it about?"

"Reg was constantly bullying Radio Voice at work. He's the janitor."

"You mean that nice man with Down syndrome?"

"Reg had a bad streak in him. Cory always looked out for Radio Voice. One day Reg pushed it too far. I thought the fight ended it. Guess it was just the start."

Kitty watched the Sheriff's expression change. He had returned to the car wreck on the highway.

"Wasn't even a skid mark." He frowned. "Neither so much as touched the brakes. Neither vehicle swerved. Damn suicide mission for 'em both."

"Come on, honey," Kitty said, trying to pull him out of his work and back to his kitchen.

"They did find a note in Reg's vehicle. Son of a bitch. How many times I could have run him to jail. Never thought him capable of what he done."

Kitty moved closer. "I know you need to work this out in your own time and your own space—"

"Well, thank you." He reached for a salad bowl to dry.

"I'm not quite through." She looked up from the sink at him. "You've been giving yourself a good thrashing on this since it happened, despite working day and night to do everything you can to build a case to give the judge exactly what she needed to rule the way she did." Kitty put down her drying towel and took his hands.

"Truth is, Thurgood, God let this happen, not you. Somewhere down the road we can only hope to find a thread of silver lining and some meaning. That said, this town needs you back here and focused on our community. I need you back here. Your health and your quality of life need you back here. It's time to get off that road and take leave of those mangled vehicles. I know that's easy for me to say. I didn't have to see it. But you know in your heart. It's time to get off that godforsaken road."

Kitty took a step closer and held the Sheriff tightly. Their size differences might have indicated otherwise, but it was she who steadied him.

Despite the cold, they kept with tradition and took an abbreviated after-dinner walk with Private. Then they settled onto the couch and flipped on an episode of *Moonlighting*. The Sheriff's heart wasn't into watching Bruce Willis bumble after Cybill Shepherd's favor.

"Do you mind if I shut if off?" the Sheriff said.

"No. We've seen this one anyway."

The Sheriff turned to her on the couch. "You know how earlier you said this town needs me back?"

"I certainly do."

"Well, it's like you were reading my thoughts. You know me—I'm a slow cooker. But before all this started with Cory, I was stewing on some disturbing events. In regard to Wayne Varkas. You know him, right?"

"Seen him. Never formally met him. The sight of that man gives me chills."

"Varkas has an unhealthy grip on this town. And he's squeezing harder by the day. Remember the news clipping you saw tacked to my corkboard? About that Varkas employee killed in an accident?"

"I do. In fact, I went to see Tammy Maddux, the man's widow. Brought her a dinner and some diapers. She's going to move back in with her parents. Says she has to find work."

"Good thing she has people close," the Sheriff said. "So I've been thinking it's about time somebody paid more attention to all the pies Varkas has his fingers stuck into. Been ignoring my gut about that guy too long."

"What do you mean?"

"Just since he bought the McKnight plant, do you know how many employees have died on his payroll?"

Kitty adjusted her position on the couch. "Overall? Or in Baudette?"

"Across all of it. The two plants, plus the paper mill. His lumberyards. His harvesting crews and logging trucks. And his construction business."

"I'm afraid to ask."

"Sixteen. If you average them out, that's more than five deaths per year since he expanded here. He's running logging trucks overloaded. He's got crews working too fast and in unsafe conditions. He's turning trees into $100 bills quicker than you can whistle Dixie. Sixteen men. That's somewhere between gross negligence and criminal recklessness in my book. Maybe worse."

"What can you do? Has he broken any laws?"

The Sheriff raised his index finger. "Now you've hit the nail on the head." He patted her knee. "Should pin a badge on you. I'm just getting back to digging into the records and the death certificates to see what law's been broke, bent, side-stepped or plain ignored. Not much of a paper trail, but pieces are falling into place. Varkas is harvesting lumber from here to International Falls and south. We're just part of hundreds of square miles that has some kind of Varkas holding on it." The Sheriff shook his head. "Lot of places to hide things.

"Over the past three years, I've heard rumors. Varkas code violations. Hazardous waste buried in the middle of nowhere. Toxic byproducts piped into the river after dark. I brushed it off. Chalked it up to tree-huggin' crackpots who know nothing about creating a business and jobs. To my reckoning, I stand with the businessmen; they've got the meat in the stew. As for the necktied EPA man, I always said there's a rat in every bureaucrat. Professional whiners at the least." The Sheriff shrugged. "Now I'm not so sure."

Kitty nodded.

The Sheriff continued. "Many of our neighbors' livelihoods are tied to that man's ambitions. Why do you think the mayor and the chambers of commerce committee and, truth be told, *I* just look the other way when Varkas does what Varkas does? People need paychecks, Varkas needs people. Seems like a fair deal. But it's damn shocking, now, going back through the records. It's like his men are little more than disposable tools."

Kitty's brow furrowed. "I think about that young widow. She's hollowed out with grief. Plum hollowed out. I talked to her but there was nothing hopeful coming back. And those little ones latched onto her."

The Sheriff bit the inside of his mouth. "Who's going to look out for the likes of her from Varkas?" He took a deep breath and exhaled slowly. "I'm going to check that accident report more thoroughly. Maybe there's restitution coming to her if she pressed charges."

"You be careful, Thurgood. That's dangerous ground."

He nodded. "Yeah. It is. But who's going to look out for the likes of her? And her little ones if it ain't me? Who's going to see to this town?"

"I don't like the sound of that."

The Sheriff nodded. "I don't much like it either."

"Isn't there another way?" Kitty asked.

"There is. And that widow Maddux you speak of, she's now living it."

HOMESKY

HomeSky remained gratefully connected to her garden, here in the dead of winter. Such is the beauty of canning.

"Canning keeps the sunshine in and the bacteria out," HomeSky told her young pupil. She and Meadow had been working together since last fall as HomeSky passed down the art of home-canned vegetables. Ironically, this art needs to be preserved, too. Otherwise, one day, its ways and secrets will be lost.

A few such secrets HomeSky shared included blanching her vegetables before canning, but in water just below a boil verses a rolling boil. And how she used canning salt, but ardently believed it was the touch of lemon juice that kept the vegetables bright in the jar.

From her canning pantry they had taken quarts of corn, carrots, beans, potatoes and a pint of beets, though she wouldn't include the beets in her soup. Pat was a baby when it came to beets.

As it simmered, the aroma of venison vegetable soup began to make its way through the farmhouse, tiptoeing around corners and up stairs. The late afternoon descent of winter's cold and dark were underway. What better foil than a pot of homemade soup?

HomeSky had often thought about Cory during those many weeks of his hospitalization. And she could not think of him without thinking of vegetable soup. Pat would call with news after yet another surgery and she imagined Cory not in a hospital bed, but here at the house, getting stronger at her kitchen table, where Joseph would have joined him. Taking in the warming broth. Taking in the homegrown vegetables given by the trinity of sun, rain and earth. *Vegetable soup is what Cory needs, body and soul*, she thought. She refused to dismiss the belief as diminutive or clichéd or sentimental. It was healing.

Her memory of those late November days remained vivid. Emergency surgery. The setting of a compound fracture. Life-threatening internal injuries. Cory was on the scalpel's edge of losing both kidneys, each severely lacerated in the collision. They searched furiously for a living donor because the wait list for a kidney was thousands deep.

Pat, HomeSky and the Sheriff turned out not to be a match. And a parent's chance of matching is only 50% because a child's genes are shared between the mother and father. Other blood relatives were an option, too.

HomeSky had wandered through those days on autopilot, waiting on updates, buried in worry. Oftentimes, she found herself in front of her canning pantry, the painted doors hinged open, staring inside. There was solace here against the unapologetic shove of life. Solace and escape in quart after quart and pint after pint of glass jars. Full. Beautiful. Labeled. Dated. Arranged. Waiting. Good must be harvested and preserved for the hard times.

HomeSky watched Meadow carefully using a large wooden spoon to stir the soup before putting it on the ceramic spoon rest. They had browned two pounds of cubed venison with flour, butter and onion, and mixed it with the boiling vegetables and broth. The simmer of time would now work its magic.

"So what is it Pat wanted you to tell me?" Meadow adjusted the cross-tie wrap she had fashioned out of a baby blanket that held sleeping Billy warm and snug to her chest. "The thing about Cory's mom?"

Glancing out the kitchen doorway to be sure they wouldn't be interrupted, HomeSky whispered. "This was all happening right when Billy was born, so most of it we didn't tell you. You had your hands full."

"It's still a blur," Meadow confessed.

HomeSky found a lid and quietly set it on the pot, leaving a sliver of an opening so the meat would soften but traces of moisture and aroma could escape. This aptly reminded her that there are times for keeping a lid on things, and times for secrets to be exposed.

"We should sit." They found their places at the kitchen table. Billy kicked, but remained fast asleep.

"So Cory's mother came to the hospital after the accident," HomeSky said. "Cory was in a coma and the doctors worried about the blood in his urine. Surgery in a coma is extremely dangerous, but both kidneys were lacerated. They were discussing removing them both."

A muffled sound was all Meadow could utter.

"A frantic search was on for a donor, which naturally led Pat to Cory's mother. You wouldn't think there would be a moment's hesitation. But she refused him."

"She what?" Meadow said, disturbing Billy's sleep. "Sorry, little one."

"She said no. There'll be no organ donation." HomeSky shook her head. "Now, you know Pat. He is a kind man, but when he feels strongly about something, he gets emotional and isn't always restrained."

Meadow nodded.

"After quite an argument, Cory's mother finally told him why. She said she was no better donor candidate than Pat. Pat, of course, was confused. Then she told him. Cory is adopted."

Meadow's lips parted. She subconsciously put her hands on her baby.

HomeSky continued. "Cory was never told. He doesn't know. Cory's mother said it's for Pat to tell him or not tell him as he wishes. She said Cory's father always wanted a boy and because he came from a family of all sisters he didn't want to risk it. So they adopted. She told Pat she and Cory never bonded. They were—I guess still are, in an unbreakable way—strangers."

Meadow lifted her hand, stopping HomeSky. The women looked at one another. Neither could find words nor answers.

"Maybe we should talk later," HomeSky said.

Meadow stood and went back to the oven. She picked up the wooden spoon, removed the lid and stirred the soup. She began speaking, hardly louder than the spoon's rhythm. "He doesn't know.

As awful as my parents are, at least I know my story. It's grotesquely comforting to know it's not all my fault."

HomeSky walked over to Meadow and Billy and put her arms around them. "Oh, my wise dear, what are we going to do?"

Meadow closed her eyes. "We have to tell him."

"Pat and I agree. Just not yet. He's dealing with so much right now. He hasn't known for this long. Let's give him a few more days. To get stronger."

Meadow walked to the sink and stared sadly out the window. The light was gone. A tireless wind moaned. "That poor little boy," she said. "All he ever wanted was to be loved. Look where it's gotten him."

LU ANN

Lu Ann had been as sharp as buckthorn with customers. To say she wasn't herself would be a gross understatement. Things had to change.

Even grasping this reality, Lu Ann felt her dread intensifying with every step Mick took toward her diner. *What kind of mistake have I gone and made?*

She watched through the clean front window as Mick came around to the car's passenger side to aid the Monsignor, who looked chipper. The two found something to laugh about as the Monsignor navigated the curb. It was like watching a silent movie. Were such a thing audible, the only sound would have been a tightening in Lu Ann's chest.

The diner was between breakfast and lunch rushes. Lu Ann had sent Mary Alice to the bank for rolls of coins and ones, a task that now made her entire body prickle. Neither she nor Mick had discussed how their diners' income would be deposited in the bank. How could they call themselves ready for what they were about to embark on with such a detail overlooked?

The Monsignor had convinced Lu Ann to go to St. Paul and run Mick's Diner while he in turn came to Baudette to run her place. A mere 320 miles, the Monsignor had said. Not much can go wrong in that span. They had settled on the month of February for the switch. Another good omen, he told Lu Ann. Twenty-eight days made it the shortest month of the year.

As the two men crossed the street, Lu Ann could see Mick's eyes assessing her diner. A calm half-smile never left his face as he attended to both the Monsignor's arm and surveying her building. The sun offered cold comfort. Midway across the frozen blacktop, their gaits stiffened in the below-zero temperature. Mick wore a light jacket, no hat, no boots, no gloves and a scarf loosely looped around his neck. Lu Ann tried with little luck to spare judgment. "City mouse," she said under her breath.

"Hello, hello, hello," the Monsignor's voice rang out as he stomped his boots on the bristle rug inside the door. "Brrr! Have you heard? They've sold out of long underwear at Gertz's Department store." His hands reached for the neat row of 15 coat pegs along the wall. Second one in was his. He removed his coffee mug before hanging his coat in its place. Many of the other regulars also had a peg with their coffee mug hooked on it. Mick kept his jacket on.

Lu Ann approached and Mick tried not to be surprised by how sad she looked. Sleeplessness pressed into her face, especially the skin under her eyes and at the drawn down corners of her mouth. She had been described to Mick as a five-foot dynamo. A hummingbird in an apron. Her energy, he could see, was dangerously low. Any nagging doubt he carried about the wisdom of the Monsignor's plan vanished. This woman needed a change of venue.

Mick appeared to Lu Ann nothing like she had imagined. He was tall and thin; she envisioned him short and rotund. He'd been described as good-natured and kind to a fault, but his large nose and blotchy rosacea cheeks made him appear indolent and perhaps too cozy around a bottle of scotch. Frankly, she wasn't sure this would work. She didn't like the way he was looking at her, either. She had little tolerance for pity. His handshake would make or break it.

She was sold. His handshake, not theatrically firm, or worse, like a wet rag, was friendly. Most importantly, his hands were chafed, raw and abrasive from the overwork of restaurant ownership.

This was a man, his handshake announced, who didn't stand idly by when bins of dirty dishes needed to be washed. His hands were thick-skinned in defense of scalding coffee, grease jumping off the griddle, hot plates and the long handle of a mop. She was envious of Monsignor Kief, who could see nothing of a person except what physical touch and spoken words revealed. The Monsignor's first impressions were keen where sight rendered hers superficial.

"Hello, Lu Ann," Mick said. As much as she had hoped not to, Lu Ann liked his voice, too.

"I'm sorry," she let slip. Then, recovered. "For this inhospitable weather. Not a chamber of commerce day." She shrugged.

Mick's eyes seemed to get the gist of what she was saying. He nodded. "Good for selling plates with gravy." He had noticed the special on the chalkboard. Hot beef commercial; a favorite at his place for sure. "What a beautiful place you have here. I'm jealous. From the neon cup over the entryway to the fact that you don't have to walk uphill to get to the kitchen." He took a careful scan of the interior. "I hope you're not disappointed when you see my diner. It's a little . . . how do I put it kindly? Off-angle."

More of Mick was slowly revealed. Lu Ann could see he too was scared and uncomfortable. He wasn't some presumptuous know-it-all from the big city. She looked at him intently. What was it she saw in him that she also recognized in herself? Then the answer was there as plain as the bulbous nose on his face. *Insecurity.*

"Please, hang your jacket," Lu Ann said. "Take Howard's peg, on the end there." She removed his coffee mug. "He and Beth are on a cruise. Lucky so-and-sos."

The Monsignor sat at the table with them. He could not have been happier if he'd just had a 20-minute nap. In front of him was a hot, early lunch. To his right and left, Lu Ann and Mick were freely exchanging lists of procedures, tips and quirks of their businesses. He was afloat in the sounds of their voices and smiled at a thought, which he kept to himself: *these two are going on a bit of a cruise, too. To somewhere new and replenishing.*

One by one, the staff stopped by their table to shyly introduce themselves.

The conversation began to wind down. Lu Ann was relieved to see the question of how to handle bank deposits was double starred on Mick's legal pad. He seemed very conscientious.

"Can I offer you the nickel tour?" Lu Ann asked Mick.

"Perfect," he said.

"I'll finish up here," the Monsignor told them, his fork and knife on a search-and-destroy mission for any final scraps of lunch.

As they reviewed the kitchen, Lu Ann suddenly broke from her instructions and turned to face him. "Mick?" she said, using his given name for the first time.

"Make sure the latch is fully shut," he repeated back to her, thinking she was quizzing him about her last tip on the old double-door commercial refrigerator.

This made her smile. Another first since they met. "No. Not that," she said. "I meant Mick, as in can I just stop the train here a minute to ask you something?"

"Sure," he said, holding eye contact.

"Has the Monsignor told you exactly why he arranged all this?" Her glance fell to the floor. "I mean specifically?"

Mick shook his head. "He has, yes."

"You know about my father? What he did?"

Mick waited for Lu Ann to look up. "Yes. Sorry for that."

"There may be some whispering when I'm gone is all. I want you to know it isn't about you."

"I appreciate the heads up."

"The town, by far and away, has been amazing. Super supportive." Lu Ann was on the verge of tears. "But a few, not so much. There have been nights where some perfectly good eggs got ruined on that front window of mine. I had to take some sandpaper and paint to the door to remove some unflattering words. I don't blame anyone. Except maybe the damn media who made a circus of this good town for weeks. Felt like the whole world was looking in on us. Left a stain. A few customers came in just to say they'd never be back."

"It's a shame you had to face that. But the mean ones get hungry just like the good ones. We don't always get to pick who sits at our counters. Let 'em whisper."

"I admire your perspective," Lu Ann said. "But you should know, we are who we are in this town. Gossip is candy and we have mouths full of cavities. Myself included."

"I'll watch out for it," Mick said. "But your point is fairly universal. We all need to be slower to judge."

Lu Ann stood impressed by the empathy of this stranger in her kitchen.

"Since we're on the subject," Mick continued, "is the word out that you're going and I'm coming?"

"I've told my closest customers. The others will spread it faster than I can."

Mick looked around the kitchen. An unfinished silence hung upon them.

Lu Ann spoke up. "You look like you may have another question. Please."

"You and HomeSky," he began and then stopped.

"It's been some time since that name has been spoken in this kitchen."

"I'm sorry."

"No, don't be. HomeSky used to peel potatoes right where we stand. She carried more plates than a person could count out to customers. We were like sisters."

"You know she worked for me. In St. Paul."

"The Monsignor told me you took her in. I can only imagine her condition after she lost Joseph."

"Very dark days. I didn't know what had happened. She didn't talk about her son or any of it. Just a little bit at the end. She wore it like a sickness."

Lu Ann decided to continue. "And that's how you met the Monsignor."

"He came for her. But she had already left. And according to the Monsignor, God nudged her into his path." Mick shrugged his shoulders. "I believe the Monsignor. I have faith in things like that."

"Me too," she said. Lu Ann absentmindedly tapped a pen on her notepad. "I think that's enough with instructions." Looking at Mick, Lu Ann smiled. "I have a feeling we'll be friends."

Mick's grin was a bit tilted, befitting his contradictions. "I hope you're right."

VARKAS

The neatly made bed groaned as Varkas rose from its corner. He smoothed the blanket and stepped toward a large bedroom window that he was proud to know was milled from Varkas lumber at the Marvin factory up the road. He'd all but monopolized wood sourcing there.

Centered in his view through the window was his vintage Baker windmill, the same make and model his grandfather sold in this region just after the century's turn. It was a monument to immigration and a tribute to the first Varkas to pursue an impossible dream that took him almost 5,000 miles from his Czech homeland to northern Minnesota. The windmill stood like his grandfather's hand, reaching to the sky, open to what it might take from the winds of fate.

His grandfather was as shrewd as he was tireless. The young windmill agent quickly recognized that real opportunity lay not in equipment for tiny farmsteads, but in the endless swallow of timberland from which humble scraps of ground were cleared.

Grandpa Varkas would have been 94 this year—and Varkas's father, 60. Both were long in the ground. Lumbering gives and takes with equal disregard. To hear Varkas, he'd say that even with all the advancements in today's equipment, death was in the very sap of the timberland. Trees fell. Men fell with them.

With Varkas's fortieth birthday now behind him, he was thinking more often of his own death. Could be it was because neither his father nor his grandfather lived to see 50. Or maybe it was last month's logging accident. In the old days, a few funerals a month in high season were common. But now there were regulators and lawyers crawling around like bugs. Hell, Varkas thought. America is losing its testicles. Replaced by shiny shoes. What good, what real product, what anything do those people produce?

They issue papers. Warnings. Citations. Subpoenas. Don't they see the irony? It was men like Varkas who harvested the very paper that they in turn pushed back at him, covered with ink. This thought made his fingers flex. He needed to get out to his tree. Swing an ax. Pull a saw. That was medicine.

Every year, on his birthday in June, Varkas took down a lone oak the old woodsman's way. Certainly, his shed was stocked with industrial-sized chainsaws with the horsepower to drop and cut that same oak in minutes. But the process of taking a tree by hand, with an ax, to buck it by hand, to let it season, to center-split and quarter it, to stack it, and finally, to take it in your hands and burn it in your hearth, this was the kind of strong-back work that seeped to Varkas's roots.

He made his way along the narrow trail, the snow hard-packed from recent trips to the downed tree. Fresh rabbit tracks crossed in front of him as his core heated up. He was appropriately dressed for the elements. There was no wind in the forest to conspire with the minus-five-degree morning.

Varkas wore no gloves; calluses were pinned to a lumberman like medals. He was dressed in cotton underclothing, wool Mackinaw pants, a flannel shirt and a red kerchief tied around his neck. Even this small bit of layering would soon be too much for the sweat-filled work ahead. One crosscut saw rested on each shoulder, carried with their razor-sharp, three-inch teeth pointed skyward. These were his grandfather's tools. Varkas would cut until the first saw dulled, then take up the other.

The oak had been dropped in June. This way, by the time winter months arrived, the branches and foliage would be dry and easy to delimb. Varkas had already completed that tedious work and was ready to start bucking the length of the trunk.

Varkas's preference was for 60-year-old oaks. Their diameter averaged about 16 inches, which quartered nicely for the hearth. The tree would be bucked into 13-foot log lengths, each weighing about 300 pounds. Varkas used skidding tongs, a rope and a leather shoulder harness to pull lengths across the snow to his woodshed like a draft horse. There, Varkas cut each log length into ten splitting-sized pieces, roughly 16-inches long, the desired length for his fireplace. These logs he stacked to season under a lean-to until dry enough to be split.

The trail ended where the tree lay. There is something profoundly dead about a tree laying in winter's white bedding. Varkas put a goodly chew of tobacco in his cheek and took out his 13-foot string to mark his cuts.

Standing back from the tree, Varkas cracked his neck. With his mighty arms lifted over and then behind his head in a slow stretch, he used one arm's resistance against the other's to lengthen his muscles. His grandfather's two saws rested on the tree stump. He tested the sharpness with the back of his hand and selected a weapon.

He would take only the heart: four log sections of 13 feet each from the middle of the oak. The filet mignon, as it was known, straight and manageable and right-sized. The thickest wood nearest the tree's base and the scrawny crown poles would be left to rot.

Sawdust flew. In fewer than 20 minutes, Varkas had dulled two saws working powerfully and steadily through a number of precise cuts. His bucking saw had become so hot that when he set it in the snow there was a quick, audible "ssst."

His heart was booming in his chest. Momentarily lightheaded, Varkas pulled a rough shirtsleeve across his face, wiping stinging perspiration from his eyes. An internal alarm sounded. Something was watching him. The hair on his skin rose. Recessed in the understory of the forest, just to his right, stood a giant wolf. The animal was motionless, save for one ear twitch. The wolf's amber-gold eyes glowed unblinking out of the morning-darkened woods. He was hardly more than a shadow.

Perspiration leaked further into Varkas's eyes. He again used his shirtsleeve to wipe the sweat, and when his sightline cleared, the wolf was gone.

Varkas's thoughts raced to his rifle back at the house. Leaving it there was a mistake he would not repeat on his next trip back. To merely carry a pistol would be a risky defense against a wolf of such size. He had read of a record 175-pound wolf killed in Alaska. The wolf Varkas just saw had to be of comparable size. It looked to have an astonishing six-foot body length.

"These are my woods!" Varkas's shout echoed. "You hear me?" His words were finally snuffed out in the snowy surroundings.

Picking up the only available weapon, Varkas strode toward the location where he saw the animal. Both hands firmly grasped his bucking saw. "My land!" Varkas's deep voice echoed. Adrenaline raced and he soon found himself stumbling in knee-high snow. His heart pounded faster.

There were no tracks in the snow. Varkas glanced back at his broken string of cut logs, looked again at the spot where he was now standing, recalculating the distance. His voice dropped to a whisper. "Had to be here." He blew out a mouthful off air, visible for a moment. "Disappeared like a breath," he muttered.

He cautiously began walking in a small circle, using where he stood as the center. Varkas was sure he'd cross paths with the wolf's exit tracks. "Have to be prints coming and going."

The snow was untouched except for where he broke it. His fast-cooling perspiration raked a shiver through his frame. No tracks.

Varkas twice returned to his cutting area and walked back to where he remembered the wolf standing. Each time he ended up in about the spot he had already searched. Everything became more trampled and confusing.

His final analysis was sweat in his eyes and low morning light must have played tricks on his vision. It was the only logical explanation. Nonetheless, Varkas unzipped his wool pants and made sure his territory was marked.

To sleigh a log to his shed, Varkas nailed four-foot squares of plywood on the front and back ends of the log. Then he rolled the log so the boards would keep the ends from biting into the snow as he pulled. Varkas attached the skidding tongs, put on his shoulder harness and, once the short length of rope was taut, leaned forward, cracking inertia.

He began his trek back, 300-pound log in tow. Once the log was riding on the well-traveled snowpack, the work got easier. Slow but sure was a philosophy Varkas harvested from his ancestry. Back at his shed in 30 minutes, Varkas was proud of his work, but not pleased with the frequent stops the heavy load demanded of him.

A hot shower and a large breakfast are infinitely more rewarding when earned. Varkas basked in this truth as he brought his breakfast dishes to the sink to rinse. He was mildly stiff through the shoulders, but thoughts of the wolf dragged his attention away from full enjoyment of the moment.

Varkas didn't like unfinished business; this mystery left him feeling tricked and vulnerable. But the washing of dishes and subsequent drying and stacking of them in the cupboards put him back in accomplishment mode. He pushed the mystery aside. He had bigger prey.

The polished mahogany dining table was rarely used to entertain, nor for that matter, to eat. Its large surface was crowded with ledgers, county plat maps and assorted notepads and paperwork. Everything was laid out roughly in accordance with its geography. That is, if something on the table had to do with Baudette business, it was placed top left or in the northwest section. Bottom right was southeast—Hibbing operations, and so on.

Varkas's hands traipsed over the various items until finding the atlas he was after. The book was folded open to the map of his home county. Varkas's large finger came down on a land parcel north of Baudette that he would purchase. A scrappy quarter section whose owner would surely jump at his generous price. His friends in the Register of Deeds office found the landowner, someone named HomeSky Blackholm. Varkas grinned, thinking: *A Native. Naïve, more likely. Probably as good a dealmaker as her ancestors.* He laughed.

Jotting down the address was an unnecessary precaution, but Varkas nonetheless did so. He had driven past that land plenty. He had a mind for directions and locations; it came from a lifetime on back roads, logging trails and the like.

As Varkas passed through the dining room, he took a moment to admire his prized possessions. Three ornate frames hung on the wall. The first held a printed woodcut map of turn-of-the-century Eastern Europe. This same map had crossed the Atlantic with Varkas's grandfather and was a family lesson in what a landless peasant can achieve in a country as great as America.

Varkas stroked his chin, which was smooth from this morning's shave. The Varkas family was careful to shave at least once a day. They quickly learned that Americans were suspicious of dark complexions and beard shadows. To leave a face unshaven was to announce potential criminality.

The second frame held a small black-and-white photograph of Varkas's grandfather and father. The corners were yellowed and creased and bent by time. Circa 1940, the photo was taken when Varkas's father was about 14 years old. The two were equal height. This was near the time of his grandfather's death, an unceremonious event that left him on the kitchen floor, his chair toppled, with one of his wife's homemade doughnuts still clasped in his hand. At age 49, he had literally worked himself into the ground.

Varkas leaned in as he had done countless times to study the photo's detail. The two each had an arm slung over the other's shoulders. They had removed their caps, which were held in their hands. A dollop of black hair sat atop their heads, the sides shaved tight. These two were more than the picture of happiness. There, standing on the edge of a wild and endless forest, they were the picture of ambition.

Held in a final frame on the wall was an oil painting of John Wayne straddling a ginger-colored stallion, one gloved hand lightly taking up the reins, the other holding a lever action Winchester across his lap. The red kerchief that Varkas wore in the field was the same style as the one knotted around the Duke's neck, ruffled in the painting by untamed wind. The John Wayne persona erected on the silver screen of countless Westerns embodied everything the Varkas men hoped to become. They actually believed this was the example of what a real American was supposed to be. He straightened the frame before grabbing his coat and keys and heading out the door. He had a visit to make.

Varkas would no sooner drive a black truck than John Wayne would wear a black cowboy hat. His white pickup pulled off the highway and ran the gravel until it slowed and stopped at a mailbox with the same address he had jotted down earlier.

Not your typical hardware store mailbox, this one was handmade, and well done at that. It was a miniature of the farmhouse that sat just ahead, off the curve of a driveway. To Varkas's eye, the home couldn't have been more than a few years old. That didn't bode well for him. Properties that were easiest to snatch up were usually on the slide.

Seeing no twisted farm equipment nor rusted-out car chassis was another check in the hard-to-buy column. He was buoyed, however, by the sight of a wheelchair ramp off the front porch. Somebody in that house had bills to pay.

Cory watched out the bedroom window as an oversized white truck rolled down the driveway, almost lost in the washed-out background of a snow-drifted bean field. A giant of a man stepped out, stretched, lifted a hand to his eyes to shield the glare and took a prolonged look.

He was dark-complected, like many Native Americans in the area, though his looks were more Eastern European, with a longer face carrying a permanent grimace and oversized ears that looked to be set too low.

The man was in no rush as he slowly pivoted in the driveway, almost as if recording the property with a camcorder. Satisfied, he walked into the wind, which could not disarrange his thick, black hair. Exhaust rose out of the tailpipe of the idling truck, partially obscuring a bumper sticker that read: *Hug a logger. You'll never go back to trees.* Next to that was an American flag sticker.

Meadow thought she heard knocking at the front door, a sound that sprung her upright. She and Billy Little Tree were upstairs napping after a long up-and-down night.

She looked out her bedroom window and saw a white truck she didn't recognize. Fear took her by the throat. The memory of her father stalking her yanked her back in time, momentarily paralyzed her. There was another knock at the door.

Cory heard the knocks and waited for the sound of Meadow's footfalls to come down the stairs. She had to have heard the knock at the door. But nothing.

Then sharper pounding came from the back door, followed by the word hello.

Meadow descended the stairs quickly. When she stepped into Cory's bedroom she looked pale.

"Somebody at the door . . ." she said nervously.

I wonder if she's sick, Cory thought.

"Do you recognize the truck?' she asked.

Cory shook his head no.

"I'll go see about it then," she said, forcing a smile. She was relieved for his company.

Varkas stood impatiently at the back door thinking about his coat, which hung over the seat of his warm truck. A young woman appeared, looking at him through the small glass panels in the door. He smiled, trying to undo her obvious concern.

"Yes," Meadow said, opening the door, but leaving the screen door between them closed.

"Hello. Sorry to intrude. Are you the owner of this house?" Varkas looked past Meadow into the kitchen. This room, too, was nicer than he had hoped.

"What's this about?" Meadow said curtly.

"I'd like to talk to the owner of this property. I'm interested in purchasing it. Is this your piece of ground, young lady?"

When Meadow looked at the man she saw deceit. His face was

disturbing: the meat of his heavy forehead heaved along his browline. Angry creases cut into the bridge of his nose between coarse, black brows. Thick eyelids hung over his dark eyes, which would not long settle on one thing.

"Are you the owner?" Varkas repeated. "Maybe I could step in out of the cold for a moment." He looked like a man who wouldn't budge, but his large boot lifted as he reached for the handle on the screen door.

"No," Meadow said louder than she had intended. She latched the hook-and-eye lock. "I am not the owner."

"I see. When do you expect the owner back?"

"Never know. Sometimes he comes home for lunch."

"I must be mistaken," Varkas said, puzzled. "I thought it was a woman who owned this property. HomeSky Blackholm."

"Yes. Well, it's kinda co-owned. Him and her, or really her and him."

Varkas cocked his head like he wasn't getting the entire story. "Please. I'm sorry if I startled you. You have nothing to be afraid of with me. My name is Wayne Varkas." He waited for some acknowledgment. When there was none, he said, "Are you aware of who I am?"

"Yes," Meadow said. "Wayne Varkas."

Varkas smiled unpleasantly. "Have I done something to offend you, young lady?"

"Not as of yet."

"You're not being very hospitable," he said through the locked screen door.

"Sorry."

"Can I ask you a favor?"

"Okay."

"Will you give my business card to Ms. Blackholm. Ask her to call me when it's convenient, although the sooner the better." Varkas's dark eyes pressed into Meadow.

She nodded.

Varkas removed a business card from a slim leather holder. Both the case and the card itself were emblazoned with an elegant cursive *V* that Meadow had seen on many of the logging trucks on the road. He held the card up for her to take.

"Please leave it in the door. I'll make sure to get it."

"Thank you," Varkas said, with a trace of sarcasm. He slid his card in the crack between the door and the jamb. "One more thing. I couldn't help but notice in front, you have a wheelchair ramp. Has there been an accident?"

"I don't see where that's your business, Mr. Varkas."

Varkas cocked his head. "But it is my business. You see, the lumber the ramp was built with is Varkas lumber. In fact, the house you stand in was made from Varkas wood. So all of this around you, sheltering you, is my business."

"Is that so?" Meadow said.

"Yes." Varkas said. "It most surely is."

"The lumber you call yours came from my trees, the native forests of the Ojibwe. The forests were stolen from me, so the lumber under me, above me and around me was, in the first place, mine."

Varkas was not amused. "That's how it's going to be, then?"

"No," Meadow replied. "That how it was. How it's going to be is not for me to say."

Varkas stood for a moment looking through the screen at Meadow. "We don't need to be enemies, young lady."

Meadow could see Varkas was a master at getting in the last word. "Okay," she said. Then she shut and deadbolted the door.

Varkas was not used to being spoken to in such a manner. As he walked to his car he had heated up considerably. *This isn't going to be easy, but it will be worth it. There's water under this ground and eventually, whoever controls the water controls their livelihood. But to accuse me of stealing? Laziness is their problem. And liquor. I'll make a fair offer, more than fair. We'll do it the easy way or we won't. We'll strike up a partnership or I'll wipe my feet with these people and scrape them off with a stick.*

Meadow counted to thirty, warming her feet and hands, rubbing her shoulders. She watched through the door as the wind pulled at Varkas's card. *Take it*, she implored. *Take it.* But the card held fast. She quickly unbolted the door and removed it. What she did next made little rational sense. But she thought, *if the card is gone maybe the whole issue will go away.* She opened the cabinet door to the trash, folded the card in half and shoved it as far down into the garbage as she could.

Cory rolled his wheelchair into the hallway and met Meadow as she was coming out of the kitchen. He tapped the words on his notepad with his pen. EVERYTHING OKAY?

"Yeah," she said. "Some guy looking to talk to HomeSky." Meadow decided that adding one more worry to Cory's burden wasn't necessary.

Cory added a second note. WHAT DID HE WANT?

Meadow shrugged. "He didn't say."

BLOOD RELATIVES

The days turned over like a bad hand of cards, one after another, revealing little in the way of hopeful surprise.

Cory sat on his bed. With sweatpants bunched around his ankles, he went about the tedious process of dressing himself. Looking at his scrawny legs left him lightheaded. The nine weeks since the accident had greedily eaten into muscle. Pasty, bony, foreign, Cory wondered whose legs these could be. He pulled up his baggy Wisconsin Badger sweatpants.

His fingers traced the 12-inch scar that began to the left of his belly button and wrapped around to his back. With the surgical staples and stitches removed, the incision was healing well, yet the scar was alien to the touch, like a giant rubber band had been glued to his skin. He was supposed to massage it to help the incision heal and recess.

Cory was told that living with one kidney would have virtually no impact on his lifestyle. He was advised to ease back into a routine of eating, exercise and daily activity. He needed to get back to his "old self," a doctor told him. What an idiotic thing to say. How dare he spit out that mouthful of bullshit. What did he know about Cory's old self? With a 30-year-old wedding band and a couple of kids smoothly through college, what could that doctor possibly know about the guilt that haunted him? Self-consumed, presumptuous prick.

Pat had left Cory's thick folder of physical therapy exercises on his dresser. It contained a number of instruction protocols featuring black-and-white photos of a man or woman demonstrating correct techniques for knee extensions, hip extensions, partial squats, hip marches, sit-to-stands as well as wrist exercises. All of these were designed to improve range of motion, flexibility and strength—and prevent clots from surgery, too.

He was also assigned stomach curls to rebuild abdominal muscle that was cut in surgery, a squeezing ball for hand and forearm strength and soup can lifts for triceps and shoulder strength.

Why were they smiling? Cory studied the faces of the people demonstrating the different exercises. He looked up at the vanity mirror. The ragged beard. The gaunt face. The lopsided hair stacked to one side because his left arm was as useful for styling hair as a fireplace poker.

Cory tossed the folder back on the dresser. What's the use? How are these smiling exercises going to get inside his head? How are they going to fix what he saw at the cabin, a future blown from its foundation? Where's the sheet of paper with the exercise for that?

A sneeze was coming on, so Cory pressed a pillow to his scar to protect the incision. Strange, when the only sound to come from your mouth is a sneeze; the volume was surreal.

There was a knock on his door, a pause, and then Pat slowly pushed it open. "Bless you," he said. "Am I interrupting anything, bud?"

Cory was worn out by Pat's over-the-top, cheery attitude. He shook his head no.

Pat saw the PT folder on the dresser with a few of the pages spilling out. "Did you do your exercises?" he asked with a tinge of hope.

Cory nodded yes.

"Truly?"

Cory shook his head no.

"What do you say we do them now. Breakfast can wait. I have to admit, I sure like having you here. I was getting tired of the drive to the rehab center."

When Cory came out of his coma and then kidney surgery, he had acute and chronic health issues. His brain trauma, as well as the dislocated hip and compound wrist fracture, created a cascading effect, each injury worsening the other.

In the first weeks of recovery, Cory wore a diaper, relearning the basics, beginning with control of bodily functions and how to chew and swallow. In the following weeks, his motor responsiveness gradually improved, but his verbal responsiveness remained unchanged.

Pat's current challenge was to help Cory regain motor control, strength and range of motion. Cory's handwriting continued to improve, but getting him on his feet, working on balance, ambulation and coordination were especially delayed by the hip injury and wheelchair.

"Let's start with sit-to-stands." Pat went into coach mode. "I know you have ten in you. Okay with that?" Cory looked at Pat blankly, then he set the right brake on his wheelchair. His broken wrist kept him from setting the left.

Pat set the left brake and gripped the handles on the wheelchair as Cory struggled to rise out of the seat. Wobbling, Cory rose to a standing position. He had had a few mild seizures when attempting to stand at the rehabilitation center, but they seemed to have passed.

Being this near to Cory, being able to study the young man's physical and emotional trauma, how it had left him a husk of the Cory Bradford he'd known, was heartbreaking for Pat. But damn it, Pat was determined not to leave it at heartbreaking. Some miracles come in tiny pieces. You need to start down on your hands and knees to find them.

Cory completed ten reps, and sat, perspiring, in the chair. Pat was as positive as a person could be, but down deep, there were doubts. He gave Cory a soft foam ball to squeeze. The muscles in Cory's left hand and forearm had greatly atrophied. Pat pushed aside worry. He thought that once they got the cast and traction rod removed, and with the hip healed, hopefully Cory's body could begin to move holistically. Complete healing could begin.

After three more exercises it was obvious Cory was done in. Pat sat on the bed, across from Cory. "Great session," he said. "No BS. Awesome job."

Cory was flushed. Blood flow opens the door to healing and this was a start. Pat wanted to keep pushing, to jump into the issue of Cory's mom, but he found some rare restraint. Cory should have breakfast on a positive note.

Pat tried to enjoy his food, but he knew what was coming. He was like a man on a raft, floating in serene waters, knowing that downstream, around the bend, there's a waterfall. The anxiety of the ensuing conversation was witnessed in his half-eaten eggs and cold, untouched English muffin. Pat looked for an answer. He found it in the morning light awakening the kitchen. It was an invitation to begin talking.

"Cory, there's something I need to tell you."

Cory looked up from his empty plate. His face immediately hardened. It struck Pat like a lash to pull Cory from an unguarded moment. "I was going to wait, but I look at this room that I built to honor mornings and light—and it strikes me we should talk here."

Pat's words were helping to relieve some of his tension, but they were having the opposite effect on Cory.

"When I was building this house, I would smash my finger or get a door jamb wrong—I fell off a ladder once, no, twice—anyway, I'd think there's no way this was going to work out." Pat sensed Cory withdrawing from his monologue.

"I swear to you Cory, I thought I'd been pushed into a deep hole. You remember how I was, right? It was like I was in a ten-foot hole and life dropped down five feet of rope. That's what I thought. What flippin' good was that going to do?"

This honesty pulled Cory back into what Pat was saying.

Pat continued. "Remember how Joseph used to say you never know who's going to throw you a rope, which was his father's saying? Remember that?"

Cory nodded.

"You have to be open to that idea. Help may very well come from the most unlikely places and people."

Cory looked down at his pad of paper. He took up his pen and wrote, HOW BAD IS IT?

"How bad is what?" Pat asked.

WHAT YOU REALLY WANT TO TELL ME.

Pat nodded. "You've always been a cut-to-the-chase guy." He took a deep breath. "After the accident, we were frantically looking for a kidney donor because the doctors thought you might lose both of yours. Your mom wasn't a match. Neither were your sisters."

Cory adjusted his weight in his wheelchair.

"That's when your mom told me." Pat looked Cory in the eye. "Cory, you're adopted."

PART FOUR

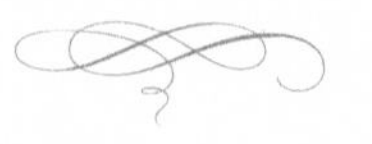

Middleton, Wisconsin

FEBRUARY

He sang the way sunlight pours through a break in the clouds. The few ears present turned toward the melody.

"Impressive. Is that your boy?" a mother at the playground asked.

The day had warmed to 38 degrees. A true February thaw.

"Um," MB said, looking at Singer, "at the moment, yes." MB both did and did not want to get into details. She stood next to a stranger—a woman who appeared maybe five or so years older, a mother of twin girls with snot running from their noses as they stopped halfway up the slide ladder to listen to Singer. MB felt an uncharacteristic pull, an urge to share. Maybe she was just lonely. "Temporary custody," MB said, edging forward.

The stranger nodded slowly. "That can be rough. For everybody." Then she deftly redirected. "Where'd he learn to sing like that?"

Should I let it drop here? Should I talk to her? MB, having forgotten her sunglasses, squinted through the brightness at the woman next to her. She wore Gucci. "Do you know something about it?" MB asked.

"Sorry?"

"Child custody. You said it can be rough."

The stranger nodded again. Her sunglasses hid her. "I'm an attorney. I don't practice family law, but I see plenty of it at the firm."

There was a budding comfort in talking. MB wondered: if you hold something inside long enough, do you reach a breaking point?

"His mother died suddenly," MB said.

"Oh, my. That's tragic."

"His biological father and mother were never married. His dad is my boyfriend. They live with me. Complicated."

The attorney pursed her lips. "So the death is recent? The courts haven't decided on custody?"

"Yes," MB said, impressed by how quickly the lawyer's mind worked. Singer stopped singing as abruptly as he had started. He waved at MB who waved back. "Our court date's in April."

"Seems like a happy child." The attorney decided to swallow any further questions; she was tired of directing conversations.

"We can talk about something else if you prefer," MB said. "Finally, weather we can't complain about."

"That's up to you."

"Well, if you don't mind. Let me ask one thing. Then I'll leave you be," MB laughed uncomfortably.

"No. It's not a problem." The attorney turned to face her. At that moment, her daughter's oversized boot slipped from the ladder. The little girl lurched sideways, her hand losing grip, causing her to separate from the ladder and fall face-down in the snowpack. A sharp cry went out of the child. Then nothing.

"Maddi, Maddi, Maddi, Maddi!" the mother said, running toward her girl, rolling her over, starting to take her daughter up in her arms. "Honey!" The girl's eyes widened as she fought to breathe. "My God," the mother said.

Then MB was at her side, on one knee. "Don't move her just yet. Let me help you." MB slipped her hand behind the little girl's head as she scooted closer to the fallen child. "Hi, honey," she said to the panic in the girl's face. MB didn't waste a moment, her eyes scanning the little girl from the feet up. Her other hand very gently, very slowly brought the girl's legs together, her knees up.

"She can't breathe!" The mother was on the edge of losing it.

All limbs were facing the right direction. No blood. The little girl could only manage a harsh squeak.

"You just have the wind knocked out of you," MB said in light tone. "You're okay, honey. Just relax a second and you'll be able to get a good full breath." MB's voice and demeanor helped the girl relax, and she was able to gather a gasping breath.

"There you go," MB said to the little girl, rubbing her back. "Just sit up, just a little, let me help you, yep just like that. Good. Wow. Fantastic. No tears. You are a lot tougher than most of the kids I see in the hospital. Okay. Feeling better?" MB nodded affirmatively.

The panic left the child's eyes as she nodded, too. MB looked at the other little concerned faces gathered, including Singer's.

"She'll be fine. When you fall hard there's a muscle called a diaphragm, here," MB touched her own chest. "It's under your lungs and it helps them take in and push out air. You use it when you cough. A hard fall can make that muscle spasm—um, stop working, but only for a few seconds—then it's fine. You're a brave girl. All better?"

The girl nodded tentatively.

"Thank you, doctor," the attorney said.

MB basked in the error. *Thank you, doctor.* Those words were an honor. Her mother used to tell her that her nickname, MB, was as close as Mary Beth would ever get to being called an MD. You lack discipline, she was told. You're too concerned with appearances and what peers think. A jolting memory.

"Actually, I'm a nurse. In the ER at St. Mary's."

"I'm Jennifer—Jenni," the child's mother said, taking her little girl up in her arms. "Darling, are you all right?" This simple question layered with mom's emotion opened the gates to tears and sobs. But soon, the girl, her sister and Singer were rocking on plastic horses as their imaginations galloped them away.

"I can't thank you enough."

"It's scarier when they're your own."

The attorney looked at MB. "I'm afraid what I do in a courtroom doesn't always translate to parenting."

"Like I said, complicated." MB brushed a little snow from the knees of her jeans.

"Don't get me started." The attorney looked at her watch. "Well, the girls and I need to get going. Piano lessons."

MB said okay.

"Say, not to push, but if there is something you need—I know you said you had a question or two about the custody hearing. Here's my card. Call me. Or we can have coffee. Or meet here. I'd like to repay you for what you did."

"That's not necessary."

The attorney held up her hand, to chide herself. "I put that poorly. I've enjoyed talking to you. If you want to talk some more sometime, give me a call. I'd like that. I frankly don't have much of a life outside of the office and my family."

MB looked at the business card. It was impressive. "Okay," she nodded. "I work some crazy hours, but, yeah. Nice to meet you, Jennifer."

"Please. Jenni. The firm makes us use our formal name. Helps rationalize a preposterous hourly rate."

"I'm Mary Beth. Everyone calls me MB."

They gave each other a shy smile.

"Can I ask you one quick question?"

Jenni nodded. "Appears we have time." The two women watched the kids playing together. "No one seems to be in a hurry to get to piano."

"This is . . . complicated, so I'm not sure it's a quick question after all."

"Give it a try."

MB nodded and gestured to Singer. "He sent a letter to the man who was engaged to his mother; the man who has also filed for custody. We wrote the letter together. In it he said he wanted to go live with him."

"With the deceased mother's fiancé?" Jenni checked to make sure she was tracking correctly.

"Yes. No response from the letter."

Jenni frowned. "That's odd."

"Yeah. I thought so, too. Now he wants to send another letter." MB looked through the sun at Jenni. "Would you do it?"

Jenni considered the question. The warm sun had softened the surface snow enough so the kids could make mini snowmen. They were making a family. "Are you asking me as lawyer, or a mother?"

"Would your answer be different?" MB asked.

"I'm afraid it would," the attorney said.

"Oh shit," MB whispered.

CHEVY

Tom and Jerry were at it again. The cunning cartoon mouse let his nemesis have it in the face. With a clothes iron. KA-WONGGG! The scene made Chevy grin on multiple levels. One, it was funny stuff. And two, here he was, on the couch, rather than on a bus bouncing toward a podunk minor league hockey venue where his head would get much the same treatment as Tom's.

The late morning snowmelt on the roof left a trickle of water drumming outside the window nearest to where Chevy reclined. It made a muffled soundtrack that synced up perfectly as Jerry tiptoed in on a sleeping Tom, slipping a stick of dynamite under his backside. Jerry lit the fuse, Chevy winced and some of his bowl of Captain Crunch spilled on the couch. MB would give him the business for that. But she and Singer were out at the playground while Chevy was reliving his childhood.

Wintertime Saturday mornings for Chevy had always been about hockey. His mom would gently rouse him from bed. They'd always rise early enough—a good hour or so before they needed to be at the arena—so Chevy could plop down on the couch, under an afghan his grandmother knitted, with a dry bowl of Captain Crunch on his lap. Mom would flip on cartoons, kiss his warm cheek and duck into the kitchen to fry bacon, scramble an egg and trim the crusts of his toast. Even when Chevy was playing at the University of Wisconsin, he'd spend Saturday mornings on the couch with his Captain Crunch and cartoons. An idyllic childhood is hard to abandon. But today, he had to go into work. He thought about showering and then said screw it. That's why baseball hats were invented.

Chevy left a note near the toaster. Call me, it said. I'll be at the salt mines slaving away on the Project.

He had told MB most of what it involved. To say she was uncomfortable with the plan was a huge understatement. She laid it right out there. It's fraud. You can't just open fake business accounts, launder money and call it nothing. It's illegal.

As Chevy pulled into the bank parking lot, his wheels splashed through a gaping, slushy pothole. It skipped his thoughts to the coming spring and summer and how he was getting sick of winter after loving it blindly for so long.

Then his thoughts swerved to MB. He saw her long, tan and lean in a bikini on a beach enjoying some of the 100K he was going to make on this harmless sleight of hand. Hell, that's all it was, he had told MB. Stop being such a drag. He was just sliding money around. No one would be the wiser. No one was getting hurt or losing money. We're just using money to make money. This was the rationale he'd been fed by Boss Allen, and this indoctrination passed from skin-deep to something now coursing through his bloodstream. Yeah, you could call it illegal. Illegal is walking across the street outside of the marked pedestrian crossing. Illegal is discarding a stray scrap of litter in any trash bin other than your own.

Chevy pulled his car next to Boss Allen's Cadillac. MB continued to run through his thoughts. Colorful bikini, smiling, carefree, wind-tossed hair. Then, as his vision of her widened out, in front of her was Singer. She chased after the little boy, who carried a sand pail and shovel, his swimsuit ruffled by an ocean breeze, their laughter swallowed in the break of the surf. Chevy's arousing scene burst like a cartoon bubble.

"Didn't expect you to be here on a Saturday. Bosses don't congregate, they delegate, right? Isn't that somewhere on the The Winner's List?" Chevy leaned on the office doorframe.

Boss Allen was wearing a blue tracksuit that produced exactly the opposite effect he had intended: he appeared paunchy and in decline. "Looking at mid-month numbers." He didn't glance up from the computer screen. "Pretty darn decent. You've opened a number of new accounts—not including the ones I imagine you're here to work on today." Boss Allen turned toward his protégé and winked.

"Yes sir. I'll have the last of our new accounts in the system for you to look at shortly." Chevy grinned slyly. "When will your investor have the deposits ready?"

Boss Allen leaned back in his desk chair, hooked his fingers behind his head and smiled. His lips, wet from coffee, had a rubbery appearance that made Chevy think of a frog. "He's waiting on us, my boy." The minimal amount of hair remaining on the top of Boss Allen's head was reinforced by an ambitious comb-over. His eyelids, typically heavy enough to deaden his eyes, lifted, giving him a spark of wild anticipation that was borderline frightening. "He's ready when we're ready."

"Give me two hours," Chevy said. The surge of adrenaline he'd been missing since hanging up the skates kissed Chevy on the mouth. He liked the banking game. He liked winning clients and holding all the aces when loaning money. He liked the neatly pressed uniform. And he especially liked the juice of this latest deal. A little deception. A little feint one way and going the other. A fake shot that tightens up an opponent as you blow by him. Banking wasn't so different from hockey. Except in this case, Chevy was getting a taste of real money.

Boss Allen was impressed with the young man. Maybe it was because he possessed so many attributes that he himself lacked. Chevy was handsome. Chevy was athletic. Chevy was witty. Chevy had natural room presence. These qualities would serve him well in financial circles. They would give him a head start. And if Chevy could show persistence, judgment and if he could seize a business opportunity as skillfully as he leveraged an opportunity on the ice, he could be a real player.

Boss Allen had not reached real player status in the Madison banking community. Much of the blame firmly rested, he believed, on the fact that Middleton was considered exactly what its name meant: a middle town. Average.

But if he could get that house in Maple Bluff, if he could secure a membership at the country club, doors would surely fly open. He'd find his way into a few high profile board appointments, perhaps become a college regent, get involved in a little non-profit work, maybe even sponsor a wing at the Children's Hospital—all the tricks the wolves used to cloak themselves in sheepskin. Appearances. That was the secret of moneymen. Just because money was their God didn't mean these men didn't attend church on Sunday.

Boss Allen rubbed his eyes. Enough scrolling through backlit columns of numbers. He turned away from his computer screen and took a yellow legal tablet from his desk's side drawer. He went to work scripting the bank's next TV commercial.

When Boss Allen took his first tentative steps into the limelight, becoming the face of the Middleton Community Bank, he was so petrified he got diarrhea. Since childhood, disparaging names had been hurled at him like rocks. Girls he smiled at would make a face like they just bit into a bruised apple.

Cameras, however, are seductive. And seeing your face on billboards and bus benches eventually inflates anyone's confidence—especially when a high school classmate who hung up on you when you invited her to senior prom is sitting on *your* bus bench, now 40 pounds heavier, smoking, twice divorced and clerking at Walgreens.

His television commercials weren't slick—usually shot by a videographer who was working on other "projects" but who needed to eat and pay rent. So he'd tolerate an insipid day in a bank working on a dull TV commercial. Boss Allen's latest idea had awakened him in the middle of the night. He wrote on his legal pad.

CAMERA OPENS ON CUSTOMER WAITING IN LOBBY.

BANKER HURRIES PAST, SAYS: I'll be with you in a minute.

CUSTOMER CONTINUES TO WAIT.

BANKER HURRIES BY AGAIN, SAYS: Just one more minute.

CUSTOMER CONTINUES TO WAIT.

BANKER HURRIES BY AGAIN, SAYS: Just one more minute.

CUSTOMER GETS UP AND WALKS OUT

Announcer: Tired of the big bank treatment? If so, Middleton Community bank is the bank you've really been waiting for.

NOW THE CUSTOMER IS IN OUR LOBBY. I COME OUT, SHAKE HIS HAND,

I SAY: Hello, John. How can I help you today?

FINISH WITH OUR LOGO AND JINGLE

Boss Allen dropped his pen on his pad and sat back in his chair with a proud grin. "That's a dagger to the heart of the giant," he said aloud. Three cups of coffee were pounding on the door of his bladder, but he had to get his brilliance down on paper first.

After a bathroom break, he stopped by Chevy's office. "Knock, knock," he said.

Chevy looked up from his computer. "Hey, if it isn't the future owner of 5,000 square feet of fine Tuscan-Mediterranean Maple Buff real estate."

Boss Allen winced, darting into Chevy's office. "Discretion," he said in a sharp voice, pulling the door shut behind him.

"No one here but us chickens," Chevy said. The look on Boss Allen's face said the reference was lost on him. "Pull up a chair. I think you're going to like the show."

Chevy pointed out how the fund manager would have access to six bank accounts aligned with six shell companies, each with a street address that was nothing more than a converted P.O. Box. The five million dollars in venture capital would get divided six ways, each account receiving a deposit of $833,333 and change. In business banking, rarely does a deposit under a million put a blip on the regulator's radar.

"So," Chevy said, "your guy's money goes quietly through these American doors and pops out safely in London, which isn't known as the money-laundering capital of the world for nothing. Now he has a sparkling-clean five-million dollar offshore account to transfer into the stock market. He piles up some nice capital gains, which aren't taxed because the money doesn't exist. After a year, his original seed money goes back into our accounts, and then back to the fund. The reporting shows that the investment in these six companies merely broke even, so they pull their venture capital. We close the accounts. Your guy is up however much the market can return in a year. Hopefully about 30% or a million five—or one point five rocks, as the Wall Street guys say."

"Perfectamundo." Boss Allen stood and stretched in his blue tracksuit. Not a pretty sight.

Chevy interrupted. "I was thinking of creating one more account."

"Huh?" Boss Allen was stunned.

"Hear me out. What's to keep this guy from cutting us out and keeping everything? There's no evidence any accounts ever existed after we hit delete."

Boss Allen's face flushed. "We have a deal. That's what would keep him!"

"No offense, but it's fair to say that this guy doesn't always tell the truth. I mean who's to say we're not just his latest patsy. Maybe this isn't his first 'Italian villa' deal."

Boss Allen sat back down. He was blinking fast. "So how does the extra account work?"

Chevy now stood. "We open it along with the others. No money goes in at first. It's just an empty shoebox. Then at the end of the year, when we're asked to transfer the money from overseas back into the accounts, our cut is routed into this extra account. Once we have our check in hand, the final 500K gets moved to the fund with the other money."

"Collateral." Boss Allen's eyes lit up like he bit into a maraschino cherry.

"You might call it that. I call it an insurance policy."

"I prefer collateral." Boss Allen looked at Chevy and slowly nodded his head. "Set up your extra account," he said. "I have to get to the gym. I'm turning 45 this year, did I tell you that?"

"Yeah," Chevy said, thinking *a million frickin' times.*

"By the way, good hedge on that extra account. Probably unnecessary, but what do we say on The Winner's List?"

"Plan for the worst but expect the best."

"Amen," Boss Allen said.

The afternoon was winding down as Chevy straightened the last items on his desk. His luminous computer screen blinked at him. The fraudulent business accounts were listed in a neat column.

He rolled his chair back so he could open the top desk drawer and remove the letter Singer had written to Cory. Chevy held it to his nose as if there might be a faint aroma. He knew what the letter said. He and MB helped the boy write it. *I want to come live with you. I miss you.*

"Singer," he said aloud. "Someday I'll show you this letter. We'll open it from the deck of our beautiful house overlooking the ocean and you'll be glad I never sent it."

A plan was starting to coalesce.

There would be a point in time—an opportunity—about a year from now, when the five million dollars that was laundered and invested offshore would be coming back through the bank. That five million, plus whatever was earned on its investment, would be momentarily and wholly under Chevy's management before it was transferred to the fund manager.

What if that money stayed in the extra account. Every cent of it. What if there were another unmailed letter, this one shown to Boss Allen and the fund manager. What if this letter were addressed to the U.S. Department of the Treasury.

Maybe this letter would include a copy of the fake bank accounts and description of the scheme and the name of the bank president and fund manager involved. It could be sent anonymously. Or not. Depending on if the bank president and fund manager agreed to part with the original five million and whatever gains were earned.

Boss Allen would only need to write Chevy a glowing letter of recommendation, throw him a heartfelt going-away party and Chevy would be out of his life forever. The fund manager would have to eat the five million dollar venture capital loss—a little scratch on the fund—nature of the beast. As long as they left Chevy's extra bank account untouched, hidden in the shadows, that letter to the Treasury would remain in Chevy's drawer—wherever he might be working in the future. Maybe sunny California. Or Florida. Maybe on the Italian coast. *Wouldn't that be ironic*, Chevy thought.

Singer's unmailed letter went back in his top drawer, tucked under the clutter. He shut down his computer. The photo of his mother stared at him from the right corner of his desk. From the left, a photo of MB. "Maybe," he said to those photographs. "Just maybe your boy has the onions to pull it off."

MOTHERS

MB paused, on the verge of hanging up the phone.

"Jennifer Taylor's office," the voice on the other end said for a second time, a bit exasperated.

"Hi. Um is Jennifer there?" MB looked down at Jennifer Taylor's business card. The words Civil Law nearly glowed in embossed golden ink.

A crisp, professional voice responded. "May I tell her who's calling?"

"It's Mary Beth. Um, MB. Tell her I'm the one she met at the playground with our kids."

"Jennifer is in court today."

"Oh. Okay. Can you leave her a message?"

"It is one of my capabilities, yes."

"Ask her to call me. MB. Are you ready for my phone number?"

"For some time now," her assistant replied.

MB had enough of the second-class treatment. "Do you enjoy making people feel like shit?"

"Excuse me?"

"Is this a regular thing for you? Or am I special?"

Now it was the assistant's turn to backpedal. "Ah, no. Um."

"I'm a friend of Jennifer's," MB exaggerated. "You need to treat every caller like a friend of your boss. Every. Person. Friend. Boss. Good rule of thumb. Yes?"

"Right. Correct."

"Are you ready for my number now?"

"Yes. Thank you."

MB gave her the number and had the assistant read it back; a small dig. Not that MB felt good about this encounter—she disliked causing discomfort, in and out of the ER. But the assistant was an elitist snob. The assumption of superiority had always put sparks in MB's eyes and made her want to run faster and compete harder.

Two days later, she and Jenni were having lunch at a restaurant equidistant from the hospital and the Madison courthouse. It was a classic Irish pub with comfort food that ushered away windchills and icy toes from your consciousness.

"My assistant mentioned that you let her have it on the phone the other day," Jenni said.

MB's look apologized for her. "I was tired. Pulled the night shift four nights in a row. She was dusting me. Kinda lost it."

Jenni smiled broadly at her new friend. "She can be a grade-A bitch. Part of her job is to screen my calls, but sometimes she enjoys it too much."

"She said you were in court. Is that case still ongoing?"

Jenni nodded. "An unfortunate reminder that two things are infinite. The universe. And man's stupidity." She hesitated.

"Is it something you can talk about?"

"Be warned. It's not the least bit appetizing."

"You know what I do for a living," MB said. "I have a pretty strong stomach."

Jenni nodded. "So there's a truck tire retreading factory in Ohio that has forever been a boys' club. You can imagine. Everywhere, testosterone and pinup calendars. But times change and anti-discrimination laws came into effect and the factory had to hire qualified women. The boys weren't too pleased."

The waiter showed up with two frothy Guinnesses.

"That sounds like a job to run from," MB said.

"Yeah. But it's a union shop. Good pay and benefits. So now a quota of qualified women are working among the boys. The factory manager said he had no hard feelings. In fact, on the work anniversary of every female employee, he'd throw a little party in the breakroom with a cupcake and a candle for her."

MB started to visibly tense up.

Jenni asked, "Have you heard about this in the news?"

"No," MB said. "But I have a bad feeling."

"Turns out, in five years, 61 cupcakes were served. All were laced with the semen of the manager and ten others."

"Sick bastards," MB said.

"They claim it was innocent fun. Luckily for our clients, this backwater factory is owned by one of the big national tire companies. Our class action suit is seeking 25 million dollars and I think we are going to get it." Jenni rapped on the wooden tabletop with her knuckle. "So, semen cupcakes. Probably a walk in the park compared to the emergency room."

MB shrugged. "The ER is either the most boring job on the planet or adrenaline gushes out like it's an open wound. Sorry, graphic alert."

Their lunches arrived in baking crocks too hot to touch. As they forked open the flaky crusts of their shepherd's pie, the steam and aroma that rose forth warmed their every cell. That and the beer had them unwinding.

"This may be an inappropriate question around food—or just a dumb one," Jenni said, "but can I ask you about veins?"

"Ah, sure," MB said.

"Is it true that veins—like I can see in my wrist here—are blue but arteries are red? And if yes, why? I always wanted to ask someone, but in law you're taught not to ask a question unless you know the answer."

"I thought that was a cliché," MB teased.

"No. Pretty much true. Which is why lawyers aren't nearly as smart as we think we are. Too many unasked questions."

"It has to do with blood color." MB pulled the sleeve of her sweater up her wrist. "Veins carry deoxygenated blood, which has been used by tissue and organs, back to the heart. Deoxygenated blood is deep red, but looks blue through opaque skin. Arteries carry blood away from the heart, so being rich in oxygen, that blood is bright red. Arterial bleeding will spurt, like you see in bad horror movies, because it's pumped."

Jenni put up her hand to say that was enough.

From there, the lunch conversation became more mundane. They talked around the edges of their relationships, exchanged tips on getting kids to eat better and spoke wistfully about sleeping past 9 a.m. Then Jenni got to the crux of why they were there.

"So, on the playground, we talked very briefly about possible child custody issues. What's the name of the boy living with you?"

"His given name is Paul, but he goes by Singer."

Jenni nodded. "Appropriate enough, judging by what I heard at the playground. And your boyfriend, Chevy, is the birth father?"

"That's right."

"You mentioned something about sending letters," Jenni said.

MB backed up the conversation a bit, including what she had learned from social services. "Singer was living with his mother and her fiancé, a guy named Cory. When Singer's mom was killed, Cory went after the guy and there was a horrific crash. The other guy died. Cory was severely injured and is now recuperating in northern Minnesota. Singer told me he wants to go and live with Cory and—"

"Can I interrupt?" Jenni asked.

"Sure."

"Is there anything unsafe or unloving at your house that would cause Singer to ask to live with Cory?"

"God no. Of course not."

"I have to ask," Jenni said, "because the question will eventually be asked by someone involved in this decision."

MB relaxed a bit. "In fact the letter said he loved living with us while Cory was in the hospital."

"What else did it say?"

MB set down her fork. Her appetite had vanished. "Singer said he wanted to go home and—" the words caught in MB's throat, "and help Cory get strong again."

"Sweet child," Jenni said. The women looked at one another. "No reply back from the letter?"

"Nothing. Odd. It's been, I don't know, three weeks. Now Singer wants to send another. Which bring me to my question. Should he—should we—send a second letter?"

Jenni leaned back in her chair and crossed her arms. Her fingers drummed on her blouse in slow regular sequences. She looked out past the restaurant's lunch bustle, through the large front window, out into the white cold of February.

"Let your feelings tell you what to do," Jenni said. "Don't let your boyfriend or an attorney—or even that beautiful little boy tell you what to do. You have instinct for this." Jenni's finger tapped her heart. "Listen to it."

LETTER TWO

Upon entering the front doors of the Maple Bluff Country Club, a person was all but submerged in richly stained hardwoods. Oak. Black Walnut. Cherry. The clubhouse was literally built on the principle that ordinary does not belong here. Only a select group of trees culled from the area's finest native hardwoods were marked, felled, milled and transported in 1917 to this 200-plus acre location. And then only the most outstanding carpenters were hired to raise and finish the building.

Ironically, or perhaps not, it was on the backs of men living at the brink of poverty that this exquisite clubhouse was erected. The building was to be a tribute to the booming wealth of the community just north of Wisconsin's capital city of Madison.

Contrary to previous visits, the moment Boss Allen stepped inside the doors of the clubhouse he was greeted like a diplomat. Their party of three was led by William Cunningham Deerg, one of Madison's leading investment bankers.

They strolled down the carpeted hallway below a succession of impressive chandeliers. On either side of the men, the walls held framed photographs that transitioned from black-and-white to four-color, marking time's passing. These were the highly regarded faces of the country club's board members. Among the more recent, there was a flattering portrait of Mr. Deerg. He used his finger to remove a bit of dust from the frame as he approached the maître d' stand.

"Those photographs need attention," he said calmly.

"Yes, Mr. Deerg." The maître d' snapped his heels together.

"Are you familiar with my guests?" Mr. Deerg turned to face Boss Allen and Chevy.

"I am indeed, sir. Gentlemen, good to see you again." The maître d' half-bowed.

Excitedly, Boss Allen extended his hand. No sooner had it hung in the air then he understood the breach. The man before him was not an equal. He was never to be recognized with anything more than a hearty clap on the back and a $10 bill discreetly tucked in the fold of his palm. Boss Allen's arm retracted like it was spring-loaded.

"Well then," the maître d' cleared his throat. "I have your usual table set for you." He looked at Mr. Deerg.

"I think something quieter today, Lester. Toward the back, closer to the trophy room."

The trophy room was a less formal meeting area, its walls heavy with taxidermy. Marble-eyed deer heads stared out from every angle. Huge, local bucks unlucky enough to step out from behind a tree to reveal antler spreads wide enough to dry a load of laundry.

The men got comfortable with water and menus. Once the waiter had left them, Mr. Deerg adjusted the knot of his tie and turned to Chevy.

"Well, young man, I'm delighted to have you on our team for this endeavor. Are there any questions you have of me?"

From the corner of his eye, Chevy could see Boss Allen shaking his head no. He nonetheless addressed Mr. Deerg. "The accounts show that everything transferred without a hitch and you've been able to access your overseas account. Have you been able to invest that money back in the market here?"

Boss Allen, blinking rapidly, was about to interject when Mr. Deerg nodded. "I have indeed. And I appreciate the smooth ride the both of you have extended to those dollars. I'm happy to say the market, and our investment, is climbing like a Swiss alpinist. All is according to plan—and then some."

Boss Allen took a shaky sip of water, hoping to steer the conversation to safer ground: falling interest rates, the strength of the dollar, weather. No such luck.

"Now, I have a question for you, young man. You've put yourself in a risk position by joining our efforts. I'm curious why." Mr. Deerg had such a twinkle in his eye upon asking, one would think the question was about a favorite ice cream flavor.

"My life has always had a certain amount of risk to it. I used to play a lot of hockey."

"I know. I fondly recall watching you leading the Badgers to a title a few years back. It's one of the reasons I agreed to meet with you today."

Chevy nodded. "I've learned risk is a key part of success. Some people are so afraid they never get very far."

"I couldn't agree more. Risk is often what separates winners from losers."

Boss Allen was not only feeling a bit left out, but he began to wonder if, in some way, he was being put in the risk-adverse loser pile. "I also agree," he said. "Up to a point."

Both men looked at Boss Allen to continue.

"Risk must be respected."

"Well put, Allen," Mr. Deerg said, hardly listening. His focus returned to Chevy, as if he were a rare breed of wild animal that he suddenly had an opportunity to study. "So it's risk you seek?"

Chevy grinned slightly. "If it were just risk, I'd walk on the wing of an airplane. But when the reward is right, the risk is to be embraced."

"To be embraced," Mr. Deerg repeated softly. "Fantastic."

Excitedly, Chevy went over the details of the meeting almost word for word with MB that night after Singer had gone to sleep. MB listened with one ear, but her heart was in a conversation she wanted to have—about Singer, about letting what was in his best interest reveal itself, about sending another letter.

"Hey, are you even listening?" Chevy asked, bemused.

"Yeah. Sure. You and Mr. Big were comparing the length of each other's risk."

"Hardy har har. Honey, I'm telling ya, it was cool. That man walks on water with million-dollar shoes. A good guy to know."

"Until he lands in jail."

Chevy frowned. "Would you quit with that. Jesus, MB, that's nothing to kid about."

"What if I'm not kidding?"

"Come on. No one's going to jail. This thing's bulletproof. It's barely a nick, money-wise."

MB knew when to push Chevy and when to back off. "If you say so. But be careful. That's a slippery slope you guys are traipsing around on."

Chevy edged closer on the couch and put his arm around MB. "How 'bout we get back to that part when we were comparing whose risk is bigger?" He gave her a squeeze and a little wink.

MB wriggled out. "Chevy, there's something I need to talk to you about."

Chevy braced himself. Those were not words he liked to hear. "What's up?" he said, minimizing.

"I'm worried about Singer. And that we haven't heard back from Cory on the first letter."

"Maybe he's too laid up to respond. Or maybe he likes things the way they are."

"I don't know." MB shook her head, confused. "Singer says he'd like to send another letter. I think we should."

Chevy almost let his emotions get the best of him. *Screw another letter! What, we're not good enough? What does the kid want that we aren't providing*? But that response, he quickly realized, was the wrong approach.

"Sure. Okay," he said.

MB was stunned. "Really?"

"Why not? If the kid—if Singer—wants to send another letter, okay by me."

"Thank you. Thank you, thank you." MB lifted his arm and slid in next to Chevy. He was warm as a furnace.

Chevy didn't like deceiving her—hated it, really. Up until now, and for the first time in any relationship, he'd been completely honest. About everything. He even told her about the bank deal. Because she was different. They were different.

But on this issue, on Singer, the boy belonged here. It gave them stability. MB was the kind of woman who could walk out just as suddenly as she walked into his life. He admired her unpredictability and independence, but it left him uneasy. She was a girl on a roof who could slide away at any time.

Write your letter. Write all the letters you want, my dear. They're not going any farther than my desk drawer.

PART FIVE

Baudette, Minnesota

KITTY

It was the final week of February in Baudette. If there is charity buried in this month, it is its length: four compact weeks. Compact. Like an ice cube.

Kitty had prepared a hot lunch of grilled cheese and tomato soup. The Sheriff, seated at the kitchen table, stared off as steam lifted from his bowl. She took a handful of last night's popcorn and sprinkled it on her soup. Then she slid the popcorn his way.

"Honey?"

No response.

"Helloo in there? Would you like popcorn?"

"What?" He looked at the puffy, white kernels riding high on her orange soup. "Oh, no thanks. Looks tasty, though."

"Now don't let your lunch go cold. It's supposed to warm you up before you have to go back out there." Kitty shivered at the thought.

The Sheriff absentmindedly picked up his spoon, but it didn't get as far as his bowl.

Kitty frowned. "Thurgood. If you're going to bring your office into this kitchen, could you at least include me?"

The Sheriff rubbed his face. "Sorry." He took a spoonful of soup. "I was letting it cool to the perfect temperature."

"Oh piffle," Kitty smiled. "By the way, that's a special aged cheddar in your sandwich."

The Sheriff took a bite. His eyes widened as he nodded. "Good thing I let it age a titch more," he said through a mouthful.

Kitty laughed. "You are full of it." Her high tone got Private off his cushion, tail wagging. He came in to check out the excitement and found a piece of popcorn to inhale off the floor. "Isn't he full of it?" Kitty scratched under Private's chin, which got his hind leg thumping the floor.

"I'm trying to think of the best way to approach Varkas."

"In broad daylight, I suggest," Kitty said. "He strikes me as more dangerous than a roller skate on a step."

Typically, Kitty had an easy, constant smile framed in a face made happier yet by her round, prominent cheekbones. Her hair was cut short and active, parted on the side. She slightly favored brunette to auburn, depending on how dialed-in the colorist was at the beauty salon.

The Sheriff set down his grilled cheese. "Now I don't need you to worry about this. We'll just have a little conversation, he and I. I won't jump right in. But 16 employee deaths in three years—that's alarming."

Kitty nodded solemnly.

"I may go by and see this latest widow," he continued. "Talk to her about the accident. Maybe there's negligence or carelessness . . . could be a wrongful death claim that'd have her recovering lost wages and such."

Kitty perked up. "I went by church the day before last. They had a pair of toddler boots, a coat, some mittens and two hats in the lost and found since last winter. I thought I might bring them over to the young widow, but with you going, it could be a good conversation-starter."

"You are cut out for police work." The Sheriff nodded. "A good idea wrapped in a good deed."

"It will get folks talking, you know. You paying her a visit."

The Sheriff shrugged. "Not much I can do about that."

Kitty reached across and patted the Sheriff's hand. "Be discreet, dear."

"I ain't really a discreet size," the Sheriff said.

"You're anything you put your mind to, Thurgood," she said surely.

"Hell, Kitty. You know as well as I do how folks want a juicy scrap of anything to gnaw on."

Kitty lifted her chin. "As Eleanor Roosevelt said, 'Great minds discuss ideas; average minds discuss events; small minds discuss people.'"

The Sheriff smiled at her. "I have nothing to add to that."

After lunch, with the lost-and-found items packed in a box in the passenger seat, the Sheriff and Private headed out in the cruiser. The Sheriff was taking Private along in the vehicle more and more. Driving was less stressful for him with a dog curled up in the back on his old Army blanket from Korea. His previous dog, a Lab named Deputy, went everywhere with him, including foot patrol. It was nice to have that companionship back.

"Well, we've got a fresh lead to pursue, right Private?" The Sheriff looked in the rearview mirror as he stuffed a stick of Big Red in his mouth. The dog listened attentively. The Sheriff had knocked on the widow's door, a tough-looking house with plastic hung across broken windows but there was no answer. Luckily, a neighbor noticed the cruiser in the driveway and came out to see if there was trouble. The Sheriff said there was not, and after listening to a protracted story about a deadbeat brother-in-law, found out that the widow had taken a job across town at the lumberyard.

Here's the thing about being a Sheriff: when you walk into a place of business and ask to see an employee, it ignites gossip and suspicion. Knowing this, the Sheriff, along with his cardboard box containing the winter items, headed right for the boss's office.

"Heya Russ," he said to the lumberyard manager.

"Sheriff. Hopin' that's lunch packed in that box. Can't seem to unstick myself from this desk." Russ folded his reading glasses onto his shirt's neckline and stretched. He was a solid guy, in every sense of the word.

"You should be so lucky," the Sheriff said.

"You still carting around licorice in those pockets of yours?"

"Not lately. Got some sugar-free gum. Just finished my last sugar piece."

"I'll pass. Must say you're looking good . . . for a guy who ain't getting any younger. Kitty still got ya eating right and church going?"

"She does. You seem to be holding up okay yourself. How's life on the shadowy side of fifty?"

Russ pursed his lips. "I'm not catching rabbits anymore. So it goes."

"How's Helen?" the Sheriff asked.

"I'd be a regular in the back of your cruiser if not for her."

"Say hello if you would."

Russ said he'd do just that. "To what do I owe the pleasure?"

"Just a heads up. Going to be talking to the widow Maddux. Heard she's been hired on here."

The manager nodded. "She's in the back, working inventory. Anything wrong?"

The Sheriff bristled. "You mean other than her losing her husband?"

"Hey, no need to swipe at me. I didn't know if there was anything else."

"Hell that's plenty."

"And then some."

The Sheriff continued. "I don't want any gossip running around, me talking to her. Thought it best to let you know what's happening so you can keep things even keel."

"Makes sense," Russ said.

Before the Sheriff picked up his box to leave, he mentioned one more thing. "I might be asking her about any negligence on the part of Varkas and his foreman out at the logging site where her husband was killed. Want you to hear that from me, Russ."

The manager put up a hand to wave the idea away. "I don't want to hear about none of that from no one."

The Sheriff frowned.

"None of it," Russ said. "Varkas is my boss, as well as hers. He's meaner than a gut-shot bear when it comes to snoopin'."

"Seriously? Russ, ain't you getting tired of all the widows on the payroll?"

"Sheriff," Russ's voice was level-set. "I don't want to talk about it. Period. End of sentence. It's a dangerous business."

"Lumbering's always been dangerous. Just not always so damn deadly."

"Sheriff, I ain't talking about lumbering. I'm talking about making Varkas's business your business."

The Sheriff took a long look at Russ. It was the first time the Sheriff ever saw the man appear anything but sure of himself. "I'll go see the widow now."

"Should find her in back. Through the first set of doors, not all the way to the drive-thru stalls."

The Sheriff turned to leave.

"Sheriff?" Russ said.

The Sheriff stopped and looked at him.

"Be careful."

The widow Maddux was on the phone when the Sheriff approached her drafty workspace in back. One overhead bay door was open as a forklift drove in and out, taking stacks of rolled insulation to the outside lot. The driver stopped for a long look at the Sheriff before getting back to work.

She was younger than the Sheriff expected, somewhat accentuated by the oversized Varkas Lumber parka she was wearing. Her stocking cap was flipped up at one ear as she went over an inventory list on the phone. Someone, the Sheriff gathered, was unhappy about the materials delivered to his construction site. She hardly looked at the Sheriff, hoping he might somehow disappear.

"Can I help you?" she said after hanging up.

"Are you Mrs. Maddux?" the Sheriff asked.

She nodded.

"My condolences on your loss."

She nodded again, this time with less resistance in her eyes.

The Sheriff set down the box he was carrying near the foot of her chair, far enough away from the glowing space heater. The overhead fluorescent lights scattered dingy rings. "I've brought you some winter things. For your kids."

"I'm no charity case," she quietly said.

"This here has gone unclaimed at the church for over a year. They wanted it out of their hair. Hate to see it end up in the trash."

She picked out a single snow boot and looked it over. "Okay," she said. "I need to get back to my work now."

The Sheriff tried to rub some warmth back into his hands. "Damn drafty back here."

"That bay door is closed most of the time. Got an order going out."

The young woman reminded the Sheriff of someone. Or maybe it was more she reminded him of a type. Tough. Alone. Exhausted. Overwhelmed. He'd seen that face more times than he cared to remember. "I want to ask you a few questions about your husband's death."

The widow anxiously looked to see if any co-workers were around.

"I talked to Russ. He knows we're speaking. He's fine with it."

She grit her teeth. "Sheriff, it's a little late for questions."

"Mrs. Maddux," the Sheriff said, "maybe something still can be done. Sometimes in the case of a wrongful death, there can be money awarded to the family if proper safety precautions were not in place, or other forms of company negligence."

The widow's eyes widened with wild energy. "Company negligence?" She stood quickly, her chair rolling away. "Company negligence!" She made a fist and punched the Sheriff in the chest. "Where am I now? Who am I working for!"

She cast her arms outstretched, breathing hard, inviting the

Sheriff to look across the cracked cement floor to the towering racks of building inventory. "I signed his paper. I took his job. Don't you see?" She lowered her voice, but only a little. "I may as well be his whore and take to his bed!" Again, she swung, hitting the Sheriff in the chest. "Where were your questions then? Where!"

The Sheriff spoke calmly. "What did you sign? Do you have a copy?"

The fury left her as quickly as it had taken possession. She hung her head and said no.

The Sheriff took her gently by the elbow and steered her to her chair.

"Leave me be, Sheriff. Please. I have a family to feed. Let it rest in some semblance of peace."

The Sheriff thought before he spoke, but spoke nonetheless. "What about the next widow?" The words rung in his ears.

The woman looked up from the floor. Her mouth hung open, mascara smudged, and her nose was running. She shook her head. "She'll get in line with the rest of us, that's what. Right at the gates of hell."

News doesn't slow down in a small town despite winter's heavy grip. It finds traction, accelerates and is waiting for you at your next destination.

As the Sheriff knocked the snow from his fur hat outside the door of Lu Ann's, he was greeted by Elrod Ames, a tractor mechanic with too much time and too little grease on his hands in the off-season. "Hey-ya Sheriff. Heard you've been questioning the widow Maddux about the death of her husband." Elrod's eyebrows lifted. "Is it true she packed his lunch box with a poisoned work sandwich?"

"Damn, Elrod. What in hell are you talking about?"

Elrod scratched his chin. "I figured that sounded sketchy." Elrod thought on it a moment. "Was it—?"

The Sheriff lifted his hat like he was going to use Elrod to knock the snow off it. That got him shuffling toward his truck.

Lu Ann's was between lunch and dinner and the few seats taken were occupied by the chronically late or early. Mick headed over to the Sheriff's table with a pot of coffee. The aroma of two cinnamon apple pies just out of the oven made the diner less empty. "Why don't you take a booth?" Mick said. "More than enough room."

The Sheriff turned his coffee cup right-side up and grimaced. "Damn. Getting harder and harder for me to muddle in and out of them booths. A hard chair sometimes best suits a person."

"There's some truth in that." Mick poured a steaming cup of coffee. "Heard you been talking to the widow Maddux."

The Sheriff brought his hand down on the table harder than intended, sloshing his coffee. "You too!"

Mick was taken aback. "What? Sorry."

"The whole town's yakkin' about my visit to the lumberyard. Is there nothing more interesting for people to discuss?"

Mick looked at the Sheriff. "It's February. In Baudette."

The Sheriff's posture slackened. "There is that."

"Elrod Ames says Varkas knows, too. Isn't happy about it."

"Elrod's always fishing off the wrong bridge." The Sheriff shook his head. "Should just take out an ad in the *Baudette Region*."

The brass bell over the front door rang out as a customer entered.

Mick lowered his voice. "Don't look now. Guess who just walked in."

Varkas filled the doorway of Lu Ann's. His eyes quickly settled on what he was looking for.

From his earliest memories on a playground, the Sheriff had always known what it was to be the biggest. Numerous inconveniences tag along with such size—shopping for clothes, finding comfort in furniture or just ritual stares from strangers—but there are definite advantages as well. None greater than the physical confidence in your every step, which you come to take for granted. Assuredness becomes second nature. Until you meet someone bigger. For the Sheriff, that someone was Varkas.

Varkas was six foot ten and weighed 300 pounds. Certainly, Varkas could stand to lose some weight, but mostly, he was huge frame and dense muscle. When the Sheriff, at six foot six and a slimmed-down 250 pounds, saw Varkas approaching his table, an unfamiliar feeling of intimidation crept over him.

"Well, well Sheriff. I see you do take an occasional break from your police work."

The Sheriff stood, presenting himself as straight and tall as possible. Varkas offered a hand to shake. Taking it, the Sheriff thought it as rough and cold as old wood.

"Varkas," the Sheriff nodded hello. "Another delightful day in the deep freeze." Both men applied extra firmness to their grip as they shook.

"Logs slide easy in these conditions," Varkas said. "I'll take it over that recent thaw we had." Varkas struggled to get his coat off his shoulders. "Hard to find coats big enough for the likes of us." The Sheriff noticed an American flag patch sewn on the right sleeve.

"What brings you to town today?" the Sheriff asked, sitting back down.

"Tying up a few loose ends. Saw your cruiser in front, thought I'd come have a word." Varkas sat without being invited.

"What can I do you for?" the Sheriff said.

Varkas waited for Mick to pour a cup of coffee and leave before speaking. "Sheriff, you seem to be curious about my business, judging by your recent sightings at my logging sites, the plant and my lumberyards. Thought it might be easier if you just told me what you're looking for. I'd like to save you some trouble."

"Well, no trouble, really. I'm just concerned over the Maddux accident, among other things," the Sheriff said.

The ledge of Varkas's heavy brow creased. One eyebrow, coarse as steel wool, lifted. "Maddux? Out at the logging site? That's long past a month ago now, isn't it?"

"That's the one."

Varkas took up the coffee mug and drank the scalding liquid like it were tap water. "There's snow over that grave, Sheriff. Why the need to disturb it?"

"There's a widow. A widow and her children."

Varkas nodded. "There is. She's working for me now, as you know. She'll be looked out for."

"How did her man die?" the Sheriff asked.

"You were there to take the report. That should tell you everything."

"Doesn't say a whole lot. Says the man was crushed by a load of logs. Says a chain broke loose. Went down as an accident."

"An unfortunate accident," Varkas said flatly. "That report is correct."

The Sheriff looked unsatisfied.

"You saw the body," Varkas said.

"I did."

"Anything you saw or what the coroner reported put in doubt that the man was crushed?"

"Nope."

"Well then, Sheriff. I'd say you know as well as I how the man died. This is a dangerous business we're talking about. That's why my men are so well compensated."

"That so?" the Sheriff said, futzing with his coffee mug.

"Everybody knows. Best pay in town."

"Was Maddux being paid overtime?"

For the first time since the conversation began, a word caught in Varkas's throat. "I'm not following."

"Overtime. Was the man being paid overtime?"

"I'm sure not. No reason to."

"Do you know the time of death at the scene?"

"Varkas's eyes narrowed. "I don't."

"Care to take a guess?"

"Sheriff, I'm not a man to guess."

"It was 6:05 in the evening."

"I'll take you at that."

"Do you recall the day of the week he died?"

"Sheriff, it was over a month ago."

"Friday. It was a Friday. That's a long day, on top of a full week, plus he's working in the dark. Wouldn't you say accidents are more frequent under those conditions?"

"Actually Sheriff, I would not. Accidents are more frequent when you lose focus. Could be in the middle of a sunny afternoon from what I've seen."

"You know who OSHA is, am I correct, Varkas?"

Varkas began to lose his patience. "Now Sheriff, I don't appreciate being talked to like I'm stupid. My family came here not speaking English, but we studied hard and caught on quick. You can't build a business in this great country of ours in these times without knowing who OSHA is."

The Sheriff continued. "OSHA says that most accidents do occur at the end of a shift. Some 60% of them. What's more, it's a federal labor law that full-time employees must be paid time and a half beyond 40 hours. I looked at his time card. Counting the hours he worked Friday, he'd put in 62. I know you're not stupid. I'm assuming you know of the overtime law and choose not to follow it."

"Sheriff, nobody tells me how much I pay my men but me. I have a business to run."

"Varkas, the flag on your coat sleeve. I'm wondering, do you consider yourself a patriotic man?"

"As patriotic as you'll find. I love this country and the opportunity it has bestowed on my family and me."

"Yet you are breaking a federal law. Maybe more than one."

Varkas all but growled. "Are you challenging my patriotism, Sheriff?"

"No I am not. I am asking why a patriotic person such as yourself would not abide by the law of the country he loves."

"That's a matter for my lawyer," Varkas said. "Me, I have a business to run. I have families and associates counting on me."

"That doesn't exempt you from the law. Or from federal safety standards."

"Sheriff, I do my best." Varkas took a paper napkin from the dispenser and dabbed up a single drop of coffee from the table. "Have you ever run a business, Sheriff?"

"No I have not."

"Have you ever had to make payroll for over 200 people?"

"No I have not."

"I'll let you in on a secret. When you add up all the regulations and taxes, it's damn near impossible to keep the lights on and the trucks fueled."

"You seem to be faring all right."

Varkas bent the conversation back on itself, catching the Sheriff momentarily off guard. "How about you, Sheriff? Are you a patriotic man?"

"I am, yes."

"Since there seems to be a lot of questions here at our table, do you mind if I ask another one?"

"Go ahead," the Sheriff said.

"Your hand. How did it happen?"

The Sheriff wore a prosthesis on his left hand where he had lost two fingers.

"Korea. Gun malfunction took 'em." The Sheriff pinged his artificial fingers against his ceramic coffee mug. "Good old PVC."

"So it was an accident."

"It was."

"And accidents happen. You didn't go after the Army for it. Or your commanding officer. Or denounce your patriotism over it. Right? You got over it."

"Yep."

Varkas continued. "That's what Americans do. We keep moving. Moving forward. You're living proof. You're a war hero."

"I'm no war hero. I was a kid who ran into some bad luck."

"Sheriff, we all run into our bad luck eventually. That's what happened to that young man out there. No more to it than that."

"Could be. But there've been too many significant accidents at your place lately. Too many young men that don't walk away just missing a few fingers."

"We're working on it, Sheriff. We're as concerned as you are."

"I hope you are."

"Well, Sheriff," Varkas said rising to leave, "good we had this talk. I wouldn't want things to get sideways between us." Varkas took a twenty-dollar bill from his wallet and dropped it on the table.

"That's an expensive cup of coffee you just drank," the Sheriff said.

"My treat, whatever you're having." Varkas wrestled his coat on.

The Sheriff looked up. "I do hope you truly are as concerned as I am about this loss of life."

Varkas stood oddly still, as though he were listening to some faint sound in the distance. "Rest assured. I am."

The Sheriff said, "Can you tell me again the name of the man who died in the accident?"

Varkas blinked. "Name? Well we just mentioned it. I believe it started with an N." Then Varkas's eyes snapped into focus and drilled into the Sheriff. "I don't appreciate the question."

The Sheriff shrugged. "It's my job to ask uncomfortable questions."

Varkas's glare did not yield. "You understand who you work for in that job of yours, right?"

"I do. I work for the welfare of this citizenry."

Varkas took a step closer and tapped the table with his rough hand. "You work for me," he said, voice lowered. "My taxes put that uniform on your back and pays your salary. That vehicle you've got parked out there and that pension sitting in the bank, that comes from taxes collected from my businesses."

"Yours, and others. I work for all taxpayers. Equally."

"But not all pay in the same. That's the point. Sure, I work for all of my customers, but hell no, not equally," Varkas said.

The Sheriff looked at Varkas with matching intensity. "Equally."

"Sheriff, yours is an elected position. The good people of this town, many who work for me, decide if you're the sheriff or not the sheriff."

"That is correct."

"Do you want them thinking you're unfriendly to their

livelihoods?"

"People can think what they want. This conversation is about what you think. I want you thinking, thinking hard, about worker safety. I am going to bring OSHA in to look at your operations. I am going to be checking up on things. The man who died in the accident, his name is Michael Maddux. He's one of 16 workers who have died in your employ over the past three years."

"Why are you stirring this up Sheriff? You know mine is a dangerous business."

"Maybe more so than it needs to be."

"Sheriff, it seems you've made up your mind." Varkas clenched his jaw. "I guess I'll be seeing you later."

"You will indeed."

"Until then." With that, Varkas turned heel and strode away.

The Sheriff's hand shook as he reached for his cup of coffee. He had a notion it might, which is why he hadn't reached for it earlier.

Sipping the last of his coffee, the Sheriff was sure of three things, none of which particularly pleased him. One, he hadn't seen his hand shake since the day he was shot at the farm. Two, Varkas was an explosive man who, above all, hated to be challenged by another.

And three, he had just lit a fuse.

WHEELCHAIR DREAM

Sitting in a wheelchair reminded Cory of Shara.

Their long talks in high school played in his head. She had said she got beyond her skiing accident. She smiled convincingly. She said you didn't wish for some events but there they were. You're powerless over them, as powerless as her legs were for her. The trick, she said, was detachment.

Cory remembered this word, detachment. How it seemed misplaced or out of character or just plain wrong. But she went on. You have to literally detach in order to get *over* something. That's how you gain freedom from what holds you down. Once she could detach from her paralysis, she said she was no longer a paraplegic; she was Shara again. And she could get her power back.

Reflecting on this, Cory thought: *Did she say these things for herself or for me? Could she somehow see this day coming? Was it a lie?* He wanted to know.

Outside his bedroom window was its own kind of infinity. Alabaster fields layered endlessly. But there, against the sky, was a lone, bare tree, ashen, gnarled as a spinster's empty hand.

Did she believe it, and then come to disbelieve? Or had she detached and gotten over her paralysis, only to relapse? Why did you kill yourself, Shara?

Cory rolled his chair over to the mirrored vanity where sheets of physical therapy exercises sat in a neat pile. He looked at the crutches leaning in the corner of the room. He lifted his hands and brought them slowly across his bearded face. *Adoption,* he thought to himself with each stroke. *Adoption.* It began to explain his disconnection with his mother, and the conditional love of his father. *What am I recovering from? How could my biological parents give me up?*

Me, myself and I had been his mantra, his ode when lost, alone, rowing on Lake of the Woods. *So who am I? A person always lost? Does this explain the cold comfort I find in retreating from others?*

His first exercise was called chair stands. With his back straight and the wheels locked, Cory stood up from the wheelchair using his hands as little as possible for leverage. Once standing, he would remain that way for ten seconds, and then sit back down for a five-second rest. Repeat 15 times. His dislocated hip, once a source of excruciating pain, now radiated mixed twinges, burns, pricks and throbs.

After finishing simple leg extensions and light squeezing exercises for his broken and good wrists, a weariness descended. Pat and HomeSky were at work. Meadow and Billy had driven to the Baudette Y to swim. Cory thought about a nap. He had an hour or so.

Needles of guilt stung him. Cory had always been most fulfilled when productive. He was intolerant of indolence. Last year as a teacher, on his homeroom blackboard he had chalked the words ACCOMPLISH SOMETHING in the top right corner; those words had a double box around them with a smaller instruction: DO NOT ERASE. Use these words, he had encouraged his students when they felt overwhelmed by a task or an obstacle. When you accomplish something, no matter how small, it gets the dominoes tipping in your favor.

Now Cory was accomplishing nothing, or so he told himself. This self-flagellation fostered no good.

Before he lay down, Cory used the bathroom. Entering by wheelchair was easier now that Pat had installed offset hinges, which allowed the door to sit flush to the jamb, widening the doorway by two inches. Once inside, he used a string attached to the doorknob to pull the door shut. It was clumsy. It was embarrassing. It was slow.

Back in his bedroom, Cory got himself on the bed. This, too, was a slow process, scooting toward the center so he could lay safely away from the edge. The quilt bunched up as he went, adding to his frustration. He closed his eyes and finally found comfort. The Dream

Spirit showed him this.

In the farmyard, Cory sat in his wheelchair in shirtsleeves. Snow whirled around him, blinding his vision, stinging his skin. There was no noise, just white violence.

Then the wind let go of the snowflakes and they dropped straightaway to the ground. A warm breeze arose that was friendly as the sun on his face. Spring caressed the farmstead as snow relinquished the ground, which became brown and soft.

Leaves, pinned under months of snowpack, were freed—unpeeled from the earth by a breeze. One dead leaf, wind-pushed, skittered along the ground before tumbling toward Cory. He watched the curled brown shape cartwheel. Closer and closer it rolled until the leaf became a brown sparrow hopping along the ground until it transformed further, feathers illuminating, now a goldfinch that took flight, lighting on his knee.

The goldfinch looked at Cory with eyes that knew. Together they absorbed the warm sun.

"You should rest," the bird said. "I won't leave you." Cory closed his eyes and slept in the peace of the strengthening sun.

When he awoke in his wheelchair, Cory was still in the farmyard, but the sun had slipped behind the horizon. He was chilled.

"You slept well," the goldfinch said. "It's time now."

Cory nodded.

Their eyes locked, and again, Cory sensed wisdom. "Honor your responsibility," the bird told him. They watched one another. Along with trust, those words began to take root.

Finally, the goldfinch fluttered to the ground and transformed into a sparrow. Wind cupped the bird and returned it to the shape of a tumbling leaf, taken across the farmyard until it went out of sight.

Cory awoke refreshed. He sat up in bed without the heaviness with which he lay down. He looked out the window. Spring was long off, but he could see it. He closed his eyes and he could smell the wet, renewed earth. He heard the words again, but this time because he spoke them aloud. "Honor your responsibility." Cory opened his eyes and the bedroom was unchanged but it held something new. Hope had entered.

The front door opened and Meadow came in. She quietly called out, "Cory? It's me." Her voice traveled the empty hallway.

"Back here," Cory said in return.

Meadow had a sleeping Billy in his car seat as she hurried to Cory's room.

She stood in the doorway, her mouth open with the beginnings of a smile. Cory was sitting on his bed.

"Did you just say that?" Her hair was still damp from swimming.

"I just said that." A dimple appeared as Cory half-smiled.

She was mystified. "What happened?"

"Before we get into that, can you bring me those crutches? I'm sick of this damn wheelchair."

VARKAS

The Baudette and Rainy Rivers meet just north of town. Near this junction, on a rise of land above the confluence, squats the Varkas Forest Products plant.

As one nears Baudette on humble highways from all directions, before you see the confluence or the city cluster, you will see, along the horizon line, what Varkas calls his signature. It's a wind-stretched, dirty plume of smoke, typically crawling west to east as it exits his plant's stacks.

Where others might see pollution, he saw progress. Where others might see emerald treetops doused in gray, he saw his signature floating across the paycheck of a growing town. And who, really, is going to argue with the name found on 200-plus paychecks every two weeks?

The plant's business model was simple enough. Processing trees into lumber is messy and inefficient. But sawmill scrap could be gathered and bonded using toxic adhesives and immense pressure to make anything from particleboard to plywood to joists to beams and trusses. It was a cacophonous, odorous, pollutant-belching business. Not to mention a profitable one.

From an observatory deck above the plant floor, Varkas looked on as giant matte black machines spat out composite wood products, and fork trucks pirouetted in and out with pallet-loads. He rapped on the office glass of his CFO and signaled for him to come out.

They stood at the railing and watched. Despite a naturally powerful voice, Varkas had to raise his to be heard. "You know the difference between those guys down there and me up here?"

The CFO said he did not.

Factory noise filled the lengthy pause. "Guts." Varkas nodded slowly, verifying the answer as his mind raced through a timeline of family history. "Some people are made to take a chance. Others are made to take a check. That simple."

"Hadn't thought about it that way, Mr. Varkas," the CFO said.

"You know all these people pretty well, wouldn't you say?"

"I would. Signed off on hiring each of them, as you know."

"Good," Varkas said. "Remind me, which one is Pat O'Rourke."

The CFO surveyed the plant floor.

Varkas continued. "He's the one I gave the envelope for the Maddux widow, correct?"

The CFO kept scanning through employees, who all looked nearly identical in hardhats. "That's right, Mr. Varkas."

"Do I remember correctly he's an ex-priest?"

"There he is now," the CFO pointed out. "At the end of plywood, line six. Looks like that line is really pushing."

"Love that new machine," Varkas said, mostly to himself.

"And yes, you have that right. He was a priest before joining us. His fifth-year anniversary is upcoming this fall. October I believe."

Varkas looked at his CFO with admiration. "Don't know how you do it," he said. "Keep all those names and numbers and dates straight as new lumber."

The CFO thought about Varkas's comment about guts. His equivalent was intellect, though he'd never say so aloud to Varkas. "Just have a knack, I guess."

"Why would a supervisor be helping at the end of a line?" Varkas was dumbfounded.

"Pat's a hands-on man."

"He's setting the wrong example. He's paid above that work. There has to be structure. People need to be clear on their place."

"He has more of a team mentality. That's why his shifts run so productively."

"Where does his shift place?"

"First, week in and week out," the CFO answered.

"Unusual," Varkas said. He reached for his wallet and took out a fold of paper with some writing on it. "Would you know his home address?"

"I might if you spoke it," the CFO replied.

"Is it 82 North—"

"North 106 Street," the CFO finished.

"You are good." He clapped the CFO hard on his narrow back.

"Is Pat married?"

"He doesn't wear a ring. I'd need to check his paperwork."

"See that you do." Varkas suddenly appeared bothered. "Who is that man who keeps walking up to Pat? He acts strange. Slow."

"Oh, that's Radio Voice."

"Who?" Varkas said, now agitated.

"Our janitor. He has Down syndrome. Pat looks out for him."

"What?"

"He has Down syndrome," the CFO repeated, speaking over the din of the plant floor.

"You mean he's retarded?"

"Yes."

Varkas studied Radio Voice as he pulled on Pat's shirtsleeve. Pat tapped his watch and pointed to the big clock on the wall. Radio Voice shuffled off.

"Can he get his work done?"

"Yes. Always on time. Never calls in sick."

"Well as long as he's a useful idiot," Varkas said. "So about that address, I've been out to the farmhouse. The assessor's office told me HomeSky Blackholm was the name on the deed. Do you know her?"

"I don't recognize that name," the CEO said.

"The door was answered by an Indian girl with a disrespectful manner I did not care for. Said the house was co-owned. Pat must be that other owner."

"Can I ask of your interest in the property?"

Varkas brightened. "Oh, I meant to bring that up with you. I'm interested in buying it. Very interested. How would I go about settling on a fair price?"

The CFO thought for a moment. "I could do some research. Talk to the bank, get some comparative market prices from my brother-in-law's real estate office. Is it for sale?"

Varkas's eyes were as blunt as his response. "Everything's for sale. This is America."

At break time, Pat sat with Radio Voice. "Don't eat your lunch now," Pat said.

"But I'm starving," Radio Voice complained.

"Did you have a breakfast?"

Radio Voice nodded proudly.

"Okay. So lunch waits till twelve. Time for a ten-o'clock snack and coffee."

Radio Voice's spirits fell. "I didn't pack a snack."

Pat improvised. "Lucky for you I brought an extra. Go get your coffee."

Radio Voice, renewed with excitement, almost knocked over a co-worker en route to getting his coffee mug out of the cabinet. His was the light blue mug that said IS IT FRIDAY YET? which he cherished. When he came back to the breakroom table, Pat had a piece of carrot cake waiting for him—Pat's lunch dessert, freshly made by HomeSky.

Radio Voice carefully set his mug next to the cake and shivered at his good luck. "Thank you for this snack. It's lucky you packed an extra."

"I am lucky," Pat said. "Beyond a doubt."

Just then the breakroom door opened and all the noise was sucked out.

Varkas stepped in, his eyes sweeping across the many faces.

"Hello everyone."

"Hello Mr. Varkas," the group said in semi-unison.

"I hear this shift continues to be our top producer, week in and week out. Congratulations."

"You're welcome," Radio Voice blurted enthusiastically through a mouthful of carrot cake.

Pat laid a hand on his arm as the others in the room laughed.

This brought Varkas's attention to Pat. "You're the shift supervisor, Pat O'Rourke. Am I right?"

Pat stood. "Yes. Hello Mr. Varkas."

"We've met before," Varkas stated.

Pat replied that they had.

"Can I see you for a moment? I know it's break time. I hope I'm not trampling on any precious workers' rights."

"No trouble at all," Pat said, following Varkas out and onto the plant floor.

The sharp, stinging smell of adhesives infused into their products hits a person on two occasions: when you first walk in the employee door to clock in, and when you step out of the coffee-rich breakroom. But the nose quickly acclimates. They stood near a massive plywood press, which hummed, its skinner saws quietly waiting.

"I have a non-work-related question," Varkas said to Pat. "If you don't mind."

"Not at all."

Varkas retrieved the fold of paper from his pocket and asked Pat if he lived at 82 North 106 Street.

Pat couldn't disguise his surprise at the question. "Yes I do."

"If I'm not mistaken," Varkas continued, "that property is owned by HomeSky Blackholm."

Pat's expression went from surprise to concern. "Is everything all right?"

Varkas held out a huge hand and rested it on Pat's shoulder. "Yes. I didn't mean to alarm you. It is her property, then?"

"It is."

Varkas thought for a moment, his hand still on Pat's shoulder. He gave it a moderate squeeze. "Do you think she might sell it?"

Pat wasn't sure he heard him correctly. "Did you say sell it?"

"Yes. I'm interested in buying the property. Have been for some time."

It was all so odd. Pat wondered for a moment if he'd nodded off while on break and was dreaming. Varkas, towering over him with his hand on his shoulder—a man he'd only spoken to a few times—now wondering if he could buy HomeSky's farm?

"It's 160 acres, am I right? However, what, maybe three-quarters of the acres are tillable? Maybe fewer?"

Pat nodded. "Yeah. It's a quarter section."

Varkas said, "Not all suitable for cash crop."

"That's right, Mr. Varkas."

"Please, call me Wayne," Varkas said. "If we're going to be doing business, we can be less formal, yes?" Varkas took his hand from Pat's shoulder and held it out to shake.

Does shaking hands mean we're doing business? Are we're agreeing to something? Pat took Varkas's hand, which surprised him in two ways. One, it was larger than any hand he had ever shook. And two, it was eerily cold.

Pat's shift ended. Clocked out, hands stuffed in his pockets, hunched over, he strode through flurries loaded in a howling wind. The employee parking lot was reasonably situated to the plant, but Pat left the closest spots for the older workers.

Rather than bending, tree branches swung in such a way that they were likely to snap in these conditions. Pat said a quiet thank you for the wind being at his back. No sooner had the petition been rendered than did two blowing snowflakes elude his coat collar, his shirt collar and make an icy landing on his bare neck. "Father, forgive me but I won't be thanking you for that," he said.

Still submerged in his earlier conversation with Varkas, he pulled out of the parking lot and turned the wrong way. After swinging a U-turn, Pat headed back toward Bonaducci's grocery store. HomeSky worked a full day Tuesdays, Wednesdays and Thursdays so she and Pat drove to and from town together.

"How was your day?" HomeSky jumped into his truck. "Brrr." She continued across the hard car seat to give Pat a kiss on the cheek and take up his arm so she could tuck under it to warm up. "Better."

Pat looked tense.

"What?" HomeSky said. "Is something wrong?" She pulled back to get a better look at Pat.

Is something wrong were three words Pat and HomeSky had discussed trying to get away from. It seemed every time someone was late or there was an unusually long pause or hard-to-read facial expression, those words came racing out. Understandably so, with what they'd been through, but the words were burdensome. They'd made an effort to not default to them.

Pat pulled HomeSky back in, close to him. "No, nothing's wrong. At least I don't think so." He drove away from the curb and turned down the radio, which did little to assuage HomeSky's concern.

Pat continued. "Had the oddest thing at work today."

HomeSky turned up the heat in the truck. "What happened?"

"Varkas came into the breakroom and asked to see me."

"Stealing office pens again?"

"Ha. Ha. I wish." Pat chewed on the inside of his mouth. "He wants to buy your farm, HomeSky."

"Now aren't you the comedian," she said with a laugh.

"I'm serious."

HomeSky was flummoxed. "Really?"

"Really."

HomeSky shook her head. "Why would he want to do that? He owns the better part of a couple counties as it is."

"He didn't say. Just said he'd had his eye on it for a long time."

"That's all well and good, but it's not for sale. I hope you told him that."

Pat shrugged. "Not exactly. I said I don't think she's selling, but—"

"Don't think I'm selling! Patrick, my family is buried on that land. I'll be buried on that land, and hopefully, when the time comes, you will too."

"I understand," Pat said, trying to slow the conversation down. "But I didn't think I could speak for you. That's what I told Varkas."

"It's your farm, too. I've told you that over and over."

"I know. I appreciate that. But like I said, this came like a bolt out of the blue. I was stunned. And Varkas doesn't like taking no for an answer."

"Tough," HomeSky said with sparks in her eyes. She drew a long breath. "Where did you leave it?" she said, quieter.

"I said I'd bring it up with you but he should call or stop by. He said he might drop by tonight."

HomeSky could only shake her head. "I don't like it. I don't want him in our house."

Pat recoiled. "That's not like you."

"Something feels wrong, is all I can say."

"He's not that bad, HomeSky. A bit intimidating, yes, but—"

"Where did he come from?" HomeSky asked.

"You mean originally or before he came to Baudette?"

"Both."

"I think his family was from Slovakia. No, Czechoslovakia. I remember the distinction was a big deal. When he bought the plant, the *Region* did an article on him and the journalist messed it up. Varkas said interchanging those two countries was like calling America Mexico." Pat shrugged. "He lived in Hibbing before here. I heard he still keeps a house there."

"How did his family end up way up here?"

Pat thought back. "My memory's fuzzy but I think the article said some Czech farming communities settled near here. I think his grandfather sold farm equipment after immigrating. Something like that. Spent a lot of time following homesteaders who were coming farther and farther north to get their 160 acres. Eventually got in the lumber business. Varkas is third generation. I remember him saying how proud he was his family helped build America."

HomeSky looked out the truck window. "Build America." She slowly shook her head. "Or steal our native land. It's a matter of how you want the story written."

Pat gave her a squeeze. "I'm sorry. I can only imagine how it must feel. To have to listen to the lies and spin. Manifest Destiny. Pioneering spirit. Making something out of nothing. They left out the part about driving families from their homeland."

"I'll never live on a reservation. And I'll never sell my farm." Pat could feel HomeSky's body tighten beneath her words. "Our farm," she corrected herself, looking at Pat now with fierce resolve.

"I completely understand," Pat said quietly. They drove in silence until HomeSky spoke up.

"How do you think we should we handle Varkas?"

"If I know him, he'll play the first card. And it will be soon."

"So we wait?"

"Unless you'd like me to say something to him first."

"No. I guess wait and see."

The truck swung into the driveway, snow crunching under the tires. HomeSky asked, "Should I get the mail?"

"That's okay," Pat said, continuing down the driveway. "I need to clear my head. A walk out to the mailbox will do that right quick. Do you mind bringing in the groceries?"

"I like that deal."

Pat drove the truck around back by the kitchen and parked using the building as a wind shelter. He made a mental note to plug in the block heater because tonight's air temperature was forecasted to be minus 33.

HomeSky hustled two bags of groceries into the house as Pat walked out to the mailbox on the road. The wind came off the corn-field and hit him in the face. Angled, late-afternoon sunlight filled the dips and whirls of the drifted snow, leaving it blue-cast.

Pat had left the last three rows of corn standing as a snow fence. It was doing a nice job of keeping the road from drifting over. Two skinny does, standing among the stalks, lifted their heads. That was the other reason he didn't harvest every row.

The mailbox was frozen shut so Pat rapped it with a gloved fist. Even that noise didn't send the hungry deer hightailing away. When it opened, he sighed. Hospital bills. Piling up like the blowing snow. For the past few months, Pat had made a point of getting to the mailbox before anyone else. He didn't want the household worried about Cory's bills.

It was a shock when Pat first learned that like most insurance policies, the fine print of Cory's had an Illegal Acts Exclusion. The insurance company had determined that because Cory's injuries were cased by an act in violation of the law, namely the negligent, purposeful, high-speed acceleration of one vehicle into another, that his injuries were not covered by his policy.

The case promised to be a P.R. nightmare, not to mention a protracted, expensive affair, so the insurance company settled out of court. The hospitals' lawyers went after their money like piranhas on a meatball. The settlement was gone in a blink of an eye. Cory was on his own now with bills still coming. Not to mention extensive physical therapy left to go. Pat didn't have the heart to bring the bills into the house and add them up. With everything they were going through, he kept it to himself.

At the truck, Pat plugged in the block heater. Then he opened the squeaky passenger door and popped open the glove box. There was a three-inch-high stack of envelopes inside. He tossed in the latest bills and slapped the glove box shut.

He looked out at the land, up to the ridge, lined with the afternoon's finishing touch of light. "Give me strength," he asked.

MICK

Mick brought very few things with him from his diner when he came to run Lu Ann's a month earlier. He did bring his cooking apron. And his coffee mug—a customer favorite—which read in bold letters: You Asked For A Half A Cup. The mug was made to look like it was cut in half from the top down, making it crescent-shaped rather than circular. He took a sip and continued.

"So St. Peter says to the drunk bus driver, 'You can enter through the pearly gates.' But he wags a finger to the priest, 'Sorry, Father. You may not.'" Mick paused to look at the rapt faces.

The mangy bunch of late-afternoon regulars sat slumped around the old wooden community table, their pie plates long cleared. They were comprised mostly of retired farmers, plus an unemployed teacher and a carpet installer who had fallen down two flights of stairs and was collecting disability. The guest of honor, at the table's head, was Monsignor Kief, who loved a good joke. But the subject matter of this one had him doubly hooked.

Mick continued. "'But St. Peter,' the priest said, baffled, 'why would a drunken bus driver be allowed through the gates of heaven when a loyal priest such as myself would not?'

"'Simple,' St. Peter said. 'The drunkard's driving led countless people to prayer. Whereas your sermons put countless people to sleep.'"

Laughter uncorked from the table. Hats, already off-kilter, were further misaligned. Rotund bellies joggled beneath wide suspender straps. The Monsignor, who was savoring a last bite of caramel roll, sent that morsel directly onto the shoulder of the carpet layer, who said he'd seen worse stains. That triggered a second wave of laughter.

When the group finally cleared out, Mary Alice came by, picked up what was left of the coffee cups and complained about the tip. Mick and Monsignor Kief were still at the table.

"Mick," the Monsignor said, "I want to congratulate you."

"As a cook or a comic?" he quipped.

"My boy, both. Yes, both." He clapped his hands together. "How superbly you fit in here in our little town! It wasn't but four short weeks ago, we were just making our way into Lu Ann's, and here you are, like family."

"I appreciate you saying so," Mick said.

"You know what especially impresses me about you, Mick?"

Mick was too humble to comment.

"How you sit."

Mick looked at the kind priest. "Sit?"

"Indeed," the Monsignor said with emphasis. "It's a lost art. Everyone these days is too busy to just sit and take in God's greatest creation: people. There are miracles happening right here, right now. But people are whizzing past. What's the hurry? Aren't we all heading toward our final destination too quickly as it is?"

"It seems we are," Mick said.

"How many times have you heard, where does the time go? or time flies? Guess what? Our behavior gives it wings!"

"So true," Mick said, remembering the first time he saw the blind Monsignor. He had come to Mick's St. Paul diner to find HomeSky and bring her back to the farm—to repair her life. Mick knew he was in the presence of a very special person, from the moment he met him.

The Monsignor continued. "You, on the other hand, take the time to sit and talk to another person. And yet, you always get your work done, too."

"Now Monsignor," Mick said suspiciously, "how would you know that? Do you have spies watching me?"

As if cued, Mary Alice showed up to top off their coffee.

"Of course I do," the Monsignor said, spreading his arms wide.

"How else can I give Lu Ann her full report of what's going on when I talk to her? In fact, I'm just back from visiting with her yesterday."

"You were in St. Paul?"

"I was. An old parishioner friend was going to the Cities to drop his daughter at the airport so I caught a ride with them. What a wonderful conversation we had down and back."

"And Lu Ann? How is she?"

"Better. Much better. The time away has been repast for her soul. I know she's more herself because she had a handwritten sign posted at your cash register, which she was known for doing here."

"I don't mean to be insensitive, but how did you know about the sign?"

"Because she read it to me, just like she always does here."

"What did it say?"

"Glad you ate here. Otherwise we'd both starve."

Mick guffawed.

"And I'm sure you're curious how your diner is?"

Mick admitted that was true.

"Buzzing," is how I'd describe it. "Busy, loud and stuffed with enchanting aromas. I had Lu Ann describe your place to me. It's much how I remember picturing it. Authentic. Hospitable. Cozy." The Monsignor underscored each word with a hand gesture. "Those are the words that come to mind."

"If authentic means not a straight line in the place then you're dead on."

"Do you miss it, son?" the Monsignor quietly asked.

Mick considered the question. "Not like I thought I would. I honestly believed I was doing this only for Lu Ann. In retrospect, I don't think that's accurate."

"Why's that?"

"I've come to realize I've slipped into a rut in St. Paul. A rut that pretty much goes from my house to my diner. And back. Coming up here, meeting new people—heck, our Wednesday dinners at your house—these are just a few of many new joys. It's been refreshing and eye-opening.

"When I go back to St. Paul at the end of the week I'm going to make a few changes. I have a very capable manager there who can open one day a week and close one day a week, for starters. There's a church group that goes bowling on Thursdays. I've been avoiding their invitation because I am, without a doubt, the world's least athletic person. Last week, out of the blue, I called them and they said there is going to be a bowling shirt with Mick stitched on the pocket waiting for me when I get home. I've already put a two-week vacation on the July calendar that includes a stopover in Baudette."

"It does my heart good to hear you say that. The learning is in the doing, no doubt. It took courage for you to come up here and take on this band of Baudette rabble-rousers and we're all better for it."

"Care to hear a confession, Monsignor?"

"Certainly," he said.

"I've spent most of my life hiding, really. I grew up unpopular for my lack of physical coordination, interminable acne and severe shyness. I never developed confidence nor really found anything I could excel at. This made me an easy target and things snowballed. Quite literally. What I mean is I was an easy snowball target."

The Monsignor offered a supportive chuckle.

"I was safest on the margins. Soon this notion of safety became somewhat thematic in my life. Why risk rejection when you can safely retreat to your parents' house?

"After high school I went to community college, kept to myself, and graduated in three years with degrees in business administration and banking. Why? Safe choices, according to my guidance counselor. 'We'll always need bankers,' I remember him saying.

"I got a job at a local bank, never pushed for a raise, lived with my parents and went to church on Sundays. When my parents passed, I continued to—and still—live in the house I was born in."

Mick exhaled. There was little more to hear than the background hum of the dishwasher. "Keep going?" he asked.

The Monsignor kindly said he should.

"What you can't see, Monsignor, but others can is I have a skin condition called rosacea. It developed in my thirties with blotchy red, bumpy facial skin. As I've gotten to my forties it has spread to my nose where, unfortunately, tissue builds up making it, well, I guess the polite term is bulbous. If you didn't know better, you'd assume I was quite the drinker." Mick laughed to break the tension.

"I know a parishioner with the same condition. He actually uses some makeup—I don't think he'd mind me confiding in you about that."

"Yes," Mick said. "My dermatologist suggested a few brands, but they seem to irritate my skin even further."

"I am sorry for that. I must say, it doesn't seem to deter you from making friends here."

"What I've come to understand, Monsignor, is the person most put off by it is me."

The Monsignor nodded his head in appreciation. "That, my son, is a pearl."

"All brains, no looks," Mick kidded.

"Well, if you had to pick one you picked the only enduring one. Is it fair to say you've kept your faith through these trials?"

"My constant and true companion, Monsignor."

"Again, you've chosen wisely. May I ask, have there been any other close companions in your life?"

Mick hesitated. "You mean like a girlfriend?"

"Yes."

"Not for many years. I did have a steady as a young professional but ultimately she was interested in convertibles. I am a sedan."

The Monsignor carefully pressed. "I sensed, when we first met at your diner last year, that you were quite fond of HomeSky."

"You are perceptive, Monsignor. I think in a way I was in love with her. Or in love with the notion of helping her or of her needing me. In a moment of romantic disillusionment I even considered asking her to marry me. But I remember looking at her—and you know how lost she was back then—and listening to my heart and thinking: our mutual loneliness is so profound a spark has no chance."

The diner's late afternoon lull allowed their thoughts to simmer. Sun angled kindly through the front window.

Tim finished bussing the dishes and came over to the table. "Sorry to interrupt. Mick, do you want the dinner popovers to go into the oven?" This was a traditional mid-week treat at Lu Ann's, and Mick had made a note to serve her signature offering at his place when he returned.

Mick checked his watch. "Let's wait on the popovers 15 more minutes, what do you say?"

"Sounds good, Cap," Tim saluted. "380 degrees?"

"Not a degree more."

"Put our soup on simmer at the same time?"

"Ten-four." Mick interjected, "Tim, I'm happy to help if you need it."

"Nah," he said. "That's what I like about you. You let me do stuff around here. Guy gets tired of straight dishes." With that he was off for the kitchen standing straighter than bus tubs typically left him.

"Do you hear what you've done?" said the Monsignor brightly. "You've given Tim a little ownership of the place. Nothing motivates like ownership."

"I'll attest to that. And though we've had a couple incidents of red eyes and smoky ovens to vent, Tim's doing great. He's clocking in on time and there doesn't seem to be any more issues with his drinking."

The Monsignor was happy to hear that news. "Now, Mick, you and I both know I love Lu Ann to death, but that's her problem. She has to do it all herself. You see, her having twins at 17 and owning this diner by 21 and raising those kids alone made her quite proficient at being independent. People can't keep up with her so they get out of the way. She could learn from you. And I think I'm the one to tell her as much."

Mick stomach tightened. "I don't want to rock the boat, Monsignor."

"Hogwash! Boats need to be rocked. A calm sea does not make a skilled sailor."

Mick shrugged. "Did she say what time she'll be back on Sunday?"

"She mentioned you were going to call her about that."

"Yep," Mick said. "It's on my packing list. Well, I better get moving."

The Monsignor smiled broadly—a mischievous smile, one that announced he held a secret. "I have one more item that I think you'll be interested in."

Mick sat up from the back of his chair. "I'm all ears."

"The mystery of the happiness triangle and the three Fs has been solved!" The Monsignor's arms shot high above his head like he just won the lottery.

"Wait. Waaait. And how are you so sure?" Mick's voice had a twinkle. "So far, only I have the answer. I've got an entire wall in my diner three-deep in napkins with admirable attempts, but for going on six years, no one has cracked the code."

"Tell me again," the Monsignor said, "how it is you came to know you had the right answer?"

Mick began the enigmatic story. "It was very early one morning, before my first customer had ventured in. I was sitting at the counter with the newspaper when I spilled my coffee, some of which seeped under the newspaper—"

"Ah yes, I remember now," the Monsignor interrupted. "And when the liquid leeched into the newsprint, it caused one word to stand out from the rest."

Mick continued. "And that word was happiness. So after I cleaned up my spill, I had a dry napkin handy so I wrote the word happiness in the center. As I was looking at that word, I guess pondering it, I swear to you, in all seriousness, three words popped into my head. All three started with the letter F. I haven't a clue where they came from, but I jotted them down, around the word happiness, one above and two below. I noticed that a line could connect those three words making a triangle around happiness. Thus the happiness triangle was born."

The Monsignor picked up the story from there. "And as you were looking at that napkin a customer came in, saw it, and asked what it was."

"Sorta," Mick said. "I had balled up the napkin and was about toss it in the trash and he said don't throw that away because it's right. It took me a moment to realize he had seen my jottings on the napkin. He said many people try to find the secret to happiness, but I had actually come to the answer."

The Monsignor nodded. "It is quite a story. And if I didn't know you better I'd say you were pulling my leg."

"I don't blame you, but I swear, I was sitting no farther from the man than I am from you now. We had the crumpled napkin between us when he abruptly paid for his coffee, wished me good day and left my diner."

"And you'd never seen this man before or since."

"Never," Mick said.

"And if I remember right, wasn't there something unusual when he left your place?"

"That's the kicker." Mick paused, shaking his head because even he had trouble believing or comprehending this part of the story. "As the man was leaving he passed a regular coming in, right at the doorway. But when I asked the regular if he'd ever seen that man before, he said what man? I said the guy you just passed coming in. He said he passed no one. He said I was standing behind the counter alone when he entered."

"That part of the story gives me goosebumps," the Monsignor said.

"Me too."

"So, with no further ado, if you'll take out a napkin," the Monsignor said, "I'll tell you what I'm quite sure is the answer to the happiness triangle."

Mick did as he was instructed.

"In the center is happiness. The top of the triangle is the word Faith, right?

"Faith is one of the words, yes," Mick said.

"Fellowship is the second," the Monsignor said. "Let's put that on the bottom left."

"Wow," Mick uttered. "Not many people get that one. And the last?"

"'The last shall be the first and the first last,' as Matthew so aptly preached."

"Are you stalling, Monsignor?"

"I am not. I've always been drawn to that passage. The last word in your triangle is Forgiveness, without which there can be no happiness in any person's heart. And the first whom we must forgive is ourselves, for our imperfections. And the second is God who lays many hardships in our path for reasons inexplicable. Which brings the triangle back to faith. And to the fellowship of those who help us navigate the hardships to rediscover the joy of life."

Mick asked, "So you're telling me the secret to happiness is faith, fellowship and forgiveness."

"I am."

"You're right!" Mick nearly came out of his chair.

"Actually, you're right," the Monsignor said. "You came up with this construct and these words. I'm just confirming them."

Mick was humbled. "But why did these words come to me, Monsignor?"

"You were open to them, would be my guess."

"But isn't it rather fantastical that two men separated by hundreds of miles for most of their lives would land on the same three words to explain happiness?"

"You'll recall," the Monsignor said, "that it took me a number of tries. You see, I wouldn't have ever dreamed of defining happiness within such a disciplined structure. The idea of three words beginning with F, that's your idea."

"Yeah, but it was a fluke."

"Perhaps. Perhaps it was much more. But for me, without the rigor, the answer to something so big would never have been emancipated. What's the old adage? The rails do not imprison the train, they set it free."

"Okay, Monsignor. Let's say we're right about the three Fs. Consider the word faith. What about all the people who aren't religious but are happy? Doesn't that invalidate one of our three?"

"Most of my contemporaries would disagree with me, but I don't think the word faith is restricted to a religious definition."

"What do you mean?"

"Faith, in a larger interpretation, is a belief in the intrinsic goodness of the world and trusting we will be rewarded by adding to it."

Mick looked puzzled. "So I could, for example, not believe in and not receive Holy Communion and still have faith and still be happy?"

"My bishop would not agree with me, but yes. However, I'm certain that faith is fortified, as is happiness, by receiving the Eucharist."

Mick reclined. His weight rested on the padded back of the old chair, sinking into the cracked vinyl. He nodded. And as his nodding became more definitive, a smile came to his face. "Makes sense. I was thinking of faith in a more traditional context."

"And there is nothing wrong with that. I've always said faith is faith, much to the frustration of those on the receiving end of that ambiguity."

Mick brightened further. "You're right. Faith is faith. How can you argue with that?"

"Now you've got it, Mick. Faith is too strong to be argued with."

Mick got up from the community table. "Thank you for the discussion." He came over and placed a hand on the Monsignor's shoulder. "Actually, thank you for the fellowship."

CORY AND MEADOW

Billy was wide awake with a gleam in his eye and a smattering of happy drool on his chin. He'd just had a bottle and the world was an endless wonder. His large, dark eyes were taking in every bright shiny object. Suddenly, Cory held his fascination.

Cory had completed his maiden voyage from his bedroom to the kitchen without the wheelchair. He was done depending on it. When Cory's mind was made up, little could undo it.

Meadow helped him get situated at the kitchen table and leaned his crutches near the doorway. She wore an over-the-shoulder flannel sling she had made for Billy. With a full twist of the fabric, it became a seat that allowed him to hang near her side and freely pump his legs. He was thrilled by this new leg power.

"Maybe he should be my physical therapist," Cory said with a half-smile.

Meadow didn't know what to say. She and Cory hadn't exchanged many words last fall when a large group gathered for dinner. They had never talked privately. And now, hearing him speak was startling. "He's quite the little kicker," she said.

Cory could see Meadow's tension. "This has to be a little weird for you. Me talking all of a sudden."

Meadow nodded. "I don't understand."

Cory considered not delving into it, but in Billy's eyes there was such wordless trust. It was liberating. "I was afraid to open my mouth." Cory looked at the tabletop. "I didn't know what might come out. I was beyond anywhere I'd ever been. I felt like I was going crazy." He looked up at Meadow with intimidating intensity. "This couldn't have happened, I kept telling myself. It was like I lost my mind."

Cory's voice was low and soft. He looked up at Billy and watched him kick and smile. Cory's eyes began to fill. "The last words out of my mouth, before what happened on the road, I couldn't risk hearing them again. Not that wrath. I was afraid if I went to speak, they might fly out. So I said nothing."

Cory looked at Meadow and she held his gaze. He brought fingers to his eyes to keep back the tears. "Then after a week or so, I got used to this silent wall. I didn't have to talk about it. To anyone. I didn't have to be consoled. I didn't have to be brave. I could just be mute. I could bulldoze it and make my silent wall higher."

Meadow risked a question. "What changed?"

"Little things. Lots of little things. Especially here. As you know, Pat's a lifesaver. He's pulled me out before and I started believing that maybe he could pull me out again. An astounding man. A gift." Cory's eyes welled up again.

Meadow nodded, thinking of where she might be without Pat.

"And HomeSky. I've done a lot of thinking about what she's been through. Yet she's here, living with the good and the bad. Facing it. Fighting back. It's not like she's won. You can see it on her face some days, some moments. But she didn't quit. She could have. Had every reason to. But there she was with my vegetable soup and a smile and leaving enough space between us for me to find my words."

Meadow closed her eyes and nodded.

"And you, Meadow."

She looked at Cory. It was the first time she heard him speak her name and he made it sound beautiful. She used to hate her name and the insults it invited. Cory made her hear her name differently.

"You and this little kicker," Cory said. "I appreciate what you said to me the other day. I was feeling sorry for myself and you backed off but you said you and Billy would keep coming back and sure enough you have. Life hasn't been a cakewalk for you, I know."

"Yeah. But like you, I have Pat and HomeSky now. And there's Billy."

Cory looked away.

"I'm sorry," Meadow said. "But does Billy remind you of Singer?"

"Sometimes. Singer and Hanna. Which ultimately is good. I'm

just not ready yet."

"Sorry."

"No. Don't be. Billy reminds me I have a purpose. A responsibility." Cory shifted, straightening his injured hip. "Did Pat tell you I was adopted?"

"Yes."

"That . . . holy shit. Hit me with my head down. I've spent probably too many hours since trying to make sense of it. Million thoughts crossing my mind. None of 'em, truthfully, making me want to get out of that wheelchair. Until today. Earlier this afternoon, to be exact."

"What happened?"

"Do you believe dreams have meaning, Meadow? I'm not trying to stereotype, but for Joseph, a big part of him and his culture was a belief in the Dream Spirit."

"I know dreams are telling," she said. Billy was starting to nod off so Meadow gently lifted and turned him so his face could press into her as he fell asleep.

"Up to now," Cory said, "my dreams have been ones you'd mostly want to avoid." Cory had this look about him that said something had changed. He shook his head in disbelief. "But this amazing dream today . . ." Cory continued. "I took a nap—something I try to avoid because it always seems lazy to me—it was while you guys were swimming. I'm pretty sure the Dream Spirit came to me."

"In what form?"

"A bird."

"Large or small?"

"Small, a sparrow at first. But when it got to me, it was, I don't know, a goldfinch I think."

"So it was bright."

"Yeah."

Meadow was excited. "That's awesome. That's good."

"I'm out in the yard in my wheelchair and it's snowing like hell and then it's suddenly springtime and this golden bird lands on my leg and says, 'Honor your responsibility.' And I woke . . . rejuvenated,

I guess that would be the word. I still am now."

"Honor your responsibility?" Meadow said. "Do you know what it means?"

"No. Not completely. I'm trying to feel what it means, rather than figure it out. I sense it has to do with a way of approaching every day. That gift. It also has a lot to do with Singer. I was supposed to be his stepdad; we made plans for that. I believe it's my responsibility to adopt him. Actually, it's my purpose. To give him a home and the . . . I don't know . . . the acceptance and unconditional love that every adopted child deserves but doesn't always get. That I didn't get.

"Singer needs more than what I was—mute in a wheelchair, hopeless. So I'm going to honor my responsibility. I'm going to find hope. It's something like that. I think. The more I live with the idea the more I'll get it."

Meadow looked at Cory. They had been talking for 15 minutes. In such a short time, the strangeness of his voice had vanished.

"I hope this doesn't sound wrong but this is kinda weird. You were adopted. You want to adopt Singer. I was going to put Billy up for adoption. And now HomeSky and Pat have kinda adopted all of us here at the farm."

Cory shrugged. "If Pat were here he'd say something like, we all came together for a reason."

Just then, Pat's truck came rolling in the driveway. Cory and Meadow looked at each other with the same thought: *no way.*

"Speaking of weird coincidences," Cory said.

"No doubt," Meadow agreed.

They watched as HomeSky got out of the truck and fished out two bags of groceries from the back seat. Pat walked toward the road to the mailbox.

Meadow smiled at Cory. "You better not actually speak out loud till they're both sitting down. One of them might faint."

Cory nodded. "My bet, Pat."

PART SIX

Middleton, Wisconsin

LAMB

Chevy asked MB to recheck the address on her slip of paper.

"Wow," Singer said from his booster seat. "It's like a hotel. Does it have a pool?"

MB flipped on the dome light. "201 Jennings. Yep, this is it."

Chevy whistled through his teeth. "Damn." He caught himself. "I mean dang." He got out of his late-model car feeling self-conscious.

"When can Singer stop riding in this booster contraption?" Chevy muttered, struggling in the dark to unbuckle the boy's seat belt.

"Yeah," Singer said.

MB was out of the car straightening her jacket. She stuck her head back in and said for all to clearly hear, "When he's 26! Too many little boys end up in the ER who wouldn't be there if they were properly restrained in their parents' cars."

"But I'm not little." Singer protested. "I'm four and a half."

"Four and a half," Chevy said, swinging him down to the ground, landing Singer on his little boots. "That's when I started skating. We need to get you some skates and a hockey stick."

"All right!" Singer squealed.

"And a helmet," MB added.

Singer looked up at Chevy. Chevy shrugged. "And a helmet," he said. "How did you meet these people?" Chevy asked for the fifth time.

MB rolled her eyes. "At the playground. They have twin girls who Singer plays with."

"Maddi and Eliza," Singer sang out as he skipped toward the house. "Eliza and Maddi," his voice trailed off. The custom-made arched front windows glowed warmly as two little alert faces gazed out.

"I've gotten together with Jenni a few times. She's cool. Very busy attorney. She has some good mom tips." MB laughed to herself. "She's funny once you get to know her."

"What does her husband do?" Chevy stared at the massive home.

"He's a lawyer, too," MB told him.

"Figures," Chevy said.

The winding brick walkway was swept clean of snow. Flickering luminaries led to an arched portico with impressive white columns. "We should get some of these," Singer said, banging his mittens on a column. "Careful," MB said aloud, but regal was the word she was thinking.

No sooner had Chevy reached for the doorbell than the heavy front door swung open. Standing there, like a photograph from an upscale home décor magazine, was Jennifer, her husband, Davis, and their two girls, Maddi and Eliza. "Welcome."

The twins were dressed in matching white dresses. Pink headbands held their carefully styled chestnut hair in place. "Singer!" they said, each taking one of his hands and pulling him though the entryway. "Come see our room."

"Girls," their mother said with just the right force. The twins stopped only long enough to speak in perfect echo. "Welcome to our home. It's nice to meet you." Then they nearly pulled Singer out of his boots and jacket before the three of them bolted upstairs.

Jenni's husband stepped forward. "They've been watching the clock since four. I'm Davis," he extended a hand first to MB and then to Chevy. They all greeted one another before Jenni whisked coats away to a side room.

Sitting alertly on a pad just inside the entryway was an athletic, cinnamon-colored dog, which Chevy first mistook for a statue. "Okay Radar," Davis said. The dog came carefully forward to give the strangers a sniff.

"Very obedient," Chevy offered. "What kind of a dog is he?"

"She," Davis corrected. "She's a pudelpointer, which is a German wirehair and poodle cross. A versatile hunting dog and a damn fine pointing breed. Do you hunt, Chevy?"

Chevy slipped into banker mode. "I've been meaning to. Such an abundance of natural resources here to take advantage of."

MB looked at him oddly but Chevy and Davis were already walking toward the living room. "I'd always hunted over flushing dogs," Davis explained. "Excuse me if I offend you, but in hindsight I find flushers the canine equivalent of high school dropouts. All brawn no brain."

MB heard Chevy ask something about upland birds, words she didn't think were in his vocabulary. Jenni locked arms with MB and walked her toward the kitchen. "What do you say we hunt down a large glass of wine?"

Every square foot was more spectacular than the last. The home was newly constructed three years ago, MB learned, after the couple bought a lot in a secluded cul-de-sac in one of Maple Bluff's most affluent neighborhoods. Jenni and Davis had outgrown their starter house, what with twin toddlers and puppy. Plus their careers provided more than enough financial security to move to a more prestigious zip code.

Davis, seven years older than Jenni, first saw his future wife not long after he'd become his firm's youngest partner at 35. As a class-action defense attorney with a fast-rising national reputation, he sat opposite her on a civil case. Jenni, not two years out of law school, wasn't lead counsel but she was instrumental to her firm's winning settlement. The home products company Davis defended was being sued for dryers that caught fire due to a design defect. The lint trap wasn't properly insulated.

A week after the decision, Davis sent Jenni, who was practicing at a firm in Boston at the time, an envelope stuffed with dryer lint and his business card. His note said if she was tired of her current firm treating her like the contents of this envelope, give him a call. She took him up on it. When Davis proposed six months later, he vowed to love, cherish and do the laundry, a romantic but nonetheless shrewd addendum to their commitment for two reasons. Most of their laundry was dry-cleaned. And with his position at the firm taking him away from home for weeks at a time, his promise, at best, was a six-month-a-year gig.

"Your kitchen is bigger than my living room," MB cracked.

"Yes. Cozy is not the word. Frankly, it's a little much, but neither of us had built a house before so we gave the designer too much leash. When my parents come to visit, Dad says he needs a skateboard to get orange juice. Jenni poured herself another half-glass of wine, noticing that MB had hardly touched hers.

"Do your parents live close?"

"No, sadly," Jenni said. "Just outside of Boston. In Brighton."

"Is that where you grew up?"

"It is."

"Are you still close with your mom and dad?"

"As close as you can be when you're 1,160 miles apart. A distance my dad regularly reminds me of. I do talk to my mom a lot. Almost everyday."

"Really?" MB said in a way that made it obvious that she did not.

"Mom is my rock. She gets me back in sync. Sometimes the career and the house and the nanny—all of it—makes me, well it doesn't make me but causes me to lose perspective."

MB let that minor confession settle. "Do you miss home?"

Jenni thought for a moment. "Not so much, anymore. Cost of living out there is absurd. And the pace is even more off the charts. But I do miss it every spring. When the baseball season starts. I miss going to Fenway with my dad. And getting dressed up with my mom in a spring dress and going into the city to shop and see the Boston Philharmonic at the Spring Mixer. You get to mingle with the musicians. One of my favorite memories."

"I noticed the grand piano. Do you play?"

"It's really just expensive furniture. But I do still play a little. Mostly the girls play now."

Jenni realized the conversation was all about her. "How about you? Are you musical?"

MB scoffed. "I wish. I do appreciate it, though."

"I remember when we first met at the playground, listening to Singer. An apt name for his prodigious talent."

"That child has a gift."

"Does he practice or take lessons?"

"If practice means singing all the time, then yes." MB took a sip of wine and smiled. "It's really cool to have singing in the house. Not something I'm used to." MB thought back to her mother's ramrod rigor. "But no. No formal lessons. At least to my knowledge."

Jenni brought out an unopened bag of pretzels and wrestled with it. "I got these for you. I know it's your one indulgence. How do you open these things?"

"One indulgence? Yeah." MB smiled, taking the bag. She quickly pulled open the seal.

"Nicely done," Jenni said.

"Plenty of practice. And thanks. For the pretzels. And the invitation."

Jenni sensed a hesitation, a vulnerability that MB rarely exposed.

"You okay? Everything good?"

"Yeah," MB exhaled deeply. "Just a confusing time. Being this surrogate mom, or whatever I am. And then my effing crazy world in the ER. All the change doesn't faze Chevy a bit, but it has me . . . what's the word? Unsettled, I guess."

"Completely understandable," Jenni said with confidence she hoped would transfer. "You're making quite a transition."

"I am and I'm not," MB said forcefully. "That's what kinda pisses me off. Is Singer staying? Am I going to be his mom? Is Chevy even staying? Am I going to be, gulp, his wife?" She took another pretzel and held it up to Jenni. "My pacifier."

"Well, it's better than mine." Jenni lifted her glass of wine before taking a sip.

The two women looked at each other, feeling the comforting bond of friendship tighten around them.

Just then Davis came into the kitchen. "Why don't you come join us? I've built a fire. Honey, did you know Chevy is the Mike Chevalier who was the captain of the Badgers hockey team that beat the Gophers for the national title? Remember we watched the game on TV and you were so overdue with the twins that you wanted to write an eviction notice on your huge belly. Remember?"

"Honey," Jenni said in a stating-the-obvious tone, "I was overdue. With twins. I don't remember anything."

Davis nodded. "Heavily redacted," he said.

The three of them laughed as he grabbed two bottles of Heineken from the refrigerator. "Hon, when did you start buying pretzels? Do you mind if I put some in a bowl?" He didn't wait for an answer.

"Oh, they're a favorite of MB's," Jenni said.

"We must have you over more often." David touched her shoulder before whisking the beers and a bowl of pretzels out of the kitchen as fast as he'd come in.

Jenni noticed the look on MB's face. "Yeah, right? At the firm they call him Wind Burn because he's in and out of conversations so quickly. He made a New Year's resolution this year to slow down. It lasted less than 24 hours."

A rack of trimmed lamb chops were in a large ceramic bowl, marinating in olive oil, lemon and garlic. This preparation was a simple secret that Davis pried out of the head chef at his favorite Indian restaurant in downtown Madison.

"What do you say we get these in the oven," Jenni said. Then her voice dropped to a whisper. "I meant to ask earlier, how's it going with Singer. And the letters?"

In the living room, Davis and Chevy sat on the couch facing a healthy four-log fire.

"Utterly primitive," Davis said. "Our attraction to fire." He looked at Chevy for a comment.

"Does make me want to eat meat," he said, testing Davis's aptitude for humor.

Davis continued. "Our ancestors' ancestors' ancestors' ancestors' ancestors stared into these same colors with senses fully engaged: Sight. Smell. Sound."

Chevy added, "Saving touch for the cavewoman next to him."

Davis looked at Chevy for one beat. Then he slapped his knee in a guffaw. "Quite right. Maybe saved taste for her as well."

They both laughed. "Here's to primitive," Chevy said. They clinked bottles.

"Tell me about your career." Davis turned toward Chevy. "Jenni said you live and work in Middleton."

"Yep. MB owns a house there we all live in."

"Is that temporary? Are you looking to move up?"

"We're good for now." Chevy paused, taken a bit off guard. "I look at this place and I think, not on my salary."

"What do you do there in Middleton?"

Chevy didn't care for the way Davis said Middleton. He seemed to linger on the Middle before adding the ton. "I work at the community bank."

"Just a stepping stone, I'm guessing," Davis said. He took a swallow of Heineken.

Chevy looked into the dancing fire and considered how to proceed. He thought about his hockey days, when he and another player were pursuing a puck into the rink's corner. Two guys. Tight quarters. One puck. One of them will come out with what he came for. The other will get the worst of it along the boards. Davis was setting a tone for their relationship, right here, right now. Asking direct questions.

Being assumptive. How should Chevy play it? Match the aggression? Or let the other player try to line him up, and then deftly avoid the onrush?

Chevy sidestepped. "What do you think I should do? Is there a future for a guy like me in a community bank in Middleton?"

Davis smiled, pleased to be asked. "Really? No. Of course not." Davis removed his glasses to clear a smudge from the lens. "Are you familiar with the word onomatopoeia?"

Chevy thought. "Words that sound like what they mean. Like sizzle."

Davis nodded. "Middleton is exactly that. A town in the middle. You don't strike me as middling."

There were a few ways Chevy could play this, but he sensed the more he let Davis command the conversation, the further it could take him.

"What would you do?" Chevy asked.

Jenni was a magician. The lamb was out of the oven and resting. Her Swiss chard, mushroom and sausage risotto was impeccably timed to be ready just as the kids' white rice finished. The ciabatta bread was warm and sliced. She plated baked asparagus for the adults and mini carrots for the kids. MB tossed the salad, but only after asking twice if she could help.

Not that Jenni needed an encore, but she nonetheless had one: she could do Jell-O. She zipped her Jell-O mold out of the refrigerator, put a platter on top, flipped it and pulled off the mold leaving a green, jiggling, two-tier, star-shaped show-stopper. MB about cried. She confessed to Jenni that she couldn't make Jell-O. She and Singer had tried three times and it never gelled correctly. She said she was going to form a support group for others who couldn't make Jell-O. But then wondered aloud if that support group would hold together. Jenni's laughter almost cost her a mouthful of wine.

Davis and Chevy weren't much help with dinner. They were immersed in a conversation that would take only a small intermission at the dining room table.

Jenni calmly interrupted "What world problem are you two so intent on solving?" A basket of warm bread had stalled at Davis's left elbow.

"What's that, honey?" Davis said.

"Can you please pass the bread?"

"Oh. Sure. Everything looks fabulous," Davis said, finally taking a moment to notice.

Jenni asked again. "What has you two so busy talking?"

Chevy spoke up. "Davis and I were just discussing banking."

"Sounds boring," one of the twins said.

"Darling!" Jenni said, trying not to laugh. "Be respectful."

Chevy gave the little girl a wink. "To tell you the truth, banking often is boring." Chevy faked a big yawn and stretch, which entertained the kids.

Jenni teased her husband. "Okay J.P. Morgan, who do you know in banking?"

"Pardon me," Davis said.

Jenni knew the counselor's parlor tricks. He was delaying. "When did you become so wise in the ways of finance?"

"Melvin Smithkenet," Davis said confidently. "He would be a good place to start."

"Oh, yeah," Jenni said. "Mel. He is a good guy to know."

"Thank you, dear," Davis teased back. "And James Eaton."

"James? Okay. A little stuffy."

"Both excellent contacts." Davis cocked his head as if to say *I rest my case.*

MB had learned that Singer's honesty could lead to him asking some zingers, but this next one left jaws dropped.

"Ms. Jenni," Singer used his fork to pick up a piece of meat, "is this lamb like the one the Joseph statue is carrying on his shoulders at church?"

Singer's gaze was as direct as his question. As proficient as Jenni was at extemporaneous speaking, she felt like she was falling backward with nothing to grasp.

Chevy spoke up. "Singer, that's not a polite question."

Singer was confused. "Why?"

The twins looked down at their dinner, mortified.

The only response Chevy could muster was it just isn't.

Jenni bravely forged ahead. "Singer, I'm guessing the lamb at your church is a baby lamb from a long time ago and far, far away across the world, right?"

"Yep," Singer said with certainty.

"Well, this is old lamb that came from the grocery store just a few blocks away."

"Oh," Singer said. "I was just thinking about Joseph's lamb when I prayed."

"When did you pray, honey?" Jenni asked.

"Before eating. We always did with Mom and Cory."

"Who's Mom and Cory?" one of the twins wanted to know.

"Let's talk about that later, okay girls?" Davis said.

MB gently spoke up. Not normally prone to swings of emotion, she was on the verge of tears. "Do you want to tell our friends about who Mom and Cory are?"

Chevy shot her a "bad idea" look.

"Sure," Singer said excitedly. "My mom went up to heaven to be with God but God kept Cory here. He's healing in a hospital."

"Oh," one of the girls said.

"God also let me meet MB and Chevy. And now you! Pretty soon we're all going to see a judge to find out if I'll live with Cory when he gets better."

Now the twins were upset. "You mean we won't see you anymore?"

Singer smiled widely. "I'll see you a lot more. We're friends for life."

It's impossible to know how much Singer could sense that the energy had left the dining room. At four and a half, he was precocious. But he was a child with a child's propensity to flit from one topic to another, one emotion to the next, unaware of the surrounding mood.

He asked, "Miss Jenni, may I have some Jell-O, please? It looks perfect!" And just as suddenly as his earlier question had flatlined the room, now the table was revived, as carefree as Jell-O.

"How about a piano recital before dessert?" Jenni asked. The girls, clearing silverware, moaned. The men were taking dinner plates away with Singer's assistance.

"Wasn't Jell-O dessert?" Singer asked.

The twins looked at him like he'd completely lost his mind.

"No, silly. Ice cream cake is dessert."

"I agree with you," Chevy said. He couldn't discern which one was Maddi and which was Eliza.

"Can we please have a recital?" Singer said to the girls. "I could sing."

It's one thing for a proud parent to prod a child about performing, but when a friend asks, all resistance vanishes.

MB guessed the five-year-old girls would play with one finger or one hand, but these girls were far beyond that. As the girls played on—now performing a duet—the less surprising their proficiency became.

Why wouldn't they be off-the-charts? she asked herself. *Two brilliant, overachieving parents with the resources to get excellent instruction and driven by steep expectations. Could I be such a mother to Singer? Could Chevy be such a father? Do we have the love, talent and money to give Singer what he needs to excel? Maybe we don't have what Jenni and Davis can offer, but can Cory offer what we can? How will he provide? How much damage physically and emotionally has been done? Maybe Singer is better off with us, with what we can expose him to here. With friends like this.*

As well as the twins performed, when Singer sang it became clear that there is a gulf between human aptitude and divine endowment. He sang his favorite solo, "Ave Maria." His soprano notes shimmered around him, unhurried, full, but with an aching evanescence. Singer's chin was tilted slightly up, mouth parted, sublime, he stared forward. His voice could be felt in one's cells. It slowed breathing and rendered peace.

Singer delighted innocently in the applause. No one was more impressed than Davis who twice looked from the boy to MB, speechless. MB hoped she misread his reaction because for an instant it said, you're not worthy.

The kids and Chevy had ice cream cake and went upstairs to play hide-and-seek. Chevy quickly extracted himself and was back where his evening had begun, in the living room, listening to a crackling fire accompany Davis's confident voice. Chevy lifted his crystal whiskey tumbler and took a sip of 15-year-old Pappy Van Winkle bourbon.

"Unbelievable," he said smacking his lips.

"Now you know why most 15-year-olds will get you arrested," Davis said. "If you'll pardon the sophomoric innuendo."

"Velvety smooth."

"Yes. Until the morning. I could make another crass comparison, but I'll show some restraint."

Chevy smiled. "Abstain might be the more lawyerly word."

"Well played," Davis chuckled. "So, if I were to arrange a meeting between you and Melvin Smithkenet, perhaps a racquetball match would be the best entrée. Do you play?"

"Yeah, but it's been a while. I might need a few games to refresh my memory."

"I imagine you can play just about any game that requires hand-eye dexterity."

Chevy shrugged.

"Well, go easy on us. Some of us are under the illusion that our game has gotten quite good." Davis smiled and tipped his tumbler for a swallow. "Every second Saturday there's singles match play at the club. Followed by drinks and dinner. The competition culminates in our annual doubles tournament. You're familiar with the Maple Bluff Country Club, I take it?"

"Beautiful place," Chevy said.

"Are you a member?" Davis asked.

Chevy laughed. "I couldn't even get a job caddying there. That's a bit out of my league."

"I know some people, on the admission board. Maybe there's something we can do. Meantime, you'll be my guest, I hope."

"Absolutely," Chevy said.

In the kitchen, in a reversal of earlier pronouncements, Jenni and MB conspired to split a piece of ice cream cake. They inhaled their halves.

"Leave no evidence behind," Jenni said to MB, turning on the chrome center-sink faucet.

"Huh?" MB said. She'd given her full self to savoring the last crumbs of gooey decadence.

"Your plate," Jenni said. "And fork. Quick. All evidence of those 450 calories must be washed and dried away."

MB handed over her plate and fork.

"So," Jenni said, "earlier we were talking about Singer. His letters. Any developments there? That is if you don't mind talking about it."

"No. God, I need to talk about it. I just don't want to heap it on you."

"Heap away."

MB's exasperation was obvious. "There's been nothing. No return letters. So strange. Why wouldn't Cory reply?"

"Maybe he's still really hurt."

"Could be. But it's been over three months since the wreck."

"Maybe he doesn't care."

"The way Singer speaks about him—that doesn't seem right."

"And you're sure you have the right address?"

"Yep. Our caseworker verified it. He's out of the hospital and at a farm way up in the northern Minnesota boonies. I'm tempted to try to call him, to find out what's up. But I don't know if they'd give me that information."

"I could probably run down a phone number if need be. We have people at the firm who are scary good at that."

MB thought about it. "I don't know."

"When are you guys in family court?"

"April tenth."

"Are you in mediation? Or in front of the judge?"

"Straight to the judge because this case doesn't involve divorce or parents in adversarial positions. They call it a best interests case, which means the judge will decide what's in the child's best interest."

Jenni nodded knowingly.

"We filled out paperwork about our jobs, living status, interests, activities. Chevy had to write a short essay about why it's in Singer's best interest to live with us. He wrote that he was Singer's father and we were starting a good life here. I had him add that Singer was doing well in school and was making friends. Like you guys." MB's voice cracked. She clenched her fist. "Jenni, how in hell am I supposed to know what's in that little boy's best interest?" She let the magnitude of that question settle. "How?" Her eyes pleaded. "Because all I want to do is that."

"You're not supposed to know," Jenni said calmly. "You can't know. Your judge has a lifetime of experience by which to make these decisions. He or she is very good at looking at cases like this and making the right decision." She nodded at MB.

"Well, what if we look good on paper. And look good in court. And we win. But we're not really right?"

Jenni looked at MB. "Is there something you're not telling me? Or that you want to tell me?"

I have many unhappy days. I use drugs. I don't know if I can be a good mother. My mother and I have no relationship. I don't know what true motherhood looks like. I don't know how to open up and tell people my feelings. Some days I have my doubts that Chevy knows what responsibility really is. Chevy is involved with fraud at his bank. I'm not sure I love Chevy but I think I might.

"No," MB said, managing a smile.

"Okay then," Jenni said. "You're smart. Give yourself some credit for that. You care. Obviously. Let your instincts guide you instead of going about it the other way around."

The conversation took a deep breath before Jenni continued. "How is Singer doing with all of it? The lack of reply from Cory."

"Unbelievably fine." MB shook her head in amazement. "He just says, well, maybe the mailman lost them. He's so upbeat. He says let's write another one. He just . . . shines on."

"He is special," Jenni said. "I don't want you to take this the wrong way, but one thing my mom always told me—and as I get older, it's starting to sink in—is that no matter what happens, no one can take away what you had. That's yours forever."

MB clawed at that advice for comfort, with no immediate success.

The ornate front door was swung open. Goodnights were quickly exchanged in the rush of cold and warm mixing at the threshold. Hurrying toward the car, MB wished aloud that Chevy had come out and started it so the interior would be warmly waiting for them. Chevy said MB was welcome to ride home on his lap to stay toasty. Singer's giggles escaped into the clear frozen night where breaths almost splintered.

MB made sure Singer was buckled in his booster seat with a small blanket over him as he hummed. Chevy was scraping frost off the windshield. As she passed he reached out and pulled MB into his arms and hugged her. "Thank you," he said. He kissed her. "Your nose is cold."

MB was taken aback. "Are you drunk?"

"Maybe a tad. But, really, thanks for tonight. I like Jenni. She's very cool. And Davis, despite being over the top, means well. And he's more connected than a politician."

MB accepted. The hug, the compliment and the moment.

Chevy turned her toward the house. "So, do you want all this?"

She looked at the home, smoke lifting from the brick chimney into a starry sky. The second-floor bedroom lights glowing softly as bedtime rituals were performed. A beautiful front door that could be left unlocked for kids to run in and out of, playing with friends.

MB searched her heart for an answer. "Yes," she said, looking over at Chevy.

Chevy remained focused on the house. "Then you shall have it."

PART SEVEN

Baudette, Minnesota

THE FARM

HomeSky glanced out the divided kitchen window as a crow flew west, a black shape in stark relief against the winter sky. A large pot of coffee brewed as she slid from-scratch biscuits out of the oven to cool.

For Pat, there was a familiarity to the scene: a comfort of closeness, a braiding of aromas, a kitchen table crowded with energy.

Over the years, they had lived different versions of this moment. Despite the kitchen being physically rebuilt, it stood on the same emotional foundation where this group had discussed funeral arrangements, letters of intent to play college hockey, adoption, marriage proposals and such events.

HomeSky missed her Joseph. How perfectly her son would fit in here alongside Meadow and Billy Little Tree. She could also imagine Joseph next to his best friend Cory, unwilling to leave him until he was strong again. And how Joseph would relish Pat and herself, their deep relationship; he would provide endless teasing support.

Her thoughts seemed to invoke his spirit. The chill of melancholy left HomeSky as warmth enwrapped her like her child's large, generous hug. She lingered for a moment, putting hot biscuits into a basket lined with a gingham towel. She took a jar of blackberry jam out of the canning pantry and silently thanked Joseph for his presence.

"Could you talk from the moment you woke up in the hospital?" Pat asked.

"I don't know. I didn't want to hear what might come out." Cory chewed the inside of his mouth. "I guess I could have."

HomeSky brought over the jam and joined them at the kitchen table.

"Is that your blackberry?" Cory asked.

HomeSky's nod had a hint of pride.

"Remember how you'd give Joseph and me two of the same size Tupperware bowls and we'd compete to see who'd fill theirs fastest?"

HomeSky shook her head, recalling their brash enthusiasm. "The scrapes on your legs. Minks couldn't have left you with more scratches. Neither of you would waste a second pulling on long pants."

Billy Little Tree's large black eyes glistened, locked on Cory, then HomeSky, with fascination. Pat was quietly pleased to hear Cory bring forward this memory. It was a healthy act.

"Joseph always showed me a few good spots but the prime berry bushes he kept close to the vest."

Pat laughed. "Problem was he ate two berries for every four he put in the bowl."

Meadow watched the fellowship open up. The three of them had crossed so many bridges together. Although she sat in the table's middle chair, she felt like an outsider.

"He was competitive, but winning, he kept in perspective," Cory said. "I envy him that."

Pat looked at Meadow, sensing her separation. He gave her a little smile. "What did Joseph always say about winning?"

HomeSky spoke. "See past winning."

"And you'll find real victory," Cory finished.

Just then Billy made a long cooing sound that got the table

laughing.

Meadow raised the baby off her lap, letting him bounce on his chubby legs. "Looks like you want to talk too. Is that right?" Her animated pitch induced more cooing. "That is right. Yes it is." Billy's smiles were contagious.

Cory's posture straightened. "Is someone at the door?" They all listened. Another knock came. HomeSky went to the widow over the sink and looked out at a pickup truck idling in the sideyard. "A white pickup with a Varkas logo on the door," she said.

Meadow hoped someday she'd get over the fear of something unknown on the other side of that farmhouse door. Sometimes all it took was a creak of a floorboard in the entryway to dry the spit in her mouth.

Cory remembered seeing the truck weeks ago when Varkas and Meadow spoke through the door.

Pat said, "My guess, Varkas has come to inquire about the property."

"Would have been nice for him to phone first." HomeSky's voice had an edge as she strode toward the front door.

"What about the property?" Cory asked.

Meadow said nothing.

"Pat?" Cory said.

Pat stood. "Something we meant to tell you. Varkas is interested in buying the farm."

Anger jumped in Cory's face.

"We were waiting for the right time," Pat said. "You had—you have—a lot on your plate."

"Buy the farm?" Cory couldn't process it. "Wait, what? When did this happen?"

"It didn't. I don't think it will." Pat heard HomeSky open the front door. "I need to be out there."

They were all seated at the kitchen table looking at Varkas, who dwarfed his chair. He said it was a custom in his family to not arrive at a home empty-handed. He'd brought *Vdolky.*

"They're Czech donuts," Varkas said. "It's best not to crowd them on the skillet, never use grease and be generous with butter and powdered sugar."

Pat took a bite. It was a delicate flaky pastry. "You made these?"

"Yes," Varkas said with obvious pride. "When I eat dessert, it's homemade. The way my mother did it."

No one else at the table had much to say. HomeSky and Cory each took a small bite of their *Vdolky.* Meadow's remained on her dessert plate untouched.

Pat pulled the blackberry jam in his direction. "Maybe I'll try a dollop of this on—"

"Oh no!" Varkas blurted. "That's not how they are meant to be eaten."

Pat apologized.

Varkas cleared his throat with a long swallow of coffee. "So, Ms. HomeSky, I was wondering if I could have a word with you and Pat about your farm."

"You may," HomeSky said.

Varkas waited for the others to leave the room. When they did not he restarted. "Is it appropriate for me to speak frankly in front of the entire household?"

"Mr. Varkas," HomeSky said. "It's imperative you speak in front of the entire household."

"As you wish. I'd like to buy your quarter section and buildings. I'm willing to pay you the going rate plus ten percent. I've brought some competitive pricing to give you a sense of the land's value." Varkas began to reach for his briefcase.

"I know the land's value, Mr. Varkas."

His stern, black eyebrows raised. "You've had it recently appraised?"

"No, I have not."

"Then I'm confused. How do you know what it's worth?"

It was difficult for HomeSky to judge his sincerity. "Mr. Varkas, to me this property is priceless."

"Is that to say you'd be unwilling to sell it?"

"Yes."

"At any price."

"At any price."

"May I ask why?"

HomeSky stood from the table, leaving Meadow, a sleeping Billy, Cory, Pat and Varkas there in silence. They all watched as she walked to the sink and looked out onto the land. "Mr. Varkas, out of respect that you are Pat's employer I will answer what I feel is a highly personal question." She turned to face him. "Every contour of this land, I can see with my eyes closed. I know where the daisies first bloom in the south pasture. I know where the goldfinch nest in the hedgerow. I know in the shadow of the stump where the spring's first snow-white trillium always arrives. I know where the creek leaves its banks during the spring melt. I know the trees my son fell out of as boy. I know what the wind chimes sound like when weather is blowing in. I know that the Creator Father asked the fox to burrow underground and raise a ridge from which I can see in all directions. This is sacred Ojibwe land. I cannot sell it. I am this land."

"We all have our attachments, Ms. HomeSky," Varkas said. "I respect yours as a strong one. But that doesn't make it a wise one."

"What would you know about that, Mr. Varkas?"

"I know that this farm isn't self-sustaining. I have friends at the bank. I know what you owe on the land and what you can hope to make in the best years of harvests."

Pat's back and neck began to burn as his temper awoke. "Mr Varkas—"

HomeSky interrupted; the last thing they needed was Pat losing his job. "Please, Mr. Varkas, say what you've come to say. Make your offer. Then I have dinner to prepare."

Varkas took a folder from his briefcase. "These are some prices of what farms in the 25-mile area sold for. All within the past three years. No doubt, the day of the small independent farm is coming to an end. You can be at the front of the line."

"Is that everything?" HomeSky asked.

Varkas could see her resolute disengagement. "I'll simply add this," he said, latching his briefcase with a snap that woke up a napping Billy. "I am a successful businessman. Whenever a deal is very important to me, I put on the others' shoes. I ask, what would I want if I were being approached? What if you came to my house and said you'd like to purchase my land and my buildings?"

Cory watched in utter disbelief. Could this man not see that HomeSky wanted only one thing: him out of her home? Cory had worked at the forest products plant, but that was before Varkas bought it, so he knew nothing of him. His instinct was sounding alarms.

Varkas continued. "If you came to me with a purchase proposal I would want market price plus 13%, not plus 10% as I originally offered. I can see you're someone who drives a hard bargain. I'm prepared to raise to market price plus 13."

HomeSky nodded. "I will give you our answer tomorrow."

Varkas stood. "And you'll look at the numbers I left here in the folder."

"Yes."

Varkas pulled on his coat and took up his briefcase. He paused. Oh, how he so wanted to ask HomeSky more about her land, especially her comment about how the creek overflows. But being too eager—especially about the water—would be showing his cards.

"Good evening to you all, then," he said, straightening. But before turning to leave he addressed Cory. "You've been injured. How are you recuperating, young man?"

"Well as can be expected," Cory said.

"I noticed a wheelchair ramp out front but the crutches here in the kitchen. That seems like significant progress."

"Everything's relative, Mr. Varkas."

"How long have you been laid up?"

Cory had no desire to answer, but doing so, he thought, might get Varkas out the door. "Since late November."

Varkas did the math. "Three months. That couldn't have been easy. Or inexpensive. If you have trouble with the medical bills don't hesitate to reach out. Pat knows where to find me."

Cory frowned, wondering if he'd heard correctly, but before he could speak, Varkas said goodbye to everyone except Meadow, whom he never acknowledged with even a glance.

"I'll walk you out," Pat said. He took his coat from a hook in the entryway and followed Varkas into the cold.

"You'll see she looks at the numbers and considers them seriously," Varkas more told Pat than asked as their boots crunched along the icy pathway. His truck was in the driveway, idling all this time, oil dripping from the exhaust pipe, leaving a black stain in the snowpack.

Pat squinted as the harsh red sun balanced on the horizon line. The cold wouldn't budge but the days were stretching out as February was all but finished. "She'll look at them."

"Can I count on you to be with me on this deal?"

"What exactly do you mean by that?" Pat asked, looking up at Varkas.

"Encourage her to take the deal. Sell the farm. Use the money to choose any number of places to live, either in these parts or in town. Perhaps put some of that money toward the girl's education, or the infant's. Life's not easy for a young Indian in this world without a father." The plume of Varkas's breath picked up a hint of red from the setting sun.

"Life isn't easy for a young Indian in this world *with* a father. I not sure I'm getting your point." Cold crept inside Pat's coat collar.

Varkas said, "Pat, we're talking about security. You've got a good-paying job with benefits. You've got mouths to feed in that house. You got a farm that's leaking money every year. You've got a injured young man with months of physical therapy in front of him. You've got a baby under your roof. My point is security. My offer is security. A good price for the farm. A good job for you. Maybe for the others if need be."

"Of all the choices, why this piece of ground?" Pat gazed over the property. "It means a lot to us, but you know what kind of yields we get out here. You did your homework. It's not like we toss seed over our shoulder and turn around to a bushel of corn."

"Like I told you, I've had my eye on this place a long time," Varkas said.

Pat looked at him. Doing so gave him an unfortunate sightline up Varkas's large porcine nostrils. Not that Pat was a small man at six feet, but Varkas had ten inches on him and higher ground for their conversation. In the long-shadow light, the baggy, ringed skin beneath his eyes made him appear older than his 40 years.

The two men looked at each other. Varkas had said what he came to say but Pat could only say so much. He was bound. He was worried. And Varkas could smell it.

"Son of a bitch," Varkas said under his breath. "There he is again."

Pat looked across the pasture toward the ridge. A hundred yards out, a large wolf stood in black silhouette.

"That's a big animal." Pat said. "Too big to be a dog."

"That's no dog," Varkas said. "You don't keep chickens or livestock on the property?"

"No we don't."

"Strange." Varkas stared out at the silhouette. "Do you keep a dog in the house or in a run in the barn?"

"No."

"Damn strange." Varkas shook his head. "I usually carry a rifle in the truck."

Pat frowned. "You won't be shooting that animal on this property," Pat said forcefully.

Varkas scoffed. "You must be kidding. That wolf is not only a trophy, you can see he's dangerous. Watching us like that. Showing no fear. You don't want that."

Pat remained silent.

"Saw that same animal at my place not long ago cutting wood. A week or so left in mating season. Only reason that makes sense for that animal to be moving around to different territory like he is." Varkas took a few sudden steps toward the wolf. Pat was the only one startled by it. "Yeah. You don't want that animal around here with women and infants and wheelchairs. Have you seen him before?"

Pat studied the wolf with his dominant high tail, slightly hunched shoulders, nose lowered. "No."

"Do you keep a rifle in the house?"

Pat looked at Varkas. Again, he swallowed a thousand words. "Yes."

"Good. Have it loaded by the door. A .270 Winchester will throw about 130 grains. Won't mess up the fur too bad." Varkas looked firmly at Pat as if to say, got it?

Pat nodded, taken aback by Varkas's confrontational eyes.

When Pat looked back to the field, the wolf was gone.

MAILBOX

Back inside the farmhouse, Pat went to HomeSky and gave her a long hug. She spoke first. "I don't want to talk about Varkas anymore. Not until after dinner."

"Me either," Pat said, not entirely honestly. "Maybe I'll see if Cory needs help with PT." Pat could hear Meadow upstairs playing her guitar, something that calmed her as much as Billy.

HomeSky faced Pat. "You're wearing quite a frown." She touched his forehead. "You okay?"

"It got frozen in place," Pat chuckled, giving it a rub. "But yeah. You're here. Cory's here. Meadow and Billy are here. I'm very okay."

"What's that in your hand?"

Pat held up a fat manila envelope. "Dunno. Came for Cory. Looks like the return address is his school." Pat shrugged.

HomeSky lifted her eyebrows as if to say, *I hope it's all good.*

"What's for dinner?" Pat asked.

"Meatloaf. Green beans. Salad." She paused. "Left-over *Vdolky.*" HomeSky managed a weak smile.

"Good to see you still have your sense of humor."

"Laugh or cry, right?" HomeSky said.

"I see Varkas left his platter," Pat said, taking note of the remaining donuts plated on the table.

HomeSky sighed. "No accident, I'll bet."

Pat agreed. "I'm going to go check on Cory."

It's a short walk from the kitchen to Cory's bedroom, a converted first-floor den that Meadow had occupied while on bed rest with Billy. The door was half-open. Pat knocked.

"Yep," Cory said.

"Still a little strange to hear your voice," Pat said, pushing open the door to find Cory in his wheelchair at the window. "Wondered if you needed help with PT?"

"Okay," Cory said. "Can you close that?"

Pat pulled the door closed behind him. "What's first on the agenda?" Pat sat on the edge of the bed, still a little chilled.

Cory turned his wheelchair around. His hair was overgrown and matted oddly in back. His beard, scraggly. His legs were stick-like in his baggy sweats. "Not sure. Maybe my psyche."

Pat puffed out his cheeks. "Sorry about all that with Varkas. Out of the blue he's interested in the farm."

"Why? Since when?"

"He said it's been on his mind a long time. Then today he pulled me out of the breakroom and started asking me about it."

"What does HomeSky say?" Cory's concern was obvious.

"She told me no way she'd sell. You heard her tonight—she and this land are inseparable."

Cory grew quiet.

"What are you thinking?"

"I don't know," Cory said.

"C'mon, Cory."

Cory's uninjured hand grabbed a fistful of hair, then ran down his face and beard. "You always say I need to have faith in things. I have to trust." Cory cocked his head at Pat. "Really?" He shrugged, despondent. "Just look at me."

"You look darn good compared to where you began."

Cory scoffed. "Pat, c'mon. I have scars all over my body. And you know that's the least of it."

Pat put his hands on his knees and leaned in toward Cory. "Let's look at what you can trust. Try that. You can trust HomeSky and me, right?"

Cory's eyes fired. "You didn't even trust telling me about Varkas wanting the farm."

"Bad decision on our part—my part, actually. That said, can you trust us? You know what I've been through. You had a front-row seat for some of it. I was at rock bottom."

"Yeah," Cory acknowledged.

"Before we met, my temper plus the alcohol, well that combo got me transferred out of more parishes than I want to talk about. When they sent me to Baudette, the Archdiocese said that was it. Last chance. And things got worse here before they got better."

"I didn't know that," Cory said.

"So, back to trust, right? How do we have faith in good when good seems to be intended for someone else?" Pat let the question linger. "When I rebuilt this house after HomeSky left, I remember how it helped me regain my faith, board by board. I had a choice. Believe. Don't believe. I just started believing she'd come back."

Pat stood from the bed and stretched his back and neck with a groan. Cory could see the man was overloaded with concerns, and that he was among them.

Pat continued. "You've seen what HomeSky has been through. God takes a husband and a son." Pat closed his eyes. "It almost killed her too. Frightening. I'm not making any comparisons here. What I'm saying is our mutual understanding of loss is why we can trust each other. Far, far beyond normal limitations."

"Okay," Cory said. "You're right. And I do trust you. And HomeSky, of course. And Meadow, for some reason, I trust her. I guess because she's been hit with the shit stick, too. But I'm not ready to trust the idea of happiness." Cory shook his head. "I've lost track of myself. Who is this bearded mess in a wheelchair? I don't know."

"I understand that," Pat said.

"Really? Do you?" Cory began to fire up. "Let's go back. I was captain of a high school hockey team on its way to a state championship. Then I wasn't. I was a college hockey player headed for a national title. Then I wasn't. I had a best friend. Then I didn't. I was going to be married. Now I'm not. I had a father, then I didn't. But wait, my real father and my real mother aren't who I thought they were. I was going to be a father to Singer. Now we'll see what the judge says. Tell me, Pat, just who the fuck am I?"

Cory's agitation was avalanching. "Seriously. What if I lose Singer? I don't know. What if Singer grows up like I did, calling someone Mom and Dad who really aren't that interested in being that? Now, I'm supposed to trust the good thing, the right thing, will come waltzing in?"

"You have no other real choice."

"I have choices," Cory flatly stated.

"What is that supposed to mean?"

"I don't know. Sometimes I just want to roll up inside of myself." Cory's sagged in his wheelchair.

"And not talk to anyone?" Pat added.

"Maybe."

"You've already proved that's no answer. Surely, that won't get Singer back where he belongs."

"So what do I do? How did you do it?"

"You have to reach for a ray of sunshine and let it pull you through," Pat said.

"That sounds a little trite."

"Maybe. But I stand before you as proof it isn't."

Cory thought about it. "You mean Joseph? How he helped you?"

"He and Monsignor Kief." Pat smiled. "Then there were a few more rays. The Sheriff—that's one friendship I would have bet against when we first met. And Lu Ann. And you. Remember the weeks we spent out here finishing the house. Painting it. Remember all you did for me?"

The men looked at each other. Cory nodded.

Pat said, "Start with whatever it was that got you to come out of your shell and talk again. What caused that?"

"What if I said I had a crazy dream?"

"I've had a few."

"Maybe it was being around the farm. All the memories."

"This is a powerful place," Pat said.

"I guess." Cory listened to his breathing. He focused on slowing it down. "I had a dream this afternoon. If I were still on pain meds, that might explain it."

"What if it just is? Doesn't need explaining."

"Could be."

Pat encouraged him. "Let's hear it."

Cory started. "So, I'm outside in the driveway. In my wheelchair. In a snowstorm. The snow suddenly stops and melts away and the wind blows an old leaf toward me. It's rolling and I'm watching it and the brown leaf turns into a bird, brown at first like the leaf, and then becomes a goldfinch hopping on the ground and then it flies up and lands on my knee."

Pat agreed that was a little unusual.

"About to really be," Cory replied. "The bird is luminous. The yellow feathers are incandescent. The day is warm, now, right? Snow is gone and everywhere, I can feel heat rising from the frozen ground."

"I like the sound of that," Pat said.

Cory looked at Pat. "I lock eyes with the bird and it says, out loud, to me: 'Honor your responsibility.' Then it stares at me like we completely understand each other."

"Honor your responsibility." Pat mulled it over.

"Yep. Watching me. Waiting for me to catch up with the gravity of the sentence. Finally, the bird flits to the ground, starts hopping away, becomes a brown leaf again, blown by the wind out of sight."

Pat smiled at Cory. "Like I said. This land has power."

"Do you think it has meaning?"

"Do you have dreams like that often?"

"No. Most dreams, I don't remember. When I do it's a recurring theme of me hitting the pipe in hockey or fumbling a punt. Failure dreams."

"This is for sure different. What do you make of it?"

Cory shook his head. "When I woke up, it didn't make much sense. But I've been thinking about it ever since. More and more it's bringing me back to Joseph. And how he gave me grief because I was constantly saying I have to do this and I have to do that. Always disciplined and scheduled."

Pat interjected. “That’s how God made you. Nothing wrong with that.”

“Yeah, but Joseph would say I had allegiance to all my responsibilities except the big one. You gotta live with joy and courage. He said that’s what the Creator wants, above all else. That’s how you honor your life.”

“Do you believe that?”

“It never made much sense to me back then. Joseph threw a lot of stuff out there. But it’s speaking to me now. I mean really, did anyone live with more joy and courage than he did?”

“Maybe Monsignor Kief.”

“Right,” Cory said. “Pretty good company.”

“The best.”

“So, back to your question about why I started talking again. Hanna’s death killed my joy. And my injuries broke my courage. Anger took over. There was no room for anything else. I am so pissed off, that as I heal outside, I wonder, will the anger ever escape? But when I spoke the words from the dream, just saying them aloud, it was a little release. So I kept saying them—”

Pat interrupted. “And the next thing you knew, you were talking.”

“Yeah. It felt good. Honor your responsibility. For some reason, saying it fit.”

“I’m proud of you.”

“Thanks.” Cory started to roll his wheelchair toward the dresser. “I want to show you something.” He bumped into the bedpost. “I can’t wait to be done with this chair.”

Pat took a step to help him maneuver around the bed.

“No,” Cory insisted. “I got this.” At the dresser he took a notepad from the drawer. Inside, he had created an elaborate hand-ruled calendar, a six-week grid with the different days of the week. He pointed. “Here’s today, and the E is for evening. This is the physical therapy I need to do tonight.”

“That’s a serious grid,” Pat was genuinely impressed. “So am I reading it right? Three times a day?”

"Yep."

"Seems like a lot."

"If I'm going to stand in front of a judge in six weeks—and I will be standing—and confidently tell him that I am the right role model for Singer, and he should be my adopted son, I have to get my ass completely out of this chair and get going. Now."

"And there's our court date, right?" Pat's fingertip pressed the last box on the grid, April tenth.

"Yep."

"You'll be ready. I don't doubt it for a minute."

Cory noticed the manila envelope on his dresser. "What's that?"

Pat had forgotten about the well-stuffed envelope he'd carried to the bedroom. "Oh, yeah. Came in the mail for you today."

Cory picked it up. "Looks like it's from school. Hefty. I hope it's not the world's longest dismissal letter." Cory managed a brave smile.

He struggled opening it. "Can you get it?"

Pat used a pen to tear along the large seal. He pulled out the contents: an assortment of 25 to 30 pieces of paper, some ruled, others not, with handwritten notes on them. He handed the stack to Cory.

Pat watched intently as Cory's eyes tracked left to right across the pages. Each note he read drew Cory's posture up straighter. After reading three he sat back with the stack on his lap. "Pretty cool," he said, exhaling deeply.

"Do you mind?" Pat put out his hand.

Cory gave Pat the notes he'd read.

Dear Mr. Bradford,

Please hurry back. Math is too easy without you.
Kinda boring, too. Hope you're feeling better and we'll see you around soon!

Mary Hernandez
P.S. Can't wait to do equation races when you get back!

• • •

Dear Coach,

I heard what happened and I offer my deepest condolences out to you.

I'm really sorry for what you had to go through. The guys and I wanted to come to the hospital but we were told you were not having visitors. We were going to sneak out anyway but then Mitch's mom called and said we shouldn't.

We've lost a few games without you on the bench, but we're starting to play better. You had us undefeated so it shows what a great coach you are.

Hope to see you soon and I just want you to know you've made a big difference for me and I appreciate you sticking by me.

Respectfully,
Tommy Hedman #14

• • •

Dear Mr. Bradford,

I know I wasn't your best student and everything but I want you to know that your class was the first time anyone in math took the time to help me and make me feel like I had a chance to get a B and not settle for a C or worse. I appreciated how you came in early to go over stuff I was stuck on. I'm not complaining, but the substitute doesn't. I have a strong faith and I'm praying for you everyday. Get better. I know you will, I just know it. You never let people give up.

God bless,
Mary Kay Wendel

Pat was reading when a tear rolled from Cory's eye onto the stack of papers, landing with an audible plop. Pat looked up. "These are amazing."

Cory's chin began to quiver but he pulled himself up straighter yet.

Pat said, "You know how you talked about honor your responsibility? This is some of it too. Your life has real impact, Cory. It has so much value. You have touched a lot of people and you give yourself little or no credit."

Cory looked at the tear splatter as it soaked into the letter. It occurred to him he had been reading off the bottom of the stack. When he flipped the pile, a note on school letterhead from his principal was on top.

Hello Cory,

I hope this note finds you healing and feeling as good as can be. I'm sorry I couldn't deliver this package of notes in person. What I wouldn't pay to see the look on your face as you read them!

Quickly, here's how they came to be. After you were hospitalized, we locked your classroom until such a time that a substitute teacher could be placed. About a day later, a note from a student was taped to your door, wishing you a speedy recovery. Soon there were three. Then six. And so on. By the time we had a substitute in your classroom, the outside of the door was full, and the inside began collecting good wishes, too.

Since they were written to you I did my best not to pry. That said, I couldn't help but read a few. They are a tribute to the quality of your teaching, coaching and character.

As you recover from your injuries, I hope you find these notes motivating. The students eagerly await your return to the classroom, as do I. Your desk will be waiting for you when you're ready.

Godspeed and all the very best,
Cliff Godfrey

Cory nodded to himself. Pat saw a glint in his gray-green eyes that had been absent for months.

"Let's start with legs," Cory said. He put the stack of letters on the dresser.

"Legs sound good," Pat said.

Cory cocked his head to an aroma coming in from the kitchen. "Meatloaf?" He looked eagerly at Pat.

"Mmmeatloaf," Pat said.

Cory cut loose a quarter-moon-dimple grin. "Hope there's still some left for you when I'm through."

Book Two

Awakening, Spring 1986

Life has few unrelated events.

—Monsignor Kief

PART ONE

March

CHEVY

It was Chevy and Davis versus the reigning doubles champs.

Be sure of this: the Maple Bluff racquetball club took their annual in-house doubles tournament seriously. It went beyond bragging rights. It went beyond a free first drink at the front bar on weekends. The champs were immortalized in a framed photograph—smiling, sweat-drenched, trophies in hand—that hung in Champions' Hallway, which was the only route from the bar to the restrooms. One might presume this a small prize, but considering the advancing age and weakening bladders of the membership, this was prime real estate.

To say Chevy stumbled into this pairing with Jenni's husband, Davis, would be insensitive. Davis's regular partner was victim to what he called a "unilateral pothole attack." While quickly crossing a street in downtown Madison, ten minutes late for a board meeting, the man unceremoniously stepped into one of the city's famously large potholes, birthed after months of assault by immense snowplows and, more recently, rapidly freezing and thawing March temperatures. His foot entered in one piece and exited in three.

Now on crutches, watching through tempered glass, the ex-partner observed as years of elite competition, and a flat-out hatred of losing, propelled Chevy around the 40-by-20-foot court like a banshee, smashing kill shots into corners and diving to keep impossible balls in play.

A gathering of other tournament players with white, freshly laundered towels draped around their necks greeted Davis and Chevy as they ducked through the small door, leaving the court. Victors always exit first.

"Hey Davis," an onlooker shouted. "I'd say you owe the mayor a phone call. Thank him for doing such a horseshit job of road maintenance." The gallery quite liked that. Even Davis's sidelined ex-partner managed a polite guffaw.

Davis put a sweaty arm around Chevy. "A burden. Me carrying the rookie." The gallery threw their towels at him.

Afterward at the bar, showered, wet hair combed back, face radiant with victory, Davis examined their trophy. It was fondly called the mini-Wimbledon, featuring a bronze cup about nine inches in diameter. "I bet you won your share of these," he said.

"Racquetball trophies?" Chevy jested.

Davis smiled. "As you may have guessed, I did not."

"You handled yourself great out there," Chevy said. "How about your kill to take the second game?"

Davis's smile got bigger before shaking his head. "I've been working furiously on my game for over three years. And you come in having played a couple one-hour warm-ups and by the end of the match, you're playing better than anyone in our league."

"I don't know about that, but I am a few years younger."

Davis waved his hand. "Sure, sure. But it was more like a switch got flipped, one that we don't have. You were not going to lose."

"Losing has never been my forte," Chevy said. "I'm pretty sure you have a similar switch in the courtroom."

Davis took a long pull off his Heineken. "That's the venue where I won my trophies. Never lettered in a sport in high school. It always chewed at me. Until I found law. That's where I earned my letter jacket."

"Sports are overrated," Chevy said, looking into the mouth of his bottle. "When the glitter settles, a lot of people have left you behind."

"How are things for you at work?" Davis held up his arm. When the bartender glanced over he made a circular motion around their empties.

Chevy perked up. "Jumping. The economy is supercharged. Companies are expanding."

"Are you making any money?" Davis raised an eyebrow.

"Yeah. But I won't be moving into your neighborhood anytime soon."

"Do you get commissions for the business loans you place?"

"We get a little taste, but nothing like what the bank hauls in with fees and interest."

"You don't get a percentage?"

"Of the loan?"

"Yes."

Chevy smirked. "I wish."

"That's what's great about civil law. The firm gets a percentage of the award. If you're a partner, you get a percentage of that, plus an additional percentage if it was your case. We call that birthing a Siamese twin."

Chevy looked at the trophy, a bit embarrassed by how much it meant to Davis.

"When we won the national college championship, we got a trophy a little bigger than this. Know what we did?"

Davis said he didn't.

"Three bottles of Jack Daniel's went in it. We passed it among the boys until it was drained."

Davis pondered that. He summoned the bartender. "Thomas, can you soap out the cup of this trophy?" Davis looked at Chevy and beamed. "We need to break it in properly."

MB and Jenni went shopping rather than watch the racquetball tournament. The two laughed among themselves about it being the easiest choice since chocolate or carrots. They planned to meet Davis and Chevy at the country club for dinner at six.

Jenni had a weekday nanny who was also available for some weekend babysitting. Singer was delighted to hear he'd be spending Saturday afternoon and evening with the twins.

"I feel guilty," Jenni said, as the sales clerk folded her new Ann Taylor blouse and slipped it in a shopping bag. The register area smelled of perfume samples. Soft retail muzak piped in from above.

"What? You look great in that blouse," MB told her.

"Oh, not that." Jenni made a lemony face. "Leaving the girls with the nanny after being so crazy preoccupied with work all week. Saturday is usually our day."

"Sorry," MB said, feeling like she was part of the problem.

Jenni put a hand on her arm. "No. It's not you. Davis was excited as a ten year old for today. He tossed and turned all night and insisted we all get together this evening. I'm just glad we were able to sidestep the tournament. I wonder if our men won."

"They won," MB said confidently. "Chevy is pretty mellow unless he's competing. Then, look out."

The two had made their way out to the atrium of the East Towne Mall where they found a bench. They talked as the world walked by.

"What's he like?" Jenni inquired. "Chevy's a hard person to read, and that's something my job required me to master."

"He's a pirate. That's pretty much the first impression I had. Still holds."

"What do you mean?"

"He takes what he wants, and with a smile on his face."

Jenni thought about that.

"Did I tell you how we first met?"

Jenni shook her head no.

"On a gurney. In the ER."

Jenni's hand went to her mouth. "No shit?"

"Yep," MB said. "He had lost control of his snowmobile, which went off the trail and ended up in a barbed wire fence. Lost a lot of blood. We patched him up. Never really gave it a second thought until that following summer when he strolled into the Lakeside with his beer-league softball team. I recognized him. Something about him stuck with me."

"Love at first suture?"

MB laughed. "Fluke? Destiny? None of the above? Anyway, Chevy didn't know me when we re-met because he was unconscious the first time, right? So I made some crack about hardly recognizing him with his clothes on. Should have seen the look on his face."

Jenni smiled. "Maybe you're the pirate."

"That was . . ." she thought for a moment, "just over two years ago. Crazy, crazy."

"So, is he the one?"

MB arched an eyebrow. "Do people really know like that? Did you know?"

"I think we're all different," Jenni said. "The romantic in me, as ignored and neglected as she may be, likes to think some take a direct arrow to the heart. Mine was more of a glancing blow."

"How so?"

"I think I was ready for something to change in my life and Davis entered on cue. Or like you said earlier, fluky, to a degree. Maybe destiny, but I'm usually too cynical for that."

MB let the pause sit, sensing Jenni had more to say.

"I love him, don't get me wrong. But I also fell in love with the notion of him. Intelligent. Good-looking. Successful. Caring. Financially secure. Someone who was ready to start a family. I could pass a polygraph test, but I'd be less than honest if I told you I woke up every morning knowing he's *the* one."

"I think Chevy might be for me. No one I know has ever challenged me *and* loved me. It was always one or the other."

"Hmm," Jenni said. Slowly she nodded. "I've never thought of it like that." Jenni smiled at her friend. "You are a smart one, do you know that?"

MB blushed.

"Forgive me for this but I have an organizationally starved brain. So now that I get Chevy better, where does Singer fit?"

MB said nothing.

"Too many questions?"

"No," MB said. "That's not it. I'm just not sure." She folded her hands and rested her chin on them. After a deep breath, she began. "I'm fighting some baggage, Jenni, not all of which I'm going to get into. Mostly, I have two questions running through my head on an endless loop. One, is Singer better off with us than with Cory? Two, am I capable of being a great wife and mom?"

Jenni was going to speak, but MB stopped her with a raised index finger.

"Cory has not responded to Singer's two letters," MB said with a frown. "That completely pisses me off. The little dear has his heart set on hearing from him. So that tells me maybe Cory is overwhelmed with the loss of his fiancée, plus his injuries. Maybe a permanent brain injury—we know from the social worker that he went through the windshield and suffered serious head trauma. I've seen stuff like that. If it's permanent, Singer could be better off here."

Jenni nodded in agreement.

"And as for me, as a wife and mother—weird to hear me say those words—well, my role model wasn't great. That scares me."

Jenni said that was understandable.

"And I've . . . I have a trap door I default to." MB looked down at the floor.

"Trap door?"

"I've pretty regularly smoked pot since high school. And I know the tricks of the trade for lifting prescription drugs from the hospital here and there. Sometimes I just need to cope. The ER, that place can crush you. You love it. You're in this amazing fight for life and you win. You hate it when you lose. And then you . . . separate. Walk out of the hospital and it's like, how am I going to go shopping for cereal right now?"

MB could see Jenni trying to keep concern from overtaking her face.

"So it's been weeks since I've had anything but an occasional beer or glass of wine. The more I have Singer around the more I want to be better. More reliable. But am I good-wife good-mom material? Dunno."

Jenni's posture straightened. "Honey, none of us are too sure one day to the next of our ranking. I'm sorry to be academic, but we don't get the results back from that test for 20 or 30 years. Maybe longer."

MB said flatly, "What if I fail Singer like my mom failed me?"

"You fail if you don't try. That much we know." Jenni looked resolutely at MB.

"If I had a gavel, I'd bring it down on the thing-a-ma-jigger. That's a strong argument." MB nodded and thought, *You fail if you don't try.*

Jenni's hands came down on her lap with a motivating slap. "Okay, I have two favors to ask. No, make it three."

MB perked up.

"Let's keep talking about these things. Your friendship and our conversations have enriched me greatly. I want you to know that."

"Sure. Thank you."

"Second, let me help you get representation for the custody hearing. I have a colleague at the firm who's a rock star in family law. He'd do it as a favor to me. Having representation like that shows the judge you're serious."

"Okay. I appreciate it."

"And lastly," Jenni added with a smile, "will you do me the great favor of going back in the store with me? I'd like to buy you a new blouse for dinner tonight. So that when we look at each other, we see the possibility of new things."

LU ANN

Two weeks had passed since Lu Ann had returned to her diner. She missed Baudette. More importantly, Baudette missed her.

It's no stretch to say her place was the town's unofficial county seat, which made Lu Ann the sorta mayor. Her first order of business was to marker up a sign she could lean against the cash register to greet her patrons.

IF YOU DIDN'T MISS ME, FAKE IT.
LEAVE A BIGGER TIP!!!

In the month she was in St. Paul running Mick's Diner, Lu Ann had plenty of time to think. Sure, managing the place had its share of unique challenges, but it was much like jumping on another person's bike: adjust the seat, test the brakes, go.

But in the evenings, when the customers had gone, when her apron was hung and the lights were off and the door was locked, Lu Ann was alone, bumping into doubts. Her process of understanding her sadness slowly unfolded. For a woman surrounded by people, as Lu Ann was, she was alone. Her kids were far from Baudette, making their way. Pat's love had found its true place with HomeSky. And her father . . . he was a murderer.

The weight of this stooped her. And if not for Monsignor Kief's hand in lifting her burden, to recommend a sabbatical from Baudette, there's no telling the toll.

Her time away reset her and shone a light on her many blessings. Beginning with the inner and physical strength with which she was endowed.

When Lu Ann was in her early twenties, not only was she a new mother, a novice diner owner, but she also discovered weightlifting and bodybuilding—she even won some regional and state contests. This was her rescue. Working with weights gave her much-needed tangible signs of advancement: from moving a pin deeper into the stack of weight she pressed to the physical attractiveness of a more muscular frame to the wash of post-exercise adrenaline that cleansed the daily grime from her spirit.

"You look darn good, Lu Ann," said Wendell, one of the two bachelor farmers finding his way to the community table. If you had to pick the more talkative of the pair, he'd be it, but words were something he more mulled over than used. They had come to town to deposit their social security checks. That act always made them hungry for pie.

"Why thank you, Wendell," Lu Ann patted him on his bony, old frame. "I'm happy to tell you I'm working out again. Hauling all this food is going to give me the posture of a question mark if I don't fight back."

"Yes, ma'am," brother Clayton said. Which doubled his word output for the day.

Lu Ann started for the coffee station when through the front window she saw Pat and Cory get out of Pat's truck across the street. The sight of Pat still made her heart skip out of rhythm. Her mouth got cottony as she smoothed down her uniform and breathed deeply through her nose, filling her diaphragm, holding it, slowly releasing.

Pat levered forward the seatback, reached into the rear seat area and what he pulled out was the last thing Lu Ann expected to see on a frosty mid-March morning. He carried the inflated, silver air mattress over to Cory, who stood leaning against the truck's hood.

Cory looked hardly like the Cory of local legend. The hockey star. The hero who pulled a pilot and his family out of a burning single-engine airplane. The ace mathematics teacher and coach who was engaged to be married to the beautiful Duluth news anchor. Was that Cory still in there somewhere under the long hair, the stained ball cap, the patchy beard and the oversized Carhartt jacket?

Cory took shuffle steps, crossing the street toward the diner. He held the air mattress out in front of him at about chin level, keeping his forward view as unobstructed as possible. Pat was at his elbow. Every three or four steps, Cory would swing the air mattress to the side, so he could see the ground in front, cautious not to trip.

The brass bell over the door announced them. Lu Ann's heart lurched again; to know that her father put all of this in front of Cory. She closed her eyes and prayed for strength and understanding.

"Greetings," Pat said, nervously loud. The couple in the rear of the diner looked up. "We're just back from an appointment in Duluth and rumor has it lunch is fried chicken and split pea soup." He smiled as best he could.

The tightness around Pat's mouth told Lu Ann that he, too, was uncomfortable and that only time would help them find an easy breath in each other's company. Lu Ann squeezed her hands together. "It is indeed. Well let's get you world travelers a booth. Or would a table be easier?" She looked to Pat for guidance.

Cory let the air mattress rest on his boot tops. "Hello, Lu Ann," he said, breaking the awkwardness, shuffling toward her. Cory could see Lu Ann's body tensing. He leaned his air mattress against a chair-back and took the last, few awkward steps with his hands free. Lu Ann felt tears building. As he approached, Cory's eyes were wet. "I hear there's chocolate cake, too." He smiled—a half-crescent dimpled his cheek.

They embraced there, by table three. The few customers fortunate enough to have come in for an early lunch were in the company of burgeoning renewal. Forgiveness is growth. Forgiveness is life. Forgiveness is God. They held one another and everyone in the diner breathed in a measure of grace.

Lu Ann didn't get up from the table to check on other customers. Not even for a quick second. She let Mary Alice attend to that. Cory started by explaining the air mattress. He had fallen while walking. His weeks in hospital beds and months in a wheelchair left his legs atrophied and unstable. His physical therapist told him if he was hell-bent on walking without crutches, he needed to carry an air mattress to serve as a landing pad. At least for the next few weeks. And while on his feet, he needed to use crutches on every other occasion to let his legs recover and rest. Cory agreed to use them 25 percent of the time.

"She's pushy," Cory told Lu Ann of his physical therapist. "I appreciate that. And she's knowledgeable. I respect that." Cory's lunch was in front of him as the diner began to fill with regulars. He struggled to cut his chicken, but both Pat and Lu Ann knew it would be fruitless to try to help. "Damn wrist," Cory mumbled. Then he rebounded. "Could stick the scrawny thing in a pencil sharpener. Amazing how fast the muscle goes."

Pat spoke up. "We had a check-up with the surgeon this morning. Says the X-rays look good. Everything's where it's supposed to be."

"Finally," Cory added.

"Did you have trouble with the bone healing?" Lu Ann asked.

"They had to re-break it after three weeks and start again. The second time they didn't use a cast. They used a fixation rod that penetrated the skin." Cory showed Lu Ann the scars on his wrist. "The thing looked like something out of the dark ages. Bumped it on every piece of furniture imaginable. Lot of fun." Cory set down his fork and made a few fists. "But it's working. Now I have to regain strength. Watch this killer workout." Cory reached over to the napkin dispenser. On the third try, he was able to pull one out. Then, slowly, he squeezed the napkin in his hand until he made a ball.

"Baby steps," he said, setting the napkin ball on the table.

"Pretty good, though," Lu Ann said with pep.

Cory and Lu Ann looked at each other like they had more to say. Pat had an idea.

"If you two will excuse me for a few, I have to go find out about corn seed at the co-op. Shouldn't be more than 15 minutes."

"Sounds good," Cory said. Lu Ann nodded.

Pat left them. Quiet replaced him at the table.

"Good chicken," Cory said.

"Thanks. Fried chicken sure makes a mess of the kitchen."

"Yep," Cory said.

Lu Ann felt tension pushing down on them both. She didn't know where to start so she just started. "I'm so sorry, Cory. For all this pain. That my dad caused." She could only look at the tabletop.

Cory leaned in closer to Lu Ann. "I don't want you to feel guilty about what happened. Really. I believe we'd drive ourselves crazy trying to understand this. Or trying to fix it."

Lu Ann looked up at Cory.

"It's not fixable, Lu Ann. It's like my wrist, or my hip. They won't be what they were. They'll work again, sure. But different. People who say move on, or forget about it, they've never been where we've been."

The diner made its sounds. Plates. Coffee brewing. A sneeze. Silverware.

Cory continued. "I was flattened by guilt. Afraid to speak. Afraid of what might come out. Couldn't say a word. Did you know about that?"

Lu Ann nodded.

"Guilt clamped my mouth shut. I thought it was anger. Anger was just a byproduct, a sliver by comparison." Cory looked off, out the window. The sun was shining. "That explosion was meant for me. Hanna died a mistaken death. I don't know why." He looked at Lu Ann. "I don't know why."

Lu Ann nodded, tears running down her cheeks.

"You've probably had this thought," Cory said. "It should have been me."

"I have had that thought." Lu Ann replied.

"That's us trying to control the world. Playing God, as Pat says."

Lu Ann said, "Do you believe in God after something like this?"

"Do you?"

"I do." Lu Ann slid her chair in closer to Cory. "I was talking with Monsignor Kief and I was telling him how furious I was with God and that I wanted to shout at Him and curse Him and he told me that was good. That I should do just that. That God would understand.

That it's okay to be angry with God at times. That God will forgive you if you forgive Him." Lu Ann's face relaxed and her eyes shone brightly. "Monsignor Kief said God sometimes asks for forgiveness, too. I took that idea and went away and thought about it. While I was running Mick's Diner I figured out what I needed. I need you to forgive me, Cory. For what my dad did."

"I do forgive you."

"Can you forgive yourself, too? Can you let go of the guilt?"

Cory shook his head. "We'll see."

"It will eat you up, Cory. It will destroy you."

"Almost did."

"I want to help. I need to help."

"You are," Cory said. "When I see you here, strong, you help me. When I see you sit with Pat—I know that's still not easy for you—you help me." He looked at her closely and whispered, "You help me."

Lu Ann put her head in her hands and sobbed. She quickly took a deep breath and wiped her face. "Sorry. Lot of pop-up showers right now. How else can I help you? There must be more."

Cory looked down, then he pushed his plate toward her with a half-smile. "You can cut my chicken."

VARKAS

One man from OSHA and a male-female team from the EPA spent two days at Varkas's Forest Products plant. They were courteously efficient. Pocket cameras flashed as they tirelessly inspected the far corners of the facility and the grounds. Low, high and in-between, they strode wordlessly in rubber boots, waving scientific instruments, recording readouts, monitoring soil probes, bagging spoonfuls of dirt, taking vials of water from the river. They moved systematically from basement to top floor, from shadow to sunlight, from employees to Varkas himself, pens at the ready, stickers at the ready, boxes at the ready. Varkas saw mice. Scurrying. Sniffing. Sampling. Running off with crumbs.

"What did they ask you?" Varkas said to one of his employees. They stood looking through an open loading dock door as the white vans exited the property.

"Said I weren't to say. Said it was a federal offense to."

"What did they ask you?" Varkas asked again, this time without casualness.

"Asked mostly about how we clean the treatment room. How we hose down them floors using the sludge trough."

Varkas's eyes widened. "You showed him the sludge trough?"

"The lady. She showed me it. Asked what it were."

"What did you tell her?"

"I said it's the sludge trough."

Varkas looked at the employee. The man had a head like a cinderblock and was without guile. "Then what?"

Varkas's man continued, his voice tightening. "The guy took out a bottle of red dye and poured it on the floor. The lady walked the conduit ditch, down to the river. To the outfall pipe. Then she raised a hand. The man up here put on the water and hosed the floor. Washed that red dye into the trough. He kept that hose on, looking down to the river after that lady. Maybe ten minutes, that lady raised her hand again. Then he shut down the water and rolled up the hose."

Varkas kept looking forward, out beyond the gates to the gravel entrance road. "The dust will settle," he said. "I want you to do as they said. Not a word to anyone."

"Yes sir," the employee said.

Varkas left him standing there and headed for the office of the CFO. They needed to get their lawyer on the phone.

The snow tires hummed on the highway. HomeSky was quieter than usual. A lightness came to Pat's stomach as his truck went over the small bridge spanning the creek that cut through their acreage. Out the side window, the creek, still frozen, was a winding scar in a snow-bound field.

"Seems like forever ago when Joseph found my car stuck out here," Pat said.

HomeSky blinked the creek into focus. "I miss him," she said.

Pat looked at her. HomeSky's hair was long and black and smooth as polished stone. It was again how it had been, with the noble addition of slim bands of streaking gray. Wisdom's legacy.

"Me too." He smiled, seeing the faint outline of Joseph's face flash in his mind. "I remember him telling me something you said about that bridge and your creek. How in early winter, before freeze-up, the open water below would cause the bridge to ice over and send many a car into your ditch. Do you remember what you said?"

The truck drove on. "The creek has a way of sending people to us," HomeSky said.

"Yeah. Wow. Funny how stuff like that just comes back."

HomeSky smiled thinly. "Maybe Joseph is among us." Then her smile grew as she looked at Pat.

It had been two weeks since Varkas had returned to the farm to ask HomeSky if she'd made a decision on his offer to buy the property. She had. And it was an answer he didn't care for.

HomeSky was firm. The land meant more to her than any price could bring. She thanked him for his interest. He responded by saying the farm could foreclose, that many neighbors were on the brink, just one bad harvest away from debt that could cascade to forfeiture.

HomeSky said their place lived on the edge, always had. Life here was like paddling a canoe, she told him. You understood it could capsize at any moment, but that didn't hold you to the shoreline. Varkas increased his offer one more time, but HomeSky simply handed him his left-behind donut tray from weeks earlier and politely mentioned she had work to look after.

"There he is," Pat blurted. He carefully decelerated the truck on the icy highway. "High on the south pasture." He brought the vehicle to a stop on the shoulder.

The wolf stood looking out at the road, perhaps 75 yards off. A magnificent animal. Surely over 175 pounds.

"Ma'iingan," HomeSky said.

Pat asked, "Is he friend or foe?"

"He is our brother."

"What does he want?" Pat asked.

"He wants us to know he's here. Watching."

"How do you know?"

"I feel it. Otherwise he'd stay to the timber."

"I saw him when Varkas first spoke to us about buying the farm."

"I've seen him too." HomeSky looked out at the animal. "Giga-waabamin naagaj," she whispered.

The wolf remained a moment longer. Then turned his head and loped back toward the treeline in the direction of the ridge.

"What did you say to him?" Pat asked.

"See you later," she replied.

HomeSky took Pat's hand. It was cold. She brought it to her cheek. "We'll be okay," she said.

"I know," Pat said. She could see the tired hanging on him.

Still a few miles from town, Pat steered the old truck back onto the highway. He drove in silence before HomeSky spoke again. "How are things at the plant?"

"Tense. Out of sync," Pat said. "The federal guys left yesterday and Varkas has pulled workers off lines and put them on all kinds of various tasks. Anyone left is doing the job of two." Pat shook his head. "Lot of mistakes and shutdowns. That's not how we do things."

"What did the inspectors find?"

Pat shrugged. "Can only guess. Hazards. Code violations. Worker safety issues. Who knows exactly. Varkas pretty much plays by his own rules."

HomeSky's eyes widened. "Are you in danger there?"

"I highly doubt it. But there is concern on the floor. If nothing else, the rumors will have to be addressed. Varkas understands that uncertainty is the enemy of productivity."

"Who cares about productivity if the environment is unsafe!"

"That, HomeSky, is why more women should be running businesses. Productivity is Varkas's obsession." Pat stared through the salt-streaked windshield as the truck drove on. "There's something I hesitate to say, because the rumors are flying." Pat's brow creased. "I need to try to keep the shift well-managed."

"What?" HomeSky asked forcefully.

"Varkas is suddenly very busy installing a bigger cement pad to park his fleet. Most of the trucks park out front. You know where I mean? Inside the gate."

"Uh-huh."

"But now he's building an additional pad alongside the plant for more parking. So yesterday, before the shift ended, I heard that when they broke through the frost line they hit an underground culvert running from the plant all the way to the river."

"He's poisoning our water?" HomeSky hissed.

"Still just a rumor, so please, don't repeat it," Pat said.

"You're not standing up for the man?" HomeSky said.

Pat squeezed the steering wheel. He was short on sleep and patience, so he took a few beats before responding. "It's a rumor. If it is actually there, the regulatory guys likely discovered it."

HomeSky wasn't listening. She said to herself, "He's going to cover up the evidence with the parking strip." Her eyes narrowed. "But a skunk has a long tail."

Pat looked at her. "What ever happened to innocent until proven guilty?"

HomeSky wasn't proud of herself, but she said what was on the tip of her tongue. "That's what white people say when they're guilty."

The tension was escalating but Pat would not engage. The wind blew hard across the hood of the vehicle. An empty logging truck heading away from town passed, rattling the pickup.

"That wasn't fair," HomeSky said. "It was reactionary. And it reduces me to the level of the man I accuse. I'm sorry."

Pat put his hand in hers. "That man signs our paychecks," he said, staring ahead at the thin black road cut out of the dirty white landscape. "Three-quarters of the town smile and look the other way when he walks by. We're all complicit."

"How'd it all get started? Routine inspection?"

"No," Pat said. "It was Sheriff Harris."

"The Sheriff?" HomeSky was surprised. "Did you know anything about it?"

"Not really. Although the other day we were playing cribbage at Lu Ann's and he brought up the workplace accidents and fatalities. Said, in his opinion, they were unusually high since Varkas bought the operation. I remember asking him what he meant, specifically." Pat shook his head as he tried to recall the details of the conversation. "I don't know. Guess he changed the subject. Probably wanted to keep me out of it."

"Can you stay out of it?"

"I hope so. But if there are real safety issues or health issues, I can't. I'd have a moral obligation."

HomeSky nodded.

As their truck came upon the bridge deck that crossed the frozen Rainy River, they both glanced at the jewel of a waterway. They couldn't help but wonder what was covered up beneath those layers of ice and snow.

Varkas stood silently on the second-story observation deck overlooking the plant floor. His CFO knew not to interrupt, just as a priest knows not to disturb someone with a bowed head. Varkas loved to watch the choreography of manufacturing. His dark eyes darted from production line to production line, calculating efficiency and looking for bottlenecks.

In particular, he had been watching Pat. Finally Varkas spoke to the CFO beside him. "The supervisor, Pat. He never stops."

"He's an important asset," the CFO said.

"Think he knows we're up here? That's why he's pushing so hard."

"I would be surprised if that were the case."

Varkas responded. "It's obvious the lines are short. It's costing us production."

The CFO let that fact hang there.

Varkas rationalized. "I needed to pull the guys. We must get the cement down."

The CEO didn't disagree. "You could always authorize some overtime."

"No. Not with all the attention we're getting from the Feds. It could lead to everyone getting paid time-and-a-half. Ridiculous."

Again, the CFO remained silent.

"Do you agree?" Varkas said.

"Might save us money, all added up. Like you said, production is lagging."

"No. They'd just expect it again next time. Overtime pay is feeding your dog from your own plate. One taste and they beg for more."

The lunch buzzer sounded and red caged lights on the walls flashed. In unison, workers on the lines sagged like one large organism. Pat stayed at it, getting the last of the treated plywood from his line stacked onto an end pallet. Then he jumped in an empty fork truck and took the load back to inventory.

Varkas spoke. "What would it cost us to lose him as an employee?"

"Pat?" the CFO said in disbelief. "You mean fire him?"

"Yes."

"Why even consider it? He's your best employee."

"He lives on ground I want. No job means no paycheck. No paycheck, no way to pay the mortgage or a line of credit or hospital bills. No way to buy seed for spring planting." Varkas asked again, "What would it cost us?"

The CFO had a mind for calculations and typically enjoyed such a challenge. He was known to sit in a duck blind and work out how many yards he needed to lead a bluebill accounting for approximate flight speed, shooting distance and the foot-per-second velocity of the shell he'd chambered. "I don't care to guess," he said to Varkas. "Too much, is what it would cost us."

"Why's that?"

Pat came back in with an empty fork truck and made his way over to line six to another full pallet. The CFO said, "He leads by example. The lines work harder for him because he never asks them to do more than he asks of himself."

"Stupid man," Varkas said. "This work is beneath a supervisor."

Just then Radio Voice came out of the breakroom. From Varkas's vantage point on the observation deck, it was hard to discern what, but Radio Voice handed Pat something. Pat patted Radio Voice on the shoulder and then shooed him back to the breakroom.

"Never mind," Varkas said. "I have a better idea."

Pat drove off with the pallet load of chipboard and a half sandwich stuck in his mouth.

HONOR YOUR RESPONSIBILITY

Cory stepped into the shower and cranked the knob toward cold but not all the way. He wasn't mentally ready for full-on cold. Not yet.

In his high school and college hockey days, he prided himself on taking cold showers. After games, his teammates wouldn't shower near him because the splash off his body or the floor was like pinpricks. They swore at him, begged him, bribed him and, finally, steered clear of him. They could make no sense of a cold shower when hot water was there for the asking. Cory told them that was entirely the point. Sometimes you have to learn what only no can teach.

The cold shower water tightened the skin surrounding his scars. Large scars, fresh, begin by feeling like they don't belong to you, like they were pasted on, numbly residing on the surface of your skin. But eventually, you own them. They recede and become as much a part of you—maybe more—than the skin God provided. They mark your life and you learn to live with that.

Cool water poured across Cory's back. After a minute, he stopped fighting it, relaxed, opened his eyes and found his washcloth. "You adjust," he said to himself. He didn't feel his aching hip. His wrist didn't throb. He didn't feel pain. He felt alive.

"Morning," Pat said, just as the toaster popped. Cory walked into the kitchen without aid from the crutches he carried. Pat hot-fingered the toast over to the cutting board. "Can I butter one of these for you?"

That is so Pat, Cory thought, leaning the crutches by the pantry. "Nah. Thanks. You better get those down before Meadow gets in here. There isn't enough buttered toast in the state to keep her at bay."

Pat smiled and took a bite. "You're up early."

"Morning routine," Cory said, matter-of-factly.

"Is it range of motion or strength this morning?" Pat wasted no time with his first piece of toast.

"Strength. Upper body. Lower body this afternoon." There were footsteps above as both men glanced at the ceiling.

"Sounds like Meadow's up," Pat said.

"Toast. A powerful alarm clock," Cory replied.

Turns out, HomeSky was the next to enter the kitchen. She couldn't disguise her surprise at the early morning bustle. Pat milked it. "Well someone sure slept in, huh Cor?"

"No kidding. Granted, we're hard to keep up with. Better she just hit the snooze."

"Snooze!" HomeSky blurted. She looked at the clock on the wall. "It's 6:20."

"No need to berate yourself about it," Pat said.

"6:20 isn't that bad," Cory added.

"For a woman," Pat finished.

HomeSky's eyes widened, but then she realized she was being played. "Aren't you two the cunning foxes." She looked over at the cutting board scattered with toast crumbs and a butter knife. "I see Pat's been cooking breakfast again. Lengthy prep time for the main course. No wonder you're up so early."

"What's wrong with buttered toast? All the food groups."

"I can't have you skinnier than me," HomeSky said. "Let me fry up some ham."

Pat looked at the clock. "I should get in. Trying to catch up a little before the shift starts."

"You need to eat."

Cory laughed.

"That goes for you, too." She gave Cory a stern look. "Your muscles need protein. If Joseph were here you know what he'd do?"

"Eat," Cory said.

"A lot," Pat added.

"He'd shoot you a deer," HomeSky said.

"Probably make me eat the heart." Cory made a face.

"Heart is delicious," she said. "And protein-rich. Maybe you two early risers should get up before sunrise and get yourselves a deer."

"HomeSky," Pat said, "they're out of season."

She looked at him squarely. "This is our land. We honor all its animals. If we were to take a spring buck, the Creator wouldn't mind."

"It's the neighbors I worry about," Pat said.

HomeSky took a leftover ham from the refrigerator. There was less left on the bone than she had remembered. And only a couple eggs. It reminded her of how Joseph would clean out the refrigerator as fast as she could stock it. The memory was a gift.

After breakfast, Cory went to his room to pull on a second sweatshirt. It was a typical mid-March morning outside with a temperature in the twenties.

In the entryway, he pulled on a wool cap, carefully managed his balance as he slid his feet into his loosely laced Sorel boots, found his thin leather work gloves and left for the barn.

It's quite unusual to see a young man come down the stairs of a farmhouse, dressed for the elements, surrounded by squinting white snowpack, carrying a silver air mattress. Cory's balance was still compromised as his hip slowly stabilized and strengthened. And with the melt-and-freeze of March, footing was treacherous.

Cory had bargained with his physical therapist: no crutches outdoors if Cory gave her one more week of carrying the air mattress instead. Should he lose balance, the air mattress would break his fall rather than the fall breaking his wrist, so she told him. Cory felt ridiculous.

The wind pulled at the air mattress. "I should just give it to you," he said as he shuffled toward the barn. He looked across the fields and imagined the wind-propelled air mattress sailing out of sight.

For his upper body exercise, Cory sat on a hay bale in the corner of the barn under a suspended work light. With a large pipe wrench in each gloved hand, he alternated between bicep curls and shoulder presses. Three sets of fifteen each.

His doctor had cautioned him, "Remember, one day equals one week." Meaning for every day spent in a hospital bed it takes a week of rehab to regain that lost strength. For a guy who used to handle fifty-pound dumbbells with ease, to break a sweat swinging pipe wrenches in a cold barn was a none-too-gentle reminder of the road ahead.

Between sets, Cory's hard breathing plumed out of his open mouth and dissipated. He thought *A life is a breath you can see, and then you don't. Dad. Joseph. Shara. Hanna. Gone.*

He observed himself sitting there. Hay bale. Sweatpants. Boots. Sweatshirts. Gloves. Wool cap. Barn. Breaths. The only thing that had remained permanent in Cory's life was his resolve. There had been a few lapses, but his resolve never truly abandoned him.

Hung on a nail near the workbench was a loop of rubber tubing from a bicycle tire. Cory held it across his chest and stretched it as wide open as he could. Again and again, until chest muscles quaked and arms burned. He also did reps with the tubing positioned more like a slingshot, pulling his hands away from each other. And finished by stretching it behind his neck to isolate shoulder and trapezius muscles.

The barn was full of items he'd improvised into workout equipment. Two galvanized buckets, each holding a large rock, were useful for lat rows. An old, iron tractor axle worked as a makeshift bench press bar. Standing pushups were done while leaning against the workbench.

For hand strength, Cory took a page of old newspaper and simply balled it up. For legs and back, he did repetitions deadlifting a ten-pound gear casing, with a goal of moving up to a 50-pound hay bale. And when boredom was setting in, he looped a long, heavy-duty rope around the tractor hitch, stood back with an end in either hand, and shook waves through the rope until he could hardly lift his arms.

Sweat leaked down his face, plopping onto the toe of his rubber boot. A chill charged through him. Wind gathered itself and whistled through the old barnwood. Cory listened to his pounding heart.

On the worktable, an old coffee can held various odds and ends. He reached in for a small pocketknife. Cory couldn't be sure, but his hunch was it belonged to Joseph. He turned it over in his hands before shuffling to the back of the barn where a week ago he had discovered letters carved into a board. JGTB. Each letter, perhaps an inch tall, was darkened and aged. Next to them, 1973.

"Joseph Good Thunder Blackholm," Cory said aloud to the quiet barn. "Boozhoo." He touched the markings, which stood about shoulder-high. "1973 was the year our fathers died. Did you carve this in the carefree days of summer? Before your dad's death? Before we met? Or after? In the cold fall? When you had to come out here and put a blade on that tractor so you could break the frostline for your father's grave?"

His finger traced across the texture of the carving. "Miss you." His eyes closed. His fingertip rode into each depression, almost imperceptible, the shallow ridges announcing each new letter and then the numbers.

Cory opened the pocketknife and pushed the sharp steel tip into the wood. The H and Y of his carving were finished yesterday. Just the small jutting leg of the R was left to be scratched in. Honor your responsibility.

He worked stooped. His carving would be no higher nor lower than the one Joseph had left so many years ago. The carvings would remain side by side, sheltered inside this humble cathedral for as long as the barn stood. When he finished, he tacked three of his students' letters and a picture of Hanna, Singer and himself to the barnwood just above.

The Dream Spirit had told him: honor your responsibility. It was contrary to Cory's nature to attribute significance to the sleep-induced tumblings of the mind—but the words so resonated. He was thankful for them. This land was the nexus of generations of great lives. Cory would rise to the sun and try to embody this message.

The barn door cracked open causing Cory to flinch. Light flooded in as he slowly made his way from the shadows. Meadow took a hesitant step inside with Billy Little Tree swaddled to her chest, a blanket over her shoulders. She was holding a bowl.

"Sorry to interrupt," Meadow said.

Cory looked at her in the flood of sunlight with her child. The low morning sun bounced off the incandescent snow leaving her in sharp silhouette. She looked strong and capable in the doorway light. At just 19, she had come so far in one year. That gave him faith in his journey ahead.

"Welcome to the gym," Cory said. "Considering a membership?"

Meadow looked around. "I don't see a pool. I'm a swimmer."

Cory smiled. "Come on in. That wind won't quit."

Meadow approached. She wore moccasins and only a blanket wrapped over her shoulders to keep her sleeping child warm.

Cory spoke quietly. "Not really dressed for the weather. Or a swim."

Meadow looked down at Billy's beautiful round face. "I guess that depends. At the Rez, when I was in high school, we got an indoor swimming pool . . . an addition to the community center. Token federal grant money to show how generous and caring the white government is. Anyway, our school formed a swim team." Meadow thought for a moment. "My freshman year." The memory left a hint of a smile.

"Practice began in October and we swam straight through March, till about this time. A lot of days, when I walked home from swimming, my hair would freeze. I'll never forget that feeling, like spiky nails on my head. I'd have my swimming hoodie. Moccasins like these. Walk home. Became immune to cold. Just like I became immune to all the shit surrounding me. Cold isn't all bad for a person. I don't want Billy to not know cold."

Cory nodded. "I get that. I used to skate for hours outdoors in the winter. Get up early before anyone was on the ice. That was good. Haven't thought about that for a while."

They looked at one another. The bowl in Meadow's hand steamed. "Speaking of cold," she said. "I made some oatmeal that's not getting any hotter. Thought you might like some."

Cory took it. The spoon held fast in the bowl. "Seems . . . substantial."

"I add milk and peanut butter, not just water. I hate swishy oatmeal."

Cory tried a spoonful. "Hmm. Not bad."

"You eat that every morning, you'll gain your weight back. That's power food."

Cory had another bite. "Honey in there?" he said with a hot mouthful.

"Oh yeah. Should be almonds, too. But I ate them all. Sorry."

Cory looked at her. "Okay," he said. "Thanks." Meadow got the translation. He was saying, *you can go now.*

She turned to leave.

"Were you a good swimmer?" Cory asked. "In high school."

Meadow turned back. "I won some races."

"Big ones?" he asked.

"I won some state races."

"A jock," Cory teased. Then he took up his bowl and shrugged. "All right, coach. Whatever you say." He had another heaping mouthful.

"You're doing the right thing," she said quickly, as though those words wouldn't get said if she didn't squeeze them in fast. "In my opinion."

"How's that?" Cory said.

"Fighting for Singer. For custody."

Cory nodded. "Thanks."

"Our situations, they're a lot the same." Meadow didn't know if she overreached, so she hedged. "Again, just an opinion."

Cory looked at the young mother. He began to see her differently. With a child slung to her chest, a blanket across her shoulders, her black hair framing a broad face that he would have called plain, but now would describe as honest. "I respect your opinion. You know what to fight for." Cory nodded at Billy.

"Took me a while."

They enjoyed the strength of the other's company for a few breaths.
"Well, I should get back at it," Cory said.
"Yep. I guess Billy got his dose of cold for the morning."
"Thanks for the oatmeal."
"Yeah. No problem."
And they each moved in opposite directions in the barn.

SINGER

March, in Middleton, is a misnamed month.

March crawls. It takes two steps forward and three steps back. It stands frozen. It does everything but march.

But after three gray days, the sun pushed out of the heavy cotton. MB had her fingers crossed. It was setting up to be a Saturday where, by late morning, she and Singer could get outside and walk to the library.

MB was happy—no, proud—to wake up on a Saturday, off from work, and not feel the lethargic press of too many drinks and etcetera from the night before. She wasn't due back to the ER until Monday afternoon. Freedom!

She slipped out of bed early and when a groggy Chevy reached for her he got an abandoned pillow instead. She was already on her way down the hall to check on Singer.

He'd had only one episode of sleepwalking in the past month. Perhaps, like the pediatrician had said, he was going to outgrow it. Or maybe he was settling in. Or both, MB wished to herself.

Singer slept on his back on his futon bed. One hand was beneath the covers, which folded across his chest, the other was straight up, over his head, like he had the answer to a question. MB was so grateful that school was going well. Singer made fast friends and was a teachers' favorite. How did this gift come to her? Why?

As she made her way down the cold hardwood floor toward the bathroom, it was as if she heard a voice. She stopped dead. But it wasn't a voice, it was a thought. A thought she hadn't had in years. *Go for a run.*

MB tried to be quiet, but finding running shoes buried in the back of her closet finally got Chevy up on one elbow in bed.

"What in hell you doing?" He had excellent bedhead going.

"Looking for my running shoes. What size are you?"

"Huh?"

"What size are your running shoes?"

"Ten."

"Close enough. I'll wear two pairs of socks."

"You hate running." Now Chevy was sitting up. "What time is it?"

"I dunno. 6:30."

"I thought the running Nazi ruined you on the sport for life."

"Go back to sleep. You're dreaming."

Chevy patted the bed. "If you get back in here I'll give you the workout you're looking for."

"Now you're really dreaming."

The run, in MB's judgment, was somewhere between pathetic and laughable. She made it a mile out and alternated walking and jogging back. But after a hot shower, she stood in the kitchen, holding a green mixing bowl, taking a whisk through the pancake batter, feeling good.

She set the bowl down on the brink of tears. *Has it been that long?* She closed her eyes. *It's not like I'm some royal fuck-up. Am I?* She quieted her breathing. MB spent a lot of time disappointed in herself.

"Can you make puzzle pancakes?" Singer wanted to know. MB had gone upstairs to wake Singer for breakfast. His face was flushed and his eyes shone with an equal share of joy and mischief.

MB leaned in. His warm bed smelled delightfully of butterscotch and Ivory soap. "What are those?"

"You've never heard of puzzle pancakes?" He was astonished.

MB shrugged. "Maybe you can teach me."

"For sure!" Singer's voice rang out. "Can we make them for Chevy, too?"

MB whispered. "Well, if you can jump on him hard enough to wake him up we sure can."

Singer eyes widened as he nodded. They had a deal.

Chevy whistled off to work after breakfast feeling quite the family man. He'd been fed Saturday pancakes, freshly made by a woman he loved. And the boy was starting to grow on him, too. They needed to get out more. *I'll get him some hockey skates. He could spend the summer walking around the back yard in skate guards to strengthen his ankles.*

At his desk, Chevy fired up his computer. He clicked open the file that held the fraudulent accounts. A satisfied smile filled Chevy's face as his hands locked behind his head. All was going according to plan. His computer showed five million dollars there, in the accounts under Chevy's management. But actually, the money had been quietly transferred to a London bank, rendering it essentially invisible, and invested in the U.S. stock market, which was on a bullish tear.

In his own way, Chevy was more bullish by the day, too. He was good at business banking. He had the touch. Charming. Easy to talk to. Plus a sprinkle of pixie dust of local fame. His first quarter numbers were the best in the department.

The $5,000 raise he received—something that would have induced somersaults the year before—felt grossly inadequate. He did, however, put on a big banker's grin when, to announce it, Boss Allen treated him to lunch at Perkins.

Five million bucks, Chevy said to himself, looking at the screen. *Plus, the way the market is rolling, another 1.5 to 1.7 mil in gains. Let's call it 6.6. Nice round 6.6, in my hands, to transfer back to the outstretched arms of the fund manager. Really? Not a chance in fuc—*

"Hey there," Boss Allen said.

Chevy nearly launched out of his chair.

Boss Allen stood in his doorway. "Shoot. Didn't mean to sneak up."

"Holy shit!" Chevy said, his arms rigid in front of him. "You scared the living crap out of me."

"Didn't mean to," Boss Allen said, like that might make a difference.

"I thought I was alone in here." Chevy exhaled.

"I just rolled in. What are you doing?"

"Nothing," Chevy said quickly.

Boss Allen furrowed his brow.

"Nothing . . . exciting. Just squaring up the accounts for our end-of-quarter meeting. What's the fourth rule on The Winner's List?"

Boss Allen beamed. "Get ahead. Stay ahead."

"Get ahead. Stay ahead," Chevy parroted while he quickly closed out the file on his screen.

"By the way," Boss Allen said, sternly folding his arms in a manner that made Chevy wonder if his boss might suspect what he was doing after all. "What's with that sticker on your car?"

Chevy was at a loss. "What sticker?"

"What sticker? You very well know what sticker."

Chevy racked his brain. *What could he be so upset about?*

"The sticker in the back window of your car. You know, that I saw when I parked next to you."

The light bulb popped on. "Oh, the country club sticker."

Boss Allen's crossed arms tightened further.

"I was going to tell you about that," Chevy said sheepishly.

Boss Allen's blank stare continued to shout at Chevy.

"Um. I'm in."

Boss Allen's rubbery mouth dropped open. "In?"

Chevy nodded.

"You're in?"

"Yep." Chevy tried not to sound very excited.

Boss Allen's words were staccato. "You're in . . . the Maple Bluff . . . Country Club. The one . . . I've been trying . . . for years . . . to get . . . INTO!" A sheen of perspiration rose on his ample forehead.

"Weirdest thing," Chevy said, forcing a laugh.

Boss Allen's eyes got beadier.

"My girlfriend slash fiancée is friends with a lawyer who's married to a lawyer who I now play racquetball with who got me in." Chevy held his hands up, innocently.

Boss Allen's eyes bounced around as he tracked the trail of the relationship in his head. "How?"

"How what?"

"Did he get you in," Boss Allen snapped.

"This lawyer husband guy, he sits on the admissions committee."

Slowly, the ice melted and Boss Allen was grinning awkwardly at Chevy. "You've got the keys to the castle."

"Not really." Chevy backpedalled. "I just know a guy."

"You just know a guy who unlocks doors. You have to get me in." Boss Allen unfolded his arms and opened them toward Chevy. "Right?"

"I could talk to him," Chevy said halfheartedly.

"Could?"

"I will talk to him."

Boss Allen took a few clumsy, lunging steps toward Chevy, unsure of the best expression of his exuberance and gratitude. He passed a little gas.

Singer's mittened hand was holding MB's. He looked up at her. "How many steps do you think it is to the library?"

"That's a tough question." MB pondered dramatically. "Hmm. I'd say more than 50 and fewer than 50 million."

Singer liked that answer. He had another question. "If the sun is so hot, how come it's cold now?" The morning sunlight played on his face as he waited for his answer. MB stopped and got down on one knee and looked at him closely. "Is it too cold for us to walk? We can turn back."

"No way!" Singer said. "It's great for walking. Just not for snowballs." There was no doubt in his eyes.

"Well," MB said, still on a knee, "I'm no sun expert, but I think it's because the sun is farther away from us now than in the summer."

"Doesn't look any farther." Singer squinted at the sky.

"Some things are so big, even though they're farther away, you can't see the difference. You can only feel it."

Singer looked at MB. "You mean like Cory?"

That was a paralyzing sentence for MB. "Huh?"

Singer looked at her closely. "Cory is farther away now and it feels different but I know it's the same Cory."

"Where do you think Cory is now?"

Singer said, "He's hurt. Like you told me."

Part of MB wanted to pull Singer close and tell him that Cory didn't even bother to write return letters. How hard could it be to check in with this wonderful little boy who had lost so much?

Singer saw the crease in MB's brow. "Don't worry," he said. "He's getting better."

MB asked him how he knew this.

"I can feel it," he smiled. "Just like the sun."

MB smiled and walked and joked the rest of the way to the library, but she was numb. Cory was like a cold shadow that would move in and out of the space between her and Singer. One moment she wanted to fight. The next, run.

They checked out a few books. Played checkers on a rug-size game board set up on the floor of the reading room. And sat together as she read him the newest Berenstain Bears tale. But it wasn't until they got to the playground to meet with Jenni and her twins that her emotions began to surface.

She was finding happiness and purpose in her role as temp mom. Not only had she noticed a side of herself that she liked, she felt she was getting the hang of it too. Then the Cory thing descends, imploding her confidence. Should she allow herself to get close to Singer? To really care? To . . . she let the thought crystallize: *To love him?*

"You seem tired," Jenni said as they watched the kids attack the rope ladder that took them up past the sidewinder slide to the playground tower house. "Tough week?"

MB said she was fine.

"Really?" Jenni asked. She lifted her sunglasses, letting them rest on the top of her head so she could see MB better.

MB turned to face her and it was obvious she wasn't fine. Her chin quivered. "I don't know how much more of this I can do."

Jenni reached out to take her hand. "What is it?" She looked into MB's eyes for answers, but found tears.

MB wiped her face and checked on Singer. He and the girls had made it to the tower deck. The slide awaited. "Just when I feel like Singer and I are forming a real bond, Cory's name comes up."

"Tell me what happened."

MB threw a hand in the air. "I ..." Words ran into each other and never got out. "Hell. One minute we're taking our walk to the library and the next he's saying he knows Cory is getting better. I see the love in his eyes when he talks about him."

Jenni exhaled. "It's tough. You're in a really hard place. But think of all you're doing for this child. He is motherless. You're stepping in. It might be for months. It might be forever. And the fact that it hurts means he's important to you. And that, no matter what happens, is good—it's your goodness coming through."

"I'm not sure being jealous of Cory is goodness."

Jenni looked at her friend. "All I'm saying is it's complicated and uncertain. Our emotional self doesn't like uncertainty. It throws us."

"Which gets me back to my first thought. How much more of this I can do, I don't know."

Jenni nodded. "You're a tough girl. I have no doubts."

That broke the tension. "You are persuasive, counselor."

Jenni reached into her jacket pocket for the business card of a family law attorney from her firm. "Here's Michael Cadder's card. He's very good. Thorough. When you show up in family court with him the judge knows you mean business."

MB looked at the card with its embossed gold logo and impressive cursive typography. "I don't think I can afford him." MB pursed her lips.

"He'll represent you as a favor to me."

"That's very generous of you both."

"It's rewarding to help nice people."

MB looked at Jenni. "But what if I'm, if we, aren't the right parents? What if—"

"I must object," Jenni said with a firm smile. "What's in Singer's best interest is for an unbiased judge to decide."

MB looked at Singer climbing the rope ladder, the twins on his heels. He appeared happy.

She thought, *Then why do I need a lawyer?*

EVEN THE SCORE

For the last few weeks, Kitty and her bridge club friends had spent Tuesday and Thursday evenings door knocking. Most of the homeowners on Baudette's busier streets were willing to put a Re-Elect Sheriff Harris sign in their yard. Kitty had ordered 100 placards and by last count, only 22 remained in her garage. After the signs were placed, there would be a postcard drop. And she was putting the final touches on the Sheriff's "I look out for Baudette" radio script, which they would record at the local 100-watt station next week.

Sheriff Harris would rather scrub toilets than campaign for his job every four years. The older he got, the less stomach he had for public tap dancing. "People know me," he'd grumble to Kitty. "Why do I have to toot my own horn?"

Kitty would give his large hand a squeeze. "People have short memories. And this town needs you."

Sheriff Harris was driving north of town thinking about his re-election when something about the car that had just turned onto the road in front of him grabbed his attention. The Sheriff shortened the distance between himself and the vehicle. Leaning forward, squinting through darkness, he could see the driver was alone. Then, sure enough, the tailfins of the Cadillac Coupe DeVille swerved. The Sheriff checked his watch. 9:22.

The vehicle swerved again, this time over the centerline. The Sheriff lit up the cherries and accelerated. He saw the brake lights of the Cadillac flash on, then go dark again. "Don't get any wise ideas about running," the Sheriff said in a low growl that got Private up and alert in the back seat. The Cadillac finally slowed and pulled over. They were about a half-mile out of town, which meant they were about a half-mile away from any road lighting.

The Sheriff always wore a holster belt, but only carried his pistol during night patrols. His hand went down and unsnapped the pistol strap. As he pulled to a stop, he illuminated the Cadillac's license plate with his mounted spotlight. He called in the plate number. Before stepping out, he redirected the beam to the vehicle's driver-side door.

"You stay," the Sheriff commanded Private as he lowered the rear window of the cruiser. "But be ready." The tone of his voice brought the hair on the Labrador's neck upright.

Before taking a forward step, the Sheriff scanned the Cadillac. He pulled his flashlight out of his holster belt. Hell if that car didn't look familiar: vintage old Coupe DeVille with fins high as track hurdles. *Who? Who? Who?* He searched his memory.

Just then the front passenger door opened and someone or something slid out of the car and crawled toward the ditch, trying to flatten itself to the dark ground.

"Hey!" the Sheriff yelled. He snapped on his flashlight. Nothing. *Damn batteries!* The Sheriff slapped the flashlight against his palm. It came on. "Hey! You!" He directed the flashlight toward the crawling shape, but the moment the flashlight was leveled it went off again. "Shitfire," the Sheriff cussed, now advancing.

I know this car. '59 DeVille. Could it be? "Benjamin Goode!" The Sheriff shouted. "Don't make me send out the dog for you!" He shook the flashlight. This time it went on and stayed on when he leveled it at the ditch. The beam found a shape on all fours trying to hide behind a patch of dead ditch grass insufficient to conceal a raccoon.

The Sheriff hollered after him. "Have you been drinking?" The man claimed to be sober as a stick. "We'll see about that. Get up from there and show me your hands." The man obliged. His hands, typically well manicured and known for working the keys of a typewriter, were cold and filthy.

It quickly became a Thursday that Benjamin Goode wished he could wad up and chuck in the wastebasket like a lousy attempt at a editorial piece. As the editor in chief of the *Baudette Region*, he had finished putting the weekly edition to bed for next Wednesday's delivery. As was tradition, he and a few of the staff headed up to the Mutineer's Jug to toast the occasion. Turned out, with his wife on a weeklong quilting cruise with her sister from Duluth, Mr. Goode stayed for a few too many. Dinner consisted of bar popcorn and martini olives. Next thing he knew, he was driving out to the highway truck stop for a pack of cigarettes when he crossed paths with the wrong man.

If the Sheriff had booked every drunk driver he'd pulled over through the years, he'd have significantly fewer friends in town. It wasn't uncommon for him to escort an impaired driver home, leaving him with a stern warning and a promise to make his life miserable should it happen again.

But Benjamin Goode left the Sheriff feeling less merciful. Goode was a self-righteous SOB. His weekly article, called Goode Neighbor, would anoint the actions of citizens he judged exemplary, but just as often, he used the column to publicly pillory those he deemed ne'er-do-wells. His commentary concluded with a prescription of corrective behavior neatly wrapped in his signature ending: That's what a Goode Neighbor would do.

By lunchtime the next day, word of Benjamin Goode's DWI had jumped from the bank to the hardware store to the dentist office to the card and candle shop to the laundromat to the post office to the barbershop to Lu Ann's, where there was no putting it down. The locals were giddy with Goode's heaping helping of comeuppance.

Goode tried to bury the story a week later on page 10A, in the circuit court news, but the letters to the editor came in such volume, a few had to be printed just to drive a stake through the heart of the misadventure. Ben Goode Been Bad was one particularly clever letter that was printed but Goode and Drunk never saw the light of day.

Varkas folded his newspaper so he could get a closer look. He sat wedged behind his desk at the plant skimming local stories. Goode's drunk driving arrest caught his eye. His finger slowly tapped the newsprint. A plan began to form. Perhaps he would have an ally in Goode; both of them had a score to even with Sheriff Harris.

For Varkas, the Sheriff's meddling led to the EPA and OSHA issuing $45,000 in fines as well as mandating a number of costly worker safety improvements over the next three months. Varkas hated that he could be told how to run his business. This was America. Success should be regulated only by an individual's will and ingenuity. The Sheriff would be sorry he stuck his nose in his business. With the election for county sheriff upcoming, maybe something unflattering about the Sheriff could find its way into Goode's newspaper. But first Varkas had to deal with Pat. And the fact that he and HomeSky had said no to his offer to buy their farm. "No" was not a word he took kindly to.

By the time Pat pulled into the plant parking lot, two employees were already waiting for him. Pat didn't like the looks on their faces.

"What's wrong?" he said as his truck window finished opening. It was a cold March morning yet they stood there without coats, blowing into their fists.

"Radio Voice locked himself in the bathroom," the first employee said.

"And he has the keys," the other added.

"Everyone is using the ladies' room for now," the first employee continued.

"Why?" Pat said.

"Because they have to go!" the employee said defensively.

Pat was exasperated. "No. Why has he locked himself in the bathroom?"

The second employee explained. "Because they fired him."

"What are you talking about?" Pat said in stunned disbelief.

Both employees simply shook their heads yes.

As they marched from the iced-over parking lot to the plant entrance, Pat's coworkers told him what they knew, most of it hearsay. Pat heard the low ringing of temper in his ears.

Radio Voice had arrived this morning, as usual, 20 minutes early for his shift. The CFO was waiting for him. Before punching in, Radio Voice went to the breakroom for his customary cup of coffee and a snack from home. This morning, it was a sandwich bag of Fruit Loops, which he offered to share with the CFO when he joined him at the long table.

Radio Voice was sobbing by the time he fully comprehended what the man was there to tell him. Radio Voice's work keys were in their usual place, on a lanyard around his neck where he wouldn't misplace them. He bolted up from the table and ran, keys jangling, sobbing, for the safety of the bathroom. He had cleaned that bathroom for over 20 years and it was where Pat found him.

"Hey buddy, it's me," Pat said, knocking gently on the men's room door. "Can you hear me? Radio Voice, it's Pat. Let me in."

"No," he said.

"Why not?" Pat asked. A small crowd had gathered.

"Because you want me to leave and never come back."

"That's not what I want. Let's talk about it. Maybe we can make another plan."

There was a long pause. "Really?" Radio Voice said.

"Yes. Really." Pat reassured him. "Let me in so we can make another plan."

"Okay. Just you. Not that guy who told me I'm fired."

"Just me," Pat said.

Pat heard the key go in the door from the other side and the lock click open. Varkas stood, unnoticed, on the observation deck above, with a newspaper folded under his arm. He checked his watch. Two minutes to eight. "The shift better run on time," he told himself.

Varkas watched as Pat dispersed the crowd, pointing to a few men and women, giving them sharp instructions. Then Pat disappeared into the bathroom. Varkas shook his head. "That's what you get for hiring a mongoloid."

Inside the bathroom, Radio Voice sat on the floor with his back against the tiled wall. Pat got some tissue from a roll of toilet paper and sat down next to him. "You better blow your nose, bud."

Radio Voice did so, and used his uniform shirtsleeve to dry his eyes.

"Tough day you're having." Pat reached over and held Radio Voice's large hand. "Your hand is cold," he said rubbing it. "Does that feel better?" Radio Voice nodded. Pat asked, "Can you tell me what the man said to you?"

"Don't want to," Radio Voice said.

"I know. But it will help us make a plan if you tell me. Plus talking about things always makes them feel better. Remember?"

Radio Voice nodded.

"Can you tell me, please?"

"He said I was fired because I work too slow." Radio Voice's eyes began to water again.

"What else?"

"I can't remember." Radio Voice avoided looking Pat in the eye.

"Try to remember," Pat said gently.

"He asked if I ever take breaks when I'm not supposed to or if I ever took anything from the plant that didn't belong to me."

"What did you say to that?"

Radio Voice looked down at the tile floor.

"You can tell me."

"I told him I took a snow globe."

"When?"

"At Christmas time. It was so pretty."

"How long ago?"

Radio Voice thought about it. "Dunno."

"A long time ago or a short time ago?"

"Long time."

Pat looked at Radio Voice. "I don't want you to feel bad about that. It was a mistake from way in the past. We'll buy one for you and bring the other one back. What do you say to that?" Pat smiled.

"I'll get a new one?" Radio Voice's posture lifted.

"Yep. Brand new."

"Okay! And they'll give me my job back." His face brightened.

"I'll need to talk to Mr. Varkas about that. Today I think you should go home and take the day off, just like it was Saturday or Sunday."

Radio Voice shook his head. "But I want to work."

"I know. Let me see what I can do."

"You'll talk to Mr. Varkas. Tell him I promise to bring back the snow globe."

Pat said he would do just that. "You ready to go?" Pat got up from the floor.

"I have to clean the bathroom first."

"Not today, buddy," Pat said as Radio Voice stood.

"Over there," Radio Voice pointed to the last stall. "I felt sick when that man told me I was fired."

Next to the stall, Radio Voice had thrown up his Fruit Loops.

Pat planned to check on the shift before seeing Varkas and then the absurdity of that idea slapped him across the face. *Why should I care about the shift?* He tried to calm himself as he went upstairs, but the closer he got to Varkas's office the angrier he became.

"Been expecting you," Varkas said as Pat stood in his doorway. "C'mon in and sit down."

Pat walked in, remaining on his feet. "Can you tell me why you let Radio Voice go?"

"I don't see how the matter pertains to you."

Pat's face hardened. "He's my co-worker. He's my friend. And he's a human being. It pertains to me."

Varkas shrugged. "Are you aware that this employee stole from me?"

Pat's mouth dropped open. "You gotta to be kidding. He took a Christmas decoration. It's a safe bet it wasn't even during your time as owner."

"Nonetheless, he stole from this company. I won't tolerate thieves working for me."

Pat's temper thrummed in his ears. "Do you have any idea what this job means to him? He's proud of what he does. He's punctual—"

Varkas pushed up from his desk. "Do not come into my office and assume to lecture me!" Then, as quickly as words roared out of his mouth, Varkas composed himself. "How about a favor for a favor."

Pat turned his head, as if he didn't hear him correctly. "A what?"

Varkas continued. "I will do you the favor of hiring your friend back if you do a favor for me."

"Sure. What is it?"

"Get HomeSky to sell me her farm."

Pat blinked. His mind raced. "Her farm? Is that what this is about? You can't be serious."

"I'm dead serious," Varkas said. "I offered more than a fair price."

Pat shook his head as he gained clarity about what he was dealing with. "Mr. Varkas, HomeSky's home and land are not for sale. She made that clear. She thanked you for the offer. Why do you persist?"

"This county was built by the persistent."

"Mr. Varkas, what if I told you I'd quit if you don't hire Radio Voice back?"

"You are a valuable employee. Unlike your friend, you do the work of two, so for the sake of business, I hope you continue your employment here."

"But what if I told you I quit?"

Varkas gave Pat a condescending scowl. "You can't quit. You have a farm that's takes more than it provides. You have a young woman and her infant depending on your income. Not to mention a man convalescing under your roof, bill-strapped I'd wager."

Pat grit his teeth. "Shameful."

Varkas sat down, seeing he'd reached checkmate. "We've wasted enough valuable time this morning for which I expect you to work through the ten o'clock break. Think about my offer. But not for too long. Remember, you have a household counting on you." With that, Varkas busied himself with paperwork.

Pat found Radio Voice in the breakroom eating his lunch. "Hey bud. How ya doing?"

"Renee said I should wait for you here and it was okay to eat my lunch. Did you make a new plan?"

Pat sat next to his friend. "No, not yet. But I'm working on it. I think you should go home for now. Here, let's save half of your sandwich." Pat helped Radio Voice reseal what was left of his sandwich in plastic wrap. "I'll come see you on my lunch break and we'll eat together, like always."

Radio Voice's eyes pleaded. "But I want to stay and work."

"I know. I just need more time to make a plan with Mr. Varkas."

"Why is he mad at me? Because I took the snow globe?"

"Radio Voice," Pat said, "can I tell you something, just between you and me?"

"You mean like a secret?" Radio Voice raised his eyebrows.

"Well, it's more like something that I don't like saying but it may help you understand what's happening if I say it."

"Okay," Radio Voice said.

"I don't think Mr. Varkas is a nice man. Sometimes people who are not nice do things that don't ever make sense."

Radio Voice thought for a moment. "They say and do mean things," Radio Voice said, nodding, in sync with Pat.

"Yes they do," Pat said, giving Radio Voice a small smile.

Radio Voice smiled back, thinking of something. "I'd rather be me than not be nice." His shoulders lifted.

"I don't think it can be put any better than that."

AN IDEA

Through the first half of the morning, Pat's jaw was set, mouth clamped, eyes locked. He was on task. He made no contact with coworkers. The muscles in his neck and back drew ever tighter, like someone was slowly turning a ratchet wheel.

Finally, he pulled his fork truck behind a towering rack of chipboard and let his head hang. *Dearest Father, Creator and Savior. Help me move beyond this. Help me let go of what's beneath me and reach for what's above me. I open myself. Strengthen me. Be here with me.*

When Pat left the plant for lunch he had no new plan to bring to Radio Voice, but he did have hope in his sails. That was a necessary start. First, he'd go see HomeSky at Bonaducci's Grocery to let her know what was happening. He hoped she wouldn't take news of Radio Voice's firing too hard or too personally. He jumped in the truck, wondering if seeing her was the right stop to make along the way. Then he was bolstered. HomeSky had weathered far worse than this. He needed her support.

When he found her in aisle three, she was putting price stickers on cans of baked beans. "Hi," he said, failing in his attempt to not startle her. Her sticker gun almost left her hand.

"Crap," she uttered, fumbling a can to the floor. She looked at Pat like she was going to let him have it.

"Sorry," he said. "I was going a little too fast I guess."

HomeSky picked up the dented can of beans and put a price sticker on it. "This one is for you."

"Haven't had my lunch yet." He smiled.

The word lunch prompted her. "What time is it? And what are you doing here?"

Pat looked at her intently. "Where's a good place to talk for five minutes?"

"We can talk here. I may get called up front to ring, but it's pretty quiet right now."

Pad nodded. "I have some not great news." He saw HomeSky brace. "But solvable. I think."

HomeSky nodded that she was ready to hear it.

"Varkas fired Radio Voice this morning."

HomeSky's face went from confusion to developing a stern frown. "What? Why!"

Pat blew out, exhaling. "The why, I'm afraid, is connected to us. He's punishing us through Radio Voice for not selling him the farm."

HomeSky shook her head, speechless.

"He said Radio Voice works too slow. And got him to admit to stealing a Christmas decoration. So he's officially fired for theft and inefficiency." Pat looked down at his can of beans as the local radio station quietly piped over the PA system. "But then Varkas tells me, let's make a deal. I get you to sell him the farm and he gives Radio Voice his job back."

"That's ridiculous." HomeSky said. Then her face transformed. "That's not what you're here for, to get me to sell."

Pat took a step forward. "No, no, absolutely I'm not. I'm here because I'm stuck and I wanted you to know what's going on."

"He's serious, isn't he?" HomeSky said. "He'd coerce us any way he can."

"Yes."

"He's a scourge. I felt it when I met him."

"Radio Voice needs that job. Not just the money, but the purpose and community—the vitality—that comes with it."

HomeSky thought as Pat continued.

"He's good at it, too," he said. "A lot of people see a janitor job as beneath them. Radio Voice loves to make things clean. He talks about sparkle and he sparkles, too." Pat dropped his head, starting to feel sadness and anger rebounding. "He loved to show me how good things look and smell when they are clean. It's something he can control. It was dirty. He makes it gleam. There's a lot of accomplishment in that if you let there be."

HomeSky was listening, but she wasn't. Her mind soared above the spoken words and then, she had an idea. "Give me three minutes." Now the sparkle was in her eyes.

Pat straightened. "Ah, okay. I thought I'd surprise Radio Voice with some licorice for lunch. What aisle?" But HomeSky had already turned and was out of earshot. "All right then," Pat said to himself. "I'll find my own licorice. Go nicely with my beans."

Turns out, HomeSky's hunch was correct. Her boss, Mr. Bonaducci, had a miserable time getting employees to clean the restrooms. And the breakroom was atrocious. For $20 per day, he would gladly pay Radio Voice to do that work. Plus he'd sell him cleaning supplies for 50% off retail. Mr. Bonaducci liked Radio Voice. More so, he was angry to hear that he was fired after 20 years of loyal service. Mr. Bonaducci was big on loyalty.

HomeSky told Pat that if they took a few days to visit neighboring businesses, they very likely could string together quite a run of clients for Radio Voice to serve.

Pat got excited about the notion. They would divide and conquer. He would take Lu Ann's side of Main and talk to the Sheriff, who held sway over the courthouse. HomeSky would take the bank side, including the hardware store, tanning salon and movie theatre. Why couldn't Radio Voice go into business for himself? Maybe the worst day in Radio Voice's life could turn out to be quite the new opportunity.

Pat arrived at Radio Voice's small apartment building feeling a million pounds lighter. The wind was in his face and the sun wasn't strong enough to dent the snow banks, but he hardly noticed. He had made two quick stopovers after leaving the grocery store: Lu Ann's and Mark's Convenience Mart. Both owners were appalled by Radio Voice's firing and said they'd be happy to be put on his janitorial schedule.

Radio Voice answered the knock on his apartment door quite

disheveled, his eyes red-rimmed. He blew into a Kleenex with one hand and with the other, gave Pat the snow globe, handling it as though it were radioactive. It featured one large snowmen and several smaller ones dancing in a circle, holding hands.

"Here," he said. Pat was just in time. The hours Radio Voice spent alone in his apartment were not good. He had ceaselessly paced the small confines of his unit, loudly muttering at the snow globe, until the tenant from below him came up, banged on the door and told him to park it and shut the fuck up.

Pat accepted the globe. "I'll leave it out in the hallway." Radio Voice was relieved.

Pat carried a small bag of groceries. Putting it down on the kitchen table caught Radio Voice's interest, but atypically, he didn't ask about it.

"Are you wondering what I've brought?"

Radio Voice nodded.

Unloading the contents, Pat provided play-by-play. "Captain Crunch, apples, buns, salami, licorice, beans, my lunch bag and a notebook." Pat and Radio Voice looked at the goods on the table. "Notice anything different from all the rest?" Pat asked.

Radio Voice studied the contents.

"Notebook?"

"Very perceptive. Whose notebook do you think it is?"

Radio Voice's shoulders shrugged.

"Yours. D'you know why?"

Radio Voice shook his head.

"Because you and I are going to plan the work you're going to do for your new job right in here." He tapped the red spiral-bound notebook against the palm of his hand.

Radio Voice brightened. "New job? Really?"

"Cross my heart," Pat said, making the gesture. "HomeSky had an idea. A great, great idea. But I don't think I can talk about it until I have a piece of that licorice."

SHERIFF

Damn, how he looked forward to five o'clock on Fridays. Wrapping up the workweek. Getting the weekend shifts scheduled and work parsed out. Then, Sheriff Harris and Private would walk down the empty hallways of the courthouse, the jangle of Private's collar mingling with the Sheriff's footfalls, turning out lights as they went.

"We'll sneak out a shade early today, huh boy," the Sheriff said to Private, holding open the back door of the cruiser. "No harm done." His watch read 4:50. "Hup." Private was in sit, but as soon as he heard the command, he jumped into the back seat and settled in on his blanket. "Atta boy," his master praised.

The Sheriff got behind the wheel, not bothering with his seatbelt. Reaching inside his jacket to his shirt pocket, he fished out a piece of Big Red. "Better unholster a stick of this," he said to Private. "Hopefully Kitty will be over to our place already. Nothing like a Friday kiss to get the weekend started." The Sheriff paused, and wrenched around to look the Lab in the eye. "That's just between us, partner."

Home on a Friday is an awfully welcome place for those in police work. Day in, day out, you "do the job." You can't escape the daily, 360-degree pressure of responsibility. When a couple days off are in front of you, when you get home and take off the uniform, hop in a hot shower, crack that first beer—for thirst—and feel the pressure normalize, it's like a different you coming alive.

Pat always enjoyed teasing the Sheriff about his "cushy" job. Hours of patrolling as paint dries, he would say. Did you arrest a disorderly caramel roll at Lu Ann's? Or put a magazine in an extended chokehold at your desk this afternoon?

The Sheriff didn't mind it like he used to. Pat was kidding, but as they say, behind every joke there's a sliver of sincerity. Many did consider the Sheriff's job easy. They saw what they wanted to see. The Sheriff drinking coffee at the diner. The Sheriff walking a patrol on a nice evening with Private at his heel. The Sheriff in his cruiser tucked off the highway, ready for speeders to race into town.

But they weren't there at a crash scene to see him go through a dead teenager's pockets to ID the victim. Or there at a modest farmhouse where a married couple of 60 years lay together, gagged and shot through the head on their new living room carpet, with entwined hands almost inseparable as their bodies were bagged. Or to listen to a mother wail and fold as you stand in her doorway telling her that her 12-year-old son won't be returning home on his bicycle.

Kitty understood, though. That made her so dear to the Sheriff. She listened. She was a woman of unusual compassion and empathy—yet spirited. She challenged him, but also comforted him. Oftentimes, in that order.

"Oh no you don't." The Sheriff came out of the kitchen, showered, holding a can of Pabst Blue Ribbon. He shook his head at his poor dog, who sat droop-eared in the living room as Kitty worked on him as one might a collapsing tent.

"Just give me a second here." Kitty kept futzing. "Sit up. We thought we'd surprise you, but—" Private stood and tried to shake. "No," she commanded. "Steady . . . there now. Perfect."

The Sheriff winced. "He looks pitiful. Will it even stay on?"

"It sure should. It has two belts."

Kitty had fashioned a makeshift sandwich board using Re-Elect Sheriff Harris posters to hang on either side of Private. "It's for our walks around town. Imagine the awareness it will generate." Kitty clipped the leash on Private's collar ring. "We've been practicing." She addressed Private. "Stay close," she commanded, with a sharp snap of the leash. As she walked, Private walked beside her. She picked up the pace, trotting an oval around the coffee table. Private, all but wrapped in cardboard, stayed with her. "Pretty good, huh?" she asked, in stride.

"Might be. For the guy I'm running against."

Kitty shot him a look. "Don't be a spoilsport." When she stopped, Private did, too. There were treats in Kitty's hand that the dog nuzzled for. "Good work," she said, petting Private.

Varkas's man had been there since noon. Had been there all week. Across the street a few houses down, he was more than happy to earn his hourly factory wage away from the plant, sitting in his truck, munching on a bag of Funyuns while he watched the Sheriff's house. He had only one job: write down what happened and when. Varkas was a stickler for good notes during surveillance.

Varkas had sent him on all kinds of similar jobs over the years. How often does the mayor golf during the workweek? What restaurants are trucking in illegally netted walleye from the Rez for their Friday night fish fry? Which city councilman slips away every Wednesday afternoon to a motel one town over, soon to be joined by his wife's sister? Which construction company is dumping demolition debris out in an abandoned pit lake? Which gas station is charging customers for premium fuel when only regular is delivered? And so on, and so on, and so on.

Varkas called it leverage. Sometimes he used this information to the advantage of his company or himself. But just as often, it served no purpose other than to offer him amusement.

With the Sheriff, though, he was by no means amused. The Sheriff had interfered with Varkas's business. The Sheriff was running for reelection. Therefore, the Sheriff should lose his election. Simple as that.

Maybe the Sheriff wasn't as untouchable as everyone in town thought. Perhaps there was a random impropriety to cloud the race. Varkas would have one of his men follow the Sheriff while another watched his house. Something would surface. Usually did. How hard did the Sheriff work for the salary taxpayers provided? Was this elected officer honest and upstanding? Any indiscretions? As the old Czech saying went, *Every potato has a little dirt to scrub away.*

There wasn't much for Varkas's man to report as he watched the Sheriff's house through the week. That is, until Friday at 12:12 in the afternoon.

A middle-aged woman scooted across the street with a crockpot, black cord swinging in the wind. She set it down on the Sheriff's front stoop, and used a key from her key ring to open his front door. In she went with the cooker.

She promptly left the Sheriff's house, retreated to hers, momentarily, before retracing her steps across the street, this time with a brightly colored overnight bag and a candle. Bad Sheriff, the man uttered to himself, making the necessary notations.

Varkas would be pleased, the man knew. A quick drive to the convenience store to place a phone call, take a piss, and re-stock his food supplies was the next order of business. The man was sure Varkas would want him to spend the night outside the Sheriff's house. More specifically, to see how neighborly the two of them got.

"Anonymous source?" Benjamin Goode said incredulously into the telephone receiver. "Mr. Varkas, excuse me, but everyone at the newspaper, as well as in town, will see such an article as a thinly veiled plot for revenge."

"Mr. Goode, you will have an anonymous letter to show your staff, and any others who question you." Varkas sat in his den, with the phone pinned under his ear as he shelled peanuts.

"My integrity will be suspect."

Varkas dropped an empty shell in a bowl. "Hell, Goode. Your integrity couldn't walk a straight line a week back. The Sheriff made that a matter of public record."

"But—"

Varkas gripped the receiver and straightened in his chair. "Listen to me. The Sheriff thinks he's bigger than this town. He needs to be brought down a peg. I'm going to write the letter, anonymously. It will simply ask, should the chief law enforcement official who is seeking public reelection in a God-fearing town be playing house with a woman out of wedlock? Your Goode Neighbor column has been a forum for addressing the virtues and failings in people for years, has it not?"

"It has," Goode agreed, seeing he was cornered.

"Write it then. Let the public be the judge."

Benjamin Goode listened to the crackle of static over the phone line. "You're sure of this relationship? I mean really, the Sheriff? You have a reliable witness?"

"I'm damn sure."

"Drop off your letter before the start of workday tomorrow. There's a slot in the front door of our office. I'll want someone else to find the letter and leave it for me."

"Consider it done," Varkas said, munching a peanut.

"One other thing," Mr. Goode said.

"What is it," Varkas answered impatiently.

"Don't type your letter. It needs to be handwritten. Journalists type. Citizens scrawl."

Varkas hung up the phone. His bowl of peanuts had been picked through, now filled with empty shells. He walked stiffly to the sliding door that led onto the back deck. He didn't bother closing the door as he made his way out. The night air had an invigorating pinch. Varkas dumped the shells over the railing.

The half-moon illuminated the old windmill standing in a corner of his long, expansive clearing. The galvanized paddles against the star-filled sky looked beautiful in the blue light. Then, out of the forest opposite the windmill, stepped the wolf. The animal moved noiselessly in the crosswind.

Varkas's yard was sizable. He had clearcut this space, eradicated its stumps, leveled its ground, added topsoil, put down seed and grown a manicured yard—to impose his will on the wild forest. Slowly, the wolf made his way across the snow-covered landscape.

There was enough light cast by the half-moon to make out the animal's shape, but little by way of detail. Varkas could not be sure, but it appeared the wolf's head was cocked in his direction as it strode across the openness toward the security of the forest on the other side.

Varkas turned from the rail and moved with equal stealth. When he returned to the rail with his rifle, the wolf had been swallowed by the night.

A CUP OF TEA

Cory had hands and knees on the ground.

It was April and the snow had left the farmyard. He closed his eyes to the uneven solidarity of the earth beneath him. As long as something registered, as long as there was feeling, there was progress. Not long ago, he felt nothing.

He had stumbled, fallen. His morning leg workout involved an exercise he called woodpile. He would remove a single split log from the stack near the farmhouse and walk it nearly the length of the driveway to the side of the barn where he would build a new pile. One by one, fifty logs to the woodpile. He had made a few trips back and forth when his foot slid in the muck. The log flung from his hands as he fell forward. There he was on all fours.

Cold puddle water sopped into the knees of his sweatpants. Mud worked up between his fingers. He felt these things. There was a stab of getting better—an uncomfortable longing for things lost. He was headed in the right direction.

Cory thought about Singer. He could feel the warmth of the boy on his lap as the child steered the tractor to the field. He felt the strap of pain that comes with filling a void with a slender hope. He was healing.

Meadow and HomeSky continued to watch from the kitchen window. They were drying breakfast dishes when Meadow's gasp made HomeSky look up from the sink just in time to see Cory, and the log he had been carrying, silently strike the ground outside. Meadow wanted to run out to help, but HomeSky placed a hand on her shoulder. "Give him a second."

Each second was agonizing. "What's he doing?" Meadow asked. "Shouldn't we help?" Her look pleaded with HomeSky.

"I think he'll be fine," HomeSky said. Inwardly she thought, *Get up. Get up.*

Cory used his fingertip to write three letters in the wet dirt. HYR. Slowly, he stood and wiped his muddy hands on his sweatpants. As he gathered up the fumbled log, he noticed the two women in the kitchen window. He waved, hoping that would ease their concern. Smiling a bit at his misstep, Cory continued to the barn where a woodpile was taking form. *Honor your responsibility.* He put the log in its place, crossways, making a solid foundation for the next and the next and the next.

Meadow looked at Billy Little Tree, who would be five months old in a few weeks. She could hardly believe it. As she strummed and tuned her guitar, Billy's eyes got heavier. Laying swaddled in his crib, he was caressed by music.

Where did the time go?
It was just here
A month goes by
Then a year

My lovely child
Let's slow it down
Let's sing our song
And dance around

Meadow hummed the melody as her fingers walked a simple chord progression. A couple times through and Billy was nearly asleep. She sang in a whisper.

Where did the time go?
It was just here
Let go of yesterday
And hold me dear.

My Little Tree
It won't be long
You'll reach the sky
Your heart is strong

Cory sat in the kitchen cupping hot tea in his hands. He was soaked through with sweat and wet from his fall. "Want some tea?" he asked Meadow as she came in.

She looked at him oddly.

He shrugged his shoulders in his defense. "I'm starting to like tea." She took a step toward the cupboard. "No, I got it," Cory told her.

"Such service," she said.

"Billy asleep?"

"Yeah." Meadow laughed to herself. "He's getting so big. Something new every day." She shook her head, dumbfounded. "I wonder if that keeps up, or it's all just new right now."

Cory poured her a steaming cup. "From what I remember, they continue to astound. Careful. I may have overdone it on the temperature." She took her cup of tea.

Meadow was learning that if you wanted to get Cory talking, you had to take a direct approach. And stick with it.

"How are you doing?" she asked.

"You mean today? Or in general?"

"Start with today."

Cory looked at his clothes. "Wet."

"You're okay?" Meadow hesitated. "From falling."

Cory shook his head. "I was trying to pick up the pace. I accelerated from slug to turtle. Had a spinout."

"What are you doing out there? With the logs?"

Cory sighed. "Good question. Four days a week, I move the woodpile. For my legs and a bit of coordination. By next week, I'll be taking two pieces at a time. The week after, an armful. Trying to build practical strength."

"What's toughest for you now?"

Cory took a sip of tea. "The legs. Zero endurance. No muscle. They're pipe cleaners."

"It was a long recovery," Meadow offered.

"I'm glad to hear you put it in the past tense." They looked at each other. Cory gave her a half-smile. "Hospital beds and wheelchairs," Cory paused for emphasis. "Suck."

Meadow was happy to hear him talking about himself. She remained quiet.

"The court date is only two weeks away. I have to get strong for Singer."

"Have you talked to him?"

Cory grit his teeth. "I asked the social worker, more than once. She advised against it. Said she has seen it before. The child begins to think that talking means things are going to change, and he'll come live with me, right away. Or he'll ask questions that I can't answer. In any case, it's confusing and frustrating, She said with temporary custody, Singer needs life to be stable as can be. All the way through, from the hearing to judgment."

"Are you scared?"

"Shitless."

"We'll all be there," Meadow said. "That will help. When the judge sees the support that Singer will have, he'll have to be impressed."

"Let's hope so," Cory said. He looked down at the table. "They have biology on their side."

"Yeah," Meadow said. "But this home is proof that family goes beyond biology."

Cory thought on that for a moment. "I just might use that with the judge." He smiled at her. "You're right."

Meadow smiled, blushing.

"How about inside?"

Cory didn't understand the question.

Meadow pointed to her chest. "In here. How are you doing?"

Cory exhaled. "You sure you want to go there?"

"Why not."

Cory chewed the inside of his mouth. "I'm pissed. I'm distrusting. But I'm trying to rewire all that, start something positive. The idea of honoring my responsibility, wherever that notion came from, has become my, I don't know . . . life raft? Direction?"

"Does it make you feel better?"

"Hard to say. It diverts my negativity, I guess."

"Can I ask one more question?"

Cory looked at her. "Have you always been so inquisitive?"

"No," she said, equaling his directness.

"All right."

Meadow looked at his bearded face, and the way the curls of his sweat-damped hair had not sprung back from the tight, wool watch cap he'd worn. "Do you pray to get Singer back?"

Cory frowned. "You mean to God?"

"Yeah. Or the Creator or Great Spirit or *Gichi-manidoo* or whatever name you have for Him."

"No."

"Why?"

"I don't believe in prayer," Cory said.

"How come?" Meadow asked.

"Prayer is a farce. Prayer is . . ." Cory thought for a moment, "a distraction."

"How do you mean?"

"Do we really want to talk about this?" Cory rubbed his beard. "Maybe we could discuss tea or something."

"Don't be afraid to talk to me, Cory." Meadow was right there. She wasn't going anywhere.

Cory nodded as if to say okay, you asked for it. "God doesn't hear your prayers. You know who does?"

Meadow said no.

"You hear your prayers. And that makes you feel good. It's selfish."

Meadow frowned. "You're saying when I pray to the Great Spirit that you'll be reunited with Singer, that's selfish?"

"It is. Because you are telling yourself you have influence. That your prayers will be heard. And you feel good for believing it. That you or I have any influence in a world that's totally, insanely, heartlessly, fucking random . . . sorry, no way." Cory was getting tired. He was pretty sure that would extinguish the conversation.

"So what if it feels good."

Cory looked up. "How's that?"

"Who cares if it feels good? Maybe prayer is just survival. If it feels good to eat a peanut butter sandwich, eat one. If it feels good to make someone a cup of tea, make one. So what? Neither are selfish."

"Yeah?" Cory challenged, now animated. "But you're not kidding yourself about the significance of a peanut butter sandwich. With prayer, it's drilled into your head, you can affect things, you can affect lives. A peanut butter sandwich . . . I don't think so."

"Maybe it can," Meadow said, cocking her head. "Maybe a peanut butter sandwich or making someone a cup of tea can have more of an effect than you'll ever know."

Cory nodded. "I guess." He looked at Meadow intently.

"What?" she said, self-consciously.

"I don't know. I didn't see you as the praying type."

"I'm not sure I am. But Pat said something to me back when I was on the run and pregnant and scared. He said, it's simple, Meadow. You can either worry or you can pray. It does no good to worry. The effect of prayer is a matter of debate, but at least it's positive." Meadow smiled at the memory.

The wet and cold of Cory's clothes were abruptly upon him. "I need to jump in the shower."

Meadow could see Cory was through with this conversation. And as he rose stiffly from the kitchen table, she couldn't blame him. His suffering was everywhere.

THE LAWYER

Now this is an office. Chevy, with his hands behind his head, swiveled left and right, wrapped in the comfort of a plush leather chair. Next to him, MB sat on her chair's edge, fidgeting with a notepad she'd brought for the meeting. Across the polished walnut desk from them, Michael Cadder used the end of his pen to scan along as he rapidly absorbed the file from the county social worker.

I could get used to this. View of downtown Madison. Underground parking. Somebody to bring you coffee. Chevy saw the lawyer had a telescope in his twelfth-floor office. *Bet there's some kick-ass window peeping.*

Michael Cadder removed his reading glasses, which were a bit of an embarrassment to him. He'd purchased them recently on the recommendation of his ophthalmologist, and despite being complementary to the savvy, salt-and-pepper lawyer archetype, they made him feel old. Especially around a young, attractive couple such as this.

"Does everybody get an office like this?" Chevy asked. They had been there fewer than five minutes. He was already bored.

Michael Cadder was a man of strong first impressions because, he had learned, judges are people of strong first impressions. "No, Mr. Chevalier. I'm sure they don't." The lawyer discreetly made a circle with a diagonal line through it next to Chevy's name in the file.

"Call me Chevy."

"You'll forgive me if I don't. I will refer to you as Mr. Chevalier and to you as Ms. Lancaster." He looked at MB, distracted by her attractiveness. He would need to quickly dispense with such unprofessional meanderings. It was time to introduce the ground rules. To rehearse. To prepare to win.

The lawyer continued. “Let me set some game day expectations. This is a child custody hearing. A decision won’t be rendered for at least two weeks after our date in family court. Rarely will a child his age be allowed in the courtroom.

“We’ll have no more than 20 minutes, perhaps as few as ten, with the judge, Judge Healy. I’ve been in Judge Healy’s court many times. Judge Healy is an outstanding jurist. Judge Healy is old-fashioned. Judge Healy’s rather humorless, but not stern. And Judge Healy is a grandfather, so he has definite opinions about children, beginning with they are this country’s most precious asset and are to be raised as such.”

MB took a few notes while Chevy’s thoughts drifted to lunch. There was a new, upscale burger bar just around the corner.

“I mention Judge Healy by name repeatedly so you can begin to get comfortable with the idea of calling him by this title. He does not particularly care to be called sir. That’s patronizing. And Judge or Your Honor doesn’t connect with him on a personal level. Mr. Chevalier, are you with me?”

“Huh?”

“How to address the judge?”

“Yeah. Um, Judge Healy.”

“Correct. And do your best to eliminate the ums. Too many ums and you knows and kindas will earn you no favor.”

Chevy nodded politely. *This guy is a real douche.*

“The first five minutes or so will go to the social worker. She will set the landscape for Judge Healy based on the meetings the three of you have had.” The lawyer’s glasses returned to his nose as he went over the notes in his folder. “A mistaken, violent death. Motherless child. Son now in temporary custody of biological father and girl-friend. Good home. Good jobs for the two of you. School is going well. Good.” Michael Cadder looked up. “Are the two of you engaged, by chance?”

Chevy said they were not.

“Any possibility of that changing in the two weeks we have before the case is heard?"

Chevy looked at MB who said there was not.

"Long-term commitments," the lawyer said aloud to himself while jotting a note. "Remind me to come back to that if I forget to cover it." He looked at his watch.

"Ms. Lancaster, you'll do most of the talking during our time with Judge Healy. He'll focus on you because his assumption will be you'll be doing most of the caregiving. Remember, he's a traditionalist.

"Your homework: Why do you want this child? Why is it in the best interest of this child to live with you?" The lawyer looked up. "You should be writing these down. What long-term commitments have you planned with each other and this child? What do you and this child most enjoy together? Expect questions of this nature. Answers should be succinct and confident."

MB wrote furiously, trying to keep up. But the heft of the questions, and the fact that answers, let alone succinct ones, were not rushing to mind, tangled her progress.

"As for you Mr. Chevalier, your homework. Have you visited the grave of the mother?"

Chevy was blindsided. "Um . . . I mean, no."

"You must visit the grave."

"But it's in Michigan. Somewhere."

The lawyer leveled a glance at Chevy. "I advise you to be able to tell Judge Healy that you have ruminated on the child's future while graveside. Have you spoken with the child's grandparents since the boy came to live with you?"

"Yes," Chevy said. "They've called a few times."

"Call the grandparents between now and the court date. Tell them what's happening with the boy. How he's doing in school. How he's going to play t-ball this spring."

"T-ball?" Chevy was confused.

The lawyer was losing his patience. "Everyday stuff. Right? Relationship stuff. The stuff that signals to Judge Healy that this child is going to grow up normally."

Chevy nodded slowly. "Like tell the grandparents we went out and got a family portrait shot and that we'd like to send them one."

The lawyer looked up, surprised. "Exactly."

Chevy continued. "Maybe I'll tell them we'd like to plan a trip out to visit them this summer. The three of us. That's a long-term plan. Which is essential to a long-term commitment." Chevy raised his eyebrows.

Michael Cadder took off his reading glasses and nodded at Chevy. "You got it."

MB had been writing as fast as she could but when Chevy mentioned a road trip to the grandparents, a chill pierced her. She looked over at him. Chevy and the lawyer shared a knowing look. Like they were wordlessly transferring the rules to some game about to played.

And it was a game played to win.

VIRTUES

It was quiet in town. Businesses were just blinking awake. Owners in front of their shops stooped to pick up newspapers. Doors were unlocked. Interior lights flick-flickered to life.

Pat and HomeSky were en route to work when they saw Radio Voice coming down Main, pulling his cart behind his bike, sporting a happy smile. A mop handle stuck up in the air with a red safety rag tied around the end as Pat had instructed.

"Hey there, entrepreneur," Pat said, rolling down the window of his truck as they pulled curbside. HomeSky leaned across Pat and waved. Radio Voice carefully slowed his bike before offering a quick wave back.

"Hi you guys," he said.

"Look at you!" HomeSky said.

"Yeah," Radio Voice agreed eagerly.

"Where's your first stop today?"

Radio Voice filled with pride. "Hardware store. I do the bathrooms. Plus the glass case where they keep the ammo. Five bucks more a time for the glass case!"

"That's called incremental business," Pat said. "Do you have it all written down in your notebook?"

"Sure do," Radio Voice said. "Wanna see?"

Pat glanced at HomeSky to make sure she had a few minutes before punching in at the grocery store. "For sure," HomeSky said. They got out of the truck for a better look.

Radio Voice was over the moon for the cart Pat had built him. Pat started with 16-inch wheels from a youth bike so it would roll smoothly. In the snow, Radio Voice would push the work cart by hand, but for almost two weeks now, he had been pulling it behind his bike. Essentially, it was a rolling plywood box, with multiple compartments for various cleaning supplies, and a special back door to load his mop and bucket.

Radio Voice had a plastic tackle box to hold his money and notebook. "See," he said, carefully opening the notebook. The top line read 8 a.m., across from that HARDWARE STORE and further across was written 2 BATHROOMS. GLASS CASE. TOTAL IS $25. Radio Voice proudly pointed to the writing. "Monday. Wednesday. Friday," he said as he flipped through the week's schedule for the hardware store. Then he whispered, "Twenty five bucks each time."

"Holy cow," Pat said. "I might have to go into business with you."

Radio Voice nodded intently. "You could."

"Nah, you're the expert," Pat said. "I'll stick to my job."

Unexpectedly, Radio Voice stepped toward HomeSky and wrapped his arms around her. "Thank you for your great, great idea. I love my new job."

Pat sat back and soaked in the moment. He hadn't had many good ones lately. Cory's medical bills continued to stack up. Grocery bills were about twice what they were less than a year ago. And making the mortgage next month while buying spring seed and fertilizer was going to take some creative math. But this made all that disappear.

"You should thank Pat, too," HomeSky said. "With your cart and your notebook, you're running your own business."

Radio Voice lifted an arm and Pat came in. "Group hug," he said, laughing.

"Well, we better get off to our jobs, too," Pat said. "Did you pack your lunch?"

Radio Voice raised the top of one of the cart's compartments and showed Pat his lunch cooler. Then he consulted his notebook. "Lunch today at 12:30, after TC's Auto Body and Tanning."

At work, Pat's spirit sunk. He wasn't able to pour his heart into his job as he once had. Varkas's firing of Radio Voice, despite its silver lining, robbed Pat of the pride he took in excelling as an employee.

He began to see Varkas's greed as more than a disappointment; it was a threat: to the ownership of their farm, to employee safety and to the environmental health of Baudette. The Sheriff was right. Varkas was dangerous. To work hard for this man, to fill his pockets with profit, in some ways endangered himself and others.

By the noon lunch break, news about the Goode Neighbor article in the *Region* had everyone at work buzzing. A few had read it, but most of the conversation was fueled by hearsay. In a word, the best way to summarize the response was stunned.

Pat had heard nothing until a coworker approached him saying he knew Pat was a friend of the Sheriff. He handed him the newspaper, folded open to the article. Pat was unpacking his lunch at the time. His lunch went uneaten.

Kitty was having an unusually quiet morning at Shields Cards and Candles. She'd opened the store as she did every day. It was Wednesday, so the weekly newspaper was waiting by the entrance of the shop, but she only glanced at the front page.

She lit a few candles—raspberry scented—in honor of the forthcoming spring, and took advantage of the lull to straighten shelves and restock a particularly popular new item. They had added a line of wooden, 24-piece children's puzzles featuring colorful jungle animals that pulled in mothers and grandmothers alike. Kitty knew how fond the Sheriff was of puzzles and stocking them made her think of him.

Just before 11:00, three ladies from the Woman's Auxiliary came in demanding an explanation. They were casual friends of Kitty and their brusque demeanor surprised her.

Slapping the newspaper down on the front counter, Mrs. Oates asked her if it were true. Kitty's smile tensed as she asked if what were true. A collaborator of Mrs. Oates snapped open the newspaper to the editorial section. All three of them pointed to The Goode Neighbor article at the top half of the fold. The headline all but screamed. Kitty, a prodigious reader who prided herself on rapid consumption without the commensurate falloff in retention, found herself stumbling through the newsprint. Knocked back. Starting and restarting lines. Comprehension spun into bits and fragments. Unable to believe the indelible words before her.

IS THIS THE KIND OF SHERIFF
OUR CITY CAN ENDORSE?

As my observant readers are most certainly aware, we are on the threshold of an election for our county sheriff. Accordingly, all across town, bold campaign placards and yard signs are springing up where the last of our snow has melted away.

Typically, this isn't news for Baudette. Deciding who holds the office of county sheriff, in years past, has been little more than a formality. We've repeatedly trusted the law enforcement and safety of our fair city to the watchful eye of Sheriff Thurgood Harris. But it has come to my attention that our Sheriff's watchful eye may be, of late, otherwise diverted.

I received a letter last week that greatly disturbed me. This citizen, who chose to remain anonymous for his protection, wrote to inform me that our sheriff is preoccupied with a number of activities unrelated to police work. Besides spending many idle hours at Lu Ann's diner, where he's well known for playing cribbage and emptying coffee pots, this letter said, our sheriff routinely leaves work early, especially on Fridays.

Why Fridays, a curious reader may ask? Brace yourself. It appears our sheriff is getting an early jump on cohabitating with a divorcee: his neighbor, Kitty Duncan. A woman who is not originally from here.

I needn't remind you, good readers, that Baudette is a city built on the solid joists of work ethic and Christian values. To shirk one's duty as well as to make a home with another outside the institution of marriage is to disrespect

> the very traditions that make Baudette exceptional. Such behavior puts us on the same moldered road as the licentious big cities to our south.
>
> A Goode Neighbor, it's my opinion, lives our traditions and exemplifies our belief system. Sheriff Harris's regular rendezvous with Ms. Duncan makes me, for one, take pause to ask: Is this the kind of sheriff that this newspaper and this citizenry can endorse? A fair question for our fair city. And one we all should take care to mull over as election day nears.

Kitty's hands trembled as she pushed back the newspaper. Her nose ran and tears filled her eyes. No one offered so much as a used tissue.

"So it is true," Mrs. Oates said, enunciating the word true, as if to throw it at her.

Kitty could not lift her eyes. The mascara from her lower lashes began to run.

"Living in sin," her second scorned.

"In the future, we'll be taking our business elsewhere."

"To be sure!"

"Shameful."

And with that Mrs. Oates and her entourage turned heel and exited.

The Sheriff spent the better part of the morning driving 40 miles northwest to Warroad and back. A stolen black Camaro was found abandoned behind the community hockey arena and the car's plates were traced to Baudette. Sheriff Harris took a drive up there because the Warroad sheriff said blood was found on the back seat. Turned out, it was ketchup from Burger King and the whole thing proved to be nothing but a joy ride involving a fast car and fast food. His colleague did, however, send the Sheriff home with a bag of frozen walleye fillets so the morning wasn't a total bust.

By the time the Sheriff put the fish in his freezer it was going on lunch hour so he sat down with a turkey sandwich, an apple and the newspaper. He nearly regurgitated the few bites he'd taken when he came across the Goode Neighbor piece.

The Sheriff had to redial the phone twice, his fingers were shaking so much.

"Shields Cards and Candles," a voice answered.

"Kitty?" the Sheriff said into the mouthpiece.

"Ms. Duncan is no longer with the company. Stop calling us."

"What? This is Sheriff Harris. Who is this?"

"Haven't you caused enough trouble?" Mrs. Shields chided before the line went dead.

The Sheriff nearly broke the phone when he hung up.

He quickly went across the street but Kitty wasn't at home. Nor was her car in the garage. Rarely was the Sheriff paralyzed by indecision. He stood, lost, in Kitty's driveway.

Kitty sat, then stood. She slumped, head in hands, then sprang to her feet, angry. She cursed, then asked for forgiveness. There was no comfort to be found in the guest chair across from the Sheriff's large, unoccupied desk. The dispatcher had tried multiple times to reach him on the car radio. No luck. Kitty had nowhere to go. He would find her, she told herself. Eventually he'll know where to find her.

The Sheriff monitored his breathing. *Slow damn down! Stop acting like a victim and start thinking like a policeman. There's plenty of time to go pay a visit to that son of a bitch Goode. Where's Kitty? Where would I go if I were her? Where is safe?*

His mind wanted to race, but he focused his attention. The Sheriff straightened, and nodded to himself. He knew where she would go. *Of course.*

The dispatcher put his phone call through to his office. The Sheriff stood in his kitchen, perspiring.

"Hello." Kitty's voice was weak.

"Hi, darling. Are you okay?"

"I guess."

"I'm so sorry about this. I don't know what to say."

"Neither do I," Kitty said.

"I called the card shop."

"She fired me. Just like that."

"That's plain wrong."

"She said she'd already received a dozen phone calls from customers saying they'd boycott the shop unless I was removed."

"Sometimes the people in this town—"

Kitty let out a sob. "I should have been more discreet."

"Kitty, nothing we are doing is wrong. I love you. You know that. You are a gift."

She did not reply.

"Stay where you are. I'm coming to get you."

"Maybe I should just go out the back way—"

"NO!" The Sheriff's voice thundered. "Sorry." He regained his composure. "You will not sneak around the back streets of our town."

Kitty started to say something but stopped.

"I'm going to straighten this out," the Sheriff promised.

"I'm afraid we are alone in this town," Kitty said.

"We are not. In fact, before I pick you up I'm going to see one of our greatest allies, Monsignor Kief."

Kitty gasped.

"Don't you worry. I've already spoken with him on the phone. And he's as upset about this as we are."

Kitty could hardly ask. "So he's on our side?"

"Very much so. He told me he's already begun drafting a letter to the paper in response."

Kitty didn't know what to say. "Hurry over," was all she managed.

They sat in Monsignor Kief's kitchen. It had been some time since the Sheriff had been over for a visit, let alone made it to the kitchen, a room that always impressed him. The efficiency and ease with which the blind priest made his way around this precisely organized space was its own kind of miracle.

"Coffee," the Monsignor said, setting down a steaming speckleware mug. "And a few ginger snaps for good measure." He produced a small plate of cookies.

"I don't mean to be inhospitable," the Sheriff said, "but Kitty's quite upset and waiting on me in my office."

"I understand. Tell me what I can do."

"Her good name has been dragged through the mud," the Sheriff began.

"And yours." The Monsignor sat down with his coffee.

The Sheriff groaned. "I have thick skin. But Kitty, she cares deeply about how she's thought of. Especially on account she didn't grow up here. She always puts in extra effort just to get a level eye."

"She's a wonderful person."

"This'll blow over, but I wonder how we can minimize the damage. You said you were planning to write your own letter to the paper."

"I am. I've been dictating it here into my tape recorder. I'll have my housekeeper transcribe it tomorrow, after I've had a night to sleep on it. We must deal with this undignified moment in a dignified way."

"I wonder if you might add one detail to your letter—to help our cause."

The Monsignor asked what that might be.

The Sheriff pulled a small ring box from his pocket. "I'd like to hand you something. Tell me if you can identify it."

The Monsignor received the ring box, his fingertips tracing its velvet cover. The Sheriff watched the Monsignor's face, waiting for the aha moment.

Slowly a smile transformed the Monsignor's face. He spun the box in his hand so he could crack it open. His fingers found the diamond ring inside. "Sheriff, will it disappoint you greatly to hear I'm not surprised?"

The Sheriff was taken aback. "Not at all?"

"I must say I prayed for this moment ever since you lost your Amanda. And knowing Kitty as I do, well, let's just say I had a strong feeling." The Monsignor handled the diamond ring. It was hard to say if his eyes or the ring sparkled more. "Is this Amanda's ring?"

"It is. I think she would want Kitty to have it." The Sheriff hung on the Monsignor's response.

"I wholeheartedly agree." He smiled fully. "Your impending marriage will make our community stronger, as all good marriages do."

"I would be honored if you would preside over the ceremony."

"I too would be honored. I will indeed. Can I assume I'm the first to congratulate you on this big news?"

"Actually, I've been talking to Pat about it for a few months, but I never found the right occasion to ask Kitty for her hand. I had decided to wait until her birthday, but now this." The Sheriff clenched his jaws. "Kitty deserves a better moment, but if she does accept my proposal, and your letter includes the news that Kitty and I are engaged and that you bless our upcoming nuptials, maybe that will get townsfolk reconsidering the accusation that we're living in sin."

The Monsignor sighed and set the ring box on the kitchen table. "When will people realize that we are all living in sin? Every one of us. It is not our earthly place to judge. That's not to say we shouldn't encourage marriage for a couple like Kitty and you. Such encouragement fully supports not only the two of you, but also our Church's values. I'm assuming Pat strongly encouraged marriage."

"He did. Yet he also understood that we were taking time to learn about each other. About compatibility. Not an easy subject, more so because I'm not an easy man to live with. And Kitty came from a not-great marriage and wasn't looking to just dive back in. We do spend weekends together, in the same home, in the same bed. You should know that if you're going to get into this and advocate for our relationship."

The Monsignor nodded, appreciating the Sheriff's forthrightness.

"Bottom line, we love and respect each other. I can honestly say, before you and God, that if not for our weekends together, I would be less ready to get married."

"God knows what's in your hearts and what's in your plans. That's how you'll be judged. I will not only have a word with Benjamin

Goode about his shameful and hurtful editorial, but I will personally deliver a counter letter to his paper that will mention that the two of you are to be married. And by me."

"A few of your neighbors might disapprove."

The Monsignor folded his hands and smiled. "I will love them nonetheless and remind them of the heavenly virtue of *Benevolentia*—kindness."

The Sheriff picked up the ring box and softly snapped it shut. "Well, I better get on to Kitty." He paused, looking at the ring box. "I must say I'm quite a bit nervous."

The Monsignor nodded. "All glory comes from daring to begin."

PART TWO

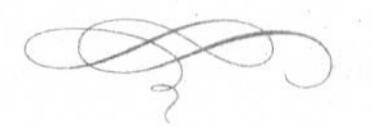

Custody

APRIL 10

Singer was born in Duluth and his birth certificate was filed in Duluth. So despite a long drive for everyone involved, the boy's custody case would be heard in Duluth's district courthouse.

For Cory and those coming with him from Baudette, it would require almost four hours to get there. For MB and Chevy, driving from Middleton, Wisconsin, it was five and a half. Their hearing was scheduled for 3:30 in the afternoon to accommodate for the distances.

April tenth was finally here.

And what a day it was. High blue sky. Flirting with 70 degrees. Sun bright enough to squint an eye closed. Pat said it was a good omen, a day like this to accompany them. Conversely, Cory couldn't seem to warm up, despite the conditions outside and Pat's continual press of optimism.

The Baudette contingent came down in two vehicles. Pat got the Toronado out from beneath its winter canvas cover in the barn and made sure it was road-ready. He, HomeSky, Cory, Meadow, and Billy, buckled in his car seat, were squeezed in his vehicle.

The Sheriff drove his police cruiser, with Kitty in front and Monsignor Kief and Radio Voice in back. The Sheriff's cruiser was never more than four car-lengths from Pat. To say who was more comforted by this proximity would be difficult.

Duluth's white stone courthouse, built in the early 1900s, was impressive, if not intimidating. It was surrounded by fountains, which had been turned on since the beginning of April. As Cory approached, he couldn't help but think of Singer. Singer loved fountains.

"Whoa," Pat said, gazing up at the three-story, rectangular structure. "Wouldn't want to be the guy cleaning gutters at this place." He was trying to lighten the mood, unsuccessfully.

They had 45 minutes before their hearing was scheduled to begin. Cory straightened his tie. Clean-shaven, his hair cut short, Cory looked more confident than he felt. "I can go in and find out where we need to go if you guys want to stay outside." He looked at the group. What an eye-catching group it was.

The Sheriff in his dress uniform. Kitty, on his arm, wore a skirt at the knee and a three-quarter sweater over a white blouse. Monsignor Kief had on his black clerical clothing. Pat and Radio Voice both in sports coats, and HomeSky and Meadow wore dark dress pants and long-sleeve oxfords that made them a little self-conscious.

"I'll go with you," Pat said. "But no need for all of us to go crowding in there just yet."

The Sheriff checked his watch. "Looks like a nice spot under those crab trees." Open benches awaited as birds lit on the bricks below to pick at lunch crumbs. Billy kicked and fussed in Meadow's arms, unhappily opening his eyes to the stunning sunlight. Producing a handkerchief from his back pocket, the Sheriff wiped a bench seat for the women to sit. The tree branches above broke the sunlight; in a month they would leaf out to become much more useful in that regard.

"Sure," HomeSky said, "let's sit." She recognized that Cory needed a quiet moment without a group trailing behind him like ducklings.

"Finally, good to be out in the warm, fresh air." The American flag over the fountains snapped sharply on its pole.

Cory and Pat stepped under the stone-arched entryway and pulled open the glass doors. The chill that Cory couldn't seem to escape rose up from the marble floor inside. He paused, closed his eyes and listened to his breathing. The words *honor your responsibility* glided across each breath drawn and exhaled.

Two security guards manned a large interior desk, looking quite bored despite the steady clatter of shoes and the whir of humanity beelining to various appointments. Cory gathered his resolve and made eye contact with the older of the two guards who lifted his chin, recognizing that Cory was out of his element.

Cory stepped forward. "Hello," he said. "I have a 3:30 hearing with Judge Healy. I'm not sure where to go."

Pat was awestruck by the massive columns rising three stories to the stone entablature above. Then he realized he'd momentarily lost Cory.

The guard nodded. "Do you have your appointment card? It should have come by mail."

Pat joined Cory at the security desk. "Yes." Cory took the card from the inside pocket of his suit coat, which hung loosely on him.

Pat regarded Cory. He had come a long way from the silent, dark of winter, mute in a wheelchair. Now neatly groomed, his limp almost imperceptible, his strength returning—confidence was sure to follow. At least Pat hoped it would.

Understandably, Cory had become tentative; his actions and decisions halting, much to his own frustration. Pat looked at the indentation and prominent scar over Cory's left eye, where he had struck the windshield as he was launched from the truck. Healing comes in desperate, fragile layers.

"You're in family court, which is courtroom A," the guard said. "Up the stairs, down the hall on your right. Look for the signs. There's a waiting area off the courtroom. Or you can take a pager and we'll buzz you five minutes before the judge is ready for you."

Cory thought about Singer. He saw their hands reaching for one another. Were they coming together or were they slipping apart? Should he take the pager or the waiting room? Should he wear the blue tie or the gold tie? Should he have left for the cabin earlier that day or stayed to correct papers? The guard, holding the pager, waited for a response, which Pat could see wasn't forthcoming.

"We'll take the pager," Pat said, putting a hand firmly on Cory's shoulder. He gave him a little shake. "Too nice of a day not to enjoy outside, am I right?" Pat extended his other hand. "Courtroom A, you say?"

The guard handed Pat the pager, watching Cory. "We'll buzz you five minutes before your time."

Chevy, MB, their lawyer and the caseworker were just finishing their 20 minutes with Judge Healy. Their time with him couldn't have gone much better. Everything had tracked as Michael Cadder had said it would. Their preparation paid off.

Judge Healy poured a glass of water from the pitcher on his desk and took a drink. He leaned back in his merlot-colored, high-back leather chair and closed the case file on his desk. "Ms. Lancaster, would you say the glass on my desk is half full or half empty?"

MB looked at the glass, then the judge. "I would say it's half empty, Judge Healy."

The judge turned his focus to Chevy "And you Mr. Chevalier?" Chevy smiled. "I would have to say it's half full."

Judge Healy nodded, showing a hint of a smile himself. "Ms. Lancaster, it's my supposition that your career as an emergency room nurse has given you a strong practical side, so I'm not surprised by your answer. I will confess, I am impressed with you and the demanding career you've chosen for yourself." The Judge paused. "Are you concerned that the taxing nature of your work could detract from the time and energy you'll be able to dedicate to this child?" Their lawyer secretly congratulated himself. They had worked on this question. *Pause,* he thought. *Don't answer too quickly.*

MB waited to answer. "No," she said, reaching over and taking Chevy's hand. "We have each other. And the support of friends and family. I am far from taking on this challenge alone. On busy days when I need support, I'll have plenty. I think modeling a work ethic, challenging myself with a meaningful profession, will make me a better parent in the long run."

Judge Healy nodded. "As for your glass-half-full answer, Mr. Chevalier, I'm also not surprised. As a loan officer and a banker, you are a purveyor of hope. I think you two balance each other quite nicely."

Chevy was hoping for a little more than purveyor of hope. He was spot-on today, mixing in anecdotes about the dedication that made him a national collegiate champion, noting also his top position at the bank in business loans, even mentioning his plan to take the whole family to visit the grandparents this summer.

"Mr. Cadder, will you approach?" Their lawyer left the table and walked up to the bench. The judge lowered his voice. "I think this is fairly cut and dried. Do you see any issues with this couple not covered here this afternoon that in your view I should be made aware of?"

"I do not, Judge Healy."

"Very well. As you know, with a child of this age, I do not want him in the courtroom, nor running into or otherwise interacting with the other parties in this case. That potential trauma does a child no good."

"Yes, Judge Healy."

The judge checked his watch. "The boy is in the waiting room?"

The lawyer answered. "Correct. With a bailiff."

"Will you escort the boy and his father to my chambers. I just need a few minutes to speak to the boy and have a look at him. Then I'll ask that you quickly usher the group out as I call the next group in."

The lawyer nodded crisply.

"Thank you, folks," Judge Healy's voice echoed in the wood-paneled courtroom as he stiffly stood. "Your counsel will inform you on next steps. Good afternoon." With that, Judge Healy retired to his chambers.

A few minutes passed and there was a knock on his door.

"Enter," a voice inside the room instructed.

Judge Healy, still in his black robe, stood to greet Singer and Chevy.

"Hello young man," the judge said coming toward the door to greet them.

"Hi, Mr. Judge," Singer said quite confidently. He had received a gold plastic badge from the bailiff that he wore pinned to his shirt.

"Please, call me Judge Healy." He put out his hand to shake. "I see you've been made a deputy bailiff. Congratulations."

Singer shook the grandfatherly judge's hand. "It's not real," Singer whispered.

The Judge winked. "And what shall I call you? Your given name is Paul but I'm told you're partial to Singer." A playful Irish lilt tipped his words in a way Chevy hadn't heard in the courtroom.

"I go by Singer. That's what everyone calls me."

"Then Singer it shall be." Judge Healy looked at Chevy. "Mr. Chevalier, do you mind if Singer and I have a few minutes to talk? Alone."

Chevy did his best to disguise his surprise. "Okay with me if it's okay with you." Chevy squatted down to look Singer in the eye.

Singer shrugged. "Sure." He looked at the judge. "Are we going to talk about Cory and stuff?"

"Mostly we'll talk about your school and your house and your friends and what you like to do. How does that sound?"

"Okie dokie," Singer said. He reached out his hand to be taken by the judge's. "Where should we go?"

Judge Healy was moved by the gesture. He held Singer's small, warm hand. "How about in here? In my office?"

Singer's brow furrowed. "Could we go out there? By your big desk? Can I sit in your chair?"

"The big courtroom?" the judge said. "Some kids think it's scary."

"No way. The wood shines. I've never seen shinier shiny wood."

And with that, they moved. Singer sat in the judge's chair, nearly swallowed by it. Judge Healy sat in the witness chair. It was the first time in his 41 years as a judge that he saw a courtroom from this perspective.

"Tell me about your school," the judge said, bringing his hands together in a playful clap.

"I'm already in preschool at Montessori. My teacher is Ms. Doyle and she's great. I can tie my shoes in bows!"

"So you like school?"

Singer lit up. "LOVE it. We do music from around the world."

"How about your house? Tell me about it." Judge Healy was mentally taking notes. *Confident boy. Outgoing. Bright. Happy.*

"It's blue. And tall. I have a bedroom where I might get a turtle."

"What do you do in your room?"

"Sleep."

"Anything else?"

Singer shrugged.

"How about read books?"

"Yep. With MB."

Judge Healy looked at Singer. "MB is who?"

"Mary Beth. You know, the lady I came here with."

"So MB is her nickname just like Singer is yours."

"Yep." The gavel on the desktop caught Singer's attention. "Can I hold that?"

The judge looked at the gavel. "You can. Do you know what it is?"

"A hammer." Singer's small hand picked it up.

"Do you know what I use it for?"

Singer thought. "To make Play-Doh pancakes, like we do in school?"

The judge smiled. "Actually I use it when I make a decision on a case and it's time for everyone to go home. I rap the hammer on its wooden base." Judge Healy pantomimed the action. "Rap!"

Singer looked at the judge. His was no longer a childish look, nor playful. "You're going to decide who I go home with, aren't you?"

The judge studied the boy's eyes. "Yes, I am."

Singer put the gavel down. "You have to be careful. Not to decide too fast."

Judge Healy blinked. He in the witness box looking up at the boy who sat in the judge's chair, spotlighted from above in omnipotent light. He perfectly understood the boy was only four and a half years old, but the child looked at the judge in a manner beyond his years.

"You'll know soon," Singer said. "Don't hit the hammer too fast."

With that Singer began to hum, his melodious voice mixing with bright courtroom lights, bounding off polished wood, surrounding the judge's bench. The quiet room filled.

Judge Healy wasn't his usual sharp self for the first five minutes with Cory and his side of the custody case.

The caseworker asked for a second time. "Sir, are these differences clear?" She had gone through the fact that Cory had spent years with Singer compared to Chevy's few months.

The judge was finally able to push aside the image of Singer—rim-lit, celestial—holding a gavel. "Forgive me," he said, clearing his throat. "Mr. Bradford," he looked at Cory, "you've been a part of the boy's life since he was an infant, is that correct?" The judge, straightening, focusing, began to feel authority replacing mystery.

"I met him when he was seven months old, yes sir."

"Good. And about how you knew his mother. Tell me about that."

"We started as friends. Singer had colic as a baby. I was rehabbing a knee. Hanna, his mother, was exhausted. So I would walk the baby for hours. Up and down the hills of Duluth. I grew closer to Hanna, as time went on. We began dating. We went on like that until eventually, I moved into her house. We were engaged to be married last summer."

The Judge nodded slowly. "We all knew Ms. Donnovan, or felt as though we did from her newscasts here in Duluth. A tragic loss. My sincere condolences."

"Thank you."

"Did you and Ms. Donnovan discuss you becoming the adoptive father of her child?"

"Yes, sir. We talked about it all the time. It's what she wanted. And it was what I wanted, too. It's what I still want."

Judge Healy adjusted his glasses and looked at his notes clipped to the case file. "And how are you recuperating from the collision you were involved in? There were significant injuries according to your file."

"I'm doing well."

"In the hospital notes I see you received trauma to your head that rendered you mute. That is concerning."

"My friends might tell you I'm now borderline verbose." Cory managed a grin, trying to relax.

Judge Healy smiled. "All joking aside, how do you explain the recovery of your voice?"

Cory directly addressed the judge. "I think time heals. There was a shock to my system that took time to resolve."

"No aftereffects? Slurring of speech? Disorientation or blackouts? Any of that?"

"None whatsoever."

Reclining in his high-backed chair, Judge Healy looked off, processing. "Cory, if you were granted custody, tell me how you see the immediate future unfolding."

Cory considered the question. "Do you mean including the rest of this school year? Or beginning with summer?"

"Let's say early June, after school is out."

Cory nodded. "I'll be at the farm near Baudette where I'm living now. Singer would live with us. If it's early June, and I remember right, the corn and soybeans would be just getting going so that would be great for him. Walk the rows of green seedlings. He loves plants. We used to grow them on the windowsill . . ."

Emotion swelled, choking Cory's words. He bowed his head, gathered himself. "We'd spend the summer on the farm. Outdoors. I'd be getting stronger, back to normal. With Singer. And with my friends.

I'm lucky for the support I have." Cory gestured to the gallery's front bench where his contingent sat.

"I see that." Judge Healy nodded at the group.

"May I introduce them to you? They all know Singer. Except the youngest one there, Billy."

Meadow took Billy's small hand and waved to the judge.

The judge checked his watch. "Certainly."

Cory went from left to right. "First is Sheriff Harris. We've known each other since I was 13. My father died unexpectedly on Lake of the Woods. Sheriff Harris was there to help. Has been ever since."

The Sheriff rose. "Pleasure to meet you, sir."

Judge Healy nodded. "Yes, I know the name. Many years of service in our northern counties. It's my pleasure, Sheriff Harris."

Cory continued. "Ms. Kitty Duncan. The Sheriff's fiancée."

"Hello," Kitty said. She hooked her arm in the Sheriff's and remained standing.

"Pat O'Rourke and HomeSky Blackholm are next. They have opened up their home and their farm to me. Incredibly generous. I also met them when I was 13. Their support and kindness is beyond words."

They, too, stood and nodded hello.

"Next is one of my best friends, Radio Voice. He and I used to work together in Baudette but he now is his own boss running a custodial engineer business."

Radio Voice sprang to his feet. "Good afternoon," he said smiling widely.

"Good afternoon," the judge responded.

"We love Cory," Radio Voice said.

"I can see that."

"We love Singer, too."

The judge nodded. "Thank you. Yes."

Radio Voice was going to add more but Pat politely stopped him.

"Next," Cory said, "is Monsignor Kief, another of my longtime friends. He is from Baudette, too. He says he's retired but every day he's in service of someone or something other than himself."

The Monsignor stood and bowed his head.

"Finally," Cory said, "Meadow FastHorse and her son Billy Little Tree. They also live at the farmhouse."

"Hi." Meadow said. "Your honor," she added.

The judge looked at the young woman and her child. She couldn't have been older than 20, he concluded. Likely younger. "Nice to meet you both," the judge said. "And how old is your child?"

"He's about to be five months." Meadow said.

"Beautiful child," he said. Then getting back to business. "Please, be seated, one and all. It's a pleasure to see such a deep and diverse support group that you have, Cory. Let's proceed." Judge Healy pulled his chair up closer to his desk. "Where were we?" Taking a sip of water, the judge thumbed through the case file. "Yes. And I see you've been invited back to teach here locally at Duluth East. Very good school. Mathematics. Outstanding subject. Excellent. Have you found a home here yet?"

Cory's posture relaxed and he crossed his legs. "I'm starting to look. I plan to get serious once the outcome of this case is decided."

The judge nodded. "Now, about the issue of your outstanding hospital bills. How do you see addressing them?" The judge straightened his glasses. "For the two of you to live on a starting teacher's salary, that can be challenging, but having this kind of debt burden makes it something quite beyond challenging."

Cory cocked his head. "Excuse me?"

"Your hospital bills. From the accident." Judge Healy found a page from the case file. "Your bills were brought to my attention by the counsel of the other party. It's my strong opinion that financial security significantly affects child development."

Cory looked at Pat sitting in the front row of gallery benches. Suddenly, there was no color in Pat's face. Cory's eyes probed deeper, as if to say, *what is this? What is he talking about?* Pat closed his eyes. Then he stood.

"Excuse me. Your honor, Cory doesn't know about the bills. It's my fault. I didn't tell him."

"Please, what is your name again?" the judge said.

"I'm Pat O'Rourke," he said, pulling at his sports jacket. "Cory is staying with us at the farm. His bills have been delivered there. I've been," Pat struggled for the appropriate word, "keeping them until I found the right time to discuss the matter with Cory, or with anyone else."

Judge Healy frowned at Pat. "Are you saying that only you know about these bills?"

"That is correct, sir. I was planning to talk with Cory, and the others, once things settled down and I had a better plan for addressing them."

The judge turned his attention to Cory. "I'm sorry to be the bearer of this news," he said, "but you have hospital and therapy bills in the neighborhood of $230,000." The judge's gaze returned to Pat. "Thank you. You may sit down."

Cory shook his head no. It couldn't be, but it was. His hand gripped the top of his head and pulled at his hair. It was happening. It was happening all over again. Make progress. Get your hopes up. Then, blindsided. Icy pinpricks invaded his skin. His stomach lurched. Muffled voices twisted in his ears. The judge's face stared out at him. Cory squeezed his eyes shut, pulling at his hair.

Then HomeSky was there at his side, her hands soothing, guiding him to release his twist of hair. The Sheriff and Pat were asked to approach the bench. Cory could feel it. A rush. Cold water closed over his head. He was sinking away from the light. Down to the depths of darkness.

VARKAS

It echoed inside his early-morning office. Varkas's sledge of a fist came down on the *Baudette Region,* which was spread open on his desk. The Letters to the Editor section of the newspaper had dedicated almost half a page to Monsignor Kief's response to the *Goode Neighbor* article. In addition, other shorter letters were printed in support of the Sheriff and his fiancée.

"That's horseshit!" Varkas sprayed the newsprint with spittle. His heart pounded. His chest burned. His face bunched in an ugly scowl. "They're going to make a saint out of the fool."

The Sheriff had risen early, waiting for the newspaper to be delivered. He quickly retrieved it, forgetting that Private had gone outside with him to do his business. A sharp bark at the door and then another pulled the Sheriff out of the newsprint to the front entryway where he apologized to his neglected Lab.

Having read the Letters to the Editor section three times over, he brought the paper across the street for Kitty. She had canceled her subscription but after some reassuring and coaxing, she sat down with the Sheriff and the newspaper at her dining room table. He held her hand as she read Monsignor Kief's reprinted letter:

> I love our small town, I truly do. Like I've always said, "A small bowl keeps the soup warmer." But as much as I want to believe in the charity and exceptionalism of our 1,202 residents, and as much as I hope we're an uncommonly welcoming community, I was recently ashamed of Baudette.
>
> It came after I read an article in our paper maligning the character of two of our finest citizens. In a so-called

Goode Neighbor editorial, Sheriff Harris, whom I have known his entire life, and Kitty Duncan, whose company I've thoroughly enjoyed since she relocated here, were publicly assailed. Why? They allegedly spend more time together than they should, according to an "anonymous source" who said such behavior wasn't becoming of a Sheriff in our town.

Firstly, dear citizens, if you put any stock in an accusation that lacks the fortitude of a name to stand behind it, then you're not using your God-given brains.

And secondly, if you wallowed in this accusation, advanced it, embellished it or became high-handed because of it, you should humbly seek God's forgiveness.

Such hurtful behavior is not why our Father gave us life and community and the breathtaking surroundings we so fortunately enjoy.

To set the record straight, if there is a more qualified candidate for county sheriff than Sheriff Harris I would like to meet the person. I mean that sincerely. Come talk to me. Until that time, there is no one I know who is better for our town, for the enforcement of our laws and the overseeing of our safety than he is.

As for Kitty Duncan, she is not only a caring, good-hearted woman, she is engaged to be married to Sheriff Harris, a wedding I am proud to say I will preside over in the near future. I hope you will give her words of congratulation, support, friendship and pray for them as a couple. If you yourself are married, you understand a marriage needs prayers. Be comforted to know I'm praying for your marriage, too.

So, finally, I ask you, Baudette: is this really your best self? If not, change your course and take the higher ground. May God be with you on your journey today and always.

Monsignor Frank Kief

Kitty closed her eyes and slipped into the Sheriff's arms. *Had the earlier slight in the newspaper been an indirect grace?* she wondered. *Did it force us closer together and strengthen our hold on what's truly important?*

"I'm so relieved," she said, crying happy tears into the shoulder of the Sheriff's uniform shirt. "Oh, look here. If I'm not careful I'll stain your uniform."

"Don't be ridiculous," the Sheriff said, holding her tightly. There was enduring warmth between them and the Sheriff could not imagine it in any other way.

"Looks like we have more than a few people in town pulling for us," he said. "Feels good, don't it."

Kitty's stronger embrace answered for her.

Varkas was on the prowl, ready to pounce. God help any employee who might be slacking. He walked the plant floor angry. Left the building angry. Inspected his lumberyards angry.

It was all the Sheriff's fault. If not for his interference, there would be no $45,000 civil penalty payment to the EPA, there would be no forced compliance with OSHA to increase worker safety. The taste was as bitter as it was lasting. He knew of one way to extinguish it.

Back home on his land, Varkas changed into his tan, Filson bib overalls, wearing a red kerchief knotted around his neck. He would head out to his massive woodshed where the remaining logs from last year's tree would be split.

Varkas eyed the three axes that hung on the shed wall. Each was a Hultafors, the classic Swedish axe known for power because of the head weight and its forged high-density steel.

He reached for the middle ax, indulging in the smoothness of the hickory handle. A simple tool able to exact such swift, simple resolution—a notion Varkas quite respected.

With his thumbnail, he checked the blade. A scrape of nail rose above the blade's edge affirming what Varkas knew: this tool had been put away correctly. A smile came to Varkas's face. He was starting to feel better. A plan was beginning to sharpen.

"C'mon, Private. Be a sport." The Sheriff gave the dog's leash a yank and Private's hindquarters disconnected from the ground. "Shitfire, boy," he urged. "You can't walk tail-tucked. It defeats our campaigning purpose."

Private had Re-Elect Sheriff Harris placards strapped to him. The dog slunk forward, a walking sandwich board for the upcoming election. Kitty had conceived of the idea, something that the Sheriff was quick to dub a propaganda contraption, but here he was, just him and his dog, taking a walk from his office to Lu Ann's for lunch.

"I'll be damned," he mumbled to a dispirited Private, "if I'll let some newspaper accusation drive me to hiding. Right boy?" The lift in the Sheriff's voice had the same effect on Private's tail. "Atta boy. Head high, tail high. We'll show this town that Sheriff Thurgood Harris will not be intimidated."

The Sheriff and his dog walked crisply toward Main, receiving a few friendly honks and waves. Car windows were lowered as the temperature rose. The sun glared off windshields making it difficult to identify faces inside the passing vehicles.

"Oh, I wish Kitty was with us." Private's ears cocked and he looked back hopefully upon hearing Kitty's name. "Nah, she's not ready to come out and draw this much attention. Not just yet." The Sheriff and his pet received another honk and friendly wave. He lifted his arm in acknowledgment. "Pretty soon, though. You know, boy, I was wrong to quickly judge her idea as foolhardy. I don't so much mind standing out like a March daffodil."

The hard shadow of man and dog and election posters moved down the sun-punched sidewalk. The air embraced them in welcome heat. A breeze slid over the Sheriff's flattop, but not before it aroused the attention of both the Sheriff's and Private's noses. They froze. Fried chicken at Lu Ann's was on the wind.

Inside the diner, replacing her typical smart-alecky sign by the register, was a fund-drive poster she made for Cory's medical bills.

A coffee can with a slot cut in the plastic lid sat next to it. The can's collection was never going to amount to a whole lot, but mountains are scaled one step at a time.

Lu Ann brought the Sheriff a steaming plate of fried chicken with a mound of mashed potatoes cupping a pool of gravy, a carrot and pea medley and a wedge of warm sourdough bread. The Sheriff gazed at the plate as one might a long-lost love. Then he shook his head.

"My dear," he said, either to Lu Ann or the food, "I hope you're not insulted but some of this has to be substituted with a salad." The Sheriff took a side plate and scraped the mashed potatoes onto it. Then he paused in silence, summoning his courage. The sourdough bread was placed on the plate next to the potatoes.

"Never thought I'd see the day," Lu Ann said, sitting down, picking up a fork, pulling the side plate toward her. "Sheriff Harris shows up to my place with a dog sandwiched in election fanfare, and then, with no arm twisting, substitutes a salad for a treasure trove of carbohydrates."

The Sheriff grimaced. "Please. A half-measure of mercy."

Lu Ann had a forkful of potatoes dripping with gravy. "Oh, my," she delighted, her mouth half-full.

The Sheriff cleared his throat. "Mary Alice," he barked at the waitress who was wiping down a booth near the front window. "Can you bring me a salad?"

"Sure, sweetie," she hollered across the diner. "What kind of dressing?"

The Sheriff glanced at Lu Ann, sheepishly. Lu Ann looked back at him as if to say, *don't you dare.*

"No dressing," he said.

Lu Ann shook her head. Then she had another forkful of mashed potatoes.

The Sheriff licked his fingers after polishing off a drumstick. "I know toting signs on my dog may look a little asinine but that mess with the newspaper raised my ire. I will not be cowed. I'm coming back punching."

"I'd expect nothing less," Lu Ann said.

The Sheriff was hoping for a little more sympathy. "Between you and me, that sucker punch knocked me to my knees."

Lu Ann raised her eyebrows. "Sometimes being on our knees gives us a perspective we can benefit from."

"I won't argue you that."

The Sheriff switched subjects. "I see you got the fund drive going for Cory. Making any headway?"

"Mostly leftover change. Maybe $50 a week. Somebody left a 20 two days ago. Nice surprise."

The Sheriff finished a bite of chicken. "Seen a lot of coffee cans around town. It'll add up, but not anytime too soon to $230,000."

Lu Ann perked up. "Funny you should say that. Almost verbatim, I said the same thing to Monsignor Kief this morning. He was in for breakfast." She paused. "You know that look he gets on his face when he's bursting with something, some news, some surprise? You know what I mean?"

The Sheriff nodded.

"I couldn't get it out of him, but he had that look."

"What do you reckon it was about?" The Sheriff wiped his chin with a napkin.

"I'm pretty sure it had to do with Cory. And the fund drive or the money."

"Why's that?"

Lu Ann continued. "Because I said there aren't enough coffee cans in all of Minnesota to take care of Cory's bills."

"And . . ." the Sheriff said.

"And he said, maybe you're right. Or maybe you're not right. And then gave me that mystifying grin." Lu Ann smiled, thinking about it.

"So what do you think that means?"

Lu Ann pensively shook her head and looked out the plate glass window at the sunshine stretched across the street, wrapping the downtown buildings in hope. "It means maybe I'm right. Or maybe I'm not right."

A stick of Big Red would suffice to quell the Sheriff's dissatisfaction with his reduced lunch portion. Gum was a bridge until stomach told brain that body was indeed sated. The Sheriff, pulled along the sidewalk by Private, stopped to let an elderly woman pass. His dog had new-found pep due to a hunk of bread slathered in mashed potatoes and gravy. It would be as close as the Sheriff would get to tasting that portion of lunch.

"Good afternoon," the Sheriff said to the elderly woman. She had a warm face, one that showed a lifetime of greeting blessings with a smile.

"I'm voting for you," she said with much vigor, poking him on the chest with a bony finger. "And my congratulations on your recent engagement."

Private continued to pull toward any and all smells that presented themselves. "Sit," the Sheriff commanded, stumbling a bit before letting the Lab feel his presence on the other end of the leash. "You'll have to forgive my dog. Spring is on the wind."

The elderly woman's eyes sparkled. "Spring. And youth. So often underappreciated."

As they exchanged words, Varkas, behind the wheel of his company truck, turned up the street.

"I thank you for your vote," the Sheriff said. "Count on me to earn it."

Varkas slowed at the sight a half-block in the distance. The Sheriff, having a sunny conversation with one of the local senior citizens. His dog, enveloped in bold election posters. *Impossible,* he thought, grimacing. *Instead of lying low, here the man stands, campaigning in broad daylight.*

The Sheriff spotted a white pickup truck with the bright red Varkas *V* emblazoned on the driver's door. The windshield glare momentarily concealed the driver's identity, but the Sheriff knew in his gut.

"A lovely day for mid-April," the elderly woman commented.

A sly grin came to the Sheriff's face as he saw it was indeed Varkas behind the wheel. He couldn't have set up this sidewalk scene any better had he commissioned Norman Rockwell to paint it.

Contempt and defeat twisted Varkas's face. The Sheriff couldn't help himself. He made eye contact with Varkas. Then he lifted a hand and offered an animated wave.

Varkas stomped the accelerator to the floorboard. The lusty diesel engine roared as the truck powered past, giving the elderly woman a start.

The Sheriff steadied her, taking her arm by the elbow.

"What a nuisance," she declared.

The Sheriff watched the truck speed away. "Yes, ma'am. And then some."

MONSIGNOR KIEF

Monsignor Kief had said his morning prayer, as usual, kneeling before the bathroom sink. Above all, he thanked his Father for this latest development for Cory. Then he took up his toothbrush and began preparing for the day.

After tidying his bedroom he went to breakfast at Lu Ann's and his excitement nearly got the better of him. But it wasn't his place to tell anyone the news yet. Events of such magnitude need an unencumbered space from which to unfold.

Now it was 11:00 his time, noon in New York, where the call would come from. The Monsignor sat near the phone. He had made himself a half tuna fish sandwich, adding a row of Fritos below the top bread slice—a practice he picked up from a friend in divinity school who called it a poor man's sardine sandwich.

Lunch sat uneaten. His plate rested next to the phone, which the Monsignor would randomly reach over to touch, just to ensure the receiver was properly cradled.

The grandfather clock had chimed out the arrival of the hour. The Monsignor flipped open the glass cover of his braille watch and felt the position of the hands. By all counts, the call would be shortly forthcoming.

This moment allowed the Monsignor to reflect on mysteries too large to fathom and too wild to direct. The clock ticked rhythmically in the great room. Outside the nearest window, the muffled chirps of birds flew in and out of earshot. Hands folded across the rosary on his lap, the Monsignor waited.

Pat's heart sank as he watched out the kitchen window. In the yard that ran from the back of the house to the barn, Cory went through his morning workout routine. And it had become routine—noticeably less energized—in the past two weeks since the custody hearing.

Judge Healy said it would be a few weeks before he rendered a decision, but Cory left the courtroom defeated. The freight of his hospital bills and the judge's words about the significance of financial security to a child's long-term development had left Cory lost. And angry. And withdrawn. It had pushed Pat to a breaking point, too.

But Pat couldn't entertain anger. Right now, he needed to be strong. Cory wasn't much for cheerleaders but Pat had to be the embodiment of optimism, even if it was transparent. The other choice was to step into the quicksand with Cory.

A tractor tire exercise had Cory squatting down, heaving the tire upright onto its tread, and flipping it over. Each flip moved Cory one tire distance closer to the barn. He flipped the tractor tire there and back. Fifteen uninterrupted minutes of grueling leg and upper body work; it was one of the best exercises for core strength and endurance.

The good news was Cory was venting his frustration using giant rubber tires and a splitting maul and by doing pull-ups in the barn where he and Joseph once had contests. The bad news was his disillusionment showed no remission.

After the court appearance, Pat told the whole group the details of the hospital bills. How the insurance company forced an out-of-court settlement. How they said they weren't liable for a penny of payout because their policy states, albeit in fine print, that an accident caused while in the act of illegal behavior—and the police report estimated Cory's vehicle was traveling over 80 miles per hour down the centerline of the road—absolved them of any liability. But, they said, because they were a company with a heart, they would make a one-time payment. Take it or leave it.

Cory's side had no legal ground to stand on, let alone counter from. The insurance company wanted to avoid the public relations nightmare of leaving Cory totally hung out to dry. A deal was struck. The money in the settlement came up well short.

Pat hadn't heard HomeSky come into the kitchen, her bare feet hardly making a sound. She joined him at the window, careful not to give him a start.

"Good morning," she said.

"Mino gigizheb," he said, putting his arm around her.

HomeSky watched out the window. "I fear I've seen this Cory before." She leaned into Pat's warmth.

"He's full of rage. I don't blame him." Pat took a deep breath. "I haven't gotten much out of him since the hearing. I know Meadow has been trying to talk to him too. He's putting up a wall. Like you say, we've been here before."

"Pat," HomeSky said.

"Hmm," he said, watching Cory, sweat working through the back of his gray hoodie, as he bent down to dead lift and flip the tire.

"Pat," HomeSky said again. Something in her voice grabbed his full attention.

He looked at her.

"We could sell."

Pat's mouth fell open.

"If we take Varkas's offer, we'd have enough to pay off the bills and some left over to rent a place in town. Until we come up with the right next step."

"Oh, HomeSky," Pat said.

Her eyes shone with resolve. "I know you love this place like I do. Your hands built it. Part of you is alive in this land as is part of me. But we can't let a possession come before Cory and Singer."

Pat closed his eyes and let his arms fall limply at his sides. "But it's your farm. It's more than home."

"Pat," HomeSky said.

He opened his eyes to her.

"If we stick together, you, me, Meadow, Billy, Cory, Singer, we'll be strong and we'll be fine. We'll find something else. We'll find a way. But if this pulls us apart, if money and bills get between Cory and Singer, between Cory and us, I fear we'll lose him. And I can't lose another son. Not for money. Not for a farm. Not for anything."

Pat reached out to HomeSky and they met inside each other's arms not as two. "I love you," he said. "If you believe this is the way, then it's the way I'll go."

Monsignor Kief hung up the phone. He pondered miracles. Of how losing his eyesight gave him a greater need for fellowship. Of Pat's arrival—a near banishment—to of all places, Baudette. Of HomeSky's Joseph and Cory's Singer and Meadow's Billy and the deliverance that children provide. He thought of the Sheriff and Kitty's upcoming marriage.

Life has few unrelated events, the Monsignor had come to know. A plan is placed in our mosaic of moments, which ultimately stands out, beckoning, as clear as a church bell.

He reached for his poor man's sardine sandwich. The Monsignor ate with gusto. The phone call confirmed it. A visitor was coming to see Cory.

JUDGE HEALY

His caseload was a labyrinth of possible outcomes held inside his head. Judge Healy navigated these cases while on walks. He drove around town with them. Inched toward decisions while waiting for the toaster to pop and while his wife spoke to him about protecting spring tulips from rabbits and while shaving in the early morning. He was a deeply conscientious man. He understood his judgments held lifelong repercussions.

He was ready to render his decision on the custody case involving Singer. He had lived silently with his decision for 24 hours, listening for any doubts or second thoughts. There were none. He instructed the court to set a date: April 21. Both parties in the case would be notified. Life would move on.

Somewhat troubling to the judge of late was that his wife had become increasingly forgetful. They did their best to joke about it, calling them her *Why am I here moments* as she stood motionless in a room or with a drawer pulled open, unable to remember what task brought her there.

On this night, she had forgotten to buy cat food, a thought jarred by a television commercial featuring a dancing cat on the 10 p.m. news. The judge was an early-to-bed early-to-rise man so she grabbed her jacket and car keys and went out to get three cans of Fancy Feast at the 24-hour convenience store.

She returned home to the tuck-under garage. Parked. And went back to watching television, an Audrey Hepburn late movie. On the couch, she snuggled under a blanket in the TV room. Below her, in the garage, she had forgotten to switch off the ignition when she parked her car.

Judge Healy woke up with a cat on his face. When he tried to push it off it was like he was mired in a dream state, his limbs too heavy to function normally. He sat up, a crushing headache at his temples. His brain shot out alerts for his body to spring into action, to get out, but the signals snagged and spun and delayed and dithered.

He fell in the bedroom. And again down the stairway. Finally, drawn by the only noise and light in the house, he stumbled into the TV room. The air was toxic. He vomited as the aperture of the room swirled and began to narrow. An intake of fresh air was the only hope. Confused by the casement windows—he had cranked the wrong direction—he found an iron bookend to throw through the glass but missed badly. Judge Healy collapsed on the carpet.

Faces raced past as he slid toward unconsciousness. Until his mind grabbed on to a particular image. A boy, a blonde boy, curly haired, in his courtroom, sitting in his bench chair, gavel in hand, wrapped in golden light. Judge Healy's consciousness hung by gossamer threads to this image he recognized as a boy from a custody case he was about to rule on. The boy looked at him and spoke. "There's still time."

Judge Healy pulled his wife off the couch and dragged her, hooking his arms under her armpits, across the room and out the front door. Oxygen-rich air quickly revived him. He screamed until hoarse, until his neighbor was there in pajamas and robe. They administered chest compressions and rescue breaths until the paramedics arrived. As Judge Healy and his wife were rushed away by ambulance, the fire department broke through the service door of his garage and shut off the idling automobile.

All of Judge Healy's cases were pushed back a month or better while he attended to the recovery of his wife. He dedicated to her his undivided attention. For the first time in as long as he could remember, he didn't think of work. With one exception. The face from the night of the asphyxiation. Singer's image remained ever-present.

CORY

Meadow imagined the gray sky as the dingy underbelly of a giant owl that had descended upon them, holding their farmstead in colorless captivity for three consecutive days. Finally, this morning, as the sun broke through and chased the clouds away, she dared to ask.

Cory had been politely withdrawn in past weeks, locked in his own purgatory of delay. Every day he awoke to anxiety, every night he retired to it. Pat and HomeSky continued to remain positive about the postponed custody decision but Cory could see that they, too, were worried. When Meadow asked if he wanted to join her and Billy on a walk, he looked out the window. The advent of sunshine offered a second invitation.

Billy faced forward in a sling knotted over Meadow's shoulder. She wore rubber boots and a hooded sweatshirt under her jean jacket. Cory and Meadow walked in silence down the driveway and looked at each other about which way to go on the gravel road. Meadow went right. Cory turned up the collar of his Carhartt jacket and followed her on the road that separated two of their fields.

Long morning shadows accompanied them along the gravel. Up ahead, light sliced through a bend in the road dividing it into equal parts, light and dark. Could one really choose on which side to live?

Meadow pointed to the fields. "It'll be beans there and corn here." Cory looked out at the idle ground—puddled, flat, untilled—and saw every shade of brown. Would Singer be with him to walk the rows when the fields were first spotted with green?

Cory grimaced noticeably.

"Did you hurt something?" she asked.

Cory shook his head, more to clear it than to provide an answer.

"No." He walked along. "Sometimes I see a moment. From the past. I have to push it away."

"Like a flashback?"

"Yeah. I guess."

"Me too," Meadow said.

They walked in sunshine. Billy kicked, let out a happy squeal, his eyes wide to the world.

Meadow continued. "I'll see my old man. Lunging out at me. Out of the shadows. Hate that."

"What do you do?" Cory asked.

"I think about Billy's face. Seeing him fills my mind, crowds everything else out. I make a slender wish."

Cory stopped and looked at Meadow, her straight black hair pulled back, her plain face, her broad nose and squarish jaw framed in the soft oval hood. "What's that?" he asked.

She stood before him. "It's hoping for little things that make life normal. It's asking the Great Spirit to give me dreams stronger than memories."

Cory's face tightened. "I don't know," he said. "Some memories . . ." He shuddered.

They began walking again, gravel crunching underfoot. In age, six years separated them. Cory felt the distance closing. She was no longer the insecure girl who would prop up her head with her hand, bending around her arm, averting her face, downcast eyes hidden in bangs and poor posture. She said, "You can change yourself. You have a chance if you have a slender wish."

"That's what you've done?"

Meadow nodded. "I've done. And others have done for me. Wished for me, too. Look at me, here. Look at us. Why here? Why us?"

The surroundings spoke. Wind whispered across fields waiting to be planted. Trees creaked, sun-bound, about to run sap. Spring was on the verge of making them forget winter ever happened.

Meadow looked at Cory. He bowed his head to the sun. She could see his breathing in the rise and fall of his jacket. He spoke to the ground. "It takes courage to ask when you've been told no so many times."

"You're right," she said. "But you can teach this world something about courage."

THE OFFER

Sunshine bathed the cab of Pat's truck. Was it a sign, he wondered, telling him to think on the bright side? His grip on the steering wheel loosened. Pat let his back settle against the seat.

He had dropped off HomeSky at the grocery store, confirming for the last time that she was sure. She said she was, so he knew what must be done. HomeSky could never bring herself to discuss the sale of her farm face to face with Varkas. He and his had been taking from HomeSky and hers for generations. She now understood why so many ancient treaties were eventually signed. One gets pushed to a desperate ledge.

Pat stood at the punch clock, timecard in hand. He was going to clock in and then speak to Varkas, making him pay for the discussion. But Pat stood there knowing he couldn't do that. It would be untruthful because he wasn't really working. He re-slotted the card in the metal rack.

Varkas was at his desk, cutting venison sausage with his pocketknife, when Pat walked into his office. Varkas was nothing if not shrewd. There was something poorly hidden on Pat's face. *What is that look?* Varkas tried to discern it. *What is the word?* Then he had it. *Concession.*

Varkas held a slice of sausage toward Pat. "Try a bite. Made it myself. The secret is in the casings."

Pat said no thank you.

"Come now," Varkas teased. "You can't negotiate a sale on an empty stomach."

The alarm that registered on Pat's face exposed him.

Varkas nodded and smiled. "Where I come from, it's an insult not to accept another's offer of food." The slice of meat balanced on the knife blade. Pat took it.

"So," Varkas said in a voice Pat had not heard before, a voice lifted a half-octave by the adrenaline of a transaction, "you're here to sell me the farm at last."

Pat would not give Varkas the satisfaction of being astonished by his insight.

"Yes," he said flatly.

"Have a seat," Varkas said. "Please. Get comfortable. We're doing business here. I help you. You help me."

Pat sat at the desk opposite Varkas.

"Now," Varkas said pulling a calculator out of one drawer and reaching in another for a crisp piece of company stationery, "we have $600 an acre, plus all buildings, dwellings and machinery on the property, multiply by—"

"That's not right," Pat said. "Your offer a few months back was $725 an acre, and that didn't include machinery. We plan to auction off as much as we can. And there's the house."

Varkas kept punching buttons on his calculator, not listening to Pat. "There," he said in an upbeat voice. He wrote a number down on his stationery and slid it to Pat. "That's what I'll give you for the place. Lock, stock and barrel."

Pat looked at the cream-white stationery with its regal, red, cursive *V* centered on top. Cold bristled his skin. The number $175,000 was underlined twice in the center of the page. "That's not enough," was all Pat could say. He was thinking about the hospital bills.

"That is my best offer."

"But just two months ago—"

Varkas did not raise his voice. "Today is today. Yes? Yesterday, you had leverage. Today I have it. That is business."

Pat stared down at the number inked into the fine paper. His ears began to fill with an unstable rumble of temper. Varkas continued to speak. "I know your situation. Hospital bills. Mortgage payments. Line of credit. Spring seed and fertilizer to be bought. If you don't sell to me, the bank will end up with it all. And I'll buy from them even cheaper."

Pat picked up the sheet of paper. "This is the best you can do?"

Varkas leaned back in his chair. He had Pat right where he wanted him. "Best I can do."

Pat brought the paper closer to his eyes for a better look. Then he turned it sideways and tore it in half. Then the halves were halved again. Then again. And again. And again. Until the pieces were too small for Pat's powerful hands to tear any further. The scraps, when he turned over his outstretched hand, floated like snowflakes down onto Varkas's desk.

"Big mistake," Varkas told him.

Pat turned to leave.

Varkas's voice roared as he rose from his chair. "Clean that up!"

Pat continued on, knowing what was coming next.

Varkas's words assaulted him in the doorway. "You're fired!"

THE VISITOR

Cory was face-down in the barn ripping off pushups when a car rolled down the driveway to the farmhouse. He neither saw nor heard it.

Billy was upstairs napping while Meadow sat in the kitchen with her blue notebook, playing with song lyrics. Her legs were folded and her moccasin had slipped off her heel, hanging from her toes. She jotted down thoughts about not letting go.

There was a sharp knock at the door.

The sound yanked her back to her father's assault only a hallway away from where she now sat. Fear gripped her throat, stifling her breathing. A second knock sprung her from her chair. Meadow ascended the stairs silently two at a time, scooped up Billy and snuck a look out the bedroom window. She couldn't see who was at the door, but she could see a four-door car that she didn't recognize. No rust, no dents, relatively new—there was nothing threatening about the vehicle but she would take no chances.

Quickly she and Billy were out the back door. They could get to the barn without being seen by whomever was at the front.

Cory was sitting on a hay bale doing bicep curls with a 15-pound fieldstone. He jumped to his feet when he saw the look on Meadow's face as she hurried into the barn.

"What is it?" he said.

"Someone's at the house. Out front. At the door." Billy started to cry.

Cory walked past her, still holding the fieldstone. "Can you safely get up in the loft?" They looked at the ladder in the corner of the barn.

"Yeah," she said. "I don't know if it's even anything."

"I'll go see."

"Sorry."

Cory looked at Meadow. "Don't be. Better safe than sorry. If anything gets started out there, I want you and Billy to go up to the loft and pull up the ladder behind you."

Cory came out into the sunlight, his hands crossed behind his back. His gray sweatpants and matching Badger hockey sweatshirt were well-worn. He had remained clean-shaven since his court date. A man stood back from the door waiting for his knock to be acknowledged.

"Can I help you?" Cory said, continuing toward the man. The stranger on the porch turned, well-dressed, Cory noticed, wearing a crisp white shirt, a blue blazer, khakis and shoes you wouldn't want to walk the property in.

The man came off the porch to the top step, lifted his hand to shield sunlight. Cory stood in the brightness. "Cory?" he said.

The men were now fewer than 20 feet apart. Cory moved the rock behind his back from his left hand to his right.

"Do I know you?" Cory stopped to examine the stranger.

"I apologize for the intrusion." The man's voice was deep and engaging. A small smile came to his face. "You don't recognize me, do you?"

The man was fit, his dark hair neatly trimmed and combed, his complexion well cared for, his teeth bright white. Cory took two steps closer. "I was in the barn exercising." He let his hands come to his sides, revealing the fieldstone. "We don't get many unexpected visitors out here."

The man calmly came down the stairs. He moved with a sense of confidence and grace. "Again, I apologize for the intrusion. I wonder if we can talk for a moment."

"Are you with the bank or the insurance company?" Cory's body tightened.

The visitor tried not to laugh. "No. Far from it. Monsignor Kief sent me."

Cory frowned. "I'm a little confused," he said as the man walked toward him.

The visitor's brown eyes had intelligence and kindness in them. "Cory, take a look at me. Do you remember what you were doing on August 15, 1984?"

Cory squinted at the man, his mind racing back in time. Then, he cocked his head slightly and a quarter-dimpled smile came to Cory's face. "No way," he said.

The visitor smiled broadly and nodded his head. "Yes," he said. "We meet again, though under slightly better circumstances this time."

"Unbelievable," was the only word that Cory could think of at the moment.

They sat at the kitchen table. Cory held Billy on his lap, who was just learning to rake Cheerios in the general direction of his mouth. Meadow made tea, listening and trying to figure out the relationship between the two men. They had made introductions outside. The stranger's name was Matthew Lancone.

"Are you still flying?" Cory asked.

"No. Not since the accident," Matthew said. "That planted my feet firmly on the ground."

"Makes sense," Cory said.

"And my wife would kill me before letting me back in the cockpit."

Meadow broke in. "Excuse me, I'm a little lost here. You were in an accident, as in, you crashed a plane?"

Matthew looked at Cory, whose face said he hadn't told Meadow about the incident. "Cory never mentioned how he's a hero?"

Meadow shook her head. "Cory isn't exactly gabby."

"Cory, do you mind?" Matthew asked.

"Be my guest."

Matthew continued. "About a year and a half ago, in August, I was with my wife and son. He was eight at the time. I took off from the Duluth airport. Late afternoon. Perfect flying conditions, visibility over 10 miles. I flew a single-engine Cessna, a four-seater, all over the country on business. Sometimes my family would come along and we'd make a long weekend of it."

Meadow brought over a steaming tea kettle. "Mind if I pour?" she asked.

Matthew thanked her. Cory made sure his cup was well out of Billy's reach. "We were flying along when there was this sudden pop under the engine cowl. Like a cap gun going off. Almost immediately the oil pressure starts to go. Not good. I knew engine failure couldn't be far off so I reduced power and altitude and looked for a place to put down.

"I was over a lake but there was a nearby field so I headed for it. When my engine stalled all I could do was bank and glide. I caught a power line and the crown of a pine tree as I came into the field, which pitched my nose down and we ended up snapping the landing gear and doing a somersault. Pretty messy."

Meadow was watching Cory and Billy as the story got more chilling. Now and again, a Cheerio made it into Billy's mouth; most were on the floor, and a few plastered to his chubby cheeks. Cory was entranced, amid the wreckage, re-living the story.

"I was in and out of consciousness, upside-down in the cockpit, and I couldn't get my harness unbuckled." Matthew shrugged helplessly. "The last thing I remember is smoke."

Cory had packed this memory far away. Suddenly, he was back staring at the debris. "When I got to the field," Cory said, "your wife had been thrown from the aircraft. I moved her to safety. By the time I crawled in the fuselage, a fire was smoldering. Like you say, smoke everywhere. I almost didn't see your son in back. He was conscious but in shock. I got him unbuckled and out. Then came back for you."

"Just in the nick of time, from what I was told," Matthew said.

"Yeah. Pretty lucky," Cory said, looking off.

"Because of the fire?" Meadow asked.

"The plane exploded," Cory said, still staring blankly. "We made it . . . by a couple of seconds. Crazy." Cory puffed up his cheeks and released a long exhale. "Seems like forever ago, doesn't it?" He looked at Matthew.

"Sometimes it feels like it happened to somebody else. You know?"

Cory nodded and smiled a little. "That's for sure." He paused, then pulled the conversation to the present. "So you said Monsignor Kief sent you?"

"A marvelous, marvelous human being," Matthew said.

Cory struggled with the connection. "How do you know him?"

"After the accident, he came and visited me in the hospital a few time before I was released. He's the kind you get to know really quickly."

Cory laughed. "He does get right to the heart of the matter."

"I remember telling the Monsignor when we first met at the hospital that I wasn't a big believer in God. And he said—and this is something I've thought about pretty much daily since—'well, God certainly is a big believer in you. Or you wouldn't still be here, able to make a difference on His behalf.'"

That thought gave Cory pause.

Matthew continued. "I never got to thank you for what you did, Cory. I thought you'd come visit me in the hospital. You never did."

"Yeah," Cory said. He both did and didn't want to get into this conversation.

"Can I ask you why?" Matthew's face was earnest.

"It's a long story." Cory adjusted Billy on his lap. "I was getting swarmed by the media. Everyone calling me a hero. I was going through a hard time. Sorry. I should have come by."

Matthew shook his head. "No, don't be. Monsignor Kief told me some of that. But I do want to say thank you to you now. Okay?"

"Yeah. Okay."

Matthew looked Cory in the eye. "Thank you for saving my life and the lives of my family. I owe you a tremendous debt."

"You're welcome."

"I'd like to begin to pay you back."

"That's not necessary," Cory said.

"Well, that's what brings me here nonetheless. After I'd come to know Monsignor Kief I told him that if you ever needed help, in any way, he should reach out to me. It was—it is—very important for me to try to repay you. I'll never be able to do for you what you did for me, but I told the Monsignor to let me know if there was anything I could do."

Cory was uncomfortable under the weight of these words.

"Cory, I imagine we have some things in common. I, personally, don't like needing help. I consider myself quite capable."

"Yeah. Same for me," Cory said.

"I had no choice but to accept help from you. I wouldn't be here if not for you. Do you understand the significance of that?"

"Probably not."

"Cory, do you like it when things are even-steven and you don't owe people anything?"

"I do. Yes."

"When Monsignor Kief reached out to me, after he found out about your hospital bills and how that debt endangered your chances of getting custody of the child in your life, I knew that was one place I could help."

"How so?" Cory asked.

Matthew spoke to Cory not with braggadocio but with truth. "I have made a lot of money in my career. Far more than my family will ever need. Ever. And the fact is, my family would not be here to appreciate any of it if not for you. I want to eliminate the possibility that a judge might let financial insecurity come between you and your boy."

"But—"

"Please." Matthew held up a hand. He was a man accustomed to being heard when it was his turn to speak. "What if I told you there are no hospital bills anymore? What if I said my lawyer has sent a letter to the judge presiding over your case showing that you're not only debt-free, but there is also a bank account with a college fund and trust set up in your boy's name?"

"Seriously?" Cory said.

"Cory, money should never be the reason you gain custody of a child. But it damn well won't be the reason you don't."

Cory looked at Meadow as if to ask, *is this happening?*

"And I'd like to do one more thing, if you'll help me."

Cory's head was buzzing. All he could say was okay.

"Monsignor Kief told me that Pat worries deeply about the mortgage and growing debt owed on this farm. I'd like you to help arrange it so I can pay that off, plus adding a little cushion so everyone who lives here never has to worry about losing their home."

Cory was dumbfounded. "I don't know what to say."

Meadow piped in. "Say yes, you dummy. Right Billy? Say yes." Meadow swooped in and took Billy in her arms and lifted him toward the ceiling. "Say yes!"

PART THREE

Decisions

MB

Two weeks ago, when MB went out and purchased a new pair of running shoes, she knew she'd turned a corner. A few months before, she would have accused anyone who might suggest she'd do any such thing as being drunk. But here she was, on a gorgeous May morning, having first walked Singer to school, now wrapped in sunshine, running.

No alcohol. No marijuana. No opiates. Her eyes were opening up. She was more decisive in the ER. She had more energy and initiative. Some of her long-lost fitness and confidence had returned. She had purpose beyond herself.

MB was not an insensitive woman, but she just wanted Judge Healy to get back to a regular court schedule so they could get the custody issue behind them. It was a time for taking next steps.

MB had pieced together a doable three-mile route that weaved through Middleton toward Lake Mendota, where the houses got larger, the lawns better landscaped and the cars more declarative of status.

Disconnected thoughts ran along with her. *Maybe we get a house closer to the lake. If Chevy is too busy when school lets out for a mini-vacation, Singer and I could go. Maybe I'll swing by Chevy's office on the way home for a surprise brunch date.*

Bent over, hands on her knees, MB caught her breath in the small parking lot of Middleton Community Bank. Chevy liked to dismiss his bank as minor league, but tucked into the quaint neighborhood, it was cozy and enduring and trustworthy—MB caught herself. She thought about the scheme Chevy and his boss were running. Her mind, awash in endorphins, left her this message. *Looks can be deceiving.*

At the front desk, the bank's receptionist of 44 years greeted MB with the news that she wasn't sure if Chevy was in his office or away on appointments. In an exasperated voice she said, "He rarely tells me anything." MB rolled her eyes and told the receptionist that she knew exactly what she meant so they might momentarily bond over Chevy's impetuousness.

"You can go back and see if he's in," the receptionist said, offering MB a root beer barrel from her candy dish. MB knew it would be unwise to decline.

His office always struck MB as a bizarre mismatch; with Chevy not at his desk, it appeared even more alien. "Whose office am I in?" she whispered to herself. She looked at his walls clogged with wildlife prints of fish and upland game birds and outdoor pursuits he had zero interest in. Chevy had told her that in the banking business they call this *presenting an agreeable buying environment.*

MB shook her head and laughed, until her eyes fell on the family portrait Chevy was so determined to have her and Singer join him in last Christmas. She studied herself. She looked detached with darkish rings under her eyes that she didn't remember ever being there. "Not your best light, sister."

MB snapped back to the now, realizing that a surprise brunch date wasn't in the cards. The least she could do, she thought, was leave Chevy a dirty note about how he missed out on an office quickie on his desk. That would make him suffer for the absenteeism.

There were no pens on his desk so she opened his drawer to get one. With none in sight, she dug under some Post-it notes, pushed aside a scissors and a Dictaphone before her fingers caught on the tip of an envelope. There was an uncomfortable prickle of familiarity as she slid the envelope forward from under the drawer's contents. The horror of what she'd found was revealed to her an inch at a time.

"No. No. NO!" The words fell hoarsely out of her open mouth. It was her handwriting on the envelope that she had addressed to Cory. "You bastard." She opened the drawer further. Her hand went searching under the pile of notepads and loose paper until she found the second letter.

"You never mailed them." MB sat, then slumped, deadened in Chevy's desk chair. She stared through tears at the two letters Singer had written to Cory. She turned them over. On the back of the envelopes, Singer's hand-drawn smiley faces looked up at her. "I'm so sorry," she whispered.

VARKAS

It was only a matter of time. Varkas knew Pat would come crawling back.

Earlier that day, Pat had emphatically rejected Varkas's lowball offer on the farm. But with bills piling up and now, no job, he'd run himself into a tight corner. Maybe Varkas would knock another twenty thousand off the purchase price for good measure. The thought slightly brightened his sour mood.

At his desk, Varkas went over a few documents. One was a land sale agreement that his lawyer had drawn up for the farm. Just get a signature at all the marked places, Varkas was instructed.

The other he could hardly look at. OSHA was hitting his company with yet another fine. The letter stated that further investigation had turned up two unreported finger amputations due to chainsaw guards being removed from power saw equipment.

When Varkas had first read the citation he immediately called his lawyer. Livid, shouting into the phone, he said that anyone who knew [expletive] anything about felling trees knows those [expletive] guards only get in the [expletive] [expletive] way!

The lawyer listened calmly and advised Varkas to have his men put the chainsaws down until the guards went back on. He further explained that this latest $20,000 citation meant the company was now on notice due to repeated willful violations and had been elevated to OSHA's Severe Violator Program. Translation: the regulators were going to be on him like wood-boring beetles.

Varkas sat at his desk, staring a hole through the letter and citation bearing the U.S Department of Labor eagle and shield in the upper left corner. What the hell, he wondered, had come of the country he so dearly loved? His grandfather and father were shining examples of how determination and industry could propel a man upward in America. They spurred the horse of capitalism. Now, damn all its fences, regulations and hobbling ropes. It was betrayal.

Increasingly, the focus of Varkas's anger was Sheriff Harris. He instigated the inspections. He accused Varkas of putting profit before people. What did the Sheriff know about the risks and realities of business? He had taxpayers to butter his bread.

The phone at his desk rang. It was his bank calling.

"Hello," Varkas said sharply.

"Mr. Varkas. It's Howard at First National."

"You better be calling with good news."

"I'm sorry to say that I am not."

Varkas covered his mouth with his huge hand. Then rubbing his chin, "Speak."

The banker's voice cracked. "You asked me to keep an eye on Pat O'Rourke's accounts, including the farm."

"And . . ."

"He's had sizable activity in his accounts. Deposits, that is."

Varkas straightened in his office chair. "How sizable?"

"Very sizable."

Varkas shouted into the phone. "Be specific, man!"

There was a pause, a shuffling of papers. "The mortgage on the farm is paid in full."

"Impossible!" roared Varkas.

"And all the farm's secondary debt—machinery loans, etcetera—has been paid. The farm's free and clear."

The words rang in Varkas's ears. He lowered his voice. "There has to be a mistake. What with these damn computers running things."

"I quadruple-checked, Mr. Varkas." The banker paused. "And that's not all."

Now Varkas stood, his height lifting the phone off the desk. "What do you mean that's not all!"

The banker's voice was barely audible over the phone. "A significant deposit has been made in his joint account with HomeSky

Blackholm."

Varkas's face contorted. He grit his teeth, squeezing the telephone receiver almost to its breaking point, saying nothing.

"Are you still ther—"

"HOW GODDAMN SIGNIFICANT!"

"There is a $300,000 balance in the account at this time."

"$300,000?"

"Yes, sir."

Varkas lightened his stranglehold on the receiver. He sat down. He took a deep breath. "Where did the money come from?" Varkas spoke without emotion.

"New York. A bank there."

"Find out who this money came from."

"Yes, sir." The banker paused to gather his courage. "Mr. Varkas, may I make a suggestion?"

On the other end of the phone, Varkas closed his eyes. "This better be good."

As it turned out, what the banker suggested was indeed that.

MB

Singer was again buckled in his booster seat, now holding his package of Sugar Babies. He promised to eat only ten. This was a boy of his word.

MB had pulled off the highway looking for a restroom, a payphone and a treat. They scored the trifecta at Casey's Convenience Store in Eau Claire, Wisconsin.

After putting a few quarters in the pay phone, MB waved at Singer, who waved back. The car was parked only a matter of feet from the storefront where a phone box hung on the brick facade. Nonetheless, she was uncomfortable leaving him in the car alone.

MB knew Jenni's direct dial, which allowed her to bypass the over-bearing executive secretary. Her friend wasn't in court this week, at least that's how MB remembered it. Maybe MB would get lucky and Jenni would be at her desk.

She picked up on the third ring. "This is Jennifer."

"Jenni, it's me."

"Hi," Jenni said cheerfully. "What a nice surprise."

"Surprise for sure. I'm in Eau Claire."

"What? I thought you were working afternoons this week."

"Called in sick."

"Are you okay?"

"I'm fine. Actually, not so fine. I have Singer. We're driving to Baudette. You know, Minnesota."

There was a pause on the line as Jenni's mind fully left the work she was doing and focused on the call.

"MB, is there is something wrong? If you can't talk just say, 'the roads are great.'"

"Jenni, seriously, I'm okay. Singer is fine, too. I'm just having a really hard day and I need a favor."

"Tell me how I can help."

MB exhaled. She stood shielded from the gusty spring winds, leaning against the sun-warmed brick. Her harbor. "Remember the letters I told you Singer wrote to Cory over the winter. The ones Cory never responded to?"

"Yeah. Jerk." Jenni said.

"I found them. Unmailed. In Chevy's desk at work. I stopped by to see him today. He wasn't there so I went to leave him a note and . . . Jesus. He never put them in the mailbox."

"Oh, MB, I'm sorry. I don't know what to say."

"Let's start with asshole. Why would he ever do that? What's he afraid of?"

"Hard to say."

MB's voice intensified. "Here I've been, judging this Cory guy as too hung up on his own recovery and pity party to write back to this wonderful, loving little boy. This changes things for me, Jenni."

"I understand you're pissed off. But don't do anything rash."

"Is that my friend talking? Or a lawyer?"

Those words stung. "C'mon. Not fair," Jenni said.

"I'm sorry. I just needed to go. To clear my head. Mostly, I need to see the two of them together."

Jenni asked, "To tell you what?"

"If they belong together."

"Honey, we've been over this. Determining the best interest of the child requires an objective third party—"

"Jenni, no. For one reason or another, I've been given this delay in the custody decision. I've been given these letters. I have a child with me that means more to me than I mean to me. I need to see Singer and Cory together. I am going to listen to my heart, not some judge who's not only distracted by what he and his wife just went through, plus his heavy caseload, but also by what now appears to be a great job of acting by Chevy."

"Are you saying Chevy doesn't love Singer?"

MB's voice lost its punch. "I think there's a reasonable chance of that."

"Then you're doing the right thing," Jenni said. "And I totally support you. What can I do?"

CHEVY

Chevy was having a fantastic morning. He lined up a new business loan with a man who had two oil-change service stores in the area and was looking to expand. He was confident that as vehicles became more sophisticated, fewer and fewer drivers would have the inclination or the knowledge to change their own oil. Chevy, always fast to dodge any and all DYI projects, couldn't have agreed more. His confidence in the man's business strategy sealed the deal.

As Chevy pulled together the necessary paperwork for an afternoon signing, he got a call from the receptionist up front. He had a guest, a Ms. Jennifer Taylor.

"Send her back," he said, frowning. He adjusted the knot of his tie. *What could this be about?* His palms went clammy.

"Hello, Jenni," Chevy said, getting out from behind his desk, putting on his best banker smile and giving her a polite hug. "How are the twins?"

Jenni considered asking him if he remembered their names, but she saw little point in that. "Everybody's great. How about Singer?"

Chevy nodded. "Yep, great too. Looking forward to summer. No school. Cartoons on the couch. Mom time. You know."

They looked at each other, as the small talk teetered.

"So to what do I owe the pleasure?" Chevy's face stiffened.

"MB asked me to stop by," Jenni said.

"MB? What's up? Have a seat."

Jenni and Chevy sat down on opposite sides of his desk.

Chevy caught himself. "I'm sorry. Can I get you a coffee or water?"

Jenni said no thank you. "I'll just jump right in," she said. "MB is driving Singer up to Baudette today to meet with Cory."

Chevy reeled. His eyes shifted back and forth as he searched for a coherent thought. "She's working double threes today."

"She called in sick."

"Why? Why would she drive up there? Did you tell her that's crazy?"

"No, I didn't."

Chevy's voice began rising. "C'mon. The judge said it's better to keep everyone apart. Until the ruling. For the kid's sake. And it could screw our chances of winning."

"Seriously?" Jenni said, trying to remain calm. "Winning? You can't actually think of Singer's situation as some sort of competition."

"I don't want to argue over words. When did she call?" Chevy paused to think. "And where was she?"

"About 30 minutes ago, from Eau Claire."

"And you didn't try to stop her?"

"No. I just listened to her."

"Why in hell would she do something crazy like that?" Chevy pulled his hands through his groomed hair.

Jenni explained. "Because she was here today. Came before lunch to surprise you. Brunch date. You weren't here. She went into your desk for paper and a pen, to leave you a note."

Chevy looked at Jenni. He still wasn't putting it together.

"The unmailed letters. She found them."

"Oh, Christ," Chevy said under his breath. He opened his desk drawer. Singer's letters were gone. He exhaled sharply, putting his head in his hand. "Stupid."

Jenni wasn't sure for whom that word was intended. "She says she wants to see them together. That will tell her where Singer belongs."

"Is she super pissed off at me?"

"I think right now she's more concerned about Singer than she is about you."

Chevy looked down at the floor and tapped his forehead with his index finger. Then he looked back up at Jenni. "We'll call the lawyer. What's his face. Michael Cadder." Chevy was grasping at straws. "Maybe he can reach her somehow. Talk her out of it. Like if MB calls again we can get the number and have him call her. Tell her this is not in the kid's best interest. Right?"

"I already spoke to your lawyer."

"What? Why?"

"Because he's a colleague of mine, remember? He's representing you two as a favor to me."

"Oh, yeah. So what did you say to him?"

"I asked for his opinion of MB's decision."

"And?"

"He said he'd recommend against it."

Chevy's eyes widened. "Did I tell you!"

"But he said he understood it nonetheless."

Chevy shook his head. "Why are you guys all against me?"

Jenni tried not to show her disappointment. "This isn't about you. This is about a young boy and doing the right thing."

Chevy's back straightened. "He's my kid. I'm the father for chrissakes. He belongs with me."

"That is now for the court to decide."

Chevy broke off eye contact. "I'm the father," he repeated.

Against her better judgment, Jenni pushed the issue. "Chevy, do you love Singer? You haven't even used his name once since this conversation began."

"Yeah, sure. I love Singer."

"Then why didn't you mail his letters?"

"I don't know."

Jenni frowned. "That's it? You don't know."

Chevy looked up at the Christmas family portrait. "It's complicated," he said.

CONTRACTS

The '66 Toronado had plenty of downward push left in the accelerator pedal, but even driving 60 miles per hour made Cory flash on memories he only wanted to forget. His right foot eased off and he sat back from the steering wheel.

Meadow rode to his right and Billy Little Tree was in the back in his rear-facing car seat. They drove the two-lane highway toward town.

"How long does he have to sit that way?" she asked. "It's gotta suck. He likes watching the world."

Cory tried to remember Singer at that age. "I think till he's about two."

Meadow shook her head. "I was bouncing around in a box in the back of a station wagon when I was Billy's age."

"That begins to explain things." Cory offered a rare quarter-dimpled smile.

Meadow, not taking the bait, opted for silence.

"Can you believe it?" Cory asked.

"Craziest thing. Ever. And I've been involved in some crazy." She paused, the hum of the wheels on the blacktop filling in. Then they both started to laugh.

After the unfathomable 30-minute pilot's visit and his miraculous generosity, Cory and Meadow sat stunned at the farmhouse kitchen table assuring each other that they weren't dreaming. Then they called Pat at work to share the great news. Cory had to ask the receptionist twice to be sure he had heard correctly, but it was true. Pat had been fired that morning.

They quickly hung up and reached HomeSky at the grocery store. At first, she thought the three of them were in cahoots, playing a practical joke: medical bills paid in full, farm and loans paid off, a hefty sum in their bank account, Pat fired from the plant—sure thing, she had said. But the more Cory insisted, the more he explained about the pilot, and then when he put Meadow on to confirm, the more HomeSky came to believe it could be true. That it was true.

But they had to hurry—HomeSky was near frantic. They had to find Pat, fast! Asked why, HomeSky told them that she and Pat had made a decision to sell the farm to pay the medical bills. Pat was talking to Varkas today. If he signed a sales contract, HomeSky said, all this good fortune would vanish in the stroke of a pen.

Varkas raced to his lawyer's office for a revised land sale agreement. That in hand, he went on the hunt for Pat. It was his banker's idea, and he quite liked it: maybe Pat didn't know about the funds transferred into his account. By law, the bank had 24 hours to notify their client. So, the banker told Varkas, if you can get to Pat with a revised offer before Pat discovers he doesn't need to sell, well maybe, just maybe, you can pickpocket him. Brilliant, Varkas concluded.

Varkas had to have it. That land had gone from a curiosity to an interest to an obsession. It began with the old plat book, a circle inked around that quarter section, and his grandfather's mysterious, one-word jotting in the margin: WATER! Later, came his dad's notation: AUGUST, NO RAIN IN 2 MONTHS. CREEK IS FULL. Varkas could almost smell the water that ran beneath HomeSky's property.

You didn't need to come from a family of windmill agents to understand the importance of subsurface water. More and more people were putting greater and greater demands on fewer and fewer resources. If Varkas could tap that aquifer there's no telling how far he could move it. Pipelines can be built by man. Water cannot. To Varkas's way of thinking, water was the gold of the future. He wondered, *Do they have any idea what they're sitting on? Maybe the Indian woman knows.*

It was lunchtime and Varkas's truck was headed toward Lu Ann's. *Where else would a man, out of a job, on an empty stomach, go?*

For some people, the pop and crunch of gravel under tires induces a transformation like no other. Pat's body began to unwind as his truck rolled down the long curved approach.

Ahead, the sight of the amber and penny-colored pipestone church gave him solace. This small building had humbly stood for over 100 years, built by hand, stone by stone, by imperfect men, to withstand heat and cold and wind and loss. Surrounded by a sentinel of century-old Norway pines, with its bell tower rising singularly above the roofline, the church where Pat was once pastor stood before him. A warm breeze. The familiar swish of pine boughs. A crow far off.

Pat had come here to reflect. He swung his pickup around so the rear was facing the building. He got out, released the tailgate and hiked himself up, sitting in the presence of peace.

What should I do, Father? Was it my temper that cost me my job and the offer on the farm? How will I provide now? Is it my pride that goeth before the fall? He closed his eyes to listen. His breathing, his shoulders, his hands, his heart, opened.

It was a dishonest offer, Father. The man's a predator. Is it right for me to collect a paycheck to pay for my daily bread and turn a blind eye to his repugnant ways? How he treats the land? How he treats his employees? Greed. Degenerate greed. Father, am I an accomplice? Is it misguided self-righteousness that makes me stand? Should I cower before his boot and ask for forgiveness? Ask for my job back? Ask for his money to at least pay for the majority of Cory's bills?

Pat bowed his head and folded his hands. The sun stroked his back. He listened for an answer, but heard only his own breathing.

He opened his eyes and found himself looking down at a good-sized throwing stone. Not too large. Not too small. A Goldilocks stone. Then his eyes rose to the bell tower, and a singular copper bell inside. He and Cory had come here about four years ago. They stood in this place and talked about how self-reliance and resilience did not preclude the need for support and community.

Pat hopped off the tailgate. He stretched his throwing arm and shoulder. Rock in hand, he took a few steps closer to the bell tower.

He let go . . . of the rock, of the worry, of the doubt. The stone rose upward as if riding a string attached to the center of the bell. A peal sung out, clear and bright.

The nesting pigeons flushed in a clatter of wings. Quickly they fell into formation, easily reaching speeds of 40 miles per hour, circling the parking lot, banking in unison, then flying the length of the church roofline, only inches apart. The streaking gray shapes made two more passes before they lit back into the tower. There were six of them now.

Varkas finished two plates of food and drank three-quarters of a pot of coffee. He was not satisfied. A white folder with the bold red Varkas *V* lay on the table across from him. Atop it, a pen.

His large head swiveled incessantly from the door, which was directly in his sightline, to the front window, which offered a view of anyone parking in front of the diner. His black eyes were restless under coarse, brushy brows.

Varkas was too large for the chair. His chest was like an oil drum under his brown flannel shirt, appointed with a miniature American flag pinned to the flap of the breast pocket. His red neckerchief, tied around his shirt collar, offered a slash of color on an otherwise dark and brooding figure. Few people said hello, let alone sat near him. He waited.

Pat was hungry. He parked in front, hoping the better part of Lu Ann's lunch rush had come and gone. He was avoiding the crowd. The thought of explaining to the regulars why he wasn't eating lunch down at the plant made his skin itch.

As he stepped out of his truck, the vented aroma of bacon cheeseburgers doubled his pace. As he reached for the door he saw Lu Ann coming his way from inside. Despite what they'd been through, their hellos were becoming less forced and their friendship more natural.

She stopped him just inside the door. "Varkas is here. He's been asking about you."

Pat stiffened. "Thank you." He touched Lu Ann's arm as he

passed her.

Varkas's mouth, lips grimly pressed together, the ends downturned, twisted into a rare smile. He stood to greet Pat.

Have faith. Pat strode toward Varkas's table, putting on bluster. "Hello, Varkas," he said, dropping the deferential Mr. before his surname. "What brings you to Lu Ann's?"

Varkas wasn't prepared for such a confident offensive. "Ah, just getting a bite to eat. Looking for you."

"And you found me. Mind if I join you?" Pat said, taking a seat at Varkas's table.

Varkas blinked, frowned and took a deep breath. "I was hoping you would, yes."

Pat knew one thing for certain about Varkas: he was a conversation leader. He had a premeditated route of directing what was said so he could walk over people. "Sorry about that spat we had in your office," Pat said. He was beginning to enjoy not living in fear of this brute.

Varkas's dull eyes suddenly had a gleam. "Okay," he slowly nodded. "I know what you're doing here and it's not going to work."

Pat returned Varkas's eye contact. "You mean eating?" He smiled.

"Pat," Varkas said impatiently.

"Varkas," Pat replied.

Varkas folded his giant hands, his fingers so thick they could hardly intertwine. He thought about that land. He thought about that aquifer. He got back on track. "I apologize for the offer I made earlier this morning. You were right. It was unfair of me to lowball from the price we had discussed." Varkas slid the folder and pen closer to Pat. "I revised the agreement back up. I think you'll be pleased."

"Thank you for that apology," Pat said. "I don't imagine you do that often."

"What?" Varkas said.

"I don't imagine you're a man who apologizes often and admits his mistake."

Varkas's eyes narrowed. "You're right about that."

"Well I appreciate it. I'm starved. I need to order. Lu Ann!" Pat raised his hand.

Lu Ann came over, stopping an arm's length from the table. She reached to pour coffee like the mug was in a wasp nest.

"What are the specials?" Pat asked.

Lu Ann recited them, but said they were nonetheless gone.

"Any pie left?"

Pat was informed they had two slices of blueberry and one raspberry.

"Apple's all gone?"

Lu Ann said it was long gone.

"Any other desserts?" Pat wanted to know.

They had lemon bars and Rice Krispy bars.

"Did you tell me the soup?" Pat asked.

Lu Ann said she had.

Meanwhile, Varkas was getting hotter than the coffee. Lu Ann got out of there lickety split with Pat's order.

Exasperated, Varkas said, "Can we discuss the offer in the folder."

"Sure," Pat said, sipping his coffee.

"Aren't you going to look at it?"

"Nope."

"What do you mean no?"

"Here's what I want you to do. I want you to double that number and then we'll discuss it."

Varkas's hands, which had been folded and resting on his midsection, became fists. His mouth curled. "You know that's never going to happen."

"That's my deal."

"But just this morning you said—"

Pat interrupted. "Now is now. Yes? This morning you had leverage. This afternoon I have it. That is business. Sound familiar?"

To have his words turned against him was Varkas's breaking point. When he rose to his feet he took a handful of Pat's shirt with him. Varkas, the size of a bear, lifted Pat to his tiptoes before pulling him across the table toward him. “Don’t mess with me, Mr. O’Rourke.” Pat smelled garlic.

In an eye blink, Pat whirled his fists overhead and slammed them down on Varkas’s arm, to break his grip. He could have struck a tree branch for the effect it brought.

“Do you hear me?” Varkas’s face twitched. “I will have that land.”

What wasn’t heard, in the toppling of both men’s chairs and the scuff of the sliding table, was the tinkle of the brass bell announcing the entrance of Sheriff Harris, with Cory, Meadow and Billy just behind.

“Varkas!” the Sheriff shouted. “Take your hands off that man!”

The Sheriff’s command hung in the noiseless diner.

Varkas’s face spoke of the disgust he held for the Sheriff. “And what are you going to do about it.”

The Sheriff moved quicker than anyone thought possible. One second he was standing at the door, then striding past the coffee station, then perched at the table with a full pot of coffee cocked at his hip, ready to be thrown in Varkas’s face. “If there is anything about your looks you value,” the Sheriff said, “you’ll take your hand off that man and quietly leave.”

Varkas looked down at the steaming open mouth of the coffee pot. And in the Sheriff’s eyes, he saw no trepidation about following through. Varkas released Pat.

Imbued everywhere, in the few customers, the waitresses, the cook who had come out of the kitchen holding a spatula, in every face, there was gawking disbelief.

“This ain’t over. Not by a little.” Varkas picked up his folder, unclicked his pen and re-pocketed it, stepped back from the Sheriff, head high, and loudly strode out of the diner.

Everyone was not only speechless, they were afraid to exhale.

Lu Ann broke the ice. “Arrest that man, Sheriff. He left without paying.”

MB

An elderly woman had fashioned a wind bonnet out of a scarf. She was out on the road at the mailbox. It was unlike her to retrieve the mail so late in the day, but she'd been to Hibbing to visit her sister, and her sister sure could talk.

MB slowed the car down and pulled off onto the shoulder of the highway.

"Why are we stopping?" Singer wanted to know.

"I'll just be a second. I'm going to go ask that woman something." MB unbuckled her seatbelt.

"What woman?" Singer asked, craning his head.

"She's back at the mailbox."

"Oh. What are you going to ask her about?"

"I'm going to see if she knows where Cory's farm is."

Singer looked surprised. "Don't you know?"

MB laughed. "You silly bean. I've never been there. And you know what else?" She turned around and gently touched him on the nose. "You are full of questions."

Singer was delighted. "I know."

From her purse, MB got a pen and one of the envelopes addressed to Cory, hoping to use them to jot down directions. She was careful not to let Singer see the envelope; it was the only paper she had. In the eight and a half hours they had been driving, she still hadn't thought of a good way to explain why she had the letters and Cory didn't.

The woman had seen the car pull over and she waited in the wind with her mail. The setting sun made luminous trophies of a few small clouds and turned the gravel into gold. MB hurried along the shoulder of the road. She waved and the woman did the same as the space between them closed. In the last week of April, once the sun touches the horizon, the warmth goes quickly, leaving a chill on the blustery flatlands north of Baudette.

Turned out the woman had lived and farmed in the area since she was married at 19. She ~~knew every backroad~~ in a 15-mile radius and drew a neat map on the back of the envelope, reminding MB twice that it wasn't to scale. MB thanked the woman who said she didn't mean to pry, but what occasion brought her to the area? Whether or not it was the wind, the elderly woman couldn't be sure, but MB's eyes teared. She said she was here for a reunion.

At the farmhouse, dinner came late. Who had time to be hungry? What with the giddy re-tellings of the story of the pilot's surprise visit, going over to thank Monsignor Kief for making it all possible, Pat driving home and then to the bank with their joint passbook to personally see updated balances, in ink, noted in their accounts. Alleluia!

They had brought home steak and potatoes and even sour cream from the grocery store, but spent another hour laughing and talking and it wasn't until Billy got fussy that they all realized they were famished. Pat and Cory got the coals started on the grill. The potatoes were rolled in olive oil and sprinkled with salt and put in the preheated oven. A salad was tossed. Cory's face hurt and it took him a moment to realize why: uncontrolled smiling.

They were just sitting down to eat when they heard a car pull in. There was enough light remaining that headlights weren't required to see, nonetheless, a beam of lights preceded the car down the driveway.

"Who can that be?" Pat said, getting up from the dining room table. Cory joined him at the window. They didn't recognize the car nor the tall young woman who got out from the driver's seat to stretch her back. They were all standing at the window when she opened the door and reached into the back seat. Even on a day that harvested miracles, they couldn't believe what they saw next.

The front door to the farmhouse banged open and Cory was the first onto the porch. He stopped before the steps. In wasn't just the failing light that made it so hard for him to trust his eyes. Life had repeatedly beaten Cory with the very trust he had extended. But he had allowed himself a slender wish.

Pat flipped on the porch light and he and the others came out.

"Cory!" Singer called out, running toward him.

Cory jumped off the porch and dropped to his knees. Singer came to him, as fast as he could, but it couldn't be soon enough. He leapt into Cory's outstretched arms, and Cory held on for his life.

MB watched from the car. She didn't bother to wipe away the tears. The reality of their love ached deep in her stomach. She placed a hand there.

Cory and Singer rocked in the low light of the farmyard. "Let me see you," Cory said, releasing the embrace, holding Singer's shoulders. "You're getting so big. I missed you very, very much." Tears streaked down Cory's face.

Singer gently pressed his small, warm hands on Cory's cheeks. In the touch of those hands came a new level of healing.

Singer was asleep in Cory's bed. Meadow was up in her bedroom with Billy. The dinner dishes were finished, crumbs swept from the table. HomeSky and Pat said they were going out for a walk under the stars. They sensed Cory and MB needed some space to talk about things left unsaid in front of Singer and the others.

"These are for you," MB said, handing Singer's letters to Cory. "They're why I came. Last winter, I gave them to Chevy to mail and he hid them at work."

"Why don't you sit down," Cory said, taking the letters. He was seated at the kitchen table.

She did. "I had created this bad guy of you," MB said, quietly. "A guy who got letters from a boy who loved him but didn't have the decency to write back. Singer asked about those letters day after day." MB shook her head. "I came to despise you."

MB shifted in her chair but her eyes remained on the wall. "I didn't know if you were too injured or too selfish to respond, but I started thinking Singer would be better off with Chevy and me." She shrugged her shoulders.

Cory looked at the small, neat map drawn on the back of one of the envelopes. He thought of all the turns that brought him here. "Does Chevy know where you are?"

"Yes. I haven't spoken to him, but a friend of mine back home did."

"You should call him. He'll be worried. Tell him everything's all right."

"Is it?" MB said with sudden fierceness. "This is so messed up. I have a boyfriend who I'm seriously thinking of starting a family with, and now I can't trust him."

"You still should call him."

"That's my decision, okay?"

Cory looked at MB. He could see how deeply she cared. "Sure."

"You know Chevy, right?"

"It's been a while. But yeah."

"Why would he not mail those letters?"

"You should ask him."

MB's eyes flashed. "Oh I will." She nodded. "I don't know if I'll get a straight answer, but believe me I will."

Cory thought about her question. "Maybe he didn't want to lose."

Those words were chilling. "What is it with you guys?"

"Don't put me in the same category."

"But it's all about winning, isn't it?"

"No. Not any more."

MB looked at Cory. He was thin. He had dark circles under his eyes. He certainly didn't have Chevy's confidence or arrogance. Maybe they were different. "You love him, don't you?"

"More than anything."

"Where would you two live?"

"Here, for the summer. I'm looking at renting a house in Duluth for the school year. I teach math at the high school. Used to coach, too. Not sure about that anymore." Cory thought about it. "It might do Singer good, me coaching. He used to love coming to our games. I need to do something that makes him proud."

"Would you have any help in Duluth?" It was like MB was interviewing Cory for the job of dad.

"We have—I have daycare help. A neighbor friend." Cory shrugged. "I'd be mostly on my own. That's never been a problem."

The two looked at each other. MB exhaled heavily and nodded. "Would it be okay if I used the phone?"

"There's one in the kitchen. Or, for more privacy, in the den off the entryway."

MB walked toward the den.

MORNING

MB wasn't a person who prayed for guidance. In fact, she considered prayer an overhyped form of self-delusion. The couch, where she insisted on spending the night, offered no solace. So she was left to restlessly toss through spotty, shallow sleep, her mind overloaded. Until the morning light illuminated what she must do.

Pat and HomeSky were up whisperingly early, padding around the kitchen, trying to hush coffee pots and quiet oatmeal pans as they tended to breakfast. Then MB was standing there in the kitchen doorway.

"Oh, good morning," HomeSky said, trying to not look startled.

"Good morning," MB said.

"Sorry if we woke you," Pat told her.

"No. I sleep, and don't sleep, funny hours. Messed up from working in the ER."

HomeSky went to the cupboard for another coffee mug. "That has to be difficult, working in an emergency room."

MB nodded but didn't expound.

"Can I get you coffee?" HomeSky asked.

MB shrugged. "Sure." She obviously had something on her mind and couldn't quite decide where to start.

"Will you join us?" HomeSky waited with a mug of coffee by an empty chair at the table.

"Thank you," MB said, taking her coffee and a seat. She looked around the kitchen at the clean, white walls and the beginnings of morning light leaking through its many windows. "You have a wonderful house," she said.

They both thanked her.

MB began. "So this isn't easy for me, intruding on you, bringing Singer here. I'd like to explain."

"Don't feel you have to," HomeSky said. "You're welcome here. We're just so glad to see Singer. He looks well."

MB proceeded. "I needed to see Singer with Cory. I guess I needed to see Singer here, too. He's talked endlessly about you, all of you. And about the farm. And about Duluth." MB paused. "I want you to know that I only want what's best for Singer."

"That's good to know," Pat said.

HomeSky watched MB. She liked her. "We appreciate you coming up. I didn't understand why you came. But I think I do now."

"Kids have giant imaginations, at least that's what I'm learning," MB said. "I needed to see all of this for myself. It's a big decision. I want you to know that I understand that."

HomeSky and Pat nodded.

"When Cory gets up I'd like to talk to him for a minute if you can watch Singer."

"Of course," HomeSky said. "But he's already up. Cory's our lark."

"Out in the barn," Pat added. "He's created a kind of gym out there. Like his physical therapy center, just with a dirt floor."

"He was hurt badly, then?" MB asked. "I've seen too many high-speed car crashes."

Pat told her straight. "He was thrown through the windshield. Head trauma put him in a coma for four days. Dislocated hip, compound wrist fracture, lacerated kidneys, one they couldn't save."

"But he's doing better now? You don't see any lasting effects . . . that could impact Singer?"

HomeSky spoke up. "Cory's been through an awful lot, but no. You wouldn't need to worry about Cory being unable to take care of Singer."

"Okay," MB said, nodding. "Good to know. Good to know."

Cory's back was to MB when she entered the barn. She shivered in the cold, stale air, watching Cory jump rope in the center of the dirt floor under a single overhead light. Rhythmically, he alternated one-foot jumps—right foot, left foot, right foot, left foot. The speed and regularity of the rope's whip-slap was mesmerizing.

She waited for his foot to catch, not wanting to interrupt. Realizing that might be some time, she walked into his peripheral vision so as not to alarm him.

He stopped upon seeing her.

"You're good at that," MB said. "I figured I might be standing there all morning."

The hood of Cory's sweatshirt was pulled up. Sweat streamed down his face, which he wiped with his dirty sleeve. "You should have seen me two months ago. Pathetic."

"You're making progress, then," MB both said and asked.

Cory was breathing hard. "Little bit every day."

"So this is your gym?" MB asked, turning a slow circle. "Pat told me about it."

"Yep. The price is right."

MB looked at Cory, really looked at him, leaning into her eye contact. "You're not what I thought you'd be."

Cory didn't know how to respond.

MB saw he was uncomfortable, so she changed gears. "It was cute last night. Watching Singer holding Billy."

Cory laughed. "He would have stayed on that couch with him all night long. But Billy won't sit for that."

"The looks on their faces."

"Yeah. They seemed pretty amazed by each other," Cory said.

"So this is where your friend Joseph grew up? This farm?"

"Yep."

"Do you mind talking about him?"

"Not really. It's fine."

"You and Chevy and Joseph all played UW hockey together?"

Cory smiled to himself. "Joseph and I go back further than that. We played against each other our senior year in the Minnesota high school hockey championship, which is kinda a big deal in these parts.

But we didn't belong on opposing sides. We always said hockey was our ticket to college together." Cory nodded.

MB dared another step. "Chevy said Joseph died too young."

"Before our junior year. Devastating. Especially for HomeSky. Joseph was all she had." Cory shrugged. "All either of us had. He was an amazing person. Left a big hole."

"Did you ever want to just run away from this place? All the memories?"

"Yeah, we both tried that. But you can't run from something like that. It'll just chase you."

MB nodded. "I know what you mean."

She stepped away from Cory and took notice of the barnwood walls, knotted, splintered, gapped from all they had endured. But still beautiful. Toward the back of the barn, a photograph and two letters were tacked to the wall. MB gestured. "Do you mind?"

"Sure, go ahead."

The light was poor, but MB looked closely at the curled photo of Cory with a smiling woman and Singer, who had a marshmallow on a stick. "Is that Singer's mom?"

"It is."

"She's beautiful."

"Yeah, she is."

"What about these?" Thumbtacks held two letters from students to the barnwood. "They're from kids I teach and coach. When I think what I do doesn't matter, I look at them."

MB read the letters. She turned to face Cory. "You're an impressive guy, you know that?"

"Not most days I don't."

MB nodded. "A person needs reminders."

"Yes. They do."

MB walked back to Cory. "Sorry for all the questions." She had a steady resolution in her eyes. "I didn't want to say anything in front of Singer, but I'll tell you now. I think Singer should be here. With you."

Cory hardly dared move. "Honestly?"

MB nodded sadly.

"Thank you," Cory said hoarsely. "Really, really thank you."

MB looked at the morning light flooding in the open barn doors. "I know it's up to the judge, but I promise you," MB had to stop, the words catching. "I promise you I'm going to do everything I can . . ."

Cory wanted to scream for joy, but he was in the presence of sadness too profound.

RETURNING

They had a long drive back to Middleton. MB tried to make it last even longer. They pulled over at roadside historic markers. Played round after round of I Spy. They sang songs. They stopped for lunch at a truck stop and each got a cowboy hat and wore them while they split a chocolate shake with whipped cream.

Singer was a real trouper. As the drive went on, every time he was about to nod off, MB would re-engage him. They practiced counting up to 20. She made up a story about two rambunctious chipmunks, Rufus and Goofus, who lived on a farm and snuck in the trunk of a car and came to the city and stirred up all sorts of trouble. She didn't want him to nap. Not until she was as close to Middleton as possible.

When Singer finally slept, MB was on the homestretch. She thought about her phone conversation with Chevy the night before. He was furious about her decision to take Singer to see Cory, but she would not be drawn in. Not over the phone. Not in someone else's home. Not with Singer under the same roof would she raise her voice and declare that she was the one person in this conversation with the right to be furious.

He kept looping back to the same question. Why won't you just leave it to the judge? And she repeated the same answer. I had to see for myself. What she didn't say was that the judge hadn't seen the farm as the sun came up nor witnessed the serenity there nor watched HomeSky and Pat momentarily hold hands while French toast cooked nor observed as Meadow quietly got up to do the dishes while others talked nor felt determination radiate off Cory as he jumped rope in the barn nor seen the look on Singer's face as he held Billy on his lap nor watched Singer run into Cory's outstretched arms. The judge had only seen file notes. The judge had met them for

30 minutes.

Chevy felt sorry for himself and asked if she had any idea how that made him feel to be left out of such a huge decision. She said how about the decision you left me out of when you didn't mail the letters?

Chevy admitted his mistake. He apologized. Said he blew it. MB didn't know if it was the truth or an act. She didn't say the words out loud, but MB didn't know if she could trust him. She was okay taking that risk herself, but this was about more than that.

Will you come home first thing? Chevy asked. He'd take the afternoon off. If she had to go to the ER, he and Singer would pal around. Have pizza. He said he heard from their social worker. The judge was back scheduling his caseload and they would be in court for the decision in a week. Just a week left to go, he told her.

When MB pulled into ER parking, Singer was zonked out. She used her pass card to go in the employee entrance hoping not to be seen. She hurried down the hall to the pharmacy. Excellent. Thomas was working. He was surprised to see her.

"Long time, gorgeous," he said, racking a prescription. He opened up his arms, walking toward her.

MB reached over the half-door countertop to give him a hug. "Sorry. Busy, busy."

"All good, I hope." Thomas stood back to assess her. "You look great. I'm jealous."

"You too, honey."

"Flattery. It will get you everywhere."

They looked at each other for a moment.

"So what's up?" Thomas asked.

MB got right to it. "I need you to misplace a bottle of Ox. Eighties."

"Whoa. Girl." Thomas lowered his voice. He poked his head over the half-door separating them and looked in both directions down the hallway. "I don't see you for a couple months and now this?"

"And now this."

"Eighty milligrams, and a bottle no less? That's no easy dip."

"Just fill it halfway. With the ones that have fallen on the floor. I know you store them in Dr. Ziploc."

"You know all too well, sweetheart," he smiled, shaking his head. "Why all of a sudden?"

"Stupid. I started running again and tripped on a curb and messed up my back. That's what I get for jogging."

"Forties should do for that," Thomas said.

MB didn't have time to argue. "I need 80s. Can you help?"

After securing the oxycodone, her next stop was the liquor store. MB was no fan of hard liquor but she had done her share of group tequila shots over the years. With Singer still asleep in the car, she went into the Bottle Shop and got a pint of Jose Cuervo. The store owner tried to convince her that he carried much better tequilas. MB said it didn't matter and paid.

Finally, she arrived where she and Singer had spent many happy hours. The day had gone blustery gray. In the dusty light of early evening, bare treetops rocked against the sky. An empty playground is a forlorn sight. The colorful slides, the spring-loaded horsies, the idle swings, childless.

MB opened the pill bottle and shook three tablets into her palm. Tears blurred the tower house and the slide that Singer always had more fun climbing up than sliding down. She swallowed the pills with a nasty, long drink of tequila. She wiped her eyes and looked in the rearview mirror at Singer. When the outside winds subsided she could hear his perfect breathing.

The pint of tequila was empty. She laid it on the car seat next to the oxycodone bottle and turned over the engine. Blood fizzed through her body. She reached up and angled the rearview mirror to reflect herself. There was no mask. Just blotched cheeks and a red-tipped nose. She watched her eyelids close in slow motion. Pain left her body in the way one's soul departs when Jesus calls you home.

The final collision lunged her forward. Her car came to rest at the rear bumper of a parked, new-model Mercedes Benz. Immediately,

MB released her grip on the steering wheel, reached over the seat and unbuckled Singer from his booster seat. She let his shoulder slide out of the strap.

"Hi," she said, giving him a little shake.

He blinked awake. "Are we there?"

"Yes we are, honey," MB said. "I want you to know everything is going to be fine now. You hear me? Everything."

Singer nodded his sleepy head.

"I also want you to know I love you. Okay? More than 100 chocolate shakes." She opened her car door.

Singer beamed. "I love you. More than two-million scoops of ice cream."

MB squeezed her eyes shut and stepped out. Staggering a step, she bent over, standing in a street that ran through Middleton's boutique shopping district. A smattering of shoppers on the sidewalk stood stock-still. Store owners ran out their front doors. MB's vehicle had careened along a row of parked cars, leaving a trail of glass and side view mirrors before coming to rest at the rear of the Mercedes. Two car alarms bleated, slightly out of unison.

CALL THE POLICE! someone screamed.

The following day, Judge Healy got a phone call from a social worker who explained who she was and the custody case she was working on. Yes, he told her, I remember you. In fact, my office was just about to call you because I've set a court date for the decision on that case. As he listened further, a deep furrow creased his brow.

"I'm sorry, what?" he said into the receiver.

The social worker repeated herself. "Mary Beth Lancaster, the woman with temporary joint custody of the child in this case, was arrested yesterday for DUI. She lost control of her vehicle and crashed into a row of parked cars—"

Judge Healy interrupted. "Just a minute. This is the woman I met? The ER nurse?"

"Yes."

The Judge was flabbergasted. "Go on."

The social worker continued. "The police found an empty liquor bottle in her car and a half-empty bottle of oxycodone. She was so high when arrested that she had urinated herself."

"Good Lord," the judge said. "Was anyone hurt?"

"Thankfully, luckily, no. But in my opinion, the most troubling offense is she had the young boy with her. And his seatbelt had been left unbuckled."

Judge Healy closed his eyes and shook his head. Never had he doubted his judgment more than he did at this moment. It was frightening.

The social worker spoke up. "Judge Healy? Are you still there?"

"I'm here." He pulled the case file out of the stack on his desk. "I have to ask, did you see any possibility of this coming?"

"None, sir. But with nurses, the pressures of the job, the availability of drugs, sadly it's not a unique story."

The judge rubbed his forehead. "Thankfully we caught it in time."

EPILOGUE

JUNE

Six weeks had passed since MB visited the farm with Singer. In that short time, things could hardly have changed more.

So it is in northern Minnesota in the lengthening days between April and June. The wallop of sun transforms the landscape more dramatically than it will at any other time. What was laid brown and barren holds a determined secret. Vivid. Bursting. Green. First, budding trees. And then the fields.

A seed struggles mightily in the dark. Until it doesn't. Until the right confluence of variables, the angle of the sun, length of the day, moisture of the earth and, finally, warmth from above calls it out. Corn and beans dare to rise. Behold. Flats of fields singing in the geometry of parallel green lines. Row upon row upon row of shoots stretch into the distance until scattering into a carpet of color.

Cory and Singer were taking their usual walk. They had come to the fields when there was nothing but a chance. Day after day, faithfully returning, stepping cautiously, despite no tangible sign of what was to come.

Then! The first plants emerged and Cory and Singer bent to them. That's how you glorify change. You stand in its midst, having witnessed before and after. Now, finally, to walk among such convincing color, how could you have ever doubted?

Varkas watched them through binoculars from his truck. He too had been attentive to the fields. Waiting. And now, with the tender shoots less than three inches tall, his time had come.

Preparations had been made. His lumberyards sold fencing materials. It was easy enough to get his shop foreman to construct heavy-duty drag mats. Varkas handed the man a sketch of what he wanted, right down to the dimensions. Eight-by-eight-foot chain link fencing banded onto two-inch diameter steel pipe. Five feet of tow chain secured to both ends of the pipe. Grab hooks at the chain ends to attach to a trailer hitch. When that steel mat was dragged through the field by truck, every shoot would be shredded.

Varkas had ten of them built. The guys would meet at the lumberyard at 2 a.m. Half the men would drag the bean fields, the other half the corn. One hundred bucks a head plus a twelve-pack.

Varkas's binoculars swept across the gravel road to a bean field on the other side. He swung past a dark mass—and then abruptly reversed—holding his binoculars on the object. Wolf. He had never been able to put glass on this animal, usually seeing it from a distance with the naked eye. Magnificent. It had to go 175 pounds. Varkas tweaked the focus and looked at the wolf's head, and then its eyes. *Are you watching me?*

The fact that the animal was protected and wasn't on ground Varkas owned meant nothing to him. He reached over the driver's seat and took his uncased rifle from the crew cab. Varkas always kept three cartridges with 130-grain Nosler bullets in the ash tray. In the seconds it took to load his rifle the wolf had vanished.

Damn ghost wolf. You've disappeared on me before. I will keep coming for you, just like I will keep coming for this land. Your coat will look fine on my wall.

The sun's position in the sky told Varkas it was about 9:00. He had a full day ahead of him and the thought made his heart beat quicker.

EPILOGUE

It was his birthday, after all. He was going to make it memorable.

In the grocery store in town, he picked up two pounds of ground beef. At the hardware store he bought a box of one-inch finishing nails. He would take his supplies home and mix up a special treat for the Sheriff's dog. Then one of his men would slip into the Sheriff's backyard late tonight. He would leave the laced meatballs where the dog would find them in the morning when he went out to do his business. The veterinarian would be helpless to save him.

Varkas grit his teeth at the thought of the Sheriff. To witness that man win re-election last week, the sight—the smugness—of the Sheriff and that woman of his parading down Main Street with that fool dog wearing election placards. As if pictures in the newspaper weren't enough, then to listen to the Sheriff boast on the radio how he would continue to serve and protect his town from all kinds of crime, including industrial pollution and unsafe work practices. The Sheriff didn't name names. Everyone knew who he was talking about.

But before Varkas would deal with the Sheriff and the farm, he would begin his birthday celebration as always: by taking down a tree. It was an annual tradition to fell a large oak and leave it in the woods where it would dry and season throughout the year. Come winter, he would hew it, buck it into hauling-size logs, and, piece by piece, pull it over the snow to his splitting shed.

He had done so with his father and his father had done so with his. With a tree on the ground, they would cut a thin cross-section from the trunk, count rings until reaching the number of the birthday they were celebrating and tap a nail donned with a ribbon in that year.

Varkas checked the zippered breast pocket of his overalls. A nail and small cutting of ribbon were right where they belonged. From inside his splitting shed, he chose one ax from the three hung on the wall. He spat in his leathery hands, which seemed more cold than usual of late.

Leaving the shed, he stood in the strengthening sunlight. He looked out across his property and in the distance saw the wheeling blades of the old Baker windmill and the towering American flag rippling on its pole. He thought, *It's the energy in men like me that keep the flag from hanging limp and the windmill from rusting into inoperation.*

The axe was cocked back on one shoulder, on the other rested a toothy 32-inch crosscut saw. Varkas closed his eyes and pictured the gray, gnarled bark of an oak trunk bearing an ideal splitting circumference, about 16 inches. His mind's eye traced up the rugged bark, 60 feet into the massive green canopy. No matter how hard his hands pushed on that trunk, the tree was immovable. But in possession of the right tools and plan, a man can swiftly place that same tree on the ground, cut it and move it in accordance to his wishes.

He walked no more than five steps into the woods before abruptly stopping. He had almost forgotten his rifle in the shed.

As of late, MB couldn't encounter light angling through windows and not be reminded of the farmhouse. She shifted, almost imperceptibly, reclined in a warm, soft chair in the community room. Looking through long panes of sun-streaked glass, she watched a drab female cardinal flit in her wooded landscape just outside the window. She wondered if the bird was happy, surrounded now by so much green. Or did she just feel out of place?

They'd be serving lunch soon. The other patients at the rehab facility were in their rooms or maybe out for a walk. It was a beautiful day. MB scrunched her long legs up in the chair like she used to when she was young. She tolerated her situation without complaint.

For her mistake, MB was issued a stiff penalty. Her license was suspended for 180 days. She paid a large fine. She agreed to 100 hours of community service. She entered a 60-day drug and alcohol rehab facility. But thanks to the strength of the nurses union and the representation her friend Jenni had arranged, she wasn't fired from the hospital. She did, however, agree to pee in a cup for the next two years.

These were small losses, comparatively. Everything had played out as she imagined. She trusted her decision. And that got her through the days and nights.

"Well, there you are," the facility's program director said, striding into the community room. "I've been looking all over for you. How about this day!"

MB nodded. "One beautiful day at a time, right doc?"

"Hey, I like that." She smiled widely, showing her high gumline, and looked at MB, trying to remember what it was that brought her there. "Oh, hey, your first letter." She held it up like a torch. The program director loved to deliver mail in person, as a way to stay connected with patients. "Special delivery for a special person."

MB hoped she cringed only on the inside. "Yeah," she said, trying to be upbeat. She accepted the letter.

The program director pulled up a chair and gazed at MB.

"Please, don't be offended," MB said. "I wonder if I can read this alone."

"Oh. Sure! Yes. Absolutely!" She put her hand on MB's knee and looked directly in her eyes. "Whatever makes you most comfortable."

MB thought that the woman's hand on her leg and extended eye contact didn't go a long way toward comfort, but what the hell. She patted the program director's hand and waited her out.

On the front of the envelope her name was printed as neatly as she'd ever seen. All capital letters, precisely the same size, spaced with equal care. On the back was a colored drawing of two smiling circular faces side by side. One face was larger with long lines of hair on either side. The other was smaller with squiggles of curly hair. An arrow pointed to each, one saying You, the other Me. Singer's command of the alphabet was improving.

A soft, repeating chime announced lunch over the intercom system. MB carefully opened the letter so as not to rip into the drawing. Cory had written Singer's letter to her, just as last winter, she had written Singer's to Cory. The symmetry gave her pause.

Hi MB!!!

I really miss you a lot. I love living at the farm. We planted corn and beans. Cory drove the tractor and I did too. Billy Little Tree is too little but not for long. We are waiting to see the seeds pop up. And I had a dream about you! You were at the playground with a little girl and you were pushing her on the swings. You both laughed and laughed. When I told Cory he said we should write. I miss you. Cory says hi and thank you very much.

I love you more than 500 cupcakes!!!
Singer

The overhead chime rang out again, but MB wasn't hungry. She wasn't sad. She wasn't happy. She was empty. MB let her head rest on the back of the soft chair, closed her eyes and hoped for little girls on swings.

Varkas found the one—an oak about 60 years old with a diameter that would center-split and quarter nicely for the hearth. Near the base of the trunk, his felling notch ate halfway into the meat of the oak, open in the direction he wanted the tree to fall. Behind and just up from the felling notch, he would make his back cut.

Breathing hard, Varkas walked away from the tree to remove his flannel shirt. He would finish the oak in his t-shirt. He took up an old woodsman's water flask that his father had once used and drank half the contents.

Upon bringing the flask down, he dared not move. He found himself 30 feet from the ghost wolf. An animal its size could cover that distance in fewer than two bounds. Varkas's ax was back at the tree. As was his rifle.

The animal's golden eyes bored into Varkas. Fear, an emotion Varkas vaguely recognized, jolted through his chest and left a metallic taste in his mouth. Varkas remained motionless.

The ghost wolf turned and melded soundlessly into the shadowy trunks of the forest. *Why would he spare me?* Varkas's heart was bombarded with adrenaline, leaving him lightheaded. As the animal's long tail disappeared from sight, Varkas regained his focus and sprang. He ran to his rifle, swept it up into his arms and pursued. Fool animal. A wicked smile came to his face, lathered in perspiration.

Now it was Varkas hunting the animal. But every time the ghost wolf was within killing range and Varkas shouldered his rifle, it would again disperse into the understory. And the chase would draw on. Finally, 40 yards ahead, the ghost wolf waited, watching, before stepping through a curtain of tamaracks into a dense swamp. Here, a wolf could live protected, unseen, with mast from trees to browse and abundant small game to eat.

Varkas splashed into the tamarack swamp. Each step required the giant man to fight to unstick his boot from the bog floor, kick it high over mats of vegetation, stride forward and then use that momentum to propel the next step. Stopping would only sink a boot deeper into the sucking mire. It was physically exhausting—mentally too—every movement demanding Varkas's complete focus to avoid loss of balance, while keeping watch for his prey.

Sunlight hardly cracked the thick, tangled pine canopy. Varkas pushed on, chasing glimpses of the wolf. In the cool boggy dark, Varkas was soaked through with sweat. His throat and lungs burning, his breathing labored, he took hold of a narrow tamarack trunk and tried to find a restoring breath. Then it hit him with nearly the force of a leaping animal.

Varkas was not pursuing the ghost wolf. The ghost wolf had lured him in. A cold drop of sweat slid down his temple.

Under an endless blanket of tamarack branches, there was no sun by which to navigate. Varkas didn't know how long or far he'd come. He'd been turned right and left and completely around by the ghost wolf's maneuverings. Lost.

Fear sprang on him. Adrenaline crashed into his heart. Blood rushed. Pressure climbed. Breathing raced, becoming shallow, raspy, labored. Varkas spun in a slow circle, teeth bared, spittle, salty perspiration, eyes bulging, gripped by desperation. He froze. In front of him, the ghost wolf's golden eyes pierced the boggy darkness.

Varkas opened his mouth but could conjure no sound. Haste and confusion rang in his ears. His hands trembled as he raised the rifle to his shoulder. And then, Varkas blinked. He felt something tiny give way in the wild.

As a newborn baby, Varkas had come loudly into the world. Large, red-faced, fists clenched, legs scissoring, but with a tiny, undetected birth defect. When the Creator took up mud and breathed life into his soul, there was an imperfection near his heart. Hidden in the walls of Varkas's aortic arch lay an abnormally thin patch of tissue.

If goodness filled his heart, the tiny defect would bear no repercussions. The organ would beat strong, blood would flow freely, the artery would grow to repair and Varkas would enjoy a long and happy life. But if his heart were inflamed by greed and evil, the weakness in his aorta could fail. An aortic dissection could occur. A rupture in the inner wall could cause blood to gush between the aortic walls, driving them apart. Massive and rapid, the blood loss would cause almost instantaneous death.

Varkas's eyes fluttered and rolled white. His rifle fell to the rich bog loam. Hands at his side, straight and giant, Varkas wobbled for a moment, canted forward, tipping, gaining speed, until he dropped directly face first, bouncing up slightly before coming to his final rest. Felled by hate.

Singer hummed. Cory listened as they lay on their backs on a checkered blanket. The wind lightly stirred. Hedge crickets chirped from the creek's buffer grass while a white-throated sparrow sang out *Oh, Sam Peabody, Peabody, Peabody.*

Their heads rested near enough to the high creek water to hear it wend and laugh over rock ledges. Were water not forced to bend around obstacles, there would be no sound sung to the firmament.

EPILOGUE

They had finished a picnic in the front pasture. Overhead, clouds with guts full of moisture billowed and morphed. Cory thought about how things change and what is sure one moment isn't the next. The key, he'd come to grasp, is you had to keep looking. Despite it all.

He took Singer's hand in his. A breeze tickled bare toes. The warm sun and ample lunch were asking for a nap. And the answer was yes.

READERS' COMMENTS

Readers value what other readers have to say about a book—as do I. While *Slender Wish* is still fresh in your mind, please go to **fivefriendsbooks.com** and share your thoughts on this novel in the Readers' Comments section.

Thanks.

ACKNOWLEDGMENTS

I'd like to recognize the pre-readers who bravely went though the manuscript looking for ill-conceived sentences and interminable typos. Kelly, Doc, Cathy, Chris, Amy, it's tough work. It's like being invited to the movies and while the film is playing, you're asked to crawl around in the dark and pick stale Milk Duds off the floor. Thank you for doing what is a thankless job.

And to those who made the book look beautiful inside and out, thanks. Photography, typography, art direction—they are crafts. You contributed greatly to both the first impression and the lasting beauty of *Slender Wish*.